To Pat

Home is a journey of the Heart

Patricia Hopper

9/23/2017

Corrib Red

Corrib Red

PATRICIA HOPPER

CACTUS RAIN
PUBLISHING

Arizona USA

CORRIB RED

Published by Cactus Rain Publishing, LLC
San Tan Valley, Arizona, USA
www.CactusRainPublishing.com

ISBN: 978-0-9962812-6-3

Front Cover Design by Ellie Bockert Augsberger/Creative Digital Studio
     www.CreativeDigitalStudio.com
Cover photos by Andrew Meek
Cover model is Liusaidh Hopper
Certified Proofreader Anita Beery. www.AnitaBeery.com

Published March 17, 2017
Published in the United States of America

DEDICATION

For my siblings:
Stephen, Margaret, Colette, Jimmy and Noel,
who stand by my side always.

ACKNOWLEDGEMENT

Many thanks to Larry Pugh who patiently edited numerous versions and who challenged me so that every nugget of the novel earned its place. Thanks to Susan Maczko who painstakingly copy-edited the novel, and for her support and friendship. To my sister Colette Hopper, thank you for vetting the novel for facts and accuracy. To Laura Treacy Bentley who provided invaluable feedback. To my grand-niece Liusaidh Hopper for agreeing to be the beautiful model on the book cover. And appreciation to my mother Elizabeth Hopper for her suggestions and loving encouragement.

Special thanks to all who brought the story of Corrib Red to life in the book video. To Liusaidh Hopper and my daughter Tara Meek who portrayed the main characters in the video. I am indebted to my son-in-law, Andrew Meek, who is an integral part of our family, and produced the video. I am also grateful to my nephew and niece, Paul and Vicki Hopper, who provided enthusiastic direction and wise counsel. Thanks to my brother and sister-in-law, Stephen and Kay Hopper, who acted as scouts for the best locations that made our project a success. And to my sister Margaret Quinn who willingly chauffeured us from place to place and offered valuable feedback.

Grateful thanks to the publishing team: Nadine Laman, owner of Cactus Rain Publishing, who treated Corrib Red with delicate and capable hands; Editor Judith McKee who first read the novel and recommended it to Nadine, which sent it on its way; Anita Beery for her indelible proofreading skills; and to Ellie Bockert Augsburger of Creative Digital Designs for her beautiful book cover.

To my family, friends and readers, thank you for your endless patience, support and encouragement. I am really lucky to have you in my life!

CHAPTER 1

Galway, December 1884

Tom held open the heavy oak door and guided Mother and me inside the railway station. I adjusted my green wool dress with its matching cloak, especially designed to make me look fashionable. Even my unruly copper-red hair had cooperated and tamed into a smooth coil at the nape of my neck. I ran my gloved hand down the front of my dress to smooth it, tried to calm the growing dread that Deirdre would find Ireland dull after Europe's disarming ways. She won't, I told myself fiercely. Kilpara is her home.

We made our way towards the platform where the Dublin train would arrive, sidestepping gentlemen in bowler hats and dark overcoats, partnered by women in long, flowing skirts and colourful cloaks. Finding an unoccupied wooden bench, we sat down to wait.

Nearby a group of men in worn suits and freshly washed faces arranged themselves in random order as they tuned banjos and fiddles. They drew curious stares from bystanders who gathered round to watch. A young man holding a fiddle glanced my way. A threadbare overcoat partially revealed a suit too tight for him, and worn shoes covered his feet. He looked about eighteen, his dark curly hair falling over a high forehead above mischievous green eyes. Our eyes met briefly; he grinned unabashedly. I looked away.

Moments later voices erupted in loud cheers when the platform attendant blew a whistle announcing the train's arrival. I peered into the distance for curling smoke, my ears strained to hear the engine. It seemed forever until the train came lunging into the station. Noisily, haltingly, it came to a standstill at the platform.

Musicians struck up a blaring rendition of "See the Conquering Hero Comes." Doors swung open, and passengers alighted into a cloud of smoke, flooding the already packed platform. Several men in black suits and dark overcoats stepped off the train, obstructing our view. People rushed forward chanting, "Parnell, Parnell." The band played frenziedly as the visitors moved through the crowd shaking hands. I searched the open doors for a glimpse of Deirdre's face.

A woman wrapped in a black woollen shawl, her wizened face adoring, shouted to one of the men, "Michael, welcome, welcome." The man moved closer. The woman shoved forward. He held out his left hand, and the woman grabbed it in both of hers and squeezed it. I looked for his right hand—there was none. The sleeve of his coat dangled empty.

Trapped in a wall of people, shoulders pushed me closer to the honoured guest. His gaze strayed from the woman's face to look over the crowd. With a jolt I recognized the gaunt features, the knitted eyebrows, the kind but determined eyes. I had seen his face in a notice pasted on the railway door. I was standing in the presence of the well-known Fenian leader, Michael Davitt.

The woman tenderly caressed his arm like a mother consoling a long-lost son. "The *United Ireland* is hailing you and Mr Parnell as heroes. Because of you, poor tenant farmers can stand up against eviction and starvation. They aren't dragged from their homes so easily these days, when landlords raise rents on a whim."

"True, we've made headway," Davitt agreed, looking at the tall thin man who stood speaking to an attentive audience. "But our struggle is far from over. There's still the fight for Home Rule."

The woman nodded. "We're fortunate brave men like yourself are willing to risk jail, and worse, to free us from tyrants."

2

"We have to reclaim our country, or we'll be forever enslaved."

The woman's gaze turned compassionate. "Demanding change only brings pain and death. But you know this already."

Davitt smiled wistfully. "We live in troubled times."

"God bless you, Michael."

He placed his hand on her shoulder and squeezed it.

Distracted by Davitt and the woman, I wasn't aware Mother and Tom had moved farther down the platform and were waving at me. I renewed my efforts to move towards them. The tall thin speech maker extracted himself from the crowd, and with a commanding nod, motioned to Davitt.

A throng of people blocked my way and shoved me closer to the revered visitor who stood aloof inspecting his surroundings with inscrutable eyes. I could see his handsome but somewhat pallid face, his neatly combed dark-brown hair, short beard and moustache. For a second time I stood in awe as I recognized Davitt's companion—Ireland's proclaimed emancipator, Charles Parnell. The band struck up again and Parnell strode away from the platform with an air of stately elegance, accompanied by his loyal followers.

At last I saw Deirdre with Mother and Tom standing next to a porter who loaded her trunk onto a trolley. I ran to them calling, "Deirdre, Deirdre."

Deirdre turned and held out her arms, her smile widening.

"You're really home," I said, hugging her tightly.

"And glad of it." She stroked my face, then stood back and studied me. "You look so—mature."

I squeezed Deirdre's hands, conscious that her face looked pasty, her blue eyes dull and strained beneath the brim of her bonnet. It was the same blue cloak and bonnet she had donned upon her departure. This took me by surprise. I expected to see her dressed in something new and dazzling, something European; her long fair hair fashionably styled, her face alive with exciting new experiences. I didn't know whether to be happy or disappointed. Linking my arm in hers I said, "I've been dying to see you. I've missed you."

"Me too," she said, her voice tired and weary.

Tom never lost his American accent. He came to Kilpara from America with his wife, Maureen, before I was born. As our head groom, Father trusted him to raise and train champion horses. He could have entrusted other grooms to drive us into Galway; instead, Tom preferred to take us himself. Wherever we went he drew attention when he spoke. Even now heads turned when he said, "Follow me, ladies."

We had stepped outside the station when we heard Father calling to us. Deirdre ran to his open arms. He swept her into an embrace then held her at arm's length. "You look tired and in need of a good meal. Maureen will prepare something special for you."

She smiled. "I can't wait to get home, Father."

"We're happy you're back."

Deirdre shivered.

"Let's get you out of the cold," Mother said.

Father nodded and escorted us to where Tom stood securing Deirdre's trunk at the rear of the carriage. After helping each of us inside, Father briefly kissed Mother. "I'll be along shortly," he said. "I've some minor details to finish up at the agency."

Tom cracked the reins. We turned away from Galway, leaving behind streets aglow with Christmas decorations that brightened the gloomy December day. Outside the town, low rock walls bordered the narrow road that led to Kilpara. Pillars of smoke rose from chimneys above thatched cottages scattered along our way, and gardens that overflowed with flowers in summer lay dormant.

To my relief Deirdre's face turned joyful when we entered the avenue bringing into view the grey ivy-covered fortress through bare trees. Her gaze drank in Kilpara, its flickering lights in tall windows bidding us welcome.

"I'm home," she said with familiar enthusiasm.

The moment we entered the vestibule, servants gathered round from all directions and lined up to greet Deirdre. The library door flew open and Grandfather rushed out, his arms outstretched.

"There you are, girlie," he said. "It's been lonely here without you. How was your journey? Wearisome, I'm sure. You're home now, and we'll see that you get rested."

Deirdre glanced about her and moved through the house as if to reassure herself nothing had changed in her absence. She gazed at her reflection in the highly polished Georgian table in the great room, ran her palm over the length of it. She touched the back of the settee in the drawing room and tapped keys on the grand piano in a moody riff.

"I've missed home *so much* and all of you," she said to a captive audience who beamed back with large smiles. Comforted by her surroundings, the strain from her journey began to vanish from her face.

We traipsed upstairs to the second floor where Deirdre looked around our bedroom. "I'd forgotten how big this room is."

"You may have your own room if you like, darling," Mother offered.

"No, I prefer things just as they are. To be here with Grace."

Deirdre smiled at me and I grinned back, her words quelling any doubts that Europe's persuasive charm had pried her away from us.

"I'll leave you to freshen up for dinner," Mother said. She looked back from the door. "It's *really* wonderful having you home again, darling."

As soon as Mother left, Deirdre flopped down on her bed.

"Are you all right?" I asked.

"Just tired, quite fatigued."

I was full of questions, yet didn't know where to begin. "You hardly wrote," I probed. "I wrote to you every week."

"I was busy."

"But I wanted to hear about everything."

Deirdre raised herself up on one elbow. "I know you think there's a lot to tell, but art school was, well—rather dull."

"That can't be. You love art and Switzerland's so different from Ireland. I was sure you were wrapped up in life there, the people, the fashions, your new friends. You never bothered to come home for summer holidays."

"I'm here now and none of it matters anymore. Let's go eat. I'm famished."

But when we sat down to dinner she pushed her food around on the plate, hardly touching it. Grandfather chattered on, and it wasn't until Mother mentioned the Sloanes were coming to dinner the following evening that Deirdre raised her head.

She frowned at Mother. "They're coming *here*?"

"Yes, darling. I know you've just arrived home, but they're anxious to welcome you back."

"They heard the news and conveniently manipulated an invitation," Father explained.

Mother looked hurt. "It's only polite, Ellis, you know that. They're our closest neighbours."

"I don't want to see them, Father," Deirdre pleaded. "I've been away for a year, and I'd rather just be with all of you. No one else."

"I understand, but I suppose we can suffer through one evening." Father words were meant to soothe Deirdre and coax Mother back into a good mood. "It'll only be for a few hours."

Deirdre looked sullen. "If only it weren't the *Sloanes*."

That night, low keening sounds awoke me. It took a moment to realize they came from Deirdre's bed. I got up and went to her. I called her name softly, but she didn't awaken. I stroked her hair the way Mother used to when we were children and had bad dreams. This seemed to calm her because the keening stopped, and she went back to sleeping peacefully.

I returned to my own bed, yet lay awake wondering what had made her fitful. She had never been uneasy in her sleep before. There were times when she awoke from the occasional nightmare like I did and had been fretful. But this was different. I wondered what happened in Switzerland to fill her with such anxiety. I continued to puzzle over this until sleep overtook me.

6

CHAPTER 2

When I awoke, wintry light speared through the gap in the heavy chintz drapes. My mind struggled to recall the previous day's events. I looked over at Deirdre tucked peacefully beneath the bedcovers, her face partially visible, her long hair spread across the pillow. I wondered if she would recall the previous night's disturbance when she awakened. I tossed back the covers and fumbled for my slippers. Pulling on a robe over my thick flannel nightgown, I quietly crossed the cold wooden floor to the vanity in the semi-darkness.

Here the light reflected better. I pulled a hairbrush through the tangled copper-red mass I inherited from Father's side of the family. I wished my hair was more like Deirdre's, whose ash-blond locks resembled Mother's. She had Mother's creamy complexion, too, and heart-shaped face, but her eyes were blue like Father's, only more striking. I had Mother's green-grey eyes; in every other way I resembled the O'Donovans.

The sun proved by far my worst enemy. Its offending rays brought out freckles across my face and over the bridge of my nose. These tiny spots became my constant companion in summertime when the sun shone brightest. I didn't let this deter my passion for riding horseback. Unlike Mother and Deirdre who travelled the countryside in the comfort of the carriage, hardly knowing what lay beyond the widely used country roads. Father and I often rode together. He said I sat a horse as well as any man, quite a compliment coming from *him*, since he was among the best horsemen in all of Ireland.

I finished dressing and arrived at the dining table the same time as Grandfather, who sat next to Mother and Father. I sat down across from them.

"Deirdre's still resting, is she?" Grandfather asked.

I nodded.

"Poor child, she's exhausted after her long journey. A few days of good food and fresh air and she'll be back to herself again." His face lit up at the mere thought of Deirdre. Anyone could see she was his favourite granddaughter. When we were together he always embraced her first, praised her first. He did this unconsciously.

I used to believe it was the order of our births that drew people to Deirdre. She was the first born, older than me by eighteen months. Later I began to suspect that she, like Mother, possessed a magnetic charm that made people indulgent. Looking at Mother sitting across the table, it was hard to imagine her young and fetching, which Father often implied when he talked about their courtship. She was a woman of convention, greatly influenced by Grandfather. I wondered if Father missed that spontaneous spirit she once possessed; if he ever wished she could be that way again.

Because I tended to be high-spirited, Grandfather protested I was growing up more like a boy than a girl. He objected to my spending so much time outdoors. Mother agreed with Grandfather, but Father never did. He understood me in ways they never could. He claimed there was time enough for frills and lace. The argument was always the same.

"She's too free, too wild," Grandfather grumbled.

"She plays the piano and has mastered French and Latin," Father would retort. "Let her ride in the countryside if she wants."

"It's not right for a girl to wander off like she does, so it's not."

Father's temper would flare, "She *prefers* the outdoors to needlepoint or painting."

"You shouldn't let her roam wherever she pleases. If she were kept closer to home, she'd develop more interest in feminine matters."

"Too much civility can stifle natural tendencies. Besides, Olam goes with her."

"As if that dimwit could do anything."

Father's look would turn to disgust. "Olam may be slow, but he's also clever. He'd lay down his life to protect Grace."

Grandfather didn't understand Father's reasoning. He wanted me to be like Deirdre and wondered why I was different. I hated sitting for hours embroidering delicate designs on sheets, pillowcases and doilies, or painting flowers on canvasses. Mother and Deirdre often sat in the company of women who spoke harshly of the world, yet knew little about its realities. They enjoyed every social amenity at their fingertips, oblivious of the trials people endured outside their tight circle.

Mother addressed Father, startling me. "You'll be home early for dinner, won't you, Ellis?"

"I've important meetings scheduled, but I should be through soon enough."

"Charles and Daphne are due at half past six. And you know Cecil is anxious to see Deirdre again."

"That whelp of an excuse for a son."

"Let's not turn Deirdre's homecoming into a circus of ill feeling," Mother implored. She covered Father's hand with hers. "Please, Ellis."

"Fine. If we must—"

"It'll be informal. Charles and Daphne understand Deirdre's been away, and Cecil has returned from his first term at Cambridge University. They're spending Christmas at Larcourt this year."

Father let out an agitated sigh. Plainly he disliked the Sloanes, and Mother's sense of societal politeness frustrated him. He rose from the dining table and pinched my cheek as he passed by my chair. Mother got up too, and as they left the room together I admired Father's strong physique, his tanned skin that lost some of its lustre in winter. Mother said the texture and colour of his complexion came from years of growing up in America. His face, characterized by a high forehead, straight nose, and strong chin, displayed the undaunted confidence of a man who faced life's challenges, and conquered them.

I left the table, stopping to kiss Grandfather's cheek. The murmur of Mother and Father's voices resounded from the vestibule. Seconds later I heard the front door close.

Deirdre had dressed when I returned to the bedroom. Remnants of a mostly uneaten breakfast sat on the writing desk, waiting to be cleared away. I searched her face for signs of the previous night's disturbance. But there were none, she looked refreshed and unconcerned.

"Let's go for a walk," she said, turning away from the vanity where she sat brushing her hair. "We can stretch our legs in the open fields and wander down by the lake."

I nodded agreeably. We gathered our cloaks and mitts to brave the cold, but sunny, winter's day. Crossing the fields we had walked some distance in silence before I said, "I suspect you'll find dinner with the Sloanes especially trying so soon after your journey. Mother means well."

"I know," Deirdre said glumly. "I emphasized in my letters to her that I wanted my homecoming to be quiet. Without fuss."

"Has she told you about the New Year's Eve ball?"

"Briefly. When it comes time I may just say I'm unwell."

I stared at her bewildered. "You can't. Mother organized it because she knows you love parties. You still do, don't you?"

Deirdre looked out across the fields. "Of course, I'm just not ready for all the fuss."

"Why? Will you find it boring after the glamorous soirees you attended in Switzerland?"

Deirdre heaved a sigh. "No. I just don't want people staring curiously at me, asking silly questions about art school. I want everything to be the way it was. Mother is convinced I should start thinking about a marriage suitor. She'll be sure to point out every eligible bachelor and his prospects. I can hear her now. Look at this one, Deirdre, don't you think he's handsome. What about him, Deirdre, he's an established barrister. Deirdre, this one will offer you comfort and security."

I started to giggle.

Deirdre frowned.

"I can't help it," I said. "You make Mother sound like she's choosing a cut of meat. Oh, this piece is nice and lean, that piece will do but without the bone, that's a lovely roast, all plump and tender."

A smile twitched at the corners of Deirdre's lips, gladdening my heart. But as quickly as it came her smile disappeared, and she looked sombre again.

"I wish Mother had listened to me," she fussed.

I touched her arm. I had been so concerned about losing her to European ways that I forgot she was old enough to marry. But she was clearly overreacting if she believed Mother's sole purpose for the ball was to find her a husband. It had been organized to celebrate her homecoming with our neighbours and friends who were anxious to welcome her back.

"I'm allowed to attend the ball," I said, hoping to ease her anxiety. "I'm old enough now."

She squeezed my hand. "I'm glad. Your being there will make it more bearable, should I decide to go."

We returned to the house in silence. In the greyness that surrounded us, a gnawing thought chewed at my mind. Deirdre admitted she wrote more often to Mother than to me. Granted, Mother had shared some of Deirdre's letters with us, but it seemed she hadn't shared everything.

Mother had first raised the question of Deirdre attending finishing school abroad after one of Lady Daphne's visits. In her usual annoying way Lady Daphne prattled on about how Irish education lacked instruction in the social graces, how these could only be acquired through attending more polished schools on the Continent. Mother wasn't educated outside Ireland, and Lady Daphne slyly undermined this fact.

I watched in quiet frustration as Mother failed to recognize that Lady Daphne's remarks were goaded by envy. Her pride suffered from her husband's obvious affection for Mother, which was within the confines of proper decorum, yet bordered on adoration.

This irked Lady Daphne, who schemed to demean Mother's confidence whenever possible.

She sensed Deirdre's reluctance to leave Kilpara and Mother's struggle between wanting to secure my sister's place in society and the desire to keep her close.

"Young ladies must be properly educated on the Continent if they're to take their place in society," Lady Daphne said on that particular occasion. "They have expert instructors there, unlike the heathens in this country."

She smiled courteously, but the insult was clear.

It was obvious Lady Daphne's intended slight lingered in Mother's mind, for she broached the subject shortly after the visit. She reminded Deirdre she was sixteen, the ideal age to attend a finishing school abroad. Deirdre immediately resisted.

"I *won't* go to some foreign country. Ever." she protested. "I'm perfectly content at home, so why should I have to leave?"

"What Daphne says is true, darling," Mother said. "Being schooled overseas will make you worldly, more poised."

"I don't care about that."

"Your father and I want you to marry well and take your place in society, that's all."

"If I must go abroad to become marriageable, then I won't marry at all."

Locked in fierce disagreement, the subject was dropped indefinitely. It came as a shock some months later when Mother announced unexpectedly that arrangements were made for Deirdre to go to La Croix Art School in Switzerland. Meetings were held between Mother, Father, and Deirdre in the library from which Deirdre emerged in tears.

I waited for the deluge of protests. Instead, Deirdre retreated into a state of despair and refused to take me into her confidence. Now that my sixteenth birthday approached, I wondered if I, too, would be sent away. I could argue the experience had not benefited my sister. If anything, it had sucked the very life out of her.

We were dressed for dinner when Clare, a junior housemaid, knocked on the bedroom door at half past six. "You're wanted downstairs," she announced. Deirdre and I looked at each other, drew deep breaths and went to the drawing room where Mother, Father, and Grandfather lounged with cocktails.

Deirdre jumped when a knock at the front door echoed through the house. "I'd forgotten how loud that door knocker is," she said with a nervous grin.

Mother reached over and patted her hand. "Don't worry, darling. You'll get used to it again."

Moments later Anthony, our butler, announced the Sloanes and ushered in Lady Daphne, Sir Charles and Cecil. Grandfather was first to greet them. Sir Charles hastily brushed his greeting aside and walked over to Mother.

He was a slender man with sandy hair combed straight back, and a thin moustache covered his upper lip. His pale freckled skin stood out against his dark evening suit.

Father scowled as Sir Charles took Mother's hand and kissed it. Sir Charles' face softened noticeably, becoming animated the moment he looked at her. She, on the other hand, seemed indifferent to his flagrant attention.

Deirdre grinned suddenly as he gazed at Mother in his usual adoring way. Head bent, she turned towards me in an effort to control her amusement. This was more like the sister I knew.

"Well, isn't this nice," Lady Daphne announced when we were seated at the long Georgian table in the great room. She wore a purple silk dress, her dark hair braided and coiled on top of her head. Her expression was one of controlled politeness. I half expected her face to break out of its mold and snarl at any moment.

"Our little group all together again, even Deirdre back home from Switzerland," she said. "I know La Croix well. Pupils are taught refined art techniques and become splendidly adept in the social graces. I'm sure you made many friends. I should know their families."

"I don't think so," Deirdre said, looking uncomfortable.

"There were different class levels. I didn't get to know any of the students well."

"Surely, you'll invite your new friends to Kilpara."

"Of course." But Deirdre sounded doubtful.

"And Morrigan, how are you these days, darling?" Lady Daphne asked sweetly.

"I'm well," Mother said.

"You look especially lovely tonight," Cecil said to Deirdre, gazing at her in the same adoring way his father looked at Mother.

At seventeen he had grown as tall as his father, had the same sandy hair and was trying to grow a moustache. Unsuccessfully. He practised twisting and curling the thin strands of hair like his father. He inherited his mother's strange eyes, piercing, though not as dark. They had that same intense stare that made me wonder what thoughts went on in their minds behind those eyes.

Lady Daphne drained her wine glass then told Clare, who was removing the soup bowls, to refill her glass. When Maureen served plates of duck covered in white sauce, along with roast potatoes, peas, and garnished parsley, Lady Daphne ignored her food until more wine was poured.

"I've missed Irish food," Deirdre confessed.

"You must be delirious, darling," Lady Daphne said. "It hardly compares to delicacies on the Continent."

Deirdre didn't answer. Instead she addressed Cecil. "How long are you staying at Larcourt?"

"Throughout the Christmas holidays. I'm glad I came." He stared at Deirdre, who looked away. He was sitting next to me and I looked directly at him. He avoided eye contact and continued to stare at Deirdre, who pretended to eat.

Lady Daphne drew everyone's attention when Clare brought more wine and she took the bottle from the girl's hand. Sir Charles glared at his wife. She refilled her glass, ignoring him.

"Several of Cecil's friends and their families will be visiting Larcourt after Christmas," she announced, taking a large swallow from her glass.

"They must come to the New Year's Eve ball," Mother said.

"That's jolly good of you, Mrs O'Donovan," Cecil said. "I'm sure they'll gladly accept your invitation."

Sir Charles turned to Father. "I heard Parnell and Davitt were campaigning for Home Rule in Galway."

"It's true," Father agreed. "They created chaos at the train station yesterday, disrupting traffic when crowds of people followed them into the streets."

Sir Charles laid down his napkin. "That can only mean trouble."

"The Irish people should be entitled to self-government."

"And the landlord class be damned?"

"You've nothing to fear. England's army crushes every rebellion."

"Parnell and Davitt are nuisances," Sir Charles protested. "They held parliament ransom with obstructionist tactics over the Land Act nonsense. Now they want to seize more control with Home Rule. Ridiculous. They're nothing more than a pair of murderous villains who should be thrown back in jail."

"Please spare us from politics, darling," Lady Daphne interrupted. She turned to Father. "There's a hunt at Larcourt on Boxing Day, Ellis. You'll come?"

Father looked thoughtful then turned to me. "It could be an opportunity to test Spitfire."

"I'd love to join the hunt," I said.

"Girls should never ride horses that are highly spirited," Lady Daphne warned. "Accidents happen."

"I agree wholeheartedly," Grandfather said.

I smiled at them both. "I can handle Spitfire."

Lady Daphne observed me through dark eyes. "Don't be overconfident, darling."

Cecil turned to Deirdre. "You'll come, too?"

"I don't care for hunts."

Cecil cast her a disappointed look.

Maureen arrived with dessert, evoking sighs of relief from Father and Deirdre.

As soon as dinner was over Deirdre asked to be excused.

"Of course, darling," Mother said.

Cecil rose and moved to follow Deirdre.

"Please stay," Deirdre said.

"It'll be my pleasure." A sickly smile tugged at his thin lips and his deep stare never left Deirdre's face.

I wondered what Cecil was up to.

When Deirdre and I were children, the Sloanes' governess brought him regularly to Kilpara to play. "He's an only child and should learn to share with other children," she told our governess, Miss Robinson. But he was devious and sly. In the company of the governesses he smiled nicely and played well, but the moment their backs were turned, he pulled our hair and ripped out our dolls' arms and legs. Then he'd appear innocent when our governess noticed us crying.

I was surprised that his attitude changed towards Deirdre shortly before she left for Switzerland. He became courteous and attentive, and cunningly placed himself next to her at social functions. Mother just smiled when Deirdre voiced her annoyance. She pointed out he was maturing and could now appreciate the opposite sex. For the most part he still ignored me. But his eyes narrowed now when I said, "I'd like to be excused, too. It's been a long day."

His piercing gaze was meant to intimidate me. I smiled back warmly, turned and kissed Mother and Father good night.

"I'll look in on you shortly," Mother said.

When we reached the staircase Cecil said, "You go on up, Grace. I'd like a private word with Deirdre."

I looked at Deirdre and could see she was in no mood to chat with Cecil. I didn't move.

Cecil stood very close and glowered. I met his gaze evenly. "Go on, Grace, leave us. I'd like to speak to Deirdre."

"I'm very tired," Deirdre said. "Let's talk another time."

She started up the stairs. Before she got very far, Cecil reached out and grabbed her arm. "When?"

"Soon." Deirdre shook his hand loose. "Good night, Cecil."

She hurried upstairs before he could protest further. I followed.

When we reached our room we fell on our beds relieved.

"Did you see how he looked at you?" I said, peering at Deirdre. This brought a wry smile to her face. "Why do you suppose he's so persistent? He's never been this bad."

Deirdre shrugged. "College, most likely. Wants to impress us with his manly charms."

"He was always such a pest. I didn't think he could get much worse."

"You never know with Cecil."

I shivered. I didn't trust Cecil with his dark piercing eyes.

Two days later we rode into Galway with Father, who divided his time between his Financier Agency and Kilpara. It was a special treat when he accompanied us in the carriage on days that we visited Mrs Collins' dressmaking shop.

Looking particularly handsome in his dark business suit and long overcoat, he talked cheerfully throughout the ride. Seated beside him, Deirdre occupied him in a lively discussion about our surroundings. Her face, not as pale now, had developed a rosy tint about her cheeks thanks to fresh air from our walks.

I was relieved that the fitful episode hadn't repeated after her first night home. Strange enough she still avoided attempts to draw her into conversation about Switzerland, which left me more curious than ever about what had happened there.

Father bid us farewell at his agency, and Tom insisted on driving us to Mrs Collins' shop that was located a few streets away. He delivered us in front of the brightly coloured storefront with a promise to pick us up at the Station Hotel after lunch.

Mrs Collins, a small round woman with a happy face, had married and borne five children. The eldest daughter, about my age, followed in her mother's footsteps and worked in the shop.

"Come in," Mrs Collins welcomed, as Mother expressed our desire to order new gowns for the New Year's Eve ball. Mrs Collins began pulling bolts of fabric off shelves . Rolls of satin, silk , lace, chiffon, and taffeta were spread on long wooden tables. She laid out sketches for us to examine.

She chose light grey silk for Mother and suggested a fitted bodice. Mother draped the fabric against her. The image that looked back from the mirror was mysterious, like someone walking out of a mist.

"Such a busy time, Christmas," Mrs Collins said. "I could work round the clock and never get finished. The same can't be said for other seamstresses whose customers are flocking to the Continent these days for their gowns."

"You do wonderful work. Your customers would never go anywhere else."

"The trend hasn't affected me, yet. Frivolous, that's what people are. Workers are crying out for jobs here in Ireland, and our *aristocrats* take their business to foreigners. It's a disgrace."

She fussed with the fabric, pinning it in place. Mother studied the effect, then nodded her consent.

Satisfied, Mrs Collins found a bolt of pale blue satin and held it up to Deirdre. "This should do you nicely," she said. "I'll use royal blue or navy material to make bows and place them where the folds meet in half-rainbows. A bit of the same fabric knotted through your hair will make it perfect. You'll be a beauty, that's for sure."

Mrs Collins turned her attention to me. "So you're attending the gala, or are you still too young for such affairs?"

"I'll be sixteen in January. Mother says I'm old enough."

"Too bad you don't have her complexion." Mrs Collins turned my face from side to side. She did this every time I came to her shop. She always fussed over Mother and Deirdre, but when it came to me, she seemed perplexed. Even though she complained, I felt she found me a challenge. "I need something special for you." She turned me around then pushed my hair back from my face. "Don't move, I have the very thing."

She went out of the room and returned with a bolt of fabric wrapped in brown paper. Deep rose red peeked through a torn hole. "I just received this bolt of velvet." She pulled out a design with a scooped neck and dropped sleeves. The bodice was tight and the waist dipped into a "V" in front. "What do you think?" she asked.

I looked at her in astonishment. The dress was very advanced. "I—er."

Mother laughed softly at my shock. "Why not?" she said. "You're a young lady now."

Mrs Collins ripped brown paper off the fabric. Mother's eyes welled up at the sight of the material.

Mrs Collins stared at her. "Try not to fret, Mrs O'Donovan. I know it's hard to accept that your childer are growing up."

"It's not that. This was Grace's grandmother's favourite colour. It's the exact same colour as the roses she loved. Blood-coloured red."

Mrs Collins touched Mother's arm. "May she rest in peace."

I stroked the smoothness of the fabric, grateful that my paternal grandmother, Ann O'Donovan, who died before I was born, had returned to Ireland after years of exile in America. I couldn't imagine growing up anywhere else. She had been ill when she arrived and knew she was dying. She wanted to be buried along with my grandfather at Kilpara. The estate was once owned by O'Donovans until they were forced to sell it a generation before. Mother's father, Grandfather Purcenell, owner of Kilpara at the time, objected to Grandmother's request, but was later persuaded to grant her permission.

Father, who made the voyage along with Grandmother from America, never counted on meeting and falling in love with Mother. After only a short courtship they married in a simple, romantic ceremony. Following their marriage Mother worked alongside Father and his brothers to care for Grandmother in the final weeks before her death.

Grandmother had stayed at St Bridget's Convent and was nursed by Grand-Aunt Sadie, the Mother Superior there. To help Grandmother's spirits during that time, Grand-Aunt Sadie grew her favourite roses in the convent garden.

Whenever I helped tend the rose garden, Grand-Aunt Sadie talked about how the roses were her sister's favourites and how much she loved them. Even now when they are in bloom, fresh bouquets are always placed on my grandparents' graves.

I visited their gravesite often with Grand-Aunt Sadie, who insisted on praying. "Your grandparents are with our Creator in his heavenly kingdom, but you must still pray for them," she said. She explained that while they were in God's glorious presence they would still benefit from our indulgences.

She worked diligently to make sure the roses thrived. It was as if by nurturing them, she felt connected to my grandmother. Mother was right. The fabric Mrs Collins uncovered was that same blood-red.

"We can look at something else, Mother," I said, wanting to erase the sadness in her face.

Mother smiled through blurred eyes. "No, it's perfect for you."

"If the dress is off your shoulders, it won't clash with your hair," Mrs Collins said. "And a white wrap will contrast it nicely."

Mother nodded.

Mrs Collins' daughter stepped in and began taking my measurements.

"That's settled then." Mrs Collins opened her date book for return fittings. "Everyone's taken care of."

We left Mrs Collins's shop and went to the Station Hotel for lunch. Tom joined us shortly afterward and accompanied us to the market where we explored stalls for Christmas gifts. I bought a journal for Deirdre, perfume for Mother, pipe tobacco for Father, a book about salmon fishing for Grandfather, and coloured pencils for Olam. The afternoon was waning when Father joined us and we left Galway. Although it was still early, darkness was closing in.

CHAPTER 3

Christmas fast approached, and the house took on a holiday atmosphere as smells of baking drifted from the kitchen and decorations were underway throughout every room. A white linen tablecloth covered the length of the dining table in the great room, and red and green holly centrepieces were set atop. In the drawing room a tall Christmas tree stood in front of the window ready for trim, and silver bells and garland made the wide mantelpiece look festive.

A few days after we visited Mrs Collins' shop I learned that Rengen intended to ride over to Mercy Hospital to visit Grand-Aunt Sadie. He and his wife Jasmine were the only black people at Kilpara, and perhaps in all of Ireland. They had arrived at St Bridget's Convent and Mercy Hospital from America with my uncles Mark and Dan, just weeks before my grandmother died. When my uncles prepared to return to America after Grandmother's funeral, Father asked Rengen and Jasmine to stay on at Kilpara. He offered Rengen work in the forge.

Rengen agreed to stay, but not because of Father's offer; he had developed a fondness for Grand-Aunt Sadie and the patients at Mercy Hospital who found their way into his heart. He sent for his two sons and his daughter, and they spent their adolescent years at Kilpara. After they reached the age of consent they returned to America. There were grandchildren now, and Rengen often talked about returning home to see them.

"I's staying only a while longer," he said.

Rengen and Jasmine had grown accustomed to people staring at them wherever they went and tended to ignore this harmless curiosity. Some people asked to touch the couple to see if they were real. Rengen would deliberately speak in his old southern American drawl to watch looks of enchantment appear on their faces.

It turned out overcast but dry the day we rode to Mercy Hospital. We galloped in silence across barren fields bordered by bare hedges, each of us caught up in our own thoughts. When we slowed to a canter Rengen lapsed into stories about his youth. Even now, after so many years, details rolled off his tongue about the time he spent as a captured slave, his escape, his travels north in search of freedom, and his eventual arrival at Stonebridge House, Father's boyhood home in Maryland. It was a strange and unusual story that had happened so long ago.

"I've been hoping you'd come, Rengen," Grand-Aunt Sadie said, when we arrived at the convent. "Mrs Murphy has been asking for you. She's afraid of falling when she gets out of bed. She's well enough to walk, but won't try it because her legs are weak. Mr Sullivan is a handful to get into his wheelchair. And that goat, Lucifer, butts everyone who goes near her."

Grand-Aunt Sadie put an arm around my shoulder and kissed my cheek. "You're like a breath of fresh air, Grace dear. Have you been saying your prayers?"

"Yes, Grand-Aunt Sadie."

"Trista, she's in the hospital, Mother—?" Rengen asked.

"Yes," Grand-Aunt Sadie said.

"I go find her to see what's needing done after I milk Lucifer."

Grand-Aunt Sadie nodded and after Rengen left, she took me into her drawing room. She eased herself into a green and white brocade chair. "Would you tell the housekeeper to make us some tea, dear?" she asked. "Rengen will need something soothing after he tackles Lucifer. If we didn't need that goat's milk for the patients, I'd give her away."

I went in search of the housekeeper, knowing that Grand-Aunt Sadie had no intention of parting with Lucifer. There was an ongoing battle between them that she was determined to win.

Upon my return, with the question of tea out of the way, Grand-Aunt Sadie motioned me into the chair opposite her. I obeyed, comfortable in this cosy room with its brocade settee and matching chairs set in front of the fireplace, its wooden floor buffed to a high gloss by the nuns.

"Let me look at you, dear," Grand-Aunt Sadie said. "You grow lovelier every time I see you."

"You see me often."

Grand-Aunt Sadie gurgled with pleasure. "Your smiling face gladdens my heart more each time. So tell me, how are your mother and sister? And I haven't seen that nephew of mine in over a fortnight."

"Father will pay a visit in a day or two. Mother is fine and Deirdre is adjusting after being away. She doesn't say much about Switzerland. Do you suppose it was truly awful there?"

Grand-Aunt Sadie looked thoughtful. "I don't know, dear. But don't press her. I'm sure she'll tell you about it in good time."

Rengen came in triumphant with a container of milk. "Well I never—" Grand-Aunt Sadie declared. "It's a miracle."

"No miracle, Mother— All you needing is to talk sweetly to poor ol' Lucifer. And that ain't no name for a female goat anyway. I call her Lucy, and she be putty in my hands."

"She may behave for you. But it's her disposition and not her name that's the problem."

We turned at footsteps on the hardwood floor. A woman who looked older than her years greeted us. "Rengen, Grace, how wonderful to see you," Trista Ryan said. "Sister Josephine told me you were here."

"Rengen will help you with Mrs Murphy and Mr Sullivan." Grand-Aunt Sadie held up the container of milk. "He's already had success with Lucifer."

Trista smiled, and when she did a hint of an energetic young woman flashed behind her eyes. She had known Grand-Aunt Sadie since she was a young girl not much older than I was now. I hadn't met her until last summer, but had heard many times how she courageously voyaged to America at Grand-Aunt Sadie's request and accompanied my infirmed grandmother on her return to Ireland. Trista continued as my grandmother's caregiver until she died. After that she left Mercy Hospital to marry a man named Liam Ryan, a sheep farmer. She joined him on his small farm near Maamtrasna Cross and Lough Mask. Her own family lived close by in Cloughbrack, and she had relatives all around. One of them, a cousin named Myles and his wife Bridget, were neighbours. While Trista waited for her own children that never came, she helped Myles and Bridget with their brood.

Grand-Aunt Sadie often received letters from Trista and kept them in a neat pile on the sideboard in her drawing room. She would read us the latest ones when we visited. Trista told of the constant struggle she and her husband faced trying to raise livestock on snipe grass at the edge of the valley. This lifestyle was especially hard on her husband, who suffered from pleurisy all his life. His condition became critical last winter when he insisted on doing his outside chores in damp weather against Trista's advice. He caught a cold, which strained on his lungs, and turned into pneumonia. The illness put fatal pressure on his heart.

Grand-Aunt Sadie visited Trista after Liam's death and pleaded with her to return to Mercy Hospital. But Trista refused. She stayed on at the farm and mourned her husband while continuing to struggle with the heavy farm work. By summer she was forced to admit she couldn't cope any longer and put one of her brothers in charge of the fields.

She returned to Mercy Hospital and poured her energy into taking care of patients. Since then we spent many hours talking about my grandmother, about Stonebridge House in Maryland that looked exactly like Kilpara, my uncles and their families, and America. I watched her turn from a hollow-eyed, under-nourished woman into someone solemn, but kind. She had filled out, no longer bearing a skeletal look.

Rengen beamed when Trista indulged him with a smile. "Where be Mr Sullivan and Mrs Murphy?" he asked.

"Come on, I'll show you," Trista said.

"Aye so," Rengen said, mocking her Irish accent. She laughed, and Rengen happily followed her to the hospital.

"So much tragedy for such young shoulders," Grand-Aunt Sadie murmured, watching Trista walk outside with Rengen. Forcing away a glum look she turned to me and said cheerfully, "Will there be a ball at Kilpara for Deirdre's homecoming?"

"Yes, on New Year's Eve."

"Good. And Christmas, how are things coming along there?"

"The whole house is in a frenzy. You'll visit on Christmas Eve, won't you?"

"I haven't missed one yet. I'll bring Trista along. She could use a bit of good cheer."

CHAPTER 4

A few days before Christmas, Father ordered every form of fowl to be delivered to Kilpara. These would be taken home by servants for their Christmas dinners after the Christmas Eve celebration. On those occasions when the servants left, the house took on an eerie feeling as silence echoed through it like an empty shell. Shadows turned into ghosts of former generations that raised their ancestral heads and roamed about freely. I told Father about noises that scourged the hallways during quiet holiday periods. He chided me for having too much imagination and accused me of being fanciful.

At the moment the house was alive with activity. During idle moments in the kitchen, knitting needles clacked and wool spun as hats, cardigans, and gloves evolved from industrious hands. Baskets filled with preserves and baked goods sat in the kitchen pantry, ready to be whisked away.

Inside the small church adjoining Kilpara, fresh red candles replaced used ones in sconces along church walls. Attached at the end of each pew, red bows lined the way to the altar where a nativity scene took centre stage. As I stood admiring the transformation, crooning filled the empty sanctuary. I looked around to find Olam, Maureen and Tom's son, singing to himself and tracing delicate patterns left by the previous night's frost on one of the stained glass windows.

"They're pretty," he said, when I greeted him. We were the same age, born only a month apart. But there had been problems during his birth that caused him to be backward in some ways. At times, when Mother didn't know I was listening, I heard her tell the women in her circle about the difficult labour she endured when I was born—but, thankfully,

I had emerged a healthy baby. She compared herself to Maureen, whose labour had also been prolonged with complications. Olam was born healthy, only to be plagued later with learning difficulties. He failed to grasp some simple concepts, yet in other ways he was quite normal.

I smiled at him.

"Window's cold," he said. "I don't like the cold. I wish it was Christmas."

"Me too."

A grin spread across his wide mouth. "I made you a Christmas present, Miss Grace, but it's a secret."

"I have a present for you too, Olam."

"What is it?"

"It's a surprise. I'll give it to you on Christmas."

He returned to the stained glass window. "Will you help me draw designs, Miss Grace?"

"Yes. Don't move. I'll fetch paper and pencils from the schoolroom."

I could hear him singing to himself again as I left the church.

Christmas Eve arrived. Servants and their families, mostly from Brandubh, gathered in the small church and were greeted by Fr Matthews in the serene, shadowy candlelight. Mother looked elegant in a black velvet dress standing next to Father in his dark evening suit. Grand-Aunt Sadie and Trista joined us in the front pew, and Deirdre glowed with pleasure as area residents welcomed her home. They accepted her return without curiosity about Switzerland, lacking interest in foreign places, which suited Deirdre. In this perfunctory atmosphere she relaxed into the familiar person townspeople adored.

A hush came over the assembly when organ music filled the church and Fr Matthews made his entrance, preceded by a small procession of altar boys. During the hymn "Away in a Manger" the priest gestured to a young couple at the back of the church. They reverently came forward, urging their toddler ahead who held the statue of the Infant Jesus in her arms.

She solemnly placed the holy figure in the crib. Father Matthews bent to pat the toddler's head, who immediately reached out and grabbed hold of his chasuble. The mother quickly unclasped the child, and there were half-grins as the embarrassed parents returned to their pew.

The congregation poured into the ballroom after the service. Grandfather, who chose to forego the church service, joined us for the festivities in the ballroom. He strode in looking the perfect image of a lord in his dark evening suit and red waistcoat.

Townspeople wished him well, praising his benefaction. Grandfather smiled broadly, allowing them to believe Kilpara's generosity was his notion, when in fact he often declared his loath of Irish peasants. He mistrusted them, feared they belonged to Fenian societies that schemed to murder landlords. He disagreed with Father's charity, said it bred familiarity and envy. Father held a different viewpoint, which was to treat people fairly and gain their respect. Still, being in a position of prestige, Grandfather expected acknowledgement and basked in its glory.

Glasses clinked as they were filled with cider or black ale. People milled around talking and greeting one another. Then came the unmistakable sound of bells and children whispered softly, "Is it Santa?"

A loud clomping through the hallway followed. Father trudged into the ballroom loaded down with two heavy sacks slung over his shoulders and bellowed out a loud "Ho, Ho, Ho." Older children ran to him while younger ones clung to their mothers, frightened by this oversized man in a red suit and white beard. Deirdre and I went to Father's side and helped him distribute presents to the children.

I didn't notice the bold fiddle player from the railway station until the music began. He appeared among the musicians, cleaned and scrubbed, his white shirt contrasting against his dark hair curled over his collar. His trousers weren't quite as worn as the ones I had seen him wear previously. Catching my look of curiosity, his green eyes sparkled mischievously above the bow of his fiddle.

I blushed at his cheekiness, which he answered with a wide grin.

People joined hands forming circles on the polished floor. Their voices shouted out gleefully as they danced to a series of reels and jigs. An hour later the band still played, but the crowd had dwindled as parents gathered up sleepy children and took them home to bed. The dark-haired youth set down his fiddle and left the other players.

I thought for a moment he was coming my way. But before he got very far, Clare, the junior housemaid, ran up to him. "Dance with me, Ruairi," she begged.

The youth took her hand and nodded at the band. They began the "Haymaker's Jig." It was easy to see the couple had danced together before, they knew each other's steps intimately.

Olam tugged my hand. "Come on, Miss Grace, let's dance." I nodded and we joined the dancers opposite Clare and the dark-haired youth, who both smiled at us. We danced towards our companions then back again. We crossed, switching partners, and I joined hands with the youth. His eyes looked mirthfully into mine. I tried to match his gaze, but lowered my eyes after a few seconds. His long fingers caressed mine before his grip tightened and we spun around. After a couple more turns I returned next to Olam again.

When the dance ended, the band took a much-needed break. The dark-haired youth settled his fiddle beneath his chin. His face contented, he entertained dancers with a medley of waltzes. People, tired from dancing, begged for a Christmas song. With confident hands the youth moved the bow across the fiddle filling the air with "Silent Night." People moved closer together joining hands, their voices raised in chorus to the music. Pleasure shrouded their faces as hushed harmony echoed throughout the large room.

Suddenly hoarse cries broke the mood, but no one reacted at first. Then the cries became louder. "Trista, Trista ... for the love of God ... where are you, Trista?" People moved apart and stared at a woman in dark worn clothing staggering into the ballroom.

"Bridget, what is it?" Trista asked, her expression changing from calm to one of fear. Detaching herself from the crowd she moved swiftly to the distraught woman who drew her into outstretched hands.

"It's me childer," the woman said, clinging to Trista. "They're sick."

"Where are they?" Trista asked.

"What's ailing them?" Grand-Aunt Sadie added, joining in.

"They're outside in the wagon and they've got burning fevers," the woman said fretfully. "Oh Trista, why did you leave the valley? It took me hours to get here."

"Shhh, you can stop fretting now, Bridget," Trista soothed. "Let's go look at the children."

Mesmerized by the scene, we followed Trista and the weeping woman outside. A man stood guard over a wagon and what looked like a bundle of coats and blankets in the back. Trista got into the wagon and pulled back the covering. Beneath were two pale faces, one of a child about seven and the other a child not much more than a toddler. The older child gave a painful little cough, bringing an anxious look to Grand-Aunt Sadie's face. "How long have they been like this?" she asked.

"A week—maybe more," the woman said. She looked at Trista. "Your brother said we'd find you here. I did the right thing to bring them, didn't I?"

Trista nodded. "Looks like a chill has settled in their chests." She moved a hand over their faces and under their clothes. "Their fever is pitched and they're dehydrated." She looked worriedly at Grand-Aunt Sadie.

"They should be in hospital," Grand-Aunt Sadie said, acknowledging Trista's concern. She turned to Father. "Ellis, order my groom and carriage. And send someone ahead to alert the hospital staff that we're coming with sick children. We'll need lukewarm baths, hot broth, and clean beds when we arrive."

"I'll go," I offered.

"Nonsense, Grace," Grandfather scoffed. "You're too young to risk such an errand. One of the servants will go."

"Grace, your grandfather's right," Father said. "It's too dangerous to ride in the dark. I'll send a groom or stable hand."

He turned to Rengen. "You can get Aunt Sadie to the hospital faster than anyone. Take her, Trista, and the children in a Kilpara carriage."

Father looked questioningly at the man standing beside the wagon and a tired-looking horse. "I'm John Lydon," the man said. "Bridget's brother."

Father motioned to Rengen. "Order Aunt Sadie's groom to follow you with Mrs Joyce and Mr Lydon in her carriage."

Father turned to Tom. "Who's our best rider that knows the shortcuts to the hospital?'

Tom rubbed his forehead. "I gave the lads the night off. By now, they'll have had too much to drink. I'll go."

Father considered it for a moment. "You don't see well at night."

"I can manage," Tom said.

Father looked at him dubiously.

The dark-haired fiddler spoke up. "I've a fast horse. I'll go. I know the way there."

"He's my brother," Clare confirmed. "He knows every inch of the countryside between here and Mayo."

"Send him," Grandfather said.

"Do you know the fastest way to the hospital?" Father asked the youth. He hesitated and Father made a decision. "Grace, you and the boy go together."

"Have you *lost* your mind, Ellis?" Grandfather sputtered, looking around for Mother who was guiding Deirdre indoors.

"Morrigan, tell your husband that Grace can't ride into the night with some indolent commoner. Think of the danger—and her reputation."

But Mother was preoccupied with Deirdre and didn't hear him. I grabbed this opportunity to escape indoors, avoiding Grandfather's forbidding gaze as I hurried past.

Grabbing my cloak I ran to the stables. I threw open the stall door, surprising Spitfire. He was hard to steady as I struggled to get the bit in his mouth.

"Here, let me help you," the dark-haired youth offered, coming into the stable with a brown mare. I stared at the mare. She was a plough horse—and old. Was this the fast horse he spoke about? It would take her hours to reach the hospital. I looked from the boy to the horse.

He shrugged. "She's all I've got. But I wouldn't mind riding that stallion over there." He nodded at Ceonig, one of Father's best horses. I glared at him. If Father hadn't ordered him along I would have told him to leave, but now wasn't the time to stand on principle.

"Get your tackle, and quick," I ordered. The boy grinned. All his mare had on her back was a thick blanket. He walked over to the stall and boldly unhooked the tackle hanging there.

"This'll do, I've never ridden with a saddle before."

"You better know the countryside as well as your sister says you do," I retorted.

"I can ride it blindfolded," he replied easily.

I pulled myself up into the saddle. The youth didn't disguise his surprise when I straddled Spitfire.

"Not very ladylike, are you?" he said, following me into the courtyard.

I gave him a withering look and urged Spitfire into a gallop.

"Right then. Lead the way, Miss Grace O'Donovan."

The carriages were already winding down the avenue as we set out across the fields along the banks of Lough Corrib. It was a moonlit night and cold air stung my cheeks. Clare and the youth were right about one thing, he knew the countryside. In no time he was out in front, treating Ceonig's speed and strength like one does a precious jewel.

"You're some horse," he said softly to Ceonig. When we jumped ditches he cautioned the stallion, "Careful boy."

The lights of Galway grew closer and clearer. It wasn't until we were upon them that the youth hesitated.

"Southwest," I said, taking the lead.

"The lady knows her reference points," he said, in a condescending voice.

"Follow me, and try to keep up," I retorted.

My feet and hands were cold and my face felt numb. I exhaled a deep breath when the convent and Mercy Hospital came into view.

When we reached the hospital I jumped down from Spitfire, handed the reins to the youth, and ran to the heavy door. I pulled the bell cord.

"Good heavens, Grace, what are you doing here at this hour, child?" Sister Josephine exclaimed heaving open the door. "And tonight of all nights. Come inside."

"Grand-Aunt Sadie ..." I said breathlessly, "sent me to forewarn you, she and Trista are on their way here with two very sick children. Grand-Aunt Sadie said to have lukewarm baths, broth, and clean beds ready."

Sister Josephine didn't wait for any more explanation. She called to other nuns and relayed the message. Then turning back to me she said, "You look half frozen. Come in beside the fire and warm yourself."

The youth joined me and we followed Sister Josephine to the waiting room where she invited us to sit in big chairs by the fireplace. She left briefly, returning with cups of steaming tea. "Drink this. It'll bring heat back into you. How old are the children? Do you know anything about their condition?"

"One's school age, the other is very young." I said.

"They looked pale," the youth added.

"What a time for this to happen," Sister Josephine fussed. She left and I hugged the warm mug in my frozen hands, trying to still my shivering body.

"Here, let me help you," the youth said. He set his mug down and knelt before me, reaching to unlace my boots. I drew back.

"I'll thank you to leave my boots alone, Mr—?"

"Kineely, Ruairi Kineely. Be sensible. If you don't take off those boots and warm your feet, you'll get chilblains. Your feet will be swollen and red. Chilblains are very irritating." He held out his hands, and reluctantly I laid a foot in them. Almost delicately he unlaced my boot and slid it off. Then he unlaced the other one.

"Are you always so bold, Mr Kineely?" I asked.

"Not bold—practical." He took my stocking feet between his hands and rubbed them vigorously. Circulation rushed to my toes. As sensation returned I became aware of his touch through my thin stockings.

"That'll do," I said. He lowered my feet to the floor, then stood up to warm his hands over the flames. A minute or two later he turned and lifted my cold hands between his and massaged them. I wanted to contest his insolence, but warmth radiated through me, spreading a velvety lassitude.

"Your sister is Clare Kineely?" I asked sleepily.

"Yes, we own a small farm near Carandulla, not far from Kilpara," Ruairi explained. "Your father is American. I am, too, or at least I was born there." He looked at me proudly. "My father emigrated to America and fought in their Civil War. After it ended he had enough money saved to return home and buy a small farm."

I eased my hands from his. He had stopped massaging them and was holding them. He picked up his mug and was drinking his tea when Sister Josephine reappeared. "Would you fetch me some water, young man?" she asked.

"Surely," he said.

Ruairi followed Sister Josephine outside. After they left, I put my boots on and sat back, dreamily watching blue and orange flames disappear up the chimney.

An hour later we heard the carriages arrive. Ruairi ran outside to assist. He came back carrying the younger of the two children. Rengen followed behind bringing in the older child. They were instructed to take the children to a quiet ward. Grand-Aunt Sadie and Trista instantly went to work, unlacing the children's shoes, removing their worn colourless clothes. The youngest child began coughing. Sister Josephine poured liquid on a spoon and placed it against her lips. She sipped it, her eyes opening momentarily. She looked around until she found her mother's face, gave a faint smile and closed her eyes again. Ruairi pulled a chair close to the children's beds and guided Mrs Joyce into it. Sister Josephine covered her with a blanket.

I left in search of the housekeeper to get fresh tea. "Glory be," the housekeeper said, groggy from sleep. "What a thing to happen, and on Christmas Eve, too. Here, young Grace, fill the teapot from that boiling teakettle."

I took the ceramic teapot, filled it, wrapped it in a tea cosy and placed it on a tray. Pointing to a cupboard she said, "The mugs are in there, dear. Those poor people. Terrible, terrible."

While I retrieved the mugs, she poured clear broth into bowls. "I must get this to Mother Superior right away for the childer," she said. "Can you manage the tea by yourself?"

I nodded. I carried the tray, mugs, and teapot into the waiting room.

"You okay, Miss Grace?" Rengen asked when I handed him a full mug of tea.

"Yes. How are the children?"

"Not good. Their fevers be high and they coughing badly." He looked towards the ward. "Mother— and Trista put them in warm baths, then steam tents to help they's breathing."

Sister Josephine came in. "Mother Superior said there's nothing more you can do here tonight. Since you must be exhausted, she wants you to make yourselves comfortable in the visitors' quarters."

Too tired to protest, we followed Sister Josephine across the frozen yard. She became apologetic when we entered the cold building. "The fires have just been lit, so the rooms will take awhile to warm up. But there's lots of covering on the beds. You won't notice the cold once you're beneath the blankets."

I hesitated when Sister Josephine opened the door to my assigned room. This was the room where my grandmother had spent her final months. Father hardly ever talked about her death, but Grand-Aunt Sadie did. She believed my grandmother existed with God in a world of everlasting love. She had shown me this room and told me how my grandmother had passed away surrounded by love in the midst of her family. Knowing this, I didn't view this room as one of sadness, which Father obviously did. But I was overcome with emotion to find myself sleeping here.

"Is something wrong?" Sister Josephine asked.

"No, everything's fine," I said.

Rengen looked at me. "You all right here, Miss Grace?"

"Yes," I said.

He squeezed my shoulder. "Get some rest."

I nodded, went inside and closed the door.

That was easier said than done. The bed was comfortable and I was soon warm beneath heavy blankets. Thoughts of my grandmother didn't haunt me, but the image of the woman who had shown up unexpectedly at Kilpara kept me awake. She was Myles Joyce's wife. Her husband had made newspaper headlines a couple of years ago.

I twisted restlessly in bed, unable to shut out the sad story Trista told Father soon after she returned to Mercy Hospital. We had ridden to the convent to visit Grand-Aunt Sadie and were leaving when Father spotted Trista resting on a bench beneath a chestnut tree. We went over. She had been back at Mercy Hospital a month then, but her sallow skin still showed the effects of malnutrition and fatigue. She looked up through hollow eyes.

"Hello Ellis," she greeted us.

Father smiled and we sat down.

"How are you, Trista?"

"Improving. I made the right decision to return to the hospital."

She joined her hands and looked down. "Here, I'm not reminded of my husband, Liam, every day. Patients occupy my mind. But I worry about my family. Especially Bridget at Maamtrasna Cross."

"Bridget?" Father asked. "The wife of your cousin who was implicated in the murder of John Joyce and his family?"

Trista nodded. "Bridget's not doing well. This is the second anniversary of when the authorities arrested Myles and nine other men in the valley."

"It was a gruesome murder," Father said.

"John Joyce wasn't well liked, but that's no reason for murder. It's rumoured by some that his killers were Fenian supporters. That they murdered him because they suspected he'd turned informant against his own kind; gave the authorities names of men likely to assassinate landlords or their agents for evicting tenant farmers from their homes. Constables hunting Fenians in the area had been paying visits to John's cottage. It didn't look good." Her voice wavered. "Personally, I think the constables initially visited John, hoping to pry information from him, but then they saw Peggy and became smitten with her. After that they were only mildly interested in interrogating him. It was Peggy they really went to see."

"Peggy?"

"John Joyce's pretty daughter. Men swarmed around her like bees to nectar. Authorities ignored the Fenian theory, and claimed Myles and the others murdered John because he stole their sheep."

Trista stared at the dark convent walls. "Myles was hanged, but he was innocent. He was a good man. Everyone in the valley knew he didn't kill John, or his family. He never would've committed such a sin, even though John was a bit of a gombeen man. Myles and John had their differences, but they were related."

"The trial made headlines."

"If you could call it a trial. Myles' only crime was that he was a simple farmer who only spoke the Irish. The judges had to punish someone, I suppose. The other two men who hanged alongside Myles proclaimed his innocence."

"The justice system failed miserably."

Trista heaved heavily. "The authorities turned a blind eye to sworn testimony and hanged him anyway. Bridget gave birth to Nora that same day. When she was strong enough she went to Galway jail and keened him for days. She was in terrible shape when we tore her away and brought her back home."

"How is she now?"

"She'll never recover from losing Myles. The other accused men escaped the hangman's rope, if you consider prison in Dublin a lucky alternative."

Father shook his head. "Perhaps justice will prevail now that Tom Carey made a public confession before the bishop and cleared Myles' name."

Tears swam in Trista's eyes. "The truth is no good now. It won't bring Myles back. And it doesn't change the fact he was an Irishman in an Englishman's court."

"Tragic."

"It's tragic for a community still mourning the innocents that died. And the family of a man wrongly hanged. Bridget is left without a husband and a father for her children. Her brother, John Lydon, helps out as best he can. I go and see her every chance I get."

Father squeezed Trista's hand. "You've had your share of troubles. You need to concentrate on getting your strength back."

"I can't help fretting over Bridget."

Trista's troubled face on that day swam through my consciousness, along with images of the distraught Bridget and the two unmoving children wrapped in the wagon, pale, already the picture of death.

Finally, I fell asleep, and when I opened my eyes, the sky appeared lighter through the small bedroom window. I got out of bed, put on my cloak and walked to the hospital. In the silent ward a nun sat vigil over the two children. Someone had put a pillow behind Bridget's head, for she slept upright in the same chair she had sat in last night. Grand-Aunt Sadie and Trista lay resting in empty beds nearby. The nun put a finger to her lips and led me back to the waiting room.

"Mother Superior and Trista have done all they can. They're worn out," she said.

"The children?" I asked.

"We'll know more when they wake up."

I sat in the empty waiting room, staring at dead ashes in the cold fireplace. A novice arrived to restart the fire and offered to bring me tea. Soon afterward Rengen, Bridget's brother, and Ruairi joined me.

It wasn't until Trista came in, her face tired but cheerful, that anyone moved. "The children's fever is hovering below the danger point," she announced. "Their breathing is laboured, but better, and they're taking medicine for their coughs. Bridget and John will stay on here for a few days. They'll return to the valley when we know for sure the children will recover."

Following Trista's announcement we prepared to leave. The groom brought the carriage from the stables, followed by Ruairi Kineely with Ceonig and Spitfire.

Rengen raised an eyebrow.

"What was I supposed to do?" I asked. "His mare was a plough horse and would've slowed us down."

Rengen looked at me reproachfully, then shrugged.

Without apology Ruairi tied the horses' reins to the back of the carriage. He and Rengen mounted up front while I took my place inside. We started down the drive, leaving Trista and Grand-Aunt Sadie framed in the doorway waving.

We jostled along the road in the frosty morning air. Families tucked cosily inside cottages along the way were already celebrating Christmas. I would too, very soon. I imagined Maureen preparing the Christmas goose. There would be presents, but none more precious than having witnessed Bridget Joyce's joy when her two children awakened and took sips of broth fed to them by the nuns.

We arrived at Kilpara and Ruairi led his mare out of the stable. He put the blanket on her and hopped up. He had retrieved his fiddle from the house with a message from Clare.

"They're waiting Christmas for me," he said.

"You'd best not delay," I said.

His eyes held mine and I saw pride and longing there. He was comparing Ceonig to his mare, his world to mine.

"Why did you fib about your horse?" I asked, before I could stop myself.

"I did it for the sake of the woman and her sick childer," he said, a hint of pride in his voice.

Jutting out his chin, he dug his heels into the mare's sides, nodded, and rode off.

"Happy Christmas, Ruairi Kineely," I whispered under my breath.

40

CHAPTER 5

Smells of gingerbread, goose cooking, and scented pine greeted me inside, all pleasantly free of antiseptic and carbolic acid. I joined Mother, Father, Deirdre, and Grandfather in the drawing room next to the fireplace. Mother rose and hugged me, relief smoothing her anxious face. "Will the children be all right?"

"I hope so," I said. "They showed improvement this morning."

"The younger one looked so still and pale," Deirdre said. "As if she were already dead. Not much older than a baby ..."

Grandfather snorted. "Balderdash. Ellis, it's abominable that you permitted Grace to ride into the night, accompanied by an ill-bred peasant. With no chaperone. Behaving no better than a common servant!"

I expected Father to retort; instead, he spoke calmly. "The children were deathly ill. They needed immediate attention. Besides, Grace is an excellent horsewoman. I trusted her to get to the hospital and warn the staff. That 'ill-bred peasant' is a reliable young man. His parents voyaged on *The White Lady* with Mother and me when we came to Ireland in '66. The boy was only a baby, but his family persevered through difficult seafaring conditions. His father's a decent man. He fought in the Civil War under the Union flag in the same regiment as my brother, Francis."

Grandfather stood up. "For God's sake, Ellis, this is no time to reminisce about the past. Times have changed. Think of the danger. That vulgar-looking young hoodlum has no rearing, no manners, yet you let him escort Grace on a midnight ride through deserted countryside. *You* gave her permission to go gallivanting with him."

I watched a flash of red work its way up Father's neck and cover his face.

"Like I said, I know the youth's parents. His sister works for us as a housemaid and is a decent young woman. You know, where I grew up, we helped the less fortunate. It's considered the Christian thing to do."

Grandfather stared at Father, then turned and stormed out of the room.

Father started after Grandfather, but Mother stopped him. "Let me talk to him," she said.

In the silence that followed. Deirdre rose, walked over to stand by the Christmas tree and looked outside, her back to us. Father slumped into a chair and stared at flames dancing up the chimney. I gazed at the different shades of wallpaper. On the east wall where the sun hit, small purple flowers had become an odd shade of lavender, deep green leaves turned lime, unlike other parts of the room where original colours remained untouched from direct sunlight. I had never noticed this before.

I found Father's admission he knew Ruairi's family surprising; that they had voyaged on the same ship that brought my grandmother back to Ireland. He had never mentioned the Kineelys, not even when he talked about my uncle Francis, killed in America's Civil War.

A low sniffle pierced the silence like a thunder clap. I stared at Deirdre's back, her slumped shoulders, folded arms, which she unfolded to raise a hanky to her nose. She hadn't commented on my late night adventure, only on the condition of the children. I recalled how she gasped when Trista pulled back the old blankets and coats to reveal the sick youngsters. Her face turned a ghastly white at the sight of their pitiful condition. Mother, equally shocked, had gathered her indoors, creating the distraction I needed to escape censure and ride over to Mercy Hospital. Deirdre would be less distraught if she witnessed the children's improvement this morning.

I rose to reassure her as Maureen entered the room, cheerfully carrying a tray with cups of hot cider. "The goose is cooking up nicely. We'll have a feast fit for a king."

She looked at me. "Olam is asking—Miss Grace—if he can give you your Christmas present now. It's hard for him to be patient. I know you've just come in, but would you mind?"

"Of course," I answered, pausing to look at Deirdre. She hadn't moved. I hurried upstairs and returned to the kitchen with Olam's present. His face brightened into a wide smile when he saw me.

He shifted from one foot to another. "It's Christmas. I can give you your present now. Close your eyes and hold out your hands."

I obeyed. He placed an object on my open palms. "Don't drop it." Satisfied that I had gripped it he said, "Now open your eyes."

I stared in delight at a replica of Spitfire carved from rich dark wood. Olam had caught his image reared-up on hind legs, every muscle flexed, his forelegs raised high. It took my breath away.

Olam clasped and unclasped his hands while I examined the statue. "Do you like it?"

"It's beautiful," I said and hugged him.

"Mam and Dad helped me," he said, beaming.

I gave him his present. He unwrapped it with the eagerness of a young child. Upon seeing the coloured pencils he said, "Let's go draw, Miss Grace."

The ground froze and thawed on Christmas Day. It was thawing again when Father and I set out for Larcourt on Boxing Day. He rode Apollo, a fast, but well-behaved stallion. I rode Spitfire. Their hooves kicked up muck as we sped across bleak hillsides, past bare trees, jumping over low rock walls and lifeless brown hedges.

The courtyard at Larcourt was filled with amiable chatter when we arrived. Riders and hounds crowded round impatiently waiting for the hunt to begin. Spitfire, disoriented by the noise and chaos, drew back and balked.

"Talk to him. Calm him," Father commanded. "He must learn to ignore commotion if he's to enter into competition."

PATRICIA HOPPER

I nodded, led Spitfire slightly apart from the crowd, dismounted and spoke softly. Satisfied with my efforts, Father joined Sir Sloane and Lord Ligham. Near them Cecil sat on a grey and white gelding, clustered in a group of young men that chatted in a lively fashion. David Ligham stood beside his father, not yet mounted. He saw me and led his horse over.

I let my surprise to see him show on my face. He had been mostly absent from social functions in recent years while studying law at Trinity College in Dublin. He didn't look anything like his father, who was a short stocky man. In fact, as he came towards me I thought he appeared taller and thinner than I remembered. His dark straight hair was combed forward, his angular face pronounced by a long pointed nose and round eyes set too close together.

"It's been a long time, Grace," he said.

"It has," I admitted.

"You look all grown up."

I laughed uneasily.

"Forgive me for staring. You really are turning into a beautiful young woman."

I averted my gaze towards Spitfire. "How've you been?"

"Quite well, I'm studying for the bar. I've considered practising law in England after my exams. But who knows, I may have been too hasty. I may have overlooked Ireland."

"I'm sure you'll do well whatever you decide."

The huntsman's horn blew, announcing the start of the hunt, and David's father motioned for him to mount.

"Good luck," he said. "See you after the hunt. Oh, and we'll be attending the ball on New Year's Eve."

I mounted Spitfire and was about to line up beside the other riders when Cecil pulled his horse alongside. "Deirdre didn't change her mind, I see."

"No," I said. "You know she doesn't care for hunts."

"But you do." Cecil's dark eyes bore into mine.

Without warning he raised his riding crop and slapped Spitfire's flank, startling him. Spitfire reared up, and if I hadn't been holding the reins tightly, I would have fallen off. I struggled to regain control.

Cecil laughed. "That'll teach you to interfere next time I want to be alone with Deirdre."

"Interfere? What?" He slapped Spitfire again who reared in protest. I pulled on the reins, but he didn't respond. The huntsman blew the starting blast. Spitfire shot forward at the sound, ahead of other riders. We were in front, galloping wildly. The metal gate was coming up fast and pulled open only halfway by two stable hands. I looked at the wall next to it. It was close to five feet. We had never jumped that high before. The only choices were to go over the wall or run into the gate. I tried to prepare, but there wasn't time. "Focus," I whispered as much to myself as to Spitfire. "We must jump the wall." But Spitfire was heedless, frightened, not reacting to my commands.

The stable hands saw us bearing down on them and hurried to get the gate open. "It's now or never, Spitfire," I said, fearing for us both. We gained momentum. We were upon the wall, up, over, cleared it, just barely. Cheers sounded behind us and hounds drew alongside barking furiously, noses to the ground. They passed us, then charged out in front. We were in close pursuit, Spitfire excited, but no longer out of control.

We were the first to arrive when the hounds cornered the fox in his den. Father wasn't far behind. He pulled alongside. Turning to face me he said, "What the devil were you thinking, Grace, to risk your neck and Spitfire's like that? You could've been killed!"

"Spitfire was spooked," I said, holding his gaze. "I had no choice but to jump the wall."

Father's frown slackened. "You gave me quite the scare. I may have misjudged Spitfire. It's obvious he's too excitable for public situations."

"On the contrary. He proved himself ready for competition. Did you see how he cleared the wall without any preparation?"

"He has the height and the speed. But if he hadn't made the jump …"

I began to tremble then, shake from head to foot. Realisation of the near-accident sank in. If Spitfire had refused to jump or couldn't make the height, we both would have been injured. By the time we returned to Larcourt I was still trembling inwardly, even as I was presented the symbolic trophy. Afterwards, I tried to hold myself steady as everyone congratulated me. Except Cecil. His dark eyes held a warning.

People began to move indoors where a buffet had been prepared. I knew my stomach would revolt at the onslaught of food, and the stagnant indoor air would make me dizzy. I whispered to Father that I'd like to be excused to return home.

"But the festivities—" he began. "You're a celebrity. A girl—er—young woman seldom takes the prize. If ever."

"That's it, you see. The excitement. I'm drained."

"I understand," Father said. "You're so tough I sometimes forget your delicate disposition. I'm really proud of you, Grace. You showed tremendous courage today. You displayed professional sportsmanship in the way you handled Spitfire. I'll arrange for a carriage to take you home."

"Thanks, Father, but I don't need a carriage. The fresh air will do me good. I can ride home. It's not far."

"I won't hear of it. You'll ride back in a carriage."

I shrugged acceptance. His insistence was a small price to pay for the escape I badly wanted.

After Father left, the courtyard was empty except for hundreds of hoof prints in the soft earth. Alone in the cold outdoors with only Spitfire for company, I stared through the windows of the great room. People in red and black riding habits passed back and forth with plates filled from the large sideboard stacked with various food dishes. Riders took their places at the long table, to eat, to mull over how I, a mere girl, was first to corner the fox. I was unaware a carriage had approached until it stopped beside me.

"Tie Spitfire to the back," Father ordered, opening the carriage door and stepping out.

"Yes sir," a familiar voice answered as the driver jumped down from the dickie. I stood face to face with Ruairi Kineely who held out his hand for Spitfire's reins.

Father hugged me and helped me inside. "I'll be home soon," he said. I pretended to believe him. By my leaving he would stay late into the night, the challenge of the hunt easing into a long poker game.

"Ready, Miss Grace?" Ruairi asked, his green eyes fixed on my face.

"Yes. Please leave the window open." Ruairi nodded, closed the door, and we started down the avenue. We began the short distance between Larcourt and Kilpara, and in the confines of the carriage, I gave in to the tremors. I put my head in my hands and cried.

I didn't notice the carriage had stopped until strong hands were on my arms and Ruairi's voice was saying, "Ah, come on, Miss Grace, don't do that."

He helped me out of the carriage and I stood heaving against his chest, his calm body steadying me. He stroked my hair and spoke softly. "You were so brave, Miss Grace, taking that wall with more guts than anyone I've ever seen. You deserve more than a prize. The bloody bastard, I'd like to kill him with my bare hands."

I drew back, and he wiped tears from my eyes with his handkerchief. "You saw. How?"

"I was helping out at the stables. They always need extra hands at these affairs and I need the money. Ours is a small farm and we're a large family. I had guided Lady Daphne on her mount to the line-up and was returning to the stable when I saw Sloane spook Spitfire. I was too far away to do anything, but I ran after you anyway." He brushed back my hair. "I was sure you'd be thrown." His eyes hardened. "I wanted to thrash the arrogant bastard."

I sniffed and he handed me his handkerchief. I took it and moved away, confused by his anger. Hearing him put into words what could have happened made my chest tighten and my breath catch in my throat.

"It was an accident," I said.

"That was no damned *accident*." Ruairi's voice rose to a roar. "It was deliberate. He intended to hurt you. Why are you defending Cecil Sloane?" He stiffened as if a thought struck him. "Unless—he's your lover? And you had a lover's quarrel. He took revenge on you because you invoked the bastard's temper."

I opened my mouth to object, but choked back a sob instead.

"So that explains it," he said stiffly. "I'd be more careful if I were you about who comes courting."

I wanted to scream at him that I despised Cecil Sloane; that he made my skin crawl, but I had no fight left in me to argue. I just wanted to go home and not think any more about Cecil or what he intended against me.

Stone-faced, Ruairi held out his hand and I got back inside the carriage. The door clicked shut, and as Kilpara drew closer. I tried to shut out my turbulent feelings. When we reached the stables I quietly handed Spitfire over to one of the grooms, then with eyes lowered I thanked Ruairi for bringing me home.

Mother looked surprised to see me carrying the trophy. After giving her only the barest details, I professed to be tired and needing rest. Escaping to my room I was grateful Deirdre wasn't there. I closed the door, laid down on the bed and gave in to pent-up sobs.

That night I drifted in and out of sleep. At one point I awakened and hugged the bedcovers, listening for sounds. Everything was quiet, yet the house felt alive. I imagined the spirits of my ancestors moving about the corridors, called back by the day's traumatic events. In their infinite wisdom perhaps they would offer sage counsel, but none was forthcoming.

The drapes were open, drawing the moon's macabre shadows into the room. I crossed the cold floor to close them. For a moment I stood mesmerized by the moon as it slid in and out behind passing clouds. It emerged from obscurity casting eerie shadows on frosted trees, spindly branches pointed upwards and outwards like gnarled fingers. A tall figure intruded onto the scene taking long strides away from the stables. I pressed my face against the window, straining to make out the apparition. Moonlight caught flecks of light hair resting above broad shoulders of a man's image whose stature reminded me of Conor Hagerty, a blacksmith who had worked at Kilpara over a year ago.

I didn't know why he popped into my mind; it was too dark to see clearly. Conor always made me think of those fearless men in stories of the Fian, warriors of olden days. The figure moving away from the stables had that mythical look of undaunted strength. Rengen was the only other man I knew whose strength and size matched Conor's. They had worked side by side in the forge, two giants, one very fair, one very dark. I commented once to Conor about the Fian. He laughed and called me farcical.

"The Fian are nothing more than fabled legends of Ireland's past glory," he remarked. "She's an oppressed country now. In the Erin of old, people were free to choose their own destiny."

"You believe Ireland should be independent of England?"

"I do. And if it's worth believing in, it's worth fighting for."

I remembered the last time I saw Conor. He stood saying goodbye to Rengen, a ticket in hand to set sail for America. He must not have felt as strongly about Irish sovereignty as he proclaimed. Or perhaps he decided his destiny lay not in Ireland, but in a progressive country like America.

The moon passed behind clouds again, and when it reappeared the figure was gone. My nerves, already fraught from the day's events, turned edgy with suspicion that a prowler was lurking about the stables. I became uneasy and knew I couldn't rest until I checked that Spitfire was safe. Stifling a soft groan, I collected my boots and wrapped a shawl around my shoulders. I glanced over at Deirdre's slumbering form as I sneaked quietly out the bedroom door and down the back staircase. Shrugging into the boots, I lit the lamp kept in the foyer at the servants' entrance and stepped outside into the cold. Bathed in yellow light I hurried along the path to the stables. Arriving without incident I paused to listen, exhaling rapid breaths of cold air that clung to me like fog.

Too late, I heard footfalls behind me seconds before a hand squeezed my shoulder. A chill shivered up my spine and I choked back a scream that rose in my throat. Raising the lamp to eye level, I swivelled around.

"Get that thing out of my face."

My knees went weak from relief. "Father?"

"Who did you think it was and what're you doing out here? You'll catch your death." The smell of alcohol wafted off his breath.

"I thought I saw a prowler and came to investigate."

"It's not safe outside at night alone," he admonished.

"I was worried about the horses."

He studied me for a moment. "I didn't encounter anyone. You probably saw one of the grooms. But if you're worried enough to risk wandering around in the dark, go check the horses and make it snappy. It's cold out here."

When the check produced nothing unusual he said, "Let's get inside."

Returning indoors I ruminated if Father was my nighttime phantom. He had the height, but not the build. The prowler was sure-footed, unlike Father who moved a little unsteady on his feet after a long night at the poker table. Now that I was calmer I began to think more rationally. It seemed likely the dark shadow was a servant or groom who had returned early after the holiday. Or maybe I had imagined the whole thing.

"Shhh," Father warned as I lit our way back upstairs. "Quietly."

We paused outside his bedroom door, and he gingerly slid inside, giving me an all-clear nod. Anxious for my own warm bed I extinguished the lamp and slipped into my bedroom. Going to the window I firmly closed the drapes, then scooted beneath the warm covers. Comforted by Deirdre's bulk across the room in the opposite bed, I fell asleep.

But my sleep was unsettled by dreams of the legendary Finn Mac Cumaill and his Fian who hunted every inch of Irish soil. Of Gráinne protesting her betrothed to Finn, a much older man, and whose heart was already given to young Diarmait, a warrior in Finn's army.

In dream-state I followed Gráinne and Diarmait's elopement and their attempts to escape Finn's wrath. I joined them on their journey as they fled from place to place across the country closely pursued by the Fian after their betrayal was discovered. They ran through fields near Kilpara and along the Corrib, the Fian closely on their heels ...

Clare's soft knock on the door and her summons to breakfast jolted me awake.

"Mmm, go away," Deirdre protested.

Sleepy as Deirdre was, I couldn't hold back telling her about Cecil. "Something horrible happened at the hunt yesterday," I said.

"Mmm," Deirdre murmured.

"Cecil deliberately spooked Spitfire."

"What?" Deirdre bolted awake. "Were you hurt? Is Spitfire all right?"

"We're fine. Cecil warned me not to get in his way."

"Of what?"

"His interest in you."

"In me. Cecil? No. Ridiculous." Deirdre made a face and hugged her knees.

"Don't trust him."

"I've never trusted Cecil. What happened?"

I told her about the hunt, the near-accident, Father's anger and my return home. I left out the scene with Ruairi Kineely.

She came over and hugged me. "You must've been terrified."

"I was. Be careful of Cecil Sloane ..."

She nodded solemnly.

Servants returned to the house and chattered as they moved upstairs and downstairs making preparations for the ball. Talk of Christmas, families, and lovers were confided up and down the hallways as Mother, Maureen, and Anthony directed them from one task to the next.

Grandfather retired to the library, Father to Galway to occupy himself at his agency. Grand-Aunt Margaret, Mother's paternal childhood guardian, arrived valise in hand and went immediately to work, making comments and suggestions even before she had settled into her room.

In all this commotion I escaped to the stables. I needed to regain my confidence after the previous day's fright; I was determined to overcome my fear and ride Spitfire. Inside the stables I strapped on his saddle and led him outside. Instead of mounting sidesaddle, I straddled his back and we struck out across the fields and along the banks of the Corrib. I steeled my nerves and fought back images of the wall rushing up to meet me, of being thrown headlong to the ground and injured, of Spitfire crushed and hurt. Spray stung my eyes from the tempestuous lake, stirred by winter winds beating against the spongy shore. We rode hard, my pulse beating fast, my breath catching in gasps. We cleared low fences and stiles, the dead earth heeding our presence. My fear began to ebb and my confidence returned. I could stand up to Cecil Sloane. I winced when I thought of Ruairi Kineely and his accusation that Cecil and I were lovers. Next time I saw Ruairi I would explain the truth.

I turned back to Kilpara feeling fortified. I was almost there when Olam rode out to meet me. "How did you know where I was?" I asked.

"Guessed," he said. "Master O'Donovan said I'm to always ride with you, remember?"

"Yes," I agreed. "But sometimes I need to be alone."

Olam looked hurt. "Why?"

"To test Spitfire," I lied. "To concentrate."

"I don't understand."

"Let's not think about it anymore. Want to race?"

He smiled widely. "Sure."

We dug in our heels and galloped back to the house. Olam grinned when he reached the stables first. "I beat you," he said. "You'll have to make Spitfire do better."

"I will," I said, looping my arm in his. "Let's see if your mammy will give us some cocoa."

CHAPTER 6

On New Year's Eve carriages arrived one after another. Men entered the house in bowler hats, gloves and long overcoats over evening suits. Women wore tailored cloaks, sequins in their hair, and a rainbow of fashionable gowns.

I struggled into the dress Mrs Collins made. I felt bare on top and tried to pull the front up higher.

Mother pushed my hands away. "Leave it alone, Grace." She handed me the wrap. "Here, put this around your shoulders."

The white velvet wrap felt soft against my skin. I closed it over my bodice.

"Stop fighting the dress," Mother ordered.

Reluctantly I obeyed and picked up my gloves. I looked at Deirdre who appeared delicate in her blue dress, her fair hair knotted into a braid and coiled on top of her head. She had a look of dread on her face. This was her first real test in public since her return home.

"I don't want to go. All those people staring at me, asking lots of silly questions," she complained when Mother left us alone.

I pulled at the front of my dress. "So much fuss to be around people we already know."

"And each one trying to outdo the other, all nosy and spoiled."

Mother came back into our room and stood observing us. "It's time, girls. You both look lovely."

Anthony, our butler, solemnly announced guests as they entered the ballroom: the Blakes, Captain Jones, the Lynches, the Stauntons, the Thompsons, Sir Manson, the Wildes, Mrs Parnell, Lord Ardilaun ... We greeted them each in turn with the same perfunctory comments. They continued into the ballroom accepting glasses of champagne offered from silver trays, then moved forward to mingle with guests.

Women's faces were pasted into smiles, elegant skirts sashaying in kaleidoscopic colour, gloved hands poised delicately around long-stemmed glasses. Men spoke loudly and strutted about in an unspoken ritual. The orchestra played softly, and after all the guests had arrived, dinner was announced. Couples entered the great room to a table laden with china place settings and crystal glassware. Mother had strategically placed families with eligible young men and women together.

Thomas Roberts and his family, good friends of the Sloanes, sat next to Deirdre. It was apparent when Thomas looked at Deirdre that he admired her. He engaged her in conversation, his voice a pleasant baritone. His face was animated with good humour, and his eyes the colour of hazelnuts held Deirdre's.

As the meal of roast pork progressed Deirdre relaxed, and by the time it was over she was conversing easily. Cecil on the opposite side of the table tried to enter the conversation, but had to resort to shouting, so he sulked.

I sat next to Lady Daphne who engaged Mrs Parnell in a discussion about her son Charles. Intrigued, I thought back to the tall thin man at the train station who spoke so elegantly in favour of Irish independence.

"So Charles spends more time at Eatham in England these days instead of Avondale," Lady Daphne remarked.

"A good place to repose between House sessions," Mrs Parnell replied.

"Willie O'Shea is most hospitable to extend an open invitation."

"A gentleman."

"I understand he's not always at Eatham himself."

"His wife is politically influential in her own right, despite the limited time she spends on current events because of the children."

"Katie's a devoted mother. But there's no denying Charles is handsome—and unmarried."

"Who did you say made your beautiful gown?" Mrs Parnell deftly changed the subject, denying Lady Daphne's thirst for intimate personal details. "I must pay your dressmaker a visit. She's in Paris?"

When the banquet was over the orchestra started a series of waltzes. By this time I had adjusted to the dress. I watched Mother and Father dance together, Mother easily the most beautiful woman in the ballroom. Mrs Collins had been right about the fabric and the dress. Mother looked like a legendary goddess from a bygone era.

"That's a departure from Mrs Collins's usual designs," Lady Daphne said observing Mother. "It gives your mother an odd look." Lady Daphne was probably the only one who thought so. She fidgeted with the frills of her own dress. It had several layers that failed to flatter her figure. She waited for her husband to request a dance, but he seemed too busy watching Mother and Father with noticeable envy.

Deirdre and Thomas Roberts joined us after the waltz ended. Thomas was telling Deirdre a story and she looked amused. Cecil didn't appear to find their tête-à-tête humourous by the look on his face. He whisked her off for the next dance when the orchestra started up again. Thomas offered me his hand, and for the first time that evening I danced with a young man.

"You're a wonderful dancer, Miss Grace," Thomas said. His gaze searched for Deirdre and when their eyes met, he smiled. "Although I must say you and your sister look nothing alike."

"What do you mean?"

"I hope I didn't sound offensive. It's just that, well, your hair for one thing, and your eyes, and well, Miss Deirdre is—"

"Delicate," I finished. I smiled up at him.

"Well yes—no—I mean, she's very becoming, that's all. Yes, that's it." He looked at me apologetically. "Not that you're not beautiful, too. I didn't mean to imply—"

"What *did* you mean to imply?" I knew he was uncomfortable, but I was determined to make him justify himself. He laughed. A conventional laugh.

"Will you please accept that I find you sister beguiling."

"That's fair. Are you in college with Cecil?"

"No, but we went to boarding school together. I'm attending Queen's College. I'm a student of engineering."

"You'll be in Galway for a while then."

"I hope so."

The dance ended and we returned to where Cecil and his friends were vying for Deirdre's attention.

David Ligham asked me to dance, and I saw Sir Charles partnered with Mother. His head was bent towards her as if trying to take in every nuance of her face. Father waltzed by with Mrs Parnell. Occasionally, David removed his hand from my shoulder to reach for his handkerchief, appearing to have a constant nose irritation. He looked at me curiously, his mouth stretched into a half smile.

"That was quite a feat you pulled off at the hunt the other day. I didn't know you were so determined to win the contest."

"I wasn't."

"But you were in full gallop before anyone else had warmed up."

"The excitement frightened my horse."

"Thoroughbreds are well known for their unpredictable temperaments. They can put their riders at risk. Not a safe thing for young ladies."

"I suppose."

"You've got such spunk and yet still manage to look beautiful. I can't help but admire you."

"Thank you." A flush crept over my face.

His mouth pushed further up into a smile.

When the dance ended David led me back to where Deirdre sat. He offered her his hand for the next waltz. I sat talking to the Misses Blake when Cecil left his group of friends and approached me.

"I do believe you promised me this dance, Grace," he said politely. But his eyes mocked me.

I took his hand, determined not to be intimidated as we moved onto the crowded floor.

"Aren't you going to thank me for what I did the other day?" he asked.

"Thank you?"

"You trapped the fox, didn't you?"

"What you did could've killed me."

"Don't be silly, Grace. I was jesting. You're a strong horsewoman. A little thing like jumping a wall shouldn't fluster you."

"It didn't," I lied. "But don't frighten my horse again, or I'll tell."

"Tell what, Grace? And to whom? No, Grace, stay out of my way and we'll get along. Cross me and there'll be hell to pay. I want to be with Deirdre, so don't meddle."

"Are you threatening me?"

"Take it any way you will." His voice was cold and hard. I felt a chill go through me.

CHAPTER 7

The ball was declared a success. It was talked about for days. The morning afterwards I returned from riding Spitfire to find Mother and Deirdre settled in their studio on the second floor. They faced the window side by side, their pinafores covered in paint splotches, canvasses perched upright on easels. They acknowledged me briefly then returned to their work, my presence blending in with stock items around the room, oil paints, watercolours, jars of brushes, mineral spirits, and blank canvasses of various sizes. I stepped behind Deirdre who daubed and brushed a stark landscape. A winter field, brown beneath a forbidding sky, tree trunks dark and leafless with branches tangled and cracked almost as if they were shrieking, a grey river cascading over angry stones. If this grim painting resembled what art masters had taught her in Switzerland, I wasn't impressed.

I was relieved when I moved behind Mother who was filling in greenery around a cheerful portrait of purple crocuses. She cocked her head to one side and posed a critical eye upon her work. "Thomas is a fine young man," she said. "He seems quite fond of you."

"He doesn't know me," Deirdre said.

"The Roberts are staying in Galway more often now that Thomas is studying at Queen's University. They're taking time away from their steamship business in Belfast. They've even bought Inishbeag Manor."

Deirdre paused in mid-stroke and raised an eyebrow.

Mother shrugged. "Small Island is a silly name for a manor on the mainland." She waved her paintbrush towards the window. "If it were possible to see across Lough Corrib, Inishbeag would be visible on the western shore."

"Why go to such trouble when the Sloanes would welcome them as guests?"

"Perhaps they've grown fond of Galway and want something permanent because they plan to spend more time here."

"Mmm," Deirdre murmured, becoming disinterested.

The following morning I was descending the staircase when I saw Cecil in the vestibule. I retreated back a few steps and sat down out of sight. I peeked cautiously through rails in the banister. Cecil stood glaring at Anthony; his voice rose, demanding to see Deirdre. The butler explained in a firm voice that Miss Deirdre had gone into Galway with Mrs O'Donovan to view a new art exhibit at the city museum. Unhappy with this news, Cecil began pacing back and forth across the vestibule, his angry footsteps echoing on the marble floor. Anthony held the front door open with a defiant look on his face. "Is there anyone else in the household you wish to speak with, Mr Sloane?"

I held my breath.

Cecil stopped pacing. "No. You're *absolutely* sure Miss Deirdre went into Galway with her mother?"

"You may check the stable for yourself, *sir*. You'll see the missus' carriage is gone."

Cecil thrust his calling card towards the butler.

"See that Miss Deirdre gets this," he demanded.

"Yes *sir*." Anthony firmly shut the door behind Cecil.

I waited until I was sure Cecil had left before heading to the stables. I saddled Spitfire and rode to Mercy Hospital to check on Bridget Joyce and her children's progress. I wondered if I would find Bridget still there; she had put off returning home twice already. Laughter spilled into the hallway outside the children's ward. I peeked inside to find Rengen carrying Nora, the youngest, on his shoulders. She was giggling in delight. Bridget sat in the same chair that had been provided upon her arrival, her haunted eyes smiling at her toddler's joy. When Rengen gave Nora back to her mother, Conboy, the older child, took hold of Rengen's hand.

"Where're you from?" he asked.

"I's from the United States of America."

"America?"

"Yes."

"Across the sea where the cowboys live?"

"Yes. You've heard about cowboys?"

"My uncle draws pictures of them when he tells us stories. You don't have a hat or a lasso like a cowboy."

"I's a Negro. There's Negro cowboys too, but you don't hear much about them."

"What's a Negro?"

"Someone with black skin like me who used to be a slave."

"Slave?"

"Yes, a slave."

"Does it hurt ... to be a slave?"

"I was a slave once, and yes it hurting a lot. When I's a boy down South, no bigger than you is now ..."

Grand-Aunt Sadie came into the ward as Rengen began his story. "This will take awhile," she whispered. "Join me for a cup of tea." I followed her to her quarters, and after we were settled by the fireplace with steaming mugs of strong brew she asked, "How was the ball?"

"A success. I was uncomfortable in my dress."

"Your grandmother used to be so elegant at those affairs when she was a young girl. Had an eye for fashion. Born to it, you might say. It was an asset when she emigrated to America."

"So you've said. Many times."

Grand-Aunt Sadie laughed. "Yes, and I've said many times she was a talented seamstress and a natural doctor. She used her genteel status to make fashionable clothes for gentry. It was her way of helping your grandfather provide for your family's survival when they first arrived in America. She was a very determined woman, your grandmother." She paused, "You have her determination."

"Do you think so?"

She nodded. "You'll know when you're faced with a difficult situation. God willing, that won't happen for a long time. Too much trial too soon can destroy one's spirit."

"Like Rengen, Bridget, and Trista?"

"God's will has tested them all. But they have the faith and strength to survive. The scars are there just the same. Never far below the surface."

That evening Mother announced we were invited to lunch next day at Inishbeag Manor.

"Delightful people, the Roberts," Grandfather said. "A well-established family."

"May I be excused from going?" Deirdre asked.

Mother looked hurt. "You must go. It's obvious Thomas and his family want to get to know you."

"But I don't want to get to know them," Deirdre mumbled under her breath, too low for Mother to hear.

I seldom rode along the western shore of Lough Corrib because of its rough terrain and rocky hillsides where sheep scaled steep inclines to grub for roots. To reach the western shore we drove into Galway then turned onto the road towards Oughterard. A few miles later we sighted Inishbeag Manor sitting on a hillside that gently sloped down to the Corrib.

The house was made of grey stucco, ivy sweeping its walls. Chestnut trees grew intermittently across the lawn and sitting-benches provided broad views of the lake. Smoke rose from twin chimneys above a steep tiled roof that seemed unusual among gentler Irish sloped roofs. The house reminded me of drawings Deirdre had shown me of Swiss chalets. I wondered if she made this same assumption as we walked up to the front door sheltered beneath a hooded alcove.

A maid greeted us and took our cloaks. She led us into a cosy drawing room filled with two pale blue settees and matching armchairs. Mr and Mrs Roberts invited us to warm ourselves by the fireplace and offered us port wine. I sank down against pillows of various colours arranged behind my back. They smelled of springtime and were so soft I found myself wanting to nod off to sleep. Thomas sat on a chair across from Deirdre and leaned forward to catch her every word.

When lunch was announced we entered the small dining room and were seated at a mahogany table with high-back chairs. Mr Roberts pointed through wide French doors to a small island on the lake. The manor's namesake, he told us. He explained it appeared even smaller in winter when its banks were buried beneath the lake's swollen swells. I peered beyond the island hoping to catch a glimpse of Kilpara on the opposite side of the lake. But it was too far away to make out any images.

The Roberts were pleasantly entertaining throughout the meal of pickled herring, roast potatoes and turnips. They recounted tales about the small island and the brave souls who have inhabited it over time. Thomas glanced furtively at Deirdre while we ate, as if she might disappear otherwise. He tried to anticipate her every movement, asked if the food was to her liking, made sure her wine glass remained full.

After lunch when we retired to the drawing room, Thomas requested a private meeting with Father in the study. Mother beamed, but Deirdre tensed like a bird in a cage. I wondered if she would have fled had Mother not taken hold of her hand. Mr Roberts immediately offered to show Grandfather miniatures of his ship collection in his study that he had transported from Belfast. Mother and Mrs Roberts were already engaged in a general discussion about spring fashions and smiled benignly when I pointed to the window pretending to see a mink near the shore. I motioned Deirdre to join me as I moved closer to get a better look.

"Can you believe it?" Deirdre said in a low whisper as we stood watching cold water ripple against the bank. "Thomas never consulted me about asking Father to come courting."

"You're sure that's why he wants to speak with Father?"

"What other reason can he have?"

I shrugged. "What will you do if Father agrees?"

Anger flickered in her eyes and there was a catch in her voice. "Pretend to be agreeable for congeniality's sake."

I clasped her hand in mine and squeezed it.

Thomas and Father returned to the drawing room looking pleased. Father announced Thomas' official request to court Deirdre. Amid the gush of pleasure that followed, only I noticed Deirdre had turned pale and had fallen silent.

At home as we prepared for bed she ignored my attempts to draw her into conversation. Instead she went to the window and stood at the same spot where I had seen a moonlit figure just nights before.

"Don't you like Thomas?" I asked for the third time.

"He's pleasant," Deirdre said at last. "It's just that he's so—"

"Predictable?"

She turned to face me and smiled wryly. "Conventional. I can tolerate his company and there's no reason why we can't be good friends. It'll be years before he finishes his studies and is ready for the responsibility of marriage."

"Could you ever love him?"

She didn't hesitate. "No."

"You should protest then."

"I will. But not right away. For now the situation is tolerable."

I didn't believe her. There was strain around her eyes. She was listless except for when she painted. She avoided visitors whenever possible, and scarcely contributed to casual conversation in the presence of company. Instead of returning to her former self, she became more reticent than ever and seemed to be sinking under mounting waves of pressure.

It came as a surprise when Deirdre finally agreed to accompany me to the hospital to visit the Joyce children. I had asked her every day since Christmas, but she refused each time. The children were almost fully recovered, and Bridget had returned home to prepare for their homecoming.

"We must take them presents," Deirdre insisted. We dragged out our old toys that were stored in the attic and began sifting through them. That's when I noticed Deirdre's favourite doll was missing, the one with the ceramic face, painted blue eyes, and stiff plaited golden hair.

"Your doll isn't here," I said.

"I took it to Switzerland," she said. "It was childish of me. I was regressing, I suppose."

"I can understand why. You loved that doll. Did you leave it behind?"

"I thought it was in my trunk, but I must've forgotten it in the confusion during preparation for my departure. I wrote and asked the principal to look for it."

"I'm sure they'll find it."

"I hope so. Let's pick something for the children." Deirdre pulled out a rag doll. "This looks like a good choice for the toddler." She adjusted the faded muslin dress covering limp legs with cloth shoes sewn over the feet.

"What about the boy?"

"He won't want dolls." Deirdre laughed, suddenly light-hearted.

"A book then?" I pulled *Gulliver's Travels* out of a box.

Deirdre nodded, and went in search of wrapping paper and ribbon.

We set out in the carriage for the hospital. The sun cast its weak winter smile, a feeble attempt to awaken the sleeping earth. On the road to Galway we passed men digging turf from the bog. I recognized Ruairi Kineely at once, even knee-deep in muck. He saw the carriage and paused. His impassive green eyes stared into mine. His look propelled me back to the day of the hunt, filling me with shame. I shivered and looked away, knowing I must talk to him if I expected to regain his respect and defend my reputation. I resolved to do it soon.

When we arrived at the hospital the children were delighted with their presents. Deirdre had remembered to bring along additional accessories for the doll. Nora immediately pulled off the doll's hat and handed it to Deirdre before adding a new one.

"Better?" Nora said.

"It's lovely." Deirdre ran her hand over the child's smooth dark hair and looked over at Grand-Aunt Sadie. "They look wonderfully healthy now. They were so ill on Christmas Eve, I feared the worst."

Grand-Aunt Sadie smiled. "We have God and his mercy to thank for their recovery."

Conboy and Trista examined *Gulliver's Travels.*

"What's it about?" Conboy asked.

"Adventures into strange worlds," Trista said. "Each adventure is different and so are the people who have them."

"I'd like Rengen to read it to me."

"Good idea," Grand-Aunt Sadie said. "You can read it together. It'll be good practise for when you return to school."

I woke up on the seventh of January dreading my sixteenth birthday. All day long I expected Mother and Father to announce that I must continue my studies abroad. I was in such a panic over my looming fate I had balked when Mother suggested celebrating my birthday with a large party. I argued it could only be a disappointment after the ball that was such a success. To my surprise Mother considered this notion and didn't make a fuss. Still, the household was in a celebratory mood. I received well wishes, presents, a large birthday cake, and my favourite dinner of corned beef and cabbage. I was greatly relieved when the day passed pleasantly without the subject of my going overseas being raised.

A few days later I rode with Olam towards the bog where I had seen men digging turf. I brought along Ruairi's handkerchief hoping for an opportunity to give it back to him, with a chance to make right his misconceptions about the hunt and Cecil Sloane.

We approached the digging site. Ruairi and several men stood in a trench, slicing into the turf with two-sided spades they used to cut out vertical blocks. They stacked the blocks loosely at the edge of the trench. The drier turf was loaded onto a cart and wheeled closer to the road for transport. Ruairi looked up when we approached, but didn't acknowledge us. We rode past and upon our return he was alone at the site.

He dug into the turf while the other men pushed the loaded cart down the hillside.

Olam and I trotted our horses to the edge of the trench. Ruairi stopped digging and looked up without saying a word. I leaned forward in the saddle and held out his handkerchief. His eyes held mine, his expression aloof. "Thank you," he said, pleasantly. He wiped his hands on his jacket and took the clean handkerchief. Noting my gaze on his mud-caked clothes, he grinned. "It makes taking a bath a pleasure."

"I appreciate you taking me home after the hunt," I said. At the mention of the hunt his eyes turned stony. "You were mistaken about me and Cecil Sloane," I added quickly.

"You don't have to explain. I interfered where I shouldn't have. It's none of my business."

Olam's horse moved a few feet away to munch on a small patch of green grass.

"I despise Cecil and he dislikes me. We're not lovers, or friends," I confided in an audible whisper. "Unfortunately, our families are neighbours, and convention prevents me from speaking plainly about his deliberate act to injure me at the hunt."

Ruairi's gaze softened. He believed me.

The men started back up the hill. "Thank you, Mr Kineely, for lending me your handkerchief," I said loudly so they could hear.

He bowed. "My pleasure, Miss O'Donovan."

I smiled and was rewarded with a cheeky grin.

The days moved slowly from cold and monotonous towards spring's welcome resurgence. Grand-Aunt Sadie complained that the cold weather made her bones ache. The Joyce children were released from hospital and returned to the valley. Their absence reminded Rengen how much he missed his own grandchildren, and he talked more about going home. Trista had reassured Bridget the children were healthy, and Grand-Aunt Sadie asked her to bring them back for regular checkups. The truth was everyone had grown fond of them and would miss them.

It became routine to see Deirdre and Thomas chatting in the drawing room on Sunday afternoons like lifelong friends. She was relieved when Cecil returned to college, only to be shocked a few weeks later when he showed up unexpectedly at Kilpara professing an impromptu break from his studies.

Deirdre and I had returned from a walk and were met by a flustered Clare at the front door. She must have been watching for us.

"Master Sloane is in the drawing room," she said in a furtive whisper.

"What!" Deirdre and I exclaimed in unison.

Clare nodded at Deirdre. "He barged in, demanded to know where you were. Anthony told him you were out, but he said he'd wait. He marched right over to the drawing room and demanded that I bring him tea. I said I would get the missus, but he insisted, and I mean *insisted,* I shouldn't disturb her. That's where he is now."

We thanked Clare who looked relieved and returned to her duties. I wanted to join Deirdre in the drawing room. She declined my presence, saying it would only agitate Cecil. I promised to stay close. I stood outside next to the door that she deliberately left ajar.

"Hello, Cecil," Deirdre said.

Footsteps sounded across the floor. "Dearest Deirdre," Cecil said. "I had to come see you."

"Is something wrong?"

"I couldn't concentrate on my studies because I kept thinking about your courtship with Thomas. I had to tell you, you're making a terrible mistake."

"Mistake?"

"You know so little about Thomas."

"Meaning?" There was an edge in Deirdre's voice.

"You don't know him like I do."

"And you left your studies to warn me?"

"He's not such a bad fellow, really. He's not right for you. You must know this already." Cecil's words came sharp as slaps.

"I find him charming, in fact."

"You're jesting." Silence followed. "You should refuse his courtship, you know."

"That would be impolite. He asked Father's permission."

"And you agreed."

"I was obliged to."

"I intended to ask your father's permission to come courting, but I wanted to ask you first."

"I had no idea you had courtship in mind. I'm sorry, Cecil."

"You don't sound sorry."

"I like Thomas."

"You can't—"

I heard Deirdre wince. "Cecil, let go, you're hurting me."

I dashed across the hall to the library, praying that Grandfather wasn't there. It was empty. I grabbed a book and walked calmly into the drawing room. I sat in a conspicuous chair, directly in front of Cecil.

He dropped his hold on Deirdre's arm. "What're you doing here, Grace?"

"Hello, Cecil," I said politely. "This is an unexpected pleasure. We didn't expect to see you until Easter."

"You're interfering again, you little witch."

Deirdre recoiled.

Cecil took a step towards her, but she backed away. "I'm sorry, Deirdre. I don't know why Grace keeps butting in."

"She's not. She's my sister and I welcome her here."

Cecil sniggered. Then he looked at Deirdre, his eyes pleading forgiveness. "Sorry, of course Grace should be here. We're still friends, aren't we?"

"Yes," Deirdre said, through tight lips.

"Agree to have tea with me then."

Deirdre looked away. "Only if you promise to go now."

"Saturday afternoon. I'll collect you."

He turned to leave the room, but bent down close to my ear first. "You're *not* invited, Grace."

He left, and after his departure Deirdre sank into a chair opposite me.

"Don't move," I said, and hurried across to the library. I poured some of Father's sherry into a glass. I had seen him give it to Mother when she was upset. I handed it to Deirdre, who made a face when she tasted it and put the glass aside. I closed the door and turned to her.

"You should've told him no," I said. "He's making a nuisance of himself."

"Please, Grace, I don't need a lecture."

"He'll keep pestering you if you don't stop him."

"I'm never going to be happy anyway, so what does it matter." She looked so tormented that my heart ached for her.

CHAPTER 8

Mick O'Rourke, a mild-mannered man, spoke with a stammer whenever he became excited, or nervous. He apprenticed as a horse trainer under Gully Joyce, Kilpara's long-time groom, whose poor health now confined him at home.

Mick taught me to jump the lower hurdles by the time I was ten. At age fourteen I itched to try the higher jumps, even if Mick disagreed. He argued I was a girl, young, and the landlord's daughter. He couldn't risk my getting injured. Determined to change his mind, I began practicing the jumps without permission. My stubbornness exasperated and worried Mick until he relented and began training me properly. Now he treated me like an equal. Ever since the incident at Larcourt, however, I stuck only to the lower jumps.

That morning when I put Spitfire through his paces Mick came to watch. "Y-you know, Miss Grace, if you were a m-man you could be a world-class jockey," he said.

I smiled at his encouragement. "You want me to jump the higher hurdles?"

"Yes." His eyes were round pools of faith, his mouth set in a heartfelt smile.

I hesitated. "What if I crash into one of them? Or injure Spitfire in a fall?"

"You won't. Trust your instincts." His voice was perfectly trained, no evidence of the stammer he worked so hard to control.

I made up my mind. "All right."

He nodded. "You'll do fine."

His callused hand closed over mine on the reins, filling me with reassurance.

I circled the paddock several times then performed one turn each on the low and medium hurdles. Mick's eyes followed me when I cantered several more laps sizing up the higher jumps. Each time I got close, visions of the gate came pouring back. Biting my lower lip, I made one more lap then lined up for the jump. As we drew close, Spitfire sensed I wasn't in control and balked.

"Try again," Mick yelled. I nodded and made another pass around the paddock. Cecil's face floated before me, gloating over my failure. Summoning my courage I concentrated solely on the jump. I lined up again, Spitfire's tension almost as high as my own. I had to relax, gain control, show more confidence.

"This is it," I whispered to Spitfire, gritting my teeth. He neighed, shook his mane. We began to canter. I focused on the hurdle, shutting out images of the gate. Spitfire was with me. We were in perfect sync. I thought only about the jump and blocked out everything else. Our timing was seamless. Spitfire leaped, his muscles flexing, his forelegs soaring over the posts where we landed perfectly on the other side. I closed my eyes and waited for the thumping in my chest to stop.

Mick appeared in front of me, relief on his face. "G-good job."

Spitfire turned to nuzzle him.

"Thank you." I dismounted and stood still for a moment to steady my shaking legs.

As appointed, Cecil arrived on Saturday afternoon. Reluctantly, Deirdre allowed him to escort her to his carriage. Because we had known Cecil all our lives, Mother trusted him completely and considered his gesture a social nicety; even Father didn't object. Yet, I couldn't shake the uneasiness that gnawed at me throughout Deirdre's absence. I couldn't settle down to any task and was already standing at the drawing room window when the carriage finally returned.

I watched Deirdre alight, her smile forced when Cecil offered her his hand. After she stepped onto the ground, Cecil continued to hold her hand. She pulled it away; he flashed a conciliatory grin before loosening his grip. Still grinning, he leaned over and whispered something against her ear. Whatever he said brought an agitated look to her face. She walked away quickly, almost ran up the steps. I heard the front door close and expected her to come into the drawing room to recount her experience. Instead she went straight to our bedroom. Later she acted as if the outing never happened, despite my attempts to broach the subject.

She didn't speak about it until two days later. I had put the incident aside after I became preoccupied with another event that occurred that same night.

I awoke feeling parched and rose to get a drink of water. The water pitcher on the small bedroom table was empty, so I started downstairs towards the anteroom next to the great room. Tea-making and other supplies were stored there for convenience because it was closer than the kitchen located on the ground floor.

In the corridor a full moon lit the way, and there was no need for a lamp. Bathed in shadowy light the house creaked and moaned. Halfway downstairs I heard a door close below. One of the servants, I reassured myself. I filled the pitcher, and then poured myself a glass of water.

Climbing back upstairs I glanced out one of the staircase windows and saw two figures running in the direction of the rundown cottage that once belonged to my great-grandparents. One figure looked suspiciously like the man I thought I saw the night after the hunt. The second shape was smaller, slimmer—a woman. A hood covered her hair and her dark clothes blended with the nighttime darkness. I moved closer to get a better look, and when I did, the figures disappeared. Was I hallucinating? Imagining ghosts again? I hurried back to the bedroom. Setting down the glass and pitcher on the table, I went to the window and pulled the drapes apart. All that was visible were bare trees, branches twisting in the wind.

I walked over to the edge of Deirdre's bed, tempted to wake her. I reached out to touch her, and then withdrew my hand. She'd be annoyed if I disturbed her and say that I was imagining things. She'd chastise me for being childish. After all, trespassers wouldn't get past the gatehouse unnoticed, and no prowlers had been reported. Only I was seeing nighttime visions.

Slipping beneath the covers I tossed and turned until I drifted back to sleep. It was daylight when I awoke again, and the whole incident seemed trivial. Yet, I began to question why I saw nocturnal images that defied explanation.

Deirdre looked desperate when she finally spoke of her afternoon with Cecil. "He asked me to marry him," she said.

"He proposed?" I was astonished.

"Yes, at the Traveller's Inn. We were having a friendly conversation when he suddenly took my hand, said he risked getting expelled from college by returning home to see me. He didn't care because he had to tell me how he felt before I made a mistake and married Thomas." She paused and shook her head as if trying to clear the image from her mind. "It would've been romantic, I suppose, if I had feelings for Cecil. But I don't."

"What did you say?"

"That his gesture was considerate, but he shouldn't feel obliged to propose because he worried Thomas and I would marry hastily. I told him we expected our courtship to be long."

"How did he react?"

"He just sat there with a silly smile on his face and caressed my hand. I dared not remove it for fear of making him angry. It was pure agony. It was a relief when I could suggest returning home."

"He has no right to interfere."

"He thinks otherwise. I'm afraid he'll appeal to Thomas to end our courtship."

"For what reason?"

Deirdre scowled. "Entitlement. That he and I were meant to be together since childhood. That Thomas's intentions have interfered with our destinies."

"You should tell Father. He doesn't care for the Sloanes any more than we do."

"I was hoping I wouldn't have to ..."

"You must avoid Cecil," I said.

"He's going to Paris with his parents for Easter. That should keep him away."

But she looked truly worried.

Father had entered Ceonig and Spitfire in the annual steeplechase festival at the Curragh in County Kildare outside Dublin. He added Spitfire after considering my suggestion that he was ready to enter the contest.

"The races are more challenging than ever," Father said one evening at dinner. "Rival horses from all over Britain are competing." He patted Mother's hand. "I've been thinking. Grace has raised Spitfire since he was a foal, she should watch him compete. In fact we should all go. We haven't been to Dublin in ages."

"It has been awhile," Mother agreed. "It'd be a treat to see the city again."

"That's settled then," Father said.

Thoughts of seeing Spitfire compete consumed me as I began preparations for our trip to Dublin. I wasn't allowed to ride him until after the race. I watched him train every day with a jockey, and afterwards I rubbed him down myself. One evening when I led him into the stable, Tom and other grooms were tending to a mare and her newborn foal. Father arrived behind me and stepped into the stall to inspect the newest addition. As the colt rose on shaky legs, Tom expressed his concern about other mares due to foal, and the need to keep grooms at Kilpara.

"We don't need as much turf for the fires now that spring is here," Father said. "The weather is getting milder. Let's take young Kineely and another fellow off turf-cutting and use them to help out at the Curragh. That should free up grooms to assist Rengen with foaling while we're gone."

Tom nodded and looked over at Spitfire's stall where I stood. "Ceonig and Spitfire should take first prize, or my name's not Tom Townsend."

CHAPTER 9

Smoke curled back from the train engine as we hurried along the platform to our compartment. When all the passengers were on board, the platform attendant blew his whistle and slammed the doors shut one by one. After the last one closed he waved a green flag.

The train moved slowly out of the station, and before long buildings gave way to green countryside and lakes. I settled back in my seat with the newspaper I had bought from a newsboy in the station. Inside the first page I was surprised to see a photo of Father with Ceonig and Spitfire at the Curragh.

The caption read: *Esteemed landowner Ellis O'Donovan, newly arrived at the Curragh, expressed high hopes of winning trophies in this year's horse racing festival with veteran contender Ceonig in the foxhunt hurdle and newcomer Spitfire in the novice hurdle. O'Donovan said, "This year's competition looks to be an exciting one, and I'm looking forward to it."*

We descended the train at Houston Station in Dublin and immediately spotted Father's face among greeters on the platform. He broke into a smile when we shouted his name and waved wildly. He signalled a porter who loaded our luggage onto a trolley. The carriage ride through Dublin always filled me with awe as we wound among streets crisscrossing in all directions. The River Liffey ran through the city, and barges shored up along quaysides swayed against stone walls.

We rode alongside horse-pulled trams on tracks that transferred people from one place to another. Women with children in tow or babies tucked inside prams passed up and down Grafton Street as our carriage moved slowly towards the quieter Merrion Row. When we halted outside the Shelbourne Hotel, a uniformed boy met us and took our luggage to rooms overlooking Stephen's Green. That evening we ate dinner in the dining room where a glass chandelier radiated mellow light over the tables. Guests who recognized Father paused to wish him good luck at the Curragh races.

The day had been unusually warm for spring, and when evening drew to a mild close, Mother asked Father to stroll with her in Stephen's Green. This allowed Deirdre and me to be as adventurous as we liked. We walked down Grafton Street, leisurely gazing at lavishly decorated shop windows that displayed fabrics, women's costumes, and jewellery.

I became absorbed in a window exhibit of eye-catching necklaces, and was captivated by one in particular made of garnets that sparkled on a velvet bust. I was about to draw Deirdre's attention to it when a reflection flashed past the shop window. I glimpsed a figure with fair hair, familiar face and wide shoulders. "Conor Hagerty," I whispered aloud.

I whipped around, but the image had disappeared; there was no one in sight. I turned to tell Deirdre, only she was gone, too. She couldn't have wandered far, so I started down the street. I had gone a few yards when I felt a tug at the hem of my skirt.

A man in ragged clothing and broken shoes propped against a doorstep had grabbed hold of my skirt.

"A copper, m'lady," he said, holding out his free hand.

"I have no money," I said. "Please, let go."

"A copper," he insisted, tightening his grip. I looked around desperately for Deirdre.

"Please—I have no money."

"A fine lady like yourself is sure to have money."

"Let go or I'll summon a constable." Fear had left me and I was growing angry.

"Gi'me a copper." He grinned, showing missing teeth, not at all frightened by my threat. He pulled me closer, doubling his grip with his other hand.

"I've no money," I pleaded. "But I have some pretty combs in my purse. Will those do?"

"Ain't got no use for combs. Gi'me a copper."

I tried to pull away but he held on tight.

Suddenly the sound of pinging hit the ground. The man grabbed for the coins dropped in front of him, releasing my skirt. I almost fell backwards.

"Grace." The sound of my name startled me. I turned to find David Ligham looking at me in consternation. I backed away from the man, stumbling into David.

"Steady," he said, holding my arm until I regained my balance. "What an unexpected pleasure meeting you here in Dublin."

I smoothed my skirts and looked into round eyes. "W-what are you doing here?"

"I'm studying for my bar exams at Trinity, remember?"

I nodded. "Sorry, I'd forgotten. Thank you for rescuing me. It was fortunate you came along when you did. I don't know what I'd have done."

"Are you alone?"

"No, we're here for the races. Deirdre and I came out for an evening stroll." I looked around. "She was here a moment ago."

As we walked away David glanced back at the man. "He didn't mean you any harm. He accosted you because he wanted money, not because he meant to hurt you. He's poor and homeless. He, and other beggars, shouldn't be allowed on the streets, but the government doesn't address the problem properly."

At that moment I spotted Deirdre turning round in circles further down the street. She saw us and I waved. She hurried towards us. "So there you are," she said, breathlessly. "I've been looking all over for you." She acknowledged David curiously. He took her gloved hand and kissed it.

"David arrived at an opportune time to rescue me from an unfortunate man who was holding me hostage for money."

"Thank you," Deirdre said to David, then let her gaze stray over me. "Are you all right? I'm sorry for wandering away. I thought you were right behind me. It took some minutes before I realized we were separated."

"I'm fine, now."

"May I offer you ladies refreshment?" David asked. "I'd like to hear about your excursion to Dublin. Where are you staying?"

We walked back towards the Shelbourne Hotel and learned that David had apartments in Harcourt Street close to Stephen's Green. He explained he had been out for a walk to clear his mind after intense poring over law books. Retiring to the Tea Room at the hotel, we chatted about our visit to Dublin.

Later that evening as Deirdre and I prepared for bed I remembered the strange apparition in the shop window. "Just before that poor man accosted me on Grafton Street, I thought I saw Conor Hagerty's face in a shop window," I said.

Deirdre stopped brushing her hair in mid-stroke. "How strange. Didn't he go to America over a year ago? It must've been someone who looked like him."

I nodded, agreeing that was the obvious explanation. It would be easy to mistake someone else for Conor in a crowded city like Dublin.

The following morning Father ordered a carriage, and we rode down to the Curragh to watch Ceonig and Spitfire at practise. City buildings and low-lying fields gave way to the Wicklow hills, green and purple in the distance. Along the way whitewashed cottages and farmhouses appeared intermittently. The sun shone brightly, and residents working in their gardens paused to wave as we passed by.

At the Curragh, stands and booths were being erected especially for the races. Excitement filled the air as canvas structures went up one after another. By race time they would be filled with souvenirs, snacks, or used for Tea Rooms.

We arrived in time to see Ceonig and Spitfire being trotted towards the racecourse for their practise runs. I went over to the rail that circled the track and leaned against it. When given the order, Tom and Ruairi Kineely led Ceonig and Spitfire onto the track. Mick walked beside them, gesturing instructions to the jockeys whose gazes were assessing the track. Mick and Father remained at the starting line while Tom and Ruairi joined me at the rails. They greeted me, and then turned their attention to the racecourse to watch jockeys canter the horses slowly around the course. As the horses passed by where we stood, Tom pointed to something amiss with Ceonig's bridle. He motioned the jockey to stop and scrambled over the fence to check the problem.

While he was preoccupied, Ruairi turned to me. "Ceonig's an incredible horse," he said. "But you know that already. He'll do well in the race."

"I hope so," I said.

"Spitfire should take a prize, too."

"He's young. This is his first year. It'll test his performance."

"You'll be here for the race?"

"The whole family will."

"Good." Ruairi's eyes held mine. I looked away as Tom rejoined us. He and Ruairi mounted the lower rung on the rail, leaning forward to watch the horses pick up speed and jump the pole jumps. Ruairi's shirtsleeves were rolled up, his arms bare. There was strength in them. His shirt collar stood open, showing a strong neck, and his dark hair fell untidily onto his forehead.

He turned sideways and caught me observing him. He grinned. Heat rushed to my face, flushing it red. I searched for something flippant to say. "Refreshing time of year," I said lamely.

Ruairi jumped down from the rail and sniffed the air. He leaned against the fence facing me, his green eyes mocking. "That's so," he said.

I pointed over his shoulder at Ceonig racing down the track. "Look."

Ruairi turned to see Ceonig flash by. "A champion indeed." When he looked at me again I wondered if he, like me, was recalling the night we rode together through darkness to the hospital.

The day before the race I walked over to Stephen's Green to feed the ducks. I stood idly tossing crusts of bread into the duck pond when I spotted them—Deirdre and Conor Hagerty strolling along the thoroughfare, deep in conversation. I stood gaping; sure my eyes were deceiving me. They approached a gate on the opposite side of the park. Keeping out of sight I followed behind. They left the park and crossed the street to a row of houses with wide granite steps leading up to brightly painted Georgian doors, each a different colour. I watched them go inside a green door.

I stared at the house asking myself a host of questions. Hadn't I seen Conor with his ticket in hand for America? He couldn't be here in Dublin. Was my mind playing tricks again? But Deirdre was with him and acting very familiar indeed. Like she knew him; she wouldn't do that with a stranger. It didn't make sense. I paced back and forth on the pavement arguing with myself what I should do next. Unable to contain my curiosity I walked over to the house, climbed the steps and lifted the silver door knocker. I waited nervously.

Conor opened the door. "Miss Grace," he said, looking surprised.

I stood awestruck, unable to speak. I looked past him down the hallway to a room where Deirdre sat in a chair next to a small table.

"Come in," he said, recovering first.

I followed silently behind him into the room with faded wallpaper and the sweet smell of lingering pipe tobacco. He offered me a chair at the small table.

"I was about to bring Miss Deirdre tea. Would you like some?"

"Thank you, yes." My voice sounded high-pitched and unnatural. When Conor left I turned to Deirdre, searching her face for an explanation.

"What's going on? Why are you with—Conor?"

She looked out the window at fluttering tree branches. "How did you know I was here?"

"I saw you with Conor in Stephen's Green.I followed you."

"I bumped into him when I went for a walk," Deirdre said slowly. "I was shocked to see him since everyone knows he went to America."

"He didn't go?"

"That's what I asked. He was so overcome to see a familiar face that he invited me here to his uncle's residence to explain the whole story."

"His uncle's residence?"

Deirdre gestured around the room. "He's staying here with his uncle. His departure was delayed because his uncle took ill. Conor is tending to him until he recovers."

"Since last year?"

"A slow recovery."

"Did you ask him if he was in Grafton Street the other evening?"

Before Deidre could respond, Conor returned with a tray bearing a teapot, cups, and a plate of biscuits. He set the tray down on the table and looked at me.

"You saw me on Grafton Street? I'm up and down there all the time. You didn't say hello?"

"I only caught a glimpse of your reflection in a shop window," I said.

"I was telling Grace how we met by chance in Stephen's Green," Deirdre said.

Conor smiled. "Yes, an unexpected surprise."

"And how you postponed going to America because your uncle took ill," she continued.

"A sudden emergency. But it's good to see you both again."

Deirdre poured the tea, and there was something practised about the act that confused me.

"When are you going to America?" I asked, looking at Conor.

"Soon, I hope. I must stay with my uncle awhile longer. He's unwell."

"May I inquire from what?"

Conor hesitated. "Nothing contagious, or even fatal. Not anymore, anyway. It's a sensitive matter—"

"Is Dublin his home?"

"No. He's here under the care of a specialist."

"We should apologise for intruding."

"No need. He's resting upstairs in his room and not accepting visitors."

I looked curiously towards the stairs. "He's been ill for over a year?"

"Roughly," Conor said. "His recovery is almost complete."

"I think it's admirable you put your future on hold to care for your uncle," Deirdre said.

Conor beamed. "Family obligation. But I'm forgetting my manners. I'd be honoured if you'd let me escort you around the city. I've come to know it well."

"Wonderful idea," Deirdre said, surprising me. I expected her usual dissonance, yet she seemed almost cheerful at the prospect of seeing the Dublin sights.

"Who will look after your uncle if you leave?" I asked.

"He only needs general assistance now. He can manage on his own for short periods."

We finished our tea then walked over to Stephen's Green where Conor summoned a carriage for hire. On impulse I glanced back. A street tram had halted nearby the house we just exited. A group of men in dark suits dismounted and proceeded to the green door. They disappeared inside. Conor caught my gaze, but didn't offer an explanation. Instead he held out his hand and assisted me inside the carriage.

When we were settled he gave instructions to the driver, who guided the horses down Grafton Street, past College Green and the Bank of Ireland. Crossing the bridge over the River Liffey, I looked down at murky water and found it hard to imagine Viking ships had once ventured up this river from the sea. We travelled up the quays and into the Phoenix Park. The driver stopped the carriage at the Viceregal Lodge, home to the Chief Secretary for Ireland, and let us admire the majestic building with gleaming whitewashed walls, a regal front porch, and graceful Greek columns. The avenue, bordered with ceremonial trees, gave way to expansive lawns and colourful flowerbeds.

"It's tragic that Lord Cavendish's life was taken as he strolled home with Undersecretary Burke from Dublin Castle to these beautiful surroundings," I said.

"You remember that?" Conor asked, a trace of bitterness in his voice. "It happened almost three years ago. You were what—thirteen then?"

"It's hard to forget photographs of the brutal violence that the newspaper printed."

"Did you also know that the day before the attack on the Chief Secretary and Undersecretary, constables fired buckshot into a group of young boys and girls following behind a band in Ballina? They killed one boy and injured others. The British charged Irish rebels for the murders they committed against Cavendish and Burke. But not one constable was charged in the Ballina debacle."

I looked into his tortured eyes, but couldn't find anything to say.

Conor motioned the driver to continue. When we came to the People's Gardens, the driver paused. Deirdre asked to dismount and Conor offered her his hand. I followed in silence. We walked along pathways flanked by white lilies and multi-coloured tulips already in bloom.

A familiar figure stood poised on the public bandstand surrounded by a seated audience that overflowed onto the sloping hillside. Without waiting for Deirdre or Conor, I walked closer to get a better look. Mr Parnell's voice carried over the crowd's heads, and he gestured with a commanding fist.

"Irish laws should be made in accordance with the wishes of the Irish people. None of us, whether we're in America or in Ireland, will be satisfied until the force of England's imperialism is removed. No man has the right to say to another country thus far shall thou go and no further. I ask your resolve to accept nothing less than to obtain for Ireland the full measure of her rights."

Applause resounded and passionate voices chanted, "Parnell, Parnell."

I glanced sideways at Conor and saw sadness and pride in his eyes.

We retraced our steps to the carriage. Returning to the hotel, I half-heartedly listened to Deirdre and Conor chat about buildings of interest. Thoughts of Mr Parnell filled my mind, as well as his words that incited the local masses into demanding Irish independence. It was disturbing to observe firsthand people's opposition to the monarchy. I thought back to those occasions when Father's acquaintances openly discussed the folly of an independent Ireland trying to manage its own affairs. They insisted that without Britain's control, the country would erupt into chaos. Conscious of this, I worried if we were on a collision course for disaster.

When the carriage pulled up a short distance from the hotel entrance, Conor helped us alight. We thanked him cordially for a pleasant afternoon. He nodded appreciatively and we shook hands.

As Deirdre and I dressed for dinner I said, "It's strange that we should see Conor here, of all places."

"It happens." Deirdre poured water from a jug into the basin. "We've met other people we know. David Ligham, for instance."

"But Conor was supposed to be in America."

"He explained his delay."

"He's been on my mind lately."

Deirdre looked surprised. "He has?"

"I not only thought I saw his reflection in a shop window in Grafton Street the other day, but I also thought I saw him at Kilpara."

"That's impossible."

"Only recently I woke up one night feeling parched and went downstairs for a drink. On my way back to bed I looked out a staircase window and saw two figures running towards the old cottage. One of them looked like Conor."

"That's impossible. What you probably saw were swaying bushes."

"But the figure had light hair and he had Conor's build."

Deirdre laughed. "You were half-asleep and the darkness played tricks on your eyes."

She was right, of course. Conor had said he was in Dublin due to his uncle's illness. As unlikely as it seemed we should bump into him here, it was absurd to believe he would be at Kilpara.

CHAPTER 10

A crowd had gathered when we arrived at the Curragh the following day. Women paraded about in wide-brimmed hats and bright dresses, while men in bowler hats and morning suits carried binoculars. The Lighams paused to greet us before taking their seats in the stands.

"You look lovely today, Grace," David said. He pointed to his program. "Ceonig and Spitfire are scheduled to run in the second and third races."

"Yes, we hope they'll do well." Nervous anticipation sounded in my voice.

The announcer's voice blared through the megaphone, shouting out the names of contenders for the first race.

"Time to get settled," Father said. We said goodbye to the Lighams and made our way through the crowds to seats overlooking the starting line.

All heads turned to the racetrack when the horses took off. Father stayed long enough to watch the first couple of laps before saying, "I must get to the barn." Mother and Deirdre nodded, busily skimming faces in the crowd through binoculars.

"I'd like to see Spitfire before he races—for good luck," I said. Mother smiled benignly and Father beckoned me to follow him.

Mayhem filled the barn as jockeys and grooms prepped to lead horses outside. Ceonig and Spitfire, restless in their confined spaces, reacted fitfully to the bedlam around them. Tom and Mick took Ceonig out of his stall and walked him in circles. Ruairi and another boy worked to calm Spitfire.

"See if you can help Spitfire, Grace," Father said, going to Ceonig.

Ruairi brought Spitfire round to face me. "Easy boy," I whispered. "You'll do great today." He whinnied, and I ran my hand along his neck. Ruairi stroked his back.

"Win a trophy for Brandubh," he urged.

I patted Spitfire's flank. At the same time Ruairi moved his hand to check the bridle. Our hands touched. His was masculine, rough, warm. I withdrew mine immediately. When I looked at him there was amusement in his green eyes.

"Spitfire's calmer," I said.

Ruairi smiled boldly. "That's so."

The second race was announced and Father said to Mick, "Ceonig seems a bit stiff."

"M-maybe a bit," Mick ran his hand down Ceonig's forelegs. "My g-guess is he'll work it out before he gets to the gate. I'll get the v-vet to double-check him."

"Will he be withdrawn?" I asked.

"It doesn't look serious," Father said. "You should get back to the stands."

I rejoined Mother and Deirdre and was relieved to see Ceonig in the line-up when horses and jockeys paraded towards the starter gate. Once they were in place, the official gave the signal and the race was on. Mother and Deirdre trained their binoculars on Ceonig as he kept pace with other horses around the course. The jockey and Ceonig adjusted their gait as the race progressed. When they rounded the last lap he was bunched up with three other horses, lagging slightly behind in fourth place.

Excitement intensified and people rose to their feet. The jockey pushed Ceonig harder. We shouted his name. Ceonig stretched out and came up beside the front-runner named Regal. But he couldn't pull ahead. Regal beat him over the finish line, Ceonig coming in a close second.

"So close," Mother fretted. "Your father hoped Ceonig would win. He was considered the favourite."

Ruairi and Mick led Spitfire out of the barn when the announcer roared out the names for the novice hurdle. The jockey, seated easily in the saddle, cantered Spitfire to the starting gate. Just before the flag dropped Ruairi looked to the stands and held up crossed fingers. I answered his sign.

They were off. Spitfire was out in front during the first lap, taking the jumps with speed and ease. He dropped back to fifth place during the next lap. I wondered if the jockey was deliberately holding him back after testing the competition. I was surprised and delighted when he urged Spitfire forward as they came up on the last lap. Spitfire responded. He ran the course at full speed and eased over the hurdles.

Mother and Deirdre were on their feet. Ruairi was jumping up and down. Father, Mick, and Tom waved clenched fists, their faces red from excitement. He was neck and neck with Supreme Commander, the favourite to win, as they raced down the fairway. Oohs and aahs echoed throughout the stands when Supreme Commander took the last jump too quickly and fell. Spitfire cleared the last hurdle and sprinted across the finish line, the announcer heralding his name as the winner.

Mother, Deirdre and I hugged each other. I ran from the stands to the finish line where Spitfire and the jockey were surrounded. Ruairi must have been watching for me. He appeared out of nowhere, picked me up and swung me around. "Did you see him, Grace? Did you see him? He was magnificent."

"I did," I said laughing. "Put me down." Ruairi swung me around once more before lowering me to the ground. Excitement from the race still pulsed in his neck as we stood close, so close I could smell the clean scent of soap.

Ruairi moved back, dropping his hands down by his sides. "It was a great race," he said almost shyly.

"It was," I agreed.

"Grace! Grace!" I pulled my eyes away to acknowledge David Ligham who arrived at my side. "Jolly good race." He took my gloved hand and shook it. Then Father was beside me, ushering me to where the jockey and Spitfire were being presented with the trophy. I looked back at Ruairi, who had turned towards the barn where Tom was already tending to Ceonig. It was time to prepare for the journey home.

The rhythm of life at Kilpara seemed dull after the excitement of Dublin. To everyone's relief, Ceonig's minor ailment turned out to be nothing more than sore joints. He was back in full form after only a couple of weeks, thanks to Mick's special care. Horse enthusiasts sent congratulatory telegrams from all over Britain, voicing sentiments for Ceonig and Spitfire's future chances in bigger races. This made Father happy and proud.

I basked in Ceonig and Spitfire's triumph only to become exasperated when Deirdre retreated into listlessness. I missed her carefree spirit that had briefly surfaced in Dublin. She hovered between gloom and indifference, a thinly veiled veneer masking her inner turmoil.

The lingering bloom from the Dublin excursion vanished the moment the Sloanes paid us an unexpected visit two weeks later. We were relaxing in the garden on Sunday afternoon when their carriage arrived unannounced.

"How strange," Mother said, laying aside the cross-stitch pillowcase she was working on. "I hope everything's all right."

Father greeted the visitors and welcomed them inside. Cecil entered the vestibule looking at us slyly, and Sir Charles for once seemed preoccupied. He looked at Mother sheepishly instead of his usual blatant admiration. Lady Daphne held her head high, her eyes confident and glaring.

Deirdre and I quickly escaped to the privacy of our bedroom. Moments later Deirdre was summoned to the drawing room. I went with her, but was asked to wait outside after I was told the meeting didn't include me. Through a narrow slit in the door before it closed I glimpsed Mother holding her hanky in her hands, and Father's drawn face. Cecil and Lady Daphne appeared smug. It was obvious they were up to something.

With my ear pressed against the closed door I caught intermittent snatches of conversation when voices were raised. "… to the point …" Lady Daphne's voice.

"… tell Thomas and the Roberts …" Cecil's voice. "… marry Deirdre …"

… "I won't …" Deirdre's voice.

"... behind our backs ..." Father's voice.

"... please consider ..." Mother's voice.

Footsteps sounded across the floor. I slipped from the hallway into the library and held the door open a crack.

"You can't *make* me," Deirdre said, flinging open the drawing room door and running up the stairs.

"Deirdre darling, *please* ..." Mother pleaded.

"Deirdre, come back here at once," Father commanded. "We're not finished."

But Deirdre was already at the top of the stairs. Father closed the drawing room door and I sneaked upstairs. Deirdre lay on the bed crying when I entered the bedroom.

I sat beside her and stroked her hair. "What is it, Dee? What's happening?"

"Cecil has ruined everything," she sobbed. "He went, he went—"

"Where? What?"

"It doesn't matter."

"Please, tell me."

"The Sloanes are in charge of my future now." She turned to face me. "They spoke to the Roberts."

I hugged her. "They've no right to interfere."

"Cecil's demanding that I end my courtship with Thomas."

"What nerve! What gives him that right?"

Deirdre looked down at her hands. "He's here to convince Mother and Father we should marry. He says he loves me, that he'll treat me with the utmost care and devotion. He was so sincere that Mother believed him. He may have swayed Father, too."

"That's impossible. Father deplores Cecil."

"He didn't outright agree—"

"He knows what Cecil's like."

"Cecil doesn't love me. He wants to possess me. He'll do whatever it takes to make me his. He refuses to give up, even when he knows I don't share his feelings. I won't marry him, Grace. I won't! You must help me find a way out."

"I will," I said. But how, was the question on my mind.

Tension rose in the house. Mother and Father had disagreed on occasion before, but never over anything significant. It was easy to see a disagreement existed now. They were divided. Father buried himself behind the newspaper at breakfast and retired to the library immediately after dinner. When Mother addressed him it was in a hurt voice. They had always sat close together, touching often. Now they avoided contact.

Deirdre moped around the house, barely speaking at all. In fact, there was hardly any communication during mealtimes. Grandfather was the only one who didn't seem fazed. He had been napping at the time of the Sloanes' visit and missed the whole fiasco. He chatted as though everything were normal.

The following Sunday the Roberts arrived, and once again there was a meeting in the drawing room with Father, Mother, and Deirdre. This one didn't last long. The Roberts departed quickly, too quickly.

"It's over," Deirdre said when she came upstairs. "The Roberts were cordial. But they politely said it was best if Thomas and I ended our courtship. They felt it would cause a rift in their friendship with the Sloanes, and it was too upsetting to see Cecil so distraught."

"I wish Thomas had put up a fight," I said.

"He didn't because he's more honourable than Cecil," Deirdre said. "He believes his stepping aside is the proper thing to do. No one's listening to me. *I don't love Cecil.*" She threw herself face down on the bed and stayed there the rest of the day.

Several days later Lady Daphne arrived and demanded to see Mother. She undid her hat and cloak with an air of forcefulness and familiarity. Mother and I were having morning tea in the drawing room, which Deirdre had declined, preferring to be cocooned in the paint studio. Lady Daphne banished me with a wave of her hand, but I managed to eavesdrop at the unclosed door.

"Cecil is changing colleges to be closer to Deirdre," Lady Daphne informed Mother. "His school year ends soon, and he plans to return to Larcourt. He'll leave Cambridge University and transfer to Trinity College in Dublin where he'll continue his education, until he and Deirdre are married. After that they can move to England or France, or wherever Cecil decides to finish his studies."

"I never imagined Deirdre living abroad." Mother's voice quivered.

"For God's sake, Morrigan, she's already *been* abroad," Lady Daphne retorted. "It won't be her first time. Now will it?"

"Deirdre prefers Kilpara and Ireland."

"A homebody just like you. To be honest, Morrigan darling, I don't know what Cecil sees in the girl."

Silence followed.

When Lady Daphne spoke again her voice was coarser and sharper than before. "Frankly, I think Cecil is too young to marry, but he's become obsessed with Deirdre."

"They're both too young to marry," Mother agreed, her voice sounded hopeful. "Perhaps Cecil should take time to experience life first."

"Oh no you don't, darling. You can't brush us off that easily. Cecil is young, but his heart is set on Deirdre, and I'll see that he gets what he wants. He'll treat her like a goddess. You should be grateful to us, considering the alternative."

After a pause, Lady Daphne continued. "You know you did me a favour by marrying Ellis all those years ago. I would've hated to see you get hurt, had Charlie persisted courting you."

"Is that another one of your threats?"

Lady Daphne laughed. "It's only a manner of speech, Morrigan darling. I found it annoying that you mesmerized Charlie the same way Deirdre casts her spell on Cecil. Deirdre doesn't deserve my son's devotion. She's very fortunate indeed."

The conversation ended soon afterward, followed by the rustle of fabric. Lady Daphne and Mother came out of the drawing room and walked to the front door.

I watched from the ante-room, their backs to me.

"I'll be back again soon," Lady Daphne said as she passed over the threshold.

She must have almost bumped into Father, for I heard her say his name. Then I saw him come inside. When the front door closed, Mother went straight to his arms, the disagreement of the past week forgotten.

"Morrigan honey, what's the matter?" he asked tenderly.

"Ellis, it's Daphne. She takes such pleasure in making us miserable."

Father guided Mother to the library. "Let's talk in here."

He closed the door and I couldn't hear any more. I went upstairs, mulling over Lady Daphne's words. What did she mean by Mother and Father should be grateful? What was she up to? Granted she had convinced Thomas Roberts to end his courtship with Deirdre, but it would be exhausting to discourage every prospective suitor who came courting. Anticipating this, had Lady Daphne connived to secure her son's prize, thus squashing rival opposition? Her statement that Cecil would treat Deirdre like a goddess was false. For all his promises he would make her life unbearable. He already had.

I was still thinking about Cecil and Lady Daphne the next time I went to Mercy Hospital to visit Grand-Aunt Sadie. I found her walking around the grounds, her fingers moving over large rosary beads, her lips silently mouthing words. She stopped praying when I approached, but kept walking. I fell into step beside her and opened up about Deirdre before I could stop myself.

"It's uncanny," I said, "that Lady Daphne and Cecil have managed to take command of Deirdre's future."

"Your father is also concerned," Grand-Aunt Sadie said.

"Then he should do something. I can't believe he and Mother are considering Cecil's proposal to court Deirdre."

"You've never liked the boy, have you?"

"No, he's evil, and so is his mother."

"Those are strong words."

"Please don't ask me to pray to be kinder, Grand-Aunt Sadie. I don't trust Cecil—or his mother. They manipulated Thomas Roberts to end his courtship with Deirdre. Can't you convince Mother and Father that Deirdre doesn't want to marry Cecil?"

"They'll do what's right for your sister. Have faith in their judgement."

"But the prospect of being courted by Cecil is making her miserable. She deserves to be happy, doesn't she?"

"Of course, and I'm sure she will be."

"Not if she's condemned to a life with Cecil."

"Everything will turn out all right. You'll see. Now come and help me with the weeding. I'm already behind."

I followed Grand-Aunt Sadie reluctantly to the building with the garden tools. I wanted her to see how unreasonable my parents were and help me convince them to reject Cecil's intentions. My heart sank, knowing I had failed to make her understand the seriousness of Deirdre's predicament.

Three nights later I was awakened by a soft noise. I thought I was dreaming when I saw Deirdre standing by the window fully dressed. Her bulging valise lay on her bed.

"What're you doing?" I asked, sitting up.

"Shhh." She put her hand over my mouth. "Be quiet."

I nodded and she took her hand away. The defeated look of the past few weeks was gone. Her eyes were bright and excited.

"I'm leaving," she said.

"Leaving?" I repeated, stupefied.

"Yes, I can't stay here anymore. I *won't* stay here anymore."

"But where will you go? And how?"

"Promise me you won't tell."

I nodded.

"Conor is coming for me. He agreed to fetch me and take me to Dublin. Once we're there, we'll book our passage for America. Cecil can't touch me if I go away. And Mother and Father won't have to worry anymore."

"*We? You're running away with Conor Hagerty?*"

"Yes. It's complicated. Conor already planned to leave for America. I'm going with him. I'll write and tell you everything."

"*That's insane. You barely know him.*"

"I don't have time to explain. Just know that I trust him completely. He'll look after me."

"How will you manage?"

"I'll be fine. Please don't worry."

"Don't go. Talk to Mother and Father."

"It won't do any good. They won't listen."

"Please don't do this."

"I have no choice."

She looked out the window again. "I have to go. I wish things could be different." She hugged me. I held her tight, tears pricking my eyes.

She picked up her valise. "I'll write. I promise."

A second later she was gone. I stood at the window in disbelief. I watched her join Conor. She handed him her valise and together they ran from the courtyard down the avenue towards the gatehouse. Once, Deirdre stopped, turned, and waved. It was then I realized, with surprise and shock, the nighttime figures I had seen through the window weren't ghosts or my imagination—they were Deirdre and Conor. I went to her bed where a lump was bulked in the shape of her body. Pulling back the covers revealed pillows rolled together to look like she was asleep.

My stomach lurched, my breath caught in my throat. It wasn't the same feeling that consumed me when she went away to Switzerland. Then I feared she would become enamoured with a different lifestyle, one more sophisticated and glamorous than anything Ireland could offer; that she would meet someone with a fine estate who would whisk her away from us. This was worse. I might never see her again.

Oddly enough, her behaviour over the past months was starting to make sense. I was convinced now it was no accident that she and Conor had met in Dublin; it was prearranged. The easy comfort in each other's presence came from a much deeper connection than a casual acquaintance. I just didn't want to recognize it at the time. But the notion that Deirdre and Conor were conspiring to be lovers—well, that was unthinkable.

Yet, when I compared Conor to suitors like Thomas Roberts or Cecil Sloane, his fearless attack on life made him far more interesting. Conor possessed a sense of honour, strength, and loyalty, yet projected a quirky sense of humour that was infectious. By comparison, Thomas and Cecil's attempts to make an impression seemed infantile. Perhaps it was believable after all that Deirdre had found Conor irresistible once they met.

Their liaison would explain Deirdre's sudden departure to Switzerland. If Mother and Father had gotten whiff of a dalliance, they would have done everything to squash it. They would vehemently object if Deirdre confessed her desire to marry Conor, and would point out to her that she and Conor lived in completely different worlds socially. That she was too young to understand that those worlds could never be bridged.

I understood now Conor's sudden decision to leave Kilpara and Ireland. Father must have left him no choice but to emigrate to America. And after Deirdre came back from Switzerland, Mother immediately initiated the process to see her settled and her future solidified. But my parents never reckoned on Conor's uncle becoming ill in Dublin and his remaining in Ireland.

They were about to be shocked.

CHAPTER 11

I lay on my bed looking at the ceiling deeply hurt that my sister had not trusted me enough to confide in me. She likely feared I was too young to understand, which was true a year ago, but not now. I had matured considerably during her sojourn in Switzerland. However, at this moment I didn't feel particularly sage as I fought back the urge to dash into Mother and Father's bedroom and scream that their attempt to force Deirdre into a futile marriage had failed. That she had eloped. The sun slowly rose, and I was still in a quandary as the house began to stir.

I was dressed and waiting when Clare knocked on the bedroom door. "Miss Deirdre, Miss Grace, breakfast is ready."

"Coming." I took several deep breaths to compose myself before going downstairs. Keeping my eyes averted, I sat down at the dining table, slowly opening my napkin and placing it on my lap. Clare set a plate of scrambled eggs and rashers in front of me. My hands shook when I picked up my knife and fork. I tried to calm myself as I listened to Mother talk about how colourful her garden was becoming.

I almost dropped my fork when Father asked, "Where's your sister?"

"She's not up yet," I said, keeping my voice steady.

"She shouldn't lay in bed all day."

"She's been under a strain lately," Mother defended.

Father frowned. "All the more reason why she should keep a regular schedule."

"You're being too hard on Deirdre," Grandfather said.

Clare came in with a fresh pot of tea. "Clare, go and call Deirdre down to breakfast again," Father ordered.

"Yes, sir."

The minutes ticked by like hours. I picked at my food, unable to eat. Clare came into the great room. "Miss Deirdre's not answering my knock."

"What do you mean—not answering?" Father demanded.

"She's still sleeping. She didn't answer."

"She's probably more tired than usual," I said.

Clare looked at me gratefully and left.

Father appeared to accept my explanation. But a few moments later, apparently still agitated, he rose from the table. "There's no excuse why that young lady can't come down to breakfast when she's called." Taking long strides, he headed for the stairs.

"Ellis," Mother pleaded, "leave her be." She looked worried, but I knew it was nothing compared to how she would look after Father found the empty bed. He came back downstairs, walking slowly, looking dazed, an envelope in his hand. "It's a letter. From Deirdre."

Mother jumped up, pushing her chair back with a clatter. "A letter?" her voice shook. "Where's Deirdre?"

"She's gone. Ran away."

"Gone?" Grandfather repeated. "She can't have just left, so she can't."

Mother fainted. Father caught her before she hit the floor. He carried her to the drawing room and laid her on the settee. "Get the smelling salts," he ordered.

I ran to find Maureen. "I need smelling salts," I said. She looked at me wordlessly, took a key from her apron pocket and opened a small cabinet.

"Who fainted?" she asked.

"Mother. Deirdre's gone. She left a note." The news would be out soon enough, no point postponing it. I took the smelling salts from a stunned Maureen and returned to the drawing room.

Father waved the bottle under Mother's nose. She coughed and opened her eyes. "Easy," he said. She sat up and Father held her.

"Is it true, Ellis? Did Deirdre really run away?"

Wordlessly Father handed her the letter. She began to cry even before she opened it. I knew its contents. It had been laid under the covers on the pillows meant to disguise Deirdre's body. A disguise she used on other occasions to fool me into thinking she was in bed when she slipped out to meet Conor. I had read the letter over and over during the last few hours.

> *Dear Mother and Father,*
>
> *Please do not hate me for leaving. I love you both dearly, but I cannot stay here any longer. Life is too unbearable so I am forced to go. I know my sudden departure will cause you heartache and I'm truly sorry.*
>
> *I do not love Cecil and I refuse to marry him. Please forgive me for stealing away in the night. I know you would never willingly give me your blessing to leave.*
>
> *As soon as I've found a place to settle, I will write and let you know I'm safe.*
>
> *Your Loving Daughter,*
> *Deirdre*

The letter fell from Mother's hands onto the floor.

I picked it up, pretending to read it then handed it to Grandfather.

Father looked at me. "What do you know about this?"

"Nothing," I lied, in my most innocent voice.

"You must've *heard* or *seen* something."

"I was sound asleep." I forced myself to ignore the urgency in his voice. "She was asleep in her bed when I woke up this morning."

"It only looked that way. At some point she sneaked out of the house. You're sure you didn't hear anything?"

I shook my head no.

"I'll contact the police," he said. "They'll find Deirdre and bring her home."

"Ellis is right," Grandfather agreed, laying the letter aside. "This is a matter for the authorities."

This was harder than I had imagined. It pained me to see my parents worried like this, yet I couldn't bring myself to divulge what I knew. I would tell them in a few days when Deirdre was safely out of reach.

Grandfather put his arm around Mother's shoulders, comforting her. Father immediately went into action and began questioning the servants, with no positive results. Tom reported none of the carriages were taken, and all the horses were accounted for. Father seemed both relieved and concerned by this news. He asked Tom to take some of the workers and search for Deirdre along the Galway Road. If he didn't find her there he should report her missing to the police.

"Good news," Tom said, when he returned from Galway. He pulled a rough sketch of Deirdre from his jacket pocket. "I showed this to the ticket master at the railway station. He recognized Deirdre, said she and a big fellow with fair hair bought tickets for the Dublin train that left early this morning."

"Hagerty," Father said incredulously. He beat his fist on the credenza. "He was supposed to go to America. She's with him. I'm sure of it."

My stomach roiled. It was unlike Father to lose his calm and forego his usual precaution to guard his words in my presence. His recklessness clearly showed he knew of Deirdre and Conor's entanglement and that he had taken action to end it.

I thought back to before Deirdre went to Switzerland and searched for clues that she knew Conor. But she never went near the forge. I often stopped by to talk to Rengen and Conor, but Deirdre never did. She had no interest in horses or anything associated with them. How then? I narrowed down the possibilities, then it came to me. Deirdre loved the little cottage that once belonged to our great-grandparents. Though it was neglected now, it was her favourite spot to paint. There was something nostalgic and forgotten about her paintings. Weeds that overtook the small yard, loose stones on the garden wall, ivy covered walls that needed whitewash, and the thatched roof in disrepair. Conor would pass by there every day if he took the shortcut to Brandubh. The more I thought about this, I felt sure that was how they met.

"Relatives," Tom said, "that's who they'll go to. Hagerty must have relatives in Dublin. And maybe some in England."

"We've *got* to find them," Father said, looking at the fading sun. "They'll be harder to trace if they leave the country."

"I'll go into Brandubh to see what I can find out," Tom offered.

"We'll both go," Father said. "Let's hope the drink will loosen some tongues." He embraced Mother. "Don't worry, Morrigan, we'll find her."

As the evening wore on, worry deepened on Mother's face, and my resolve to keep quiet began to waver. Uncertainty began to gnaw at me. Deirdre's impulsive elopement, as romantic as it seemed, could damage not only her reputation, but the good name of the family, too. And if she and Conor had gone to Dublin, was she safe at his mysterious uncle's residence? From what little I knew about Conor, he obviously supported the fight for self-rule, a conviction I assumed his uncle also held. I thought about the group of men who came to visit that day in Dublin. They could be members of an illegal society, one that committed murders in the name of Irish autonomy. Deirdre could be walking straight into danger.

The front door banged loudly, and Father and Tom came into the drawing room a little unsteady on their feet. Father produced a piece of paper. "Four addresses," he announced.

"Three in Dublin, one in Meath," Tom added.

Mother helped Father off with his coat. "We'll leave before first light," Father told her.

"May I come?" I asked. Things were bound to get difficult if Father found Deirdre.

"No," Father said with conviction.

"I could help convince Deirdre ..."

"No convincing. She's coming back home. And Hagerty will be charged with kidnapping."

Father turned to Tom. "Be ready in a few hours."

Tom nodded and stumbled off to bed. I left Mother and Father talking. It had been a long, worrisome day. I changed into my nightclothes and paused at Deirdre's empty bed. Looking out the window at the darkened fields, I wondered if she was thinking about us and knew we were worried about her. My anxiety rose as time continued to pass, my thoughts fluctuating between Deirdre's irrational decision to escape with her forbidden love, Cecil's conniving manoeuvres to force her into an unwanted marriage, and the misery her leaving inflicted on the whole family. I desperately wanted confirmation she was safe.

I slept little, and when I came down to breakfast next morning, Father and Deirdre's absence at the dining table was an immediate reminder that a search was underway. Mother and Grandfather were both quiet, and we sat through the meal in silence. Throughout the day Mother looked idly out the long window in the paint studio, her easel and canvas left untouched next to Deirdre's. Grandfather spent most of his time with Mother, reassuring her. The whole house was waiting, watching. When Father didn't appear that night, we grudgingly went to bed. The following day became a repeat of the previous one.

By afternoon I couldn't stand the silence any longer. I saddled Spitfire and rode out across the fields. Taking the trail to a cove tucked away on the shores of the Corrib, I found refuge there on the grassy bank. I stared at the dark mountains on the opposite side of the lake, opposing, silent and menacing. It was unbearable not knowing what was happening in Dublin.

Grass rustled behind me and I looked up, startled. Ruairi Kineely, atop his old mare, stumbled down the embankment to the cove. I watched in surprise as he dismounted and came to sit by me.

"Clare told me about Deirdre," he said unceremoniously. "I saw you riding across the fields like the Devil, hell bent after a soul. I was sure you'd break your neck, so I followed you." He looked at the old mare. "Or tried to."

"You shouldn't have bothered," I said moodily.

"You're worried about your sister?"

"I know where she is."

"You told your father, so you're feeling guilty about betraying her confidence."

"No."

"No—what?"

I stared at him fully. "I didn't tell him. He found out by himself."

"You're not making sense."

I explained about Cecil demanding that Deirdre and Thomas end their courtship. I didn't add anything about Conor, I just said Deirdre had rebelled and ran away.

"No offence," Ruairi said. "It's hard to believe your sister had it in her. To run off like that. She's so—"

"Submissive," I finished.

"No. Aristocratic."

"You don't know her."

"You do. You should tell your father what you know so he can fetch her back. The world outside Kilpara is too cruel for the likes of her."

"It can be cruel inside Kilpara, too."

He stared at the mountains before speaking. "You've no idea what it's like to be forced to do just about anything to survive. Your family has status and wants for nothing."

"You're saying we're spoiled?" I felt annoyance creep into my voice.

He rubbed his chin with his hand. "Let's see. Kilpara has maids, footmen, grooms, butlers, and coachmen. Hardships to be sure."

"You're being impertinent."

He shrugged. "No, just honest."

"I thought you followed me here to share your concern," I said. "Instead you came after me to berate me about my family's status. Well, like you, I didn't choose the family I was born into. I'm sorry about your misfortune."

I went to where I had tied Spitfire to a tree. Ruairi put a hand on my arm as I gripped the reins and was about to mount. "Grace, I didn't come after you to argue." His eyes softened. "I was concerned about you."

I shrugged his hand off and looked at him. He gazed back with sincerity despite his tactless methods. He gently brushed back hair the breeze kept blowing in my face.

"Your sister'll be all right."

I nodded, and mounted Spitfire. Without looking back I rode swiftly towards Kilpara.

Father still wasn't home. I woke several times during the night and stared out at the darkness, the moon casting uneven shadows on the hillsides. I wished Father had taken me with him. The address for Conor's uncle's house was not on the piece of paper he had shown us, and I regretted now not giving him that information. Already, he may be too late to discover Deirdre and Conor's whereabouts. Tears of despair began to spill onto my cheeks. I might never see my sister again.

The following morning Lady Daphne arrived, demanding to see Mother. I was coming downstairs when Anthony dutifully invited her inside. "The missus is not receiving visitors, ma'am," he explained.

"She'll see me," Lady Daphne said.

"She gave strict orders, ma'am," he insisted.

"She'll see me, I tell you." Anthony didn't respond, and he didn't move. He was standing his ground.

"I'll take care of Lady Daphne," I said.

"Take me to see your mother, Grace," Lady Daphne demanded.

"Follow me," I said, leading Lady Daphne into the library.

"Where's Morrigan?" she asked, looking round.

"Mother isn't well."

Lady Daphne stood very close. "Listen to me, you pasty-faced child, I know what's going on here. And Cecil does, too. I wrote him. That wayward sister of yours ran away, didn't she?"

"Yes," I said, without flinching.

Taken aback by my honesty she said breathlessly, "Well!"

Silence followed. The clock ticked loudly as she paced back and forth. Abruptly she stopped and said, "Your Father will bring her back. A bargain is a bargain."

Another time I would've wondered what she meant, but today I just wanted her to leave. "When Father and Deirdre return, we'll send word to Larcourt," I said.

"I'd rather hear that from Morrigan," Lady Daphne insisted.

"She's resting. This has been a terrible shock for her."

"You wouldn't lie to me?"

I put on my most surprised look. "I've no reason to."

"Morrigan has always been—well—unpredictable," Lady Daphne said, thoughtfully. "See that I'm informed the moment your sister and father return."

"I will." I escorted her to the door.

When her carriage departed I leaned against the wall and sighed.

Mother remained in her room all day and took her evening meal there. Grandfather and I ate in the great room, neither of us saying much. I went to the library with Olam afterwards. He wanted to show off his new skill at playing chess. Tom had been working with him, but Olam hadn't yet grasped an understanding of the game. When he wrongly claimed my pieces or when he moved his own pieces incorrectly, I didn't object.

At one point Olam became taut. "They're here," he said.

I listened for voices. There weren't any. "Nobody's here."

"They *are* here," he persisted.

"You're mistaken."

He shook his head vigorously. "It's them."

"I don't hear anything," I said, unconvinced.

"Listen." He put a hand behind his ear. I shook my head.

He got up, took my hand, and pulled me towards the front door. We went outside into the chilly night air. There was a faint noise in the distance. As we stood shivering in the doorway, the sound of horses' hooves and grinding wheels became more distinct. Soon the carriage came into view. I looked at Olam and he grinned.

"How did you know?"

"Dunno," he said. "Just did."

When the carriage stopped, a pale-faced Deirdre jumped out and ran past us into the house. Tom started to take the carriage to the stables and Olam hurried to help him. Father walked tiredly up the steps.

"Tell your mother I'm home," he said, unbuttoning his overcoat.

I went to fetch Mother.

"Thank God you found her, Ellis," she said, going to him. Father put his arms around her. Mother looked around. "Where is she?"

"Upstairs. Let's talk first." Mother looked longingly at the stairs as they went into the drawing room and closed the door. I hurried up to our bedroom. Deirdre lay face down on her bed.

"I didn't say anything," I said.

Deirdre turned around and put out her arms. We hugged for a long time before she said, "I know you didn't give me away. I'm sorry I involved you, Grace. Made you choose between me, and Mother and Father. Everything's so messed up."

I squeezed her hand. "Please tell me what's going on."

She didn't speak immediately. When she looked at me again it was through pain-filled eyes. "I first met Conor by accident on a beautiful clear autumn day when I had sneaked away to paint the colours of the mountainside that you see on the far side of the Corrib behind our great-grandparents' old cottage. Tom had taken Mother and Father into Galway, and you were in the classroom with Olam. I gathered up my easel and paints, and headed for the cottage. I was sitting there painting when Conor happened along. He was late getting to the forge that day because his father had broken a cartwheel, and he had to help him get it sorted."

"He walked up looking completely natural against the landscape like he commanded every inch of this land. I just sat there and stared at him. I expected him to raise a sword or something, or order a charge. It was uncanny. He paused and said politely, 'fine day.'

"I answered 'yes it is,' and next thing I knew I was sharing my lunch with him that I had foraged from the pantry. Do you know he loves poetry?"

I shook my head no.

"He does. After that first day I arranged to be at the cottage painting when he walked home to Brandubh at the end of his work day."

"Was it you and Conor I saw outside the window at night?"

Deirdre sat up and dangled her feet over the edge of the bed. "Yes, and please believe me when I say I hated putting you off—"

"Conor said he was going to emigrate last year. He showed everyone his ticket."

"He planned to leave, but he couldn't bring himself to go. And he had a good excuse to stay. His uncle was ill."

"Were you sent to Switzerland because of him?"

Deirdre looked away. "Yes. I told Mother and Father about Conor and me. They were furious and arranged for me to go to Switzerland. They refused to believe we were old enough to make our decision to get married."

"And now?"

Deirdre smiled weakly. "Father found us in Dublin. We were staying with Conor's cousins. We wanted to get married, then leave for America. But even the smallest wedding takes time to arrange. I should've known it was useless."

"Father showed up and threatened Conor with arrest. I tried to stand up to Father—told him I'll be eighteen in a couple of months, old enough to make my own decisions. He threatened to disown me, and I said I didn't care. He said if I didn't come home voluntarily, he would turn Conor over to the authorities for kidnapping. But I stood my ground. I said I would marry him no matter what." She looked at me defiantly. "I'll keep running away if I have to, until Mother and Father realize they can't make me stay here."

"What did Father say?"

"He raved at Conor and me, but we held together. After he calmed down he plaintively asked us both to come home. Said we would talk things through."

"Conor is here?"

"Yes, in Brandubh with his family."

A knock sounded at the door and Mother came in. She went to Deirdre with outstretched arms. "Deirdre darling, my poor baby," she said. "Are you all right?"

"Yes, Mother," Deirdre said despondently.

"I was worried sick about you. That was an irresponsible thing you did."

"Yes," Deirdre mumbled.

Mother put her hand under Deirdre's chin. "You're worn out. We all are. Get some rest and we'll straighten this whole mess out in the morning."

"Yes, Mother."

"Promise you won't do anything like this again." Deirdre didn't answer. "You know we want what's best for you."

Deirdre nodded.

Mother bent and kissed us both good night. She was right about one thing, we were all tired. Despite everything that happened, I slept more soundly that night than I had in days.

It was comforting to see Deirdre in the opposite bed when I awoke. She had a look of quiet resolve, the kind that settles on people when their minds are made up. The house was abuzz with news of her return. When she went to breakfast Grandfather hugged her, chastised her for being impulsive, and said now that she was home safe and sound, no harm was done.

At ten o'clock precisely Conor knocked on the front door. Deirdre rushed to open it ahead of Anthony. Conor looked at her shyly, and when their eyes met there was a connection between them that I had not observed in Dublin. Linking her arm in his, she led him into the drawing room then hurried out to find Mother and Father. I seized that opportunity to slip into the room. I wasn't going to be left out of this discussion.

"Hello, Grace," Conor greeted me. I nodded curtly and sat in a corner chair that I hoped would obscure me from everyone's view.

"I'm sorry we deceived you." His gaze wandered uneasily around the room.

"I'm not sure I can forgive you for that," I said softly.

"I'd move heaven and earth for Deirdre, if I could." He said this with quiet sincerity, and I saw from the intensity in his eyes that he meant it. With that short statement he won me over.

Father strode into the room full of purpose, and Mother and Deirdre followed behind. Father's face was taut as he went to stand by the cold fireplace. He avoided looking at Conor, his gaze resting on me instead. For a moment I thought he would dismiss me. He seemed to be deciding if I should be allowed to stay and hear grown-up matters. Then he began to talk. With one arm resting on the mantel, he looked directly at Conor, his eyes hard and implacable.

"When you left Kilpara and Brandubh, it was understood you would go to America," he said.

Conor shifted uneasily in his position behind the settee where Deirdre sat with Mother. "Yes—well sir, I had every intention of leaving," he said. "But I couldn't."

"You were told never to show your face here again," Father said.

"Yes sir. That was the bargain." Conor stuck out his chin and a prominent vein pulsed in his forehead.

"You dared to break that promise? To come back and disrupt my family?"

"That's not fair, Father," Deirdre spoke up. "You know how I feel about Conor. I wanted to be with him whatever the cost. It was *me* who wouldn't let *him* go."

"And *that* makes it right?" Father stared coldly at Conor. "Marriage will never work between you two. You're ill-matched."

"Was it so different with you and Mother?" Deirdre pleaded.

"You dare to compare this infatuation that has no substance to your mother and me?" He moved in front of Deirdre and rubbed a hand across his forehead. "Your mother and I were different in some respects, but we came from similar backgrounds. And I never—"

"Ellis!" Mother warned, nodding in my direction.

"You never what, Father?" Deirdre shot back. "Say it—*say* it. You did everything possible to win Mother over. Yet, you object to Conor because he is neither powerful, nor rich."

"Observe the differences," Father said.

"Explain that *difference* to me. Please, Father." Deirdre's voice quivered. "Or don't you think poor people should have ambitions?"

"Deirdre, don't be disrespectful," Mother cautioned.

"Some situations are too difficult to overcome," Father said, sounding less agitated and more philosophical. "You're accustomed to a lifestyle that Hagerty can't provide. It will eventually cause resentment between you, and the marriage will sour."

"Ellis, remember how it was when we were young," Mother said, trying to ease the tension. "Our feelings for each other—"

Father stared at Mother then tried another tactic. "How do you propose to support my daughter?" he asked Conor.

"We've talked about it at length," Conor said. "I'll work hard and do the best I can. Deirdre has agreed to accept what I provide."

"It's naive to think my daughter will accept your meagre lifestyle." Father's voice sharpened. "If you truly love her, you won't expect her to."

Conor bristled. "Deirdre knows I love her, and whatever I have will be hers."

"At last count that was nothing," Father said. "Love will not suffice when my daughter has to scrub floors, wash clothes, her hands turning raw and worn. She will be dressed in rags, her skin wrinkled and dried up from lack of decent food—"

Deirdre began to cry. "You're cruel, Father. Cruel. This is not why I came home. It is not what you promised. I'll pack this very moment and leave again."

"No!" Mother squeezed closer to Deirdre and held her in a tight embrace. "I won't be put through that worry again."

Father looked at Conor in disgust. "If you were a decent man, you'd have kept your promise and left my daughter alone."

Silence followed, except for Deirdre's soft sobs. Father turned his back to us and stared into the fireplace. His shoulders slumped, and when he looked at us again his voice sounded distant.

"If it was my decision alone, I'd order you to forget this man," he said. Deirdre sobbed louder. "But you'd disobey me and run away again, and that would break your mother's heart, so I'll offer a compromise."

He paused, Deirdre waited. She looked like a criminal about to receive her sentence. "If you have your heart set on Hagerty, then I give you my permission to marry him; but only on condition that the courtship lasts a full year. For your dowry I'll give you three hundred acres and the small cottage your great-grandparents lived in after they were forced to sell Kilpara. It's in need of repair. You'll be given workers to assist with making it habitable."

Deirdre stopped sobbing. A shadow of relief crossed her face. "Thank you, Father. That's very generous."

"You a have a job here," Father said to Conor.

"Thank you, sir," Conor said, "but I've been offered employment with the Lighams."

It was the worst thing he could have said. Father's jaw tightened.

"No offence, sir," Conor added quickly. "My father is the blacksmith there. He needs an assistant."

Father stared at Conor with intense dislike. Mother intervened before Father could revoke his decision. "Please, Ellis," she said softly.

Father looked at Deirdre and Conor as if he wanted to physically tear them apart. Distraught, he abruptly left the drawing room. Mother hesitated, gave Deirdre a quick hug and followed him.

Deirdre and Conor didn't move. Until this moment they were unsure what the outcome might be. Father held the power to keep them at Kilpara or to force them away. I was happy they were staying. Like Mother, I didn't want to be torn away from Deirdre again. I had already spent a long, lonely year without her companionship and affection. I went to her now, her earlier sobs having subsided into soft whimpers. Conor restrained himself from comforting her, his hand suspended inches above her shoulder. He seemed fearful any gesture in her direction would bring immediate dismissal from this house where he felt unwelcome. I hugged her while he stood by awkwardly.

CHAPTER 12

The news swept through the house with the wild uncertainty of a summer storm. Servants went about their business up and down hallways, swapping snippets of information in excited whispers, as if to speak loudly would bring down the wrath of some unknown force upon them. They wrestled with the question of how Conor, as Deirdre's suitor, threaded into the O'Donovan fabric. Oddly enough, Deirdre seemed to rebound from the previous day's scene. She had received permission to marry Conor, and her relief was obvious. However, she avoided Mother and Father, fearing they might have a change of heart and take back their decision.

To escape this unsettled milieu I wandered out to the flower garden to walk among azaleas, peonies, salvias, phlox, and red roses. Breathing in the mixed scent of flowers and watching birds flit among tree branches calmed my restive mood. My solitude was short-lived, when out of the corner of my eye I saw the Sloanes' carriage winding up the avenue.

I tensed, sure that Lady Daphne had found out about Deirdre's return and had come to pay Mother a visit. I expected her to dismount; instead, it was Sir Charles who stepped out of the carriage. Mother hurried out to greet him. They sat on the bench in the gazebo, too far away for me to hear what they said, yet close enough for me to make out their expressions.

Mother could barely sit still, her body a motion of agitation as she looked at Sir Charles, perhaps pleading for Deirdre's release from the unwanted courtship with Cecil. Sir Charles sat still, his brow furrowed into a frown; but under Mother's imploring gaze, her hands clasped tightly together begging for understanding, his face gradually relaxed, and his resistance weakened. He nodded in agreement to whatever Mother struggled to convey. Then he laid his hand on Mother's to comfort her. When they stood up and started towards the house, I moved quickly in their direction and caught up with them as they went up the steps.

"I'll do my very best, Morrigan," Sir Charles said.

"That's all I ask," Mother said.

He looked sideways at Mother in his usual adoring way. They went into the drawing room. I continued straight through the house and out the back door, then circled back around to the front garden. After a while Mother walked Sir Charles to his carriage. She offered him her hand, and he held it for a moment before lifting it to his lips and kissing it gently.

Whatever hopes Mother had that Sir Charles would influence his wife evaporated the next day. Early in the evening the Sloanes' carriage arrived without warning. This time Lady Daphne hoisted herself out and rushed up the steps to the front door, Sir Charles following timidly behind. Instead of waiting for the usual salutation, Lady Daphne brushed Anthony's greeting aside and headed straight into the drawing room. "Tell your employers I'm here," she ordered the butler.

"Yes, ma'am," he said. "They should return momentarily from their walk. Please make yourself comfortable." Sir Charles paused to look at Anthony apologetically then noticed me. I had been out riding when their carriage approached the house. I hurried through the back door, hoping to avoid them and escape up to my room.

"Hello, Grace," Sir Charles said.

"Good evening," I replied. The front door opened just then, and Mother and Father came in. Mother smiled at Sir Charles and Father said stiffly, "Charles."

Footsteps clattered across the drawing room floor, causing everyone to turn. Lady Daphne returned to the vestibule and stopped in front of Mother, who looked frozen in place.

"Why wasn't I informed that Deirdre had returned home?" Lady Daphne demanded. "I had to hear the news from Charlie. What's this nonsense about her marrying someone else? You know Cecil won't stand for it."

Father moved Mother aside slightly and faced Lady Daphne. "Where Deirdre is, or whom she marries, is none of your business."

Lady Daphne put her hands on her hips. "I've made it my business, Ellis. *Remember?*"

"Then remember this. I don't give a *damn!*"

Mother and Lady Daphne gasped in unison. My hand flew to my mouth.

Regaining her composure, Lady Daphne glared at Father. "How dare you! Quite the American barbarian, aren't you. If you break our agreement, I'll make sure everyone from here to Kingdom come knows that your daughter is *despoiled.* Even *you* care about that."

Father's knuckles turned white, and I feared he might hit her. Instead he responded through gritted teeth. "You'll only succeed to inform people that Deirdre chooses to marry a peasant over your precious son." He pointed to the door. "*Now, get out!*"

The insult went straight to Lady Daphne's vanity and her head sank into her shoulders like a hen whose cluck got stuck in her throat. "Well I *never* ..."

"You've done enough damage, Daphne. Let's go home," Sir Charles said. With his hand firmly on her elbow he guided her outside to the carriage.

"Defend my honour, Charlie. How dare he?"

Sir Charles ignored her and she shouted over her shoulder, "This isn't finished, Ellis. Cecil will set things straight. You'll see. *You'll* pay for this!"

Sir Charles opened the carriage door. "Shut up, Daphne, and get in," he ordered sharply.

We all stood in the doorway silently watching Lady Daphne and Sir Charles leave. From behind us the clatter of dishes and giggling broke the tension.

Maureen stood with a tea tray in her hands, trying to stifle her giggles. "The look on her face was precious," she said, and started back towards the kitchen. There was another giggle and she was off laughing.

Deirdre sat on her bed in awe when I reported what had happened. She grinned when I demonstrated how Father had ordered Lady Daphne out of the house.

"Do you think it will discourage Cecil?" she asked. I shook my head doubtfully.

A few days later gossip filtered over from Larcourt that Lady Daphne had gone to her English residence to escape her coarse Irish neighbours. Deirdre and I sighed with relief and silently wished Cecil would join her there.

CHAPTER 13

Olam's final school term came to an end. He had difficulty grasping that he was no longer expected to spend time in the classroom. He became anxious about the change and repeatedly asked for explanations, which only satisfied him briefly. After mulling things over he'd become anxious all over again. I was beginning to despair that he would ever understand when Tom found a solution. He told Olam there was no more school because he was old enough to work in the stables. This seemed to calm Olam's sense of displacement, and he became content now that he knew his purpose.

One afternoon I took a long walk through the fields alone to contemplate the changes that were taking place. A refreshing breeze from the west accompanied me as I wandered over the hills and along the lakeshore. I finished up on the path next to the gatehouse and started up the avenue back towards the house. Deeply immersed in thought, I didn't hear the carriage approach behind me.

"Watch out. *Watch out, miss*," the coachman shouted. Belatedly his words reached my distracted mind, and when I looked up, I was directly in the horses' path. I reacted, jumping aside just seconds before I would have been trampled. Farther along the carriage stopped, the door opened, and footsteps ran towards me as I tried to get up. My left foot hurt when I attempted to move.

"Grace, didn't you see the carriage?" an anxious voice said.

I looked up into David Ligham's concerned eyes.

"You almost got yourself killed."

I tried to stand, but pain shot through my foot. "I think I may have twisted my ankle."

David put his arm around my waist and helped me up. "I'm on my way to see your father. Let's get you to the house and look at that ankle."

I leaned on him and hopped to the carriage on my good foot.

We drove up to the door, and I stayed in the carriage while David sought help. Anthony immediately assisted. He picked me up and carried me into the drawing room. Mother came to my aid, testing the swollen skin already turning blue. She claimed there were no broken bones, although my ankle looked badly bruised and sprained. To be sure, she asked Tom to fetch Grand-Aunt Sadie to do a thorough examination.

David stopped to see me before he left. "Nasty bit of luck," he said, noting the puffiness and discolouration around my ankle. "I feel terribly responsible."

"It was my fault," I said. "I wasn't paying attention."

"Still, I'd like to make it up to you. May I take you to lunch in Galway one day next week, or if the weather's fine, a picnic by the lake? If you feel up to it by then."

"That's very generous. But you shouldn't feel obligated. Really."

David smiled. "It'll be my privilege. Shall I collect you—say—next Thursday at one o'clock?"

I was in too much discomfort to protest. It was easier to accept his offer and ease his conscience than to disagree and prolong his leaving. I nodded my agreement.

Later that evening Grand-Aunt Sadie arrived with her medical bag to examine my swollen ankle. She confirmed Mother's predictions that there were no broken bones, just a nasty sprain. "Stay off the foot for a few weeks," she ordered. She had the foresight to bring along crutches to help me get around. "There'll be no riding for you, young lady, until this heals."

I had difficulty finding a comfortable sleeping position that night and by the next morning my ankle looked even worse. It took all my strength to hobble downstairs and sit on the settee. Deirdre gathered her paints and easel and came to sit close by, busily sketching me in my handicapped position. She opened the windows, and breezes floated in carrying with them the scent of roses and sounds of crows cawing.

I marvelled how quickly discontentment and distress had disappeared from her face. She blossomed under Conor's attention, her skin restoring itself to its creamy complexion, heightening colour in her cheekbones. Her eyes that had lacked vigour were animated. She was sleeping better, and the dark circles of worry had almost disappeared.

"What's it like to be in love?" I asked.

Deirdre giggled softly. "I think of Conor all the time. My heart beats faster when I see him, hear his voice. When he smiles his face is so tender, yet masculine. And when he holds me—it's, well, you know, comforting and exciting all at once."

"Sounds complicated."

"There's no easy way to explain it. You'll experience it for yourself someday."

We were absorbed in our conversation and hadn't noticed a third person quietly enter the room.

"Hello, Deirdre," Cecil said. We both jumped. "The butler said you were here. I hope you don't mind that I came unannounced." He looked at my swollen ankle. "How did it happen?"

"I fell," I said.

He nodded offhandedly and turned his attention back to Deirdre. "Mother is upset that our courtship has ended even before it began."

Deirdre stiffened, her eyes turning sharp. "Didn't you receive my letter of apology?"

"Yes, but I wanted to hear the news from you in person."

"I'm sure your mother has done a good job explaining everything."

"She has. I'm in shock. A *commoner,* Deirdre?"

"He's a good man and I love him."

"I suppose that's that then." He threw his hands out in defeat.

Deirdre stared at him in surprise. "You accept my decision?"

"Well, yes, of course I do. Your mind is made up, isn't it?"

"Yes. I'm sorry it couldn't be you, Cecil—but—"

"We're still friends, right?"

"Of course."

"Someday I'll meet a woman who'll love me the way you love—?"

"Conor."

"Ah, yes. The Ligham's blacksmith."

"He's an exceptional man."

"*Good* and *exceptional*." Cecil's look shifted from scorn to apologetic. "I've behaved beastly in the past. Say you forgive me. That we can let bygones be bygones."

Deirdre looked puzzled, unsure if he meant to be facetious or sincere.

"Yes," she said simply.

He drew nearer and held out his hand for hers. She rose, but instead of kissing her hand, he gathered her into an embrace and kissed her lips. He tried to pull her closer, but she leapt backward as if startled by a flash of lightning. Reaching down, he took her limp hands in his and caressed them. "If you need anything—anything at all, say you'll call on me?"

Deirdre kept her distance. I waited for her to express her disgust, instead she spoke calmly, "Thank you. I will."

Cecil smirked in my direction as he strode out of the room, smugly unaware there was anything untoward about his behaviour. His shallow attempt at graciousness revealed his refusal to release Deirdre from their arranged courtship. There had been something else in his expression: self-righteous passion.

Deirdre flopped down beside me, her legs giving way from under her. I folded her into my arms.

True to his word, David arrived a week later.

My foot had turned from several shades of purple to yellow.

Grand-Aunt Sadie returned to check on my progress and said another week or two and I should be recovered.

"Does it still hurt?" David asked.

"Not so much anymore," I said. "I'm ready to walk on it, but Grand-Aunt Sadie is being extra cautious. She says I shouldn't do that yet."

He looked outside. "It's such a beautiful day, I asked the cook to pack us a picnic. I hope that's agreeable."

I nodded, picked up the crutches and hobbled out to the carriage. The air was warm, the sky clear blue. In spite of myself I began to look forward to sitting by the lake. David and the coachman helped me inside. Instead of turning south towards Galway, we headed north to Headford. At the village we followed a narrow road that wound down to the lake.

We passed Ross Abbey, a ruined monastery that once belonged to a community of monks, and tidy whitewashed cottages with fuchsia overhanging strong rock walls. We came to a grassy area sprinkled with bluebells that spread out before us like a velvet carpet and ran to the water's edge. In plain sight sat Inchnaghoill, the largest island in the middle of Lough Corrib.

David spread a blanket on the ground and opened the picnic basket. We sat listening to water lap against the bank and watched a steamer traverse the lake, making its daily run from Cong to Galway.

David spoke first. "You look especially pretty today, Grace."

I smiled at him. He was a nice man, if dull.

He took a handkerchief from his pocket, swabbed his nose and coughed nervously.

"It's very peaceful here," I said.

He gazed at me, pleased. "I'm glad you like it. I'm truly sorry about your foot. It pains me to think you could've been seriously hurt."

"You shouldn't feel responsible. You've been very kind."

"It's easy to be kind to you, Grace." His eyes held mine until I looked away.

"Have you completed your bar exams?" I asked.

"Yes. I'm now a fully fledged barrister. I've been assigned to the mentorship of barristers in both Galway and Dublin, so I'll be commuting back and forth between the two towns."

"That's tedious."

"Not at all. I especially like being back in Galway, and near you."

I glanced at the picnic hamper.

"You must be hungry," David said, pulling out thick slices of soda bread, ham, eggs, beets, cheese, and rhubarb tart for dessert.

"Your cook looks after you well," I said.

"She fears I'm too thin because I don't eat enough. The truth is, I have a highly active constitution."

I nodded, not quite understanding, but hoping to avoid further explanation.

He opened a bottle of red wine. The only time I was permitted to drink was during celebrations like Christmas, and then only a very small amount. I didn't want to appear immature, so I accepted the goblet he handed me.

The wine tasted cool and sweet. I sipped it slowly. The meal passed pleasantly, and afterwards David sat a little closer and held my hand. Normally this would have distressed me, but not today. I was uplifted by my surroundings and clear water that was weightlessly propelled onto the bank by soft breezes under a calm blue sky.

"I forget how young you are sometimes," David said. "You've grown into, well, a beautiful young woman. Have you given any thought to marriage?"

I laughed, embarrassed. "Not yet. And probably not for some time. Not until after my coming-out season. Besides, one should be in love first. Don't you agree? Have you ever been in love?"

"No, but I'm sure it's like finding the Mona Lisa. A delicate treasure."

I giggled, I didn't know why. "I'm sorry."

"Don't be," he said. "You're even more beautiful when you laugh." He leaned in close, his round eyes growing larger. "I hope when you do consider marriage, you'll think of me."

I should have been surprised and wanted to be, but I was having difficulty expressing myself. Mistaking my silence for approval, he moved closer and pressed his lips against mine. My eyes were open and I stared at his closed ones, round even now, his eyelashes dark brown and stunted. There was no sensation, only stiffness. David's lips pressed harder, tasting of wine, his breathing coming in rapid spurts. He put his hand on my neck and pressed my face tighter against his. This was my first kiss, yet all I felt was pressure against my lips. I wanted to do something—push him away, but my limbs would not respond. The kiss ended as abruptly as it started, leaving me gasping for air.

David drew back. I must've looked a bit strange because he said, "I shouldn't have done that. It was impulsive, but you must know I find you irresistible."

I looked down, feeling disconcerted.

He lifted my chin. "I admire you greatly, Grace. But I can see I've surprised you. I promise to restrain myself in future." He stroked my cheek and looked at me longingly. "I'm a patient man. I can wait until you're ready."

I giggled. "David, I'm not sure—"

"Shhh," he put a finger to my lips. "We won't talk about it anymore for now."

He went to find the coachman. I sat staring at inky green waves that drifted ashore nudged by nature's gentle hand. Thick reeds grew at the water's edge, and in their midst sprouted sparse white water lilies. Their stifled beauty marooned amid reeds stirred my muddled mind.

I remembered the night at the convent when Ruairi Kineely unlaced my boots, rubbed my frozen feet with his coarse hands until my toes tingled with warmth. His face spun before me, cold with hatred for Cecil after he spooked Spitfire during the hunt at Larcourt.

I could still feel my abandonment in Ruairi's arms the day Spitfire triumphed at the Curragh. Still feel his strength when he picked me up and swung me around, spinning the world at our feet. I remembered his sudden appearance on the old mare at the lake where I sat wrestling with my conscience after Deirdre ran away. His gaze, his stride, told me he understood my confusion. Our lips had never met, yet the moments I shared with Ruairi Kineely were closer to a real kiss than the one I had just experienced with David Ligham.

On the way home I tried to unravel my thoughts, but only succeeded in becoming more befuddled. David obviously decided the outing had gone well, for he chatted the whole way. He abstained from touching me, but when he spoke he caressed me with his voice and his eyes sought to hold mine. When I turned away he attributed this to shyness instead of the embarrassment I felt. I wanted to release him from any hope, any possibility of ever marrying him, only I couldn't think of the right words to express myself. In the end I thanked him for a lovely time, which brought renewed expectation into his eyes.

Although his mentorship would keep him busy for the next few weeks, he asked if I would have dinner with him one evening before he returned to Dublin. I agreed. It would be an opportunity to tell him how I felt after my mind cleared sufficiently to sort my feelings into words. He kissed me briefly on the cheek, a parting reminder that his desire for intimacy lurked beneath the surface.

I wanted to confide in Deirdre about David, but she was preoccupied. Somehow I already knew what she would say. If I admitted to drinking wine, she would accuse me of misconstruing events due to intoxication. Looking back on the picnic unhampered by alcohol, it was possible I overreacted to David's clumsy advances. Admittedly, he was not the spontaneous type, so who was to say the wine had not affected him, too.

"I want to see the cottage," Deirdre announced suddenly.

"The cottage?" I asked, puzzled. We had been sitting quietly in the gazebo.

"Our great-grandparents' cottage, silly."

"Oh. But it's too small to live in."

Deirdre made a face. "It was big enough for our great-grandparents who lived there after they sold Kilpara to Mother's grandfather for a pittance."

"They hated giving up Kilpara, but had no choice, according to Grand-Aunt Sadie." I picked up the crutches. "I can't put weight on my ankle just yet, so how will I get there?"

"You can ride on Ladybug. She's very docile, not at all like Spitfire. I'll lead her."

"And how do you propose that I mount Ladybug?"

"Leave that to me. Are you coming or not?"

I hobbled to the stables. Olam was there, and when he saw us he brightened. Deirdre told him we were going to the cottage. He immediately understood, for he brought Ladybug out of her stall. She was a good-natured brown and white Shetland pony who was used for pulling small wagon loads of materials around Kilpara. Deirdre steadied the pony while Olam fetched a set of wooden steps from the corner of the stables. He put them in front of Ladybug. It was such a comical sight that I laughed. Olam misinterpreted my reaction and looked disappointed.

"Did I do something wrong?" he asked. "Miss Deirdre said to make them for you."

"They're perfect," I said, leaning on his shoulder while I clambered onto the first step. "I couldn't manage without them." He grinned, happy again. Once I was comfortably settled side-saddle, Deirdre took the reins and Olam picked up the crutches. We set off across the fields.

It felt good to ride again, if only side-saddle and only on Ladybug. When we got to the cottage, Olam caught me as I slid to the ground on my good foot. Deirdre handed me the crutches and walked ahead to the cottage. It was longer and wider than most cottages, ivy growing wild over what were once white-washed walls. Parts of the garden wall had crumbled and the gate had rusted. Deirdre stepped over some crumbled stones and tried to open the gate. She looked at us helplessly when the rusty hinges wouldn't give way. Olam motioned her to stand aside, and with one swift tug broke the gate off the post.

"We'll need a new one anyway," Deirdre said and grinned.

Some of the windows were intact, while others had loosened and were blown out by strong winds. Deirdre tried the key in the door. It squeaked and moaned before reluctantly giving way. She and Olam went inside first, and I followed carefully behind. The main room wasn't very large, but it had a fireplace that was still intact. Moss and roots were growing through cracks in the stone floor, and moisture had caused paint to peel off the thick walls.

"What do you think?" Deirdre asked.

"It needs a lot of repair," I said.

She looked around thoughtfully. "Yes, but it's fixable."

There were three more rooms, two bedrooms and a latrine. "A wall will have to be knocked out to make one of these rooms into a kitchen," she said. "The latrine is small but manageable."

We went back into the main room and stared at the wide fireplace where a worn, black crane was attached to the hearth with a pothook to hold pots over an open fire.

"Just imagine, our great-grandmother cooked meals here," Deirdre said.

"It's very crude compared to the kitchens at Kilpara," I said.

Deirdre unlatched the top half of the back door and looked out at what used to be a large vegetable garden. "Look Grace, our great-grandparents may have given up most of Kilpara, but they saved the best for themselves. Isn't this the most wonderful view?" I had to agree. My gaze took in the different hues; green meadow, blue water lapping against the lakeshore, Inchnaghoill and smaller islands in deeper shades of green scattered throughout the length of the lake. All this took up the foreground with bare grey mountains rising up on the opposite side of the lake in the background.

She unlatched the bottom half of the door and we went out on the stoop. "What a wonderful place to gather in vegetables," she said. "I can almost see plants thriving here." She pulled up wild onions that were growing in spite of neglect. And strawberries appeared through strangled vines. I could see ideas churning in her mind as we went back inside. "It's small, Grace, but with the walls restored and drapes on the windows and a new floor, it could be cosy."

I grimaced at her excitement.

"Let's see what's in the attic," she said. She bounded up the stairs. I hobbled behind while Olam continued to walk around aimlessly, not quite sure why we were here.

"You're not going to believe this," Deirdre shouted.

"What?" I asked, climbing the steps one at a time. She called for Olam, who squeezed past me and joined her in the attic. He pulled several dusty trunks to where I sat at the doorstep. "I wonder why these were left behind," Deirdre said.

She blew on the lid of one trunk, causing dust to go everywhere. Inside were threadbare seasonal clothes that had been stored away. Deirdre pulled out a hat from a decaying cardboard box and put it on. "What do you think?" I scrunched my nose as she paraded about.

Another trunk produced worn blankets and handmade quilts, another stored paintings, and some very old crockery.

"There's enough here to set up housekeeping," Deirdre said, picking up the paintings. Buried beneath were two portraits. One was of our great-grandparents. They were much older in this one than in the ones in the gallery at Kilpara. Their clothes weren't nearly so elegant, and their faces were lined and worn, former visages of masters of the land reduced to struggle and defeat.

Deirdre picked up the second one. A woman with an engaging smile and a man with red hair peered out from the canvas. Sitting between them were two boys that bore a resemblance to our Uncles Dan and Mark in America.

"This must be Grandmother and Grandfather." Awe crept into her voice. She held it out and studied it. "I'm sure it is. You know how everyone says you look like the O'Donovans? You bear the resemblance; you have that strange variation of Grandfather's red hair. And see how Father resembles Grandmother? His likeness is evident here."

Deirdre was right. Their smile was the same, although Father's was more masculine. "These belong in the gallery," I said.

"Hello, anybody in there?" a male voice shouted from outside.

"We're here, Conor," Deirdre said. "Be right down."

She hurried out of the attic, ordering Olam to push the trunks back in their original place. I closed the door and leaned on Olam, who carried the portraits while I eased myself carefully down the steps.

Outside Deirdre was in Conor's arms, and he was smiling down at her. "How did you know we were here?" she asked.

"I was going to call on you at the house, but then I saw Ladybug and decided to investigate. It's a nice surprise finding you here."

"The fireplace is intact," she said in an excited voice. "One of the smaller rooms can be made into a kitchen, and you must see the view of the lake out back. We found old portraits in the attic."

"Hang on," Conor said, laughing.

"Let's look at the orchard," Deirdre said, taking his hand and running the few yards to the orchard.

Olam and I followed. Conor examined a tree loaded with budding crab apples. He tested the trunk. "The tree is sound enough and could fully produce again, but its branches need pruning." He walked over to a gooseberry bush. "Weeds are choking this."

"Some of the orchard is salvageable?" Deirdre asked.

"Most of it is. With treatment."

"We'll be able to grow our own fruit and vegetables then," Deirdre said. She didn't normally concern herself with such things. As she spoke, Conor's face clouded over. Was he remembering what Father said about Deirdre never having to labour before?

Conor picked me up and sat me on Ladybug's back with the ease of a lion picking up a cub. When we returned to Kilpara, he lifted me down off Ladybug and handed the reins to Olam. He carried me up the steps and put me down just inside the front door. He turned to Deirdre and drew her to him with naked longing in his eyes. It was several moments before he let her go reluctantly. He refused to come inside, explaining that he should be getting back to Brandubh. I wondered if this was an excuse to avoid Mother and Father.

Deirdre sighed and watched him leave. She began chattering about the cottage. I leaned on my crutches and gazed about at the silent countryside. In the distance I saw the outline of a rider. The rider was too far away to see clearly, but I recognised the horse as one belonging to the Sloanes' stables. Almost instantly both horse and rider disappeared into the woods and were swallowed up by trees. As I followed Deirdre inside, I wondered about the mystery spy from Larcourt.

CHAPTER 14

Father looked at the portraits, first our great-grandparents, then our grandparents and uncles. "I've never seen these before," he said. "Where did you find them?"

"In the cottage. In the attic," Deirdre said. She pointed to the portrait of our grandparents and uncles. "We recognised the resemblance to Uncle Dan and Uncle Mark."

A flicker of displeasure flashed across Father's face at mention of the cottage. "Yes, it's Dan and Mark."

"The portraits were buried at the bottom of a trunk," Deirdre said.

Father ran his hand over the faces of his brothers. "They must've sat for this portrait shortly before Mother and Father left for America. Mark looks only a year old, Dan not yet three. So long ago. So much has happened since then. I'll hang them in the gallery where they belong."

After Father left Deirdre said, "Do you suppose he misses his brothers?"

"Of course," I said. "You see how he pores over their letters."

I didn't tell her that when I was alone in the library I took the letters from the drawer in Father's desk and read them. Holding the paper, seeing blue ink scrawled across it was more real to me than listening to him read the letter aloud. I searched for words that made his face light up about news of Maryland's hot summer weather, swimming in cool mountain streams, riding across open fields. When Uncle Dan and Uncle Mark wrote about tracking bear or deer, Father would reminisce about when he used to go hunting and fishing. He spoke about how the whole family worked alongside servants to preserve vegetables and cure meat in the autumn so that food lasted through harsh winters, about how farm animals had to be protected against deep snows.

But the letters Father didn't read aloud came in perfumed envelopes that were addressed from a woman in Father's past named Astelle who lived in Baltimore. These letters he kept in a locked box. I read them whenever the box was unintentionally left open. It was a mystery to me why they were considered special; their contents were general. Astelle's very precise female penmanship told mostly about the comings and goings of people and family life, and what avid riders her three children were, two boys and one girl. She sought Father's advice about raising horses. He never mentioned this woman, and I wondered if he ever saw her during his infrequent trips to America.

Mother had accompanied him to Maryland once and became homesick almost before they left the harbour. She didn't like rural Maryland; she found its remoteness bleak, yet she was content at Stonebridge House, Father's family home built to resemble Kilpara. She sketched drawings of Stonebridge and of Father's family. She later turned the sketches into paintings that Father had framed. Mother said she preferred Baltimore with its city dwellings, its busy streets, the people and former business acquaintances that Father knew. When she talked about the people she met there, she never once mentioned anyone named Astelle. I found this very mysterious.

As Deirdre's birthday approached, she asked Mother and Father's permission to invite Conor to her party, a request they could hardly refuse without further straining their already frayed relationship. Especially since this was her eighteenth—a milestone. The affair would be reduced to a small family gathering instead of the large celebration that Mother had envisioned to announce Deirdre's engagement to Thomas Roberts.

A week before the event I seized an opportunity to go into Galway alone in search of Deirdre's birthday present. Tom and Rengen had left for Dublin to deliver colts contracted to an estate owner there, and Father accompanied them to conduct other business. At the last moment they took Olam along, who was turning out to be quite useful in the stables. Mother was immersed in conversation with the gardener about the flower garden when I told her about my excursion. She didn't object, presuming Olam would accompany me, unaware he had gone to Dublin with Tom.

It was market day in Galway, and the road was packed with farmers transporting livestock and produce for sale. When the groom brought the carriage to a halt outside Station Hotel, I instructed him to meet me there later and set off by myself for the marketplace. Women passed me carrying baskets of vegetables and fish, some clasping bunches of freshly cut summer flowers. Others seemed to have an organised agenda, moving from stall to stall, accumulating linens, crockery, and household items. Farm animals were gathered for auction on the square, and farmers haggled over prices with buyers for freshly cut sheep's wool.

I wove through the crowd and stopped at a stall where several women lingered, examining various kinds of jewellery. I picked up a bracelet made from silver with inlaid blue hearts. I tried it on, twirling it around my wrist, noting that the colour matched Deirdre's eyes. Unexpectedly, a hand reached out and grabbed my arm. I was locked in a male grip. I turned to find Cecil staring at me.

"Hello Grace," he said. "Your ankle's better?"

"Yes—yes," I stammered, trying to recover my surprise.

"Where's Deirdre?" He looked around for her presence.

"She didn't come. I'm here to buy her birthday present."

He frowned. "Her birthday's next week, isn't it?"

"Yes."

"And the invitations to the party …?"

"There won't be a party. Not the usual kind, anyway."

"I see." He let go my arm. I took off the bracelet and pretended to study it to avoid his stare.

"A good choice," he said.

"It's quite nice. I think I'll buy it." I handed it to the vendor who put it in a box. I paid him and as I waited for my change

Cecil said, "May I offer you some refreshment? There's an elegant café with scrumptious cakes just across from the square."

I stared at him. He stood smiling, yet his eyes were dark and unsettling. I put my change away slowly. "I'd love to, but I have to—" I frantically searched for an excuse. The last thing I wanted was to be trapped in a confrontation with Cecil and no way to escape.

"There you are, Miss Grace," a voice said from behind.

I jerked my head around and locked eyes with Ruairi Kineely. I wanted to hug him, but nodded politely instead.

"Are you ready to return home? The horses are getting restless."

"Coming," I said. I held out my hand to Cecil. "Another time perhaps."

"It'll be my pleasure."

I followed Ruairi a safe distance before asking, "What're you doing here?"

"My father brought in sheep's wool to be sold. He's held up haggling over the price. I was wandering around when I saw you in the crowd with Sloane. You looked like a fly caught in a spider's web, so I intervened. Was I correct?"

"Cecil is always difficult," I said.

"I'd like nothing better than to give the bastard a good thrashing, but I can act civilly, occasionally." I tried to read his expression to see if he was serious. It was hard to tell because he grinned back at me.

We had wandered over to the auction place. Ruairi pointed to two men, faces intent, hands waving.

"That's my father." Ruairi indicated a tall, thin man with thick black, curly hair, greying at the sides. "By the looks of things, he'll be there awhile. He won't give up a penny."

At that moment young children who had been chasing each other bumped into me from behind, accidentally knocking me forward. I would have fallen if Ruairi hadn't caught me.

"Rascals," Ruairi said, good-naturedly, "never looking where they go." He picked up my bonnet that had been jarred loose. Instead of handing it to me, he attempted to set it back on my head, smoothing my hair first. Involuntarily I closed my eyes as his hand tenderly brushed against my cheek.

"Are you all right?" he asked.

I opened my eyes. "Just a little dizzy."

Ruairi looked over at his father, who hadn't let up in the debate. Putting his hand under my elbow he asked, "Would a lemonade help?"

"That'd be nice," I said.

We returned to the carriage and Ruairi instructed the groom to drive down narrow streets away from the market. We eventually stopped in front of a Public House. Ruairi helped me out of the carriage and led me towards the door. I hesitated. "I can't go in there."

"It's fine." He pointed to the sign printed across the front window, *Kineely's Public House* and centred below it *Wines and Spirits*. "It belongs to my uncle," he explained. "It's too early to open for business, but he'll serve us." He took my hand and we went inside before I could protest.

So this is a Public House, I thought, looking around while Ruairi went to find his uncle and request lemonade. There was a long bar with stools in front. In the middle of the counter were several tall, brass handles with black tops. Bottles of all sizes stood behind them on stocked shelves. Some bottles contained clear liquid, while others were filled with dark liquid. I recognised one bottle with brandy, similar to what Father kept in the library.

Ruairi returned with a smile on his face. "Auntie is making up fresh lemonade." He guided me towards a table by the window and sat across from me.

"That smell, what is it?" I asked.

"It's hops and yeast." He pointed to the hand levers sticking above the bar. "Guinness is kept on tap back there. Pull those levers and it pours out."

"It does? Amazing."

A short, round woman with a rosy complexion came out carrying a tray. "So you're Missy O'Donovan," she said, "the girlie who's feeling faint. You do look a bit pale, mind you. The market's no place for a slip of a thing like you, getting jostled about like a sack of potatoes by big country farmers. Drink this up and you'll be right as rain." She set a tall glass in front of me and one in front of Ruairi. Wiping her hands on her apron, she smiled at us.

"You're very kind," I said, taking a sip of the tart liquid.

"Not at all, girlie. I'd gladly do anything for me nephew here, and the charmer knows it."

"Please Auntie," Ruairi said, flushing red.

She picked up the tray, tousled his hair and returned to a room in back.

Ruairi grinned and there was softness in his eyes when he spoke. "Auntie tends to be like that sometimes." We sipped the lemonade in silence. "Are you feeling better?" he asked at length.

"Much. You have a large family?"

"Yes, indeed. We've planted every inch of soil we own. And the sheep roam freely on a steep hillside. We need all the farm produces to keep everyone fed. My older brother Hughie has gone off to America. He and I were born there, you know." I nodded, encouraging him to go on. "Says life is better over there. I've been thinking about emigrating myself."

My heart flipped. "I didn't know."

"There's no limit to what you can do in America."

"My father says it's a large, rough country."

"But free. Free to think and do as you please. There's no ancient monarchy with their thumbprint on you."

"Won't you get homesick?"

"I'll have my brother there, and I can come back if I feel the need. There's no future for me here. Our farm is too small." His eyes held mine. "Have you ever thought about emigrating, Grace?"

"No," I said immediately.

"In America, people are treated the same. Equal. There's opportunity for everyone."

We looked at each other without speaking. I wondered what it would be like if we came from the same circumstances. If his upbringing was similar to David Ligham's and he had asked permission to come courting. I would welcome outings with Ruairi, unlike merely tolerating David Ligham's company. But that was wishful thinking. An impossible barrier lay between us, and the risks for crossing it were as imposing as scaling a rigid mountain. Hadn't I watched the liaison between Deirdre and Conor almost tear our family apart? Yet Ruairi's suggestion to leave Kilpara and start fresh in a country where our differences could be overcome was a thought I wouldn't entertain.

"I should be getting back," I said. "I've dallied too long."

Ruairi nodded. We thanked his aunt and uncle and went outside to the waiting carriage in silence. Ruairi opened the door. As I mounted he took my hand. "It could be very different in America," he said, as if reading my mind.

"I could never leave Kilpara," I said.

He touched my cheek with his hand. "Think about it. It'll be awhile before I have enough money saved."

I didn't answer and he closed the door.

The carriage moved away. I looked back at him until he was out of sight. He never moved from his spot.

I kept myself busy in the following days. Whenever Ruairi's face protruded into my thoughts with his questioning gaze, I pushed it aside. Common sense told me I should avoid contact with him if I were to escape further involvement. What he hinted at was hopeless. To explore a life filled with uncertainty in a large country like America was too remote to think about. With a heavy heart I knew that he would go, and the thought saddened me. From the fierceness in his eyes it was evident he would never accept living a mediocre existence. He was too vital for that. Our futures seemed destined to pull us in opposite directions.

Deirdre's birthday dawned bright and warm, and she decided the party should be held in the garden. A long table was carried outside and fresh flowers arranged into a festive centrepiece of red, yellow, blue and green. Deirdre had previously brought up the notion of inviting Conor's family to share in the celebration, much to Mother and Father's dismay.

Their presence would have made an awkward situation worse, and we all knew it, except Deirdre. Mother tactfully pointed out to her that we should get to know Conor first, that the courtship would be a long one and there was time later to meet his family. Deirdre accepted this proposition, much to Mother's relief.

Maureen brought out the birthday cake that was beautifully decorated with pink and yellow sugared flowers clustered on white icing. Deirdre looked radiant, her blue eyes happy, and her skin healthy and glowing. Normally she would have worn her best gown for this occasion; instead, she chose a simple peach muslin dress. Matching peach ribbon was braided through her hair. Plainly dressed, she looked like a medieval princess.

Grand-Aunt Margaret arrived and fussed and rearranged dishes. Grandfather looked at the table. "Very colourful," he commented, embracing Deirdre. "How's my birthday girl?"

"Wonderful, Grandfather," Deirdre answered happily.

Grand-Aunt Sadie and Trista arrived. All the guests were present, but there was still no sign of Conor. The smile on Deirdre's face slowly faded into a worried look.

"Where can he be?" she asked several times over. "He wanted this to be grand. He even arranged to arrive in a carriage to impress Mother and Father."

"It's just a slight delay," I said.

"But where *is* he?"

Half an hour passed and Conor didn't appear. Father looked at Mother more with relief than concern. But Mother, seeing Deirdre's distress increase with each passing moment, coddled her in a motherly embrace. "I'm sure Conor will be here soon," she said. "Still, it's growing late, and we shouldn't keep our other guests waiting."

"You're right," Deirdre said, through tearful eyes that she kept glued to the avenue.

"Let's blow out your candles, darling," Mother prompted, softly. She drew Deirdre into our midst and Maureen lit the candles. Deirdre closed her eyes and paused for a long moment before blowing out the flames. Father poured wine and made a toast. Still no Conor. Deirdre forced herself to cheerfully open her presents and thank each person in turn.

As soon as it was permissible she left the party and went indoors. She ordered Anthony to find a groom immediately. Writing a quick note, she told the groom to take it to Conor's family in Brandubh and return at once with a response. She went into the drawing room to wait, and I followed her.

"I'm sure there's a simple explanation," I said hopefully.

Grand-Aunt Sadie and Trista came in to say goodbye, and soon afterwards Grand-Aunt Margaret left as well. Tired of waiting indoors, Deirdre went to sit on the front steps. I joined her. Twilight descended and still we waited. Deirdre was quiet while I rambled on about happy memories. Finally a carriage approached and she ran towards it.

"It's him," she shouted over her shoulder as I hurried to catch up.

But it wasn't Conor. It was his brother Sean. He dismounted, hat in hand. He wasn't as tall or broad as Conor, but he had the same fair hair, the same strong features and blue eyes. He wore work breeches, and his shirt was stained and worn. He looked as if he had stopped whatever he was doing and came straight away without taking time to clean up first.

He looked at Deirdre shyly. "I'm sorry, Miss O'Donovan," he said. "Conor left the house to attend your birthday party early this afternoon. I don't know why he isn't here. He did say he was a bit nervous, but that's to be expected, coming to this grand castle and all. Decked out in his Sunday best, he was."

Deirdre staggered as if she might faint. "Where is he then, if he's not here?"

Sean shrugged. "I don't know. That's why I came. I wanted to tell you meself. Something's not right. We looked all along the road for an accident, but we didn't see any."

"Could he have gone somewhere else?" Deirdre asked.

Sean looked puzzled. "Where? He knew he was supposed t' be here."

"Maybe he left. Altogether."

Sean shook his head. "No—No," he protested. "Conor was all dressed up t' come here. He said he was going to your birthday party."

"He left once before."

"Not without saying goodbye. He'd never leave without saying goodbye to our Ma and Da. And not without his clothes."

"Unless he wanted nobody to know."

"Conor's afraid of no one or nothing—'cept women, maybe." He grinned tentatively at his own humour.

Deirdre and I stared at him.

"I don't mean you, Miss O'Donovan," he added quickly. "Course he's not afraid of you. He wants to marry you."

"What about the carriage?" I asked.

"Carriage?" Sean looked at me, mystified.

"Yes, did you see an abandoned carriage along the road?"

"Why would I look for an abandoned carriage?"

"Conor was coming in a carriage."

"You must be mistaken, miss. We don't own a carriage. And we don't know anybody who does. Those are just for grand people like yourselves."

I looked at Deirdre. "Didn't you say Conor was coming in a carriage?"

"Yes. But he didn't say whose carriage. Maybe he rented one in Galway."

Sean spoke up. "He wouldn't have the money to rent a carriage. He never mentioned a carriage. I thought he was taking our horse and cart. Course I went to feed the chickens right before he left the house. But I did see him all spiffed up."

"Maybe he borrowed the Ligham's carriage," I said hopefully.

Deirdre looked at me sadly. "I think he lost his nerve. He knows how Mother and Father feel about him. He got scared and ran away. There's no other possible explanation."

Sean frowned. "Not at all, miss. You might be grand people, but Conor would never run from that. He's no coward. He might not like it that you're a station above him, but he lives for you, miss. That much I'm sure."

We are getting nowhere. "We should notify the constabulary," I said.

"It won't do any good," Deirdre said. "He's gone. I feel it in my heart." She walked indoors in a trance.

"Take Mr Hagerty to the constabulary," I ordered the groom. I turned to Sean. "Tell them everything that's happened."

"What if Conor shows up?" Sean asked.

"Then we won't require their services. Do as I say."

"Yes, miss," Sean said, and got into the carriage.

It was impossible to think that Conor had left without a word to anybody. It didn't make sense that he would prepare to come to Kilpara, then change his mind. I felt there had to be another explanation, like an accident, or he had taken ill. There were other times he could have left that were more convenient. But he hadn't. So why now and why today? I tried to think of a logical explanation, but when none presented itself, the only answer was to wait until the constables investigated.

I went inside the house where Father sat in the drawing room looking triumphant. "This was sure to happen," he said. Mother didn't answer. She looked downcast and unhappy.

"Conor's brother said he left to come here," I said. "I sent Sean to report Conor's disappearance to the constabulary."

"A futile quest," Father said. "The boy finally got some sense and realised marriage wouldn't work between him and Deirdre. Took him long enough to make the right decision. He's probably in Dublin, or on his way to England by now."

"How can you say that, Father? Conor loves Deirdre. He'd sacrifice everything for her. I *know* he would."

"You're naive, Grace. The best thing Hagerty can do for Deirdre is to stay away. He doesn't love her. It's more primitive than that."

"He *does*. You're too blind to see it." I was reckless, irritated by Father's lack of understanding. He behaved as if Deirdre had lost a favourite toy that could be replaced with a similar one.

I turned and ran out of the room.

"Come back here, Grace—this very minute," he shouted. I could hear him say to Mother. "What's gotten into these girls, Morrigan? First Deirdre and now Grace. What's going on?"

I reached the landing and Father's voice faded. I opened the bedroom door and heard soft sobs. I went to Deirdre. She sat up and put her arms around me.

"Do you believe God punishes you if you've sinned?" she asked, sobbing against my shoulder.

"You've never sinned, not intentionally, anyway," I said. "There's no reason God should punish you."

"We're told to keep His commandments," Deirdre said. "I've broken them, so I'm being punished."

"I don't think falling in love with Conor Hagerty is breaking God's commandments."

Deirdre smiled weakly at my attempt at levity.

"You're distraught. We'll find out what happened to Conor tomorrow. We'll get to the bottom of this."

"You really think so, Grace?"

"Yes. Conor loves you. I'm sure of it."

"He does, doesn't he?"

"Shhh," I said. "I'll get you some warm milk. It'll help you sleep."

"That would be nice."

On my way to the kitchen I thought more about Deirdre and Conor. How they were emotional hostages caught up in a twist of fate. Everything else was secondary in their minds. If Conor had temporarily lost his nerve, I was sure he would rally around, if not today then tomorrow, shamefaced and full of apologies.

I returned with two glasses of warm milk and we sat on the edge of Deirdre's bed sipping them. "We'll find out tomorrow. We'll know what happened to Conor," I said.

"Yes," Deirdre said. She lay down, pulled the covers up around her chin and stared at the ceiling.

The following morning she wouldn't get out of bed. I went downstairs and began preparing a tray for her from the buffet on the credenza.

"Where's your sister?" Father asked.

"She's not feeling well. I'm taking breakfast up to her."

Mother rose to join me.

"She should get up," Father insisted.

"She's had the biggest shock of her life. She's distraught."

Father slammed down his napkin. "She should've expected this from Hagerty."

I forced myself not to wince. "Please, Father, stop treating us like children. Deirdre can't forget Conor just because you demand it."

"Careful, young lady. You're treading a fine line."

I put a plate of food on a tray and didn't budge when Father pushed back his chair and stomped out of the room towards the front door.

"You think your father is unfair, Grace," Mother said, turning to me. "He loves Deirdre and wants what's best for her."

"Just because Conor is poor—" I began.

"It's more complicated than that," Mother interrupted.

"Why?"

"His family could live for weeks on what one of Deirdre's dresses cost. That's just one example of the differences between them. Don't be so hard on your father. He sees things you don't."

Mother left to follow Father.

Deirdre didn't leave the bedroom all day. There was no news about Conor. I sent the groom into Brandubh to check with the Hagerty family. They sent back a note saying Conor hadn't come home the previous evening. Nobody had seen him. Not his friends. Not his family. Sean had reported his disappearance to the constabulary, who agreed they would conduct an investigation because the matter concerned a prominent family like the O'Donovans.

Early next morning a constable arrived at Kilpara and questioned everyone in the household. Deirdre came down to the drawing room looking dishevelled. The constable pretended not to notice, but his voice was kind when he asked her questions about Conor. After he finished he said there didn't appear to be any foul play. What it looked like, in his opinion, was a case of voluntary disappearance. Deirdre sat staring into space.

Mother and I accompanied the constable to the vestibule. When Anthony opened the front door, Cecil appeared on the threshold with a wrapped parcel in his hand. He looked curiously at the uniformed man.

"I'll be in touch if there's any news," the constable said. He nodded at Mother. "Good day, ma'am." He acknowledged Cecil as he went down the steps.

Cecil handed Mother the wrapped parcel. "Father asked me to drop off these papers for Mr O'Donovan."

Staring at the constable's back, Mother said, "How are your parents?"

Cecil followed her gaze. "Father's at Larcourt. Mother is visiting her sister in Kent." He looked at Mother. "Is there a problem?"

Mother turned the parcel over in her hands. "Conor was invited to Deirdre's birthday party on Sunday. He never arrived and nobody knows what happened to him."

"I'm sorry to hear that," Cecil said. "But it's not such a surprise. You're aware some people in Brandubh would consider his involvement with Deirdre unforgivable."

"Unforgivable?"

"Yes, tenants don't view us any better than we view them."

"We've always had a good relationship with the people of Brandubh."

"This is different. It involves one of their own aspiring to marry the landlord's daughter."

"I see," Mother said, worry deepening her face. "Do you think someone would—hurt him?"

"Possibly. But let's not jump to conclusions."

"The constable thinks Conor left Brandubh. So far, there's no sign of foul play."

Cecil considered this. "They shouldn't be so quick to rule out that peasants had a hand in his disappearance."

Mother nodded her agreement.

"How's Deirdre?"

"Devastated."

"Rightfully so. May I see her?"

"She doesn't want visitors."

"I'll only stay a minute. I want to help."

Mother pointed to the drawing room. "Just don't upset her."

"I don't think—" I began, but Cecil was already halfway down the hallway. I started to follow him, but Mother stopped me.

"He seems genuinely concerned," she said.

I opened my mouth to disagree then closed it again. I was sure Deirdre would object to Cecil's presence. He may have fooled Mother into thinking he had Deirdre's welfare in mind. I suspected he would look upon Conor's disappearance as an opportunity to take advantage of my sister when she was most vulnerable. I paced outside the drawing room and was about to intervene when he opened the door and said, "Ask a maid to bring us tea and something light to eat."

I took the order to Maureen then returned to find him sitting beside Deirdre, entertaining her with funny little stories. When she didn't laugh he said, "I know another story that is sure to make you smile." Deirdre's lips moved faintly at his persistence.

When Clare brought a tray with tea and daintily cut cucumber sandwiches, Cecil nodded at me. I poured the tea and handed him a cup. He immediately placed it in Deirdre's hands. She looked like she would refuse it. But Cecil gave her a stern look. "You promised you'd try."

She picked up the cup without protest and began sipping. Cecil placed a sandwich on a plate and set it beside her. I sat mesmerised when she picked it up and began eating. Cecil seemed to have accomplished more with Deirdre than anyone else so far. When he readied to depart he kissed her hand, promising to organise his own search party and look for Conor himself. Deirdre smiled wanly at him through grateful tears.

After that Cecil arrived each afternoon with an update on how the search was progressing. He kept an optimistic outlook that if anything had happened to Conor, he would soon know. The constabulary was providing full assistance, and together they would search every nook and cranny. Deirdre began living for Cecil's reports, hanging on desperately to every small morsel of hope.

Father's bad temper left him now that Deirdre was up and about. Since my outburst I had hardly spoken to him. Strangeness existed between us that had never been there before. I was sure he felt it, too.

On the third morning after Conor's disappearance Deirdre arose without prompting and dressed with a purpose.

"Where are you going?" I asked.

"To the cottage," she said.

"Do you think that's wise?"

"I don't know. I just have a desire to go there."

"I'll come with you."

It was one of those clear days with hardly a cloud in the sky. The breeze blew gently off the Corrib. Bees buzzed from flower to flower and butterflies flitted all about us. The fields smelled of freshly cut hay as we walked over the worn track in silence.

When we got to the cottage we sat on a crumbling wall and looked at the lake spread out before us. "Such a view should cure the ache I feel in my heart," Deirdre said, sadly. "But it does not. I feel so betrayed—cheated. Conor and I could've been happy here. I loved him and thought he loved me."

"You're giving up too soon," I said.

"He's gone. He sent a clear message when he didn't come to my birthday party."

"Something or someone must've stopped him."

"There's no evidence of an accident, no altercation, he hasn't taken ill."

"Sean said that he set out for Kilpara. He was dressed in his best clothes."

Deirdre's gaze pleaded with me. "Why didn't he come? He broke my heart. I would've sacrificed my life for him. I love him that intensely."

"He loves you, too."

Deirdre blinked back tears that moistened her cheeks.

We sat in silence. At last, she hiccupped and heaved a shivery sigh. "Do you think he was forced to leave?"

"It's possible."

"Who would threaten him?"

"Nobody knows."

"If that's true, he'll find a way back."

She got up and walked to the orchard. "I was happier here than I've ever been, planning our future together."

I looked at the crab apple tree. Some apples had been shaken off. I noticed spots of blood around the bark and on the ground. As I followed Deirdre back to the cottage, the dark trail led to a broken window. Deirdre started towards the door.

"Don't!" I warned. "Look." I pointed to the blood. "There might be a rabid animal in there."

"It could be just hurt," Deirdre said.

"And dangerous. We don't have anything to defend ourselves."

"I suppose." She sounded disappointed. "We'll ask Tom to take a look."

She stood back and stared at the cottage. "I'm going to fix it. Word will travel and Conor will know."

Had I been hasty to encourage false hope; if in reality Conor had been unable to cope with the surmounting obstacles to their marriage and had just walked away. It would take an undaunted spirit to face shunning by the genteel class, and the hostility towards landlords by locals who wanted Home Rule, yet were forced to subsist on crumbs from their employer's table. Deirdre may only succeed in building a shrine to her broken heart and un-kept promises.

We returned to Kilpara and told Tom about the blood leading into the cottage. He agreed that a hurt or rabid animal could have gotten inside and we were right not to bother it. He promised to send a farmhand over with a rifle.

Cecil arrived as usual that afternoon. He frowned when Deirdre told him about her visit to the cottage and her plans to restore it.

"It's a rundown old place," he said. "Not worth the bother."

"I find it peaceful, with the best views to paint landscapes," Deirdre insisted.

Cecil's eyes darkened and his jaw tightened. But the next instant his mood lightened and his expression turned cheerful. He cajoled Deirdre into walking with him in the garden.

I wondered if I had imagined Cecil's dark mood; it was so easy to suspect the worse, but he had shown a better side lately. His attention to Deirdre had helped her improve. For that alone I could tolerate him.

Father didn't object to Deirdre's desire to refurbish the cottage and said as much when we rode to Mercy Hospital the following Sunday. She had failed to mention she hoped word of improvements would reach Conor's ears and lure him back.

Father said he always meant to restore the premises, but had never gotten around to it. Now it was unsafe to the point that it attracted stray animals, like the feral pig the farmhand found after our visit. It had been badly attacked and had gotten inside through a broken window to seek refuge. It was time to bring the old building back to its original form.

He talked on and I listened, making appropriate responses. Not once did he mention Conor's disappearance or how Cecil had begun to monopolise Deirdre's time.

I half expected to feel tension between us, a need to clear the air. Instead Father seemed to have forgotten about our earlier disagreement and behaved as he always did. I decided to test the waters.

"If Conor left, where do you suppose he is?" I asked.

Father sighed. "Hard to say. He has a wanderer's spirit."

"But there's no trace of him. Someone should've seen him."

"With clever planning he could disappear unnoticed."

I wondered if Father was remembering how Conor and Deirdre had slipped away unseen and came close to leaving without a trace. "But Conor struck me as solid, dependable, caring."

"More like a rogue. He encouraged Deirdre to run away. If he cared about her welfare, he would've thought foremost about her reputation. As I've said before, Grace, you've a lot to learn about the ways of the world."

"Please don't patronise me, Father. Stop treating me like a child."

He pulled on his horse's reins, stopped, and leaned forward in the saddle. "You think I've forgotten what it's like to be young," he said. "I remember it all right. But the world's not what you think it is. Nothing's that simple. Events happen that pull us along—spin us around in all directions. It isn't until much later, in hindsight, that you see the mistakes."

"Did you make a mistake by leaving America?"

"For Christ's sake, Grace, of course not. Sure, I think of Stonebridge House and my brothers all the time. But I love your mother, you, and Deirdre. That's enough to keep me here, and happy."

"But you go back for visits."

"It's my childhood home. America is a country like no other that tests the human spirit. It makes men tough and resilient."

"I'm not afraid of challenges, Father. I know you want what's best for Deirdre and me. But we're old enough to make our own decisions. Like you did."

"It's different for girls. I'm your father and it's my duty to protect you. Kilpara, too. It's your heritage."

"I know that, but—"

Father picked up his reins. The discussion was over. We trotted towards the hospital.

"Even on a day like today," he said, changing the subject, "Mercy Hospital looks grey and depressing. Who would believe that people are cured inside those walls?"

But I wasn't paying attention. I reflected on his paternal desire to shield Deirdre and me from what he obviously considered our inability to make practical decisions. Deirdre's determination to marry Conor had proven to him her judgement was unreliable, and any choices she made were sure to result in disaster. But would he take a different view if

Conor hadn't disappeared and had married Deirdre and theirs was a good marriage? Would he trust our judgement then? So much relied on finding Conor. I wondered for the umpteenth time how a man with such distinct features could vanish. Someone must have seen him.

When we returned to Kilpara after our visit with Grand-Aunt Sadie, I sent a note to David Ligham accepting his invitation to dinner. Conor had worked for the Lighams. David dealt in legal matters; he came in contact with the improbable. He might offer insights into Conor's disappearance beyond what others assumed.

CHAPTER 15

Deirdre became obsessed with renovating the cottage, and within a week it showed improvement. A new coat of whitewash brightened the exterior, and broken windows were replaced. Workers arrived from Brandubh to re-thatch the roof, accompanied by curious onlookers who came to watch the transformation. She ardently hoped word would spread and reach Conor wherever he was and entice him back. Inwardly, I shrank from witnessing her disappointment when the work was finished and Conor didn't reappear.

Almost overnight Cecil had made himself a permanent fixture at Kilpara. He visited often and accompanied Deirdre to the cottage to view improvements. With each passing day Deirdre came to rely on his support more. He encouraged her dependency, especially now that the search for Conor had halted. I still felt he had underlying motives, but Mother, grateful for his devotion to Deirdre, readily accepted his visits. Father, always cordial but never overly friendly, gave the impression he tolerated Cecil for Deirdre's sake. I kept my reservations to myself, confiding only in David Ligham on the evening we went to dinner.

He arrived at Kilpara early on the appointed day and closeted himself with Father in the library until it was time to leave. I dressed simply in a plain beige silk dress, not wanting to call attention to myself. Even so, when he came out of the library with Father, his round eyes lit up with appreciation as he greeted me. He was so well trusted by my parents that they didn't insist on a chaperone.

"Enjoy yourselves," Father said, as David offered me his arm.

"I'll take good care of her, sir." David bowed respectfully and escorted me to the waiting carriage.

Evening sun shone through the long windows at the Traveller's Inn where a maître d' escorted us to a corner table in the half-empty dining room.

"You look captivating this evening," David said. He pulled out my chair, then leaned forward and touched my hair lightly. "And you smell wonderful."

"Thank you," I said stiffly, chiding myself for applying aromatic body lotions that were a matter of habit.

David sat down and looked at me with concern in his eyes. "Is everything all right?"

Anxious to move past this awkward moment, I said what was foremost on my mind. "It's Deirdre. I'm worried about her."

"Your father is furious with Conor over his treatment of Deirdre, and rightly so," David said sympathetically.

"Then you know he was invited to her birthday party, but never showed up. He even arranged to arrive in a carriage to make an impression. Why go to all that bother if he planned to disappear?"

"It seems puzzling."

"He, or his family, don't own a carriage," I continued. "His brother said he had little money so it's unlikely he rented one. Did he request a loan of your family's carriage by chance?"

David's eyebrows shot up in surprise. "No. That would be highly unlikely."

"Current opinion is he up and left without a word to anyone."

"A logical conclusion. He could board a ship to England, France, or even America before he was detected missing."

"He'd need money."

"He may have had money his brother didn't know about."

Our soup arrived and conversation lapsed as we sipped the creamy carrot broth.

"What about foul play?" I resumed. "Lough Corrib is deep. A body could be cast into its depths and never found again."

David dabbed his mouth with his napkin. "Conor doesn't appear to have any enemies, so there's no motive. If foul play were involved and his body was disposed of, there's a good chance it would've washed ashore. My opinion is he ran away."

I shivered at the thought of Conor going undetected in a watery grave. "The locals may have objected to his marrying Deirdre—because of her social status."

"The residents of Brandubh have long memories. Your family is well known for their fairness. You're Irish, except for your grandfather, of course. People would view the marriage between Deirdre and Conor as a compliment to their kind, and cheer your parents for welcoming a commoner for a son-in-law. On the other hand, Deirdre and Conor would be scorned and ostracised by aristocrats. By choosing him, Deirdre struck a wedge between herself and the genteel class."

"And Conor was too weak to stand up to them?"

"That would be my assumption." David looked at me intently, uncertain if he had been too forthright. The server took our bowls and returned with steaming plates of lamb, potatoes and asparagus.

"No matter how difficult the truth is, it's better to know what happened for sure," I said.

"There is one possibility that may have been overlooked—"

"What's that?"

"That he's a member of a revolutionary society. From time to time unrest in the country causes tensions to rise. Many quarrels have been settled outside the law using violence in the name of patriotism."

"Are you suggesting Conor is involved in something illegal?"

David laid his hands flat on the table and studied me as if he was about to address a jury. "Illegal according to British rule, but not in the eyes of Irish patriots. If he's a member of a secret society like the Fenian Brotherhood that seeks Irish independence, his betrothal to a landlord's daughter would be traitorous to their cause.

"There were rumours Conor's uncle was a member of the Invincibles, a radical group who claimed responsibility for the Phoenix Park murders back in '82. You may recall hearing that Chief Secretary Lord Cavendish, and Undersecretary Mr Burke, both decent Englishmen, were struck down in cold blood. Conor's uncle disappeared around the time of the incident. He was someone of interest to the authorities, but they never tracked him down for questioning."

I kept my gaze on David's face as he continued to embellish details about the Phoenix Park murders and their aftermath. He explained the charges against the convicted murderers and their court sentences. His voice grew monotonous as my thoughts drifted back to the day I followed Conor and Deirdre to the house in Dublin, where Conor's uncle supposedly lay ill.

If David was correct and Conor's uncle was involved in a revolutionary group, then Conor could pose a security risk to them by intending to marry Deirdre; a risk they couldn't afford. They could order him not to marry her, threaten him if he did, and insist he leave the country or suffer worse consequences. If Conor refused their demands out of loyalty to Deirdre, they could order him killed.

"Many rumours about the Phoenix Park murders were untrue," I said, trying to rein in my thoughts. "False accusations were aimed against Mr Parnell who advocates self-rule for Ireland through political reform. He's no murderer, yet he was forced to defend his reputation."

"Parnell defied the government by forming an Irish parliamentary party. He'd be a prime suspect in such a heinous crime. The constables were just doing their job."

"Do you think the notion of Conor's uncle's involvement in the Phoenix Park crime is far-fetched?"

"Who's to say without proof? But if it's true, it could factor into Conor's disappearance."

David leaned over the table and took my hands in his. "You look a bit pale. I didn't mean to upset you."

I tried to smile. "I'm all right. It's a bit stuffy in here. It's been rather warm today."

David looked relieved. "Perhaps a stroll outside, or a little wine might help?"

"A stroll would be nice."

David quickly paid by cheque and we walked outside. We ambled towards the park. Watching children play as the long evening drew to a close made me sad. I wanted to regain that same innocence for Deirdre and myself.

I looked at David who was observing me. "Does my father suspect Conor is involved in rebel activities?"

"He's considered the possibility. I doubt your mother has any suspicions."

I nodded. "Promise you won't say anything to my sister."

"That would be a beastly thing to do." David took my hand in his. His touch felt warm, and his grip tightened as if trying to infuse that warmth into my limp response. His voice turned wistful when he said, "It's best to leave well enough alone, Grace."

We didn't talk much on the journey back to Kilpara. The moon shadowed the sun that slipped below the horizon when the carriage pulled up in front of the steps. I didn't wince or resist when David tilted my chin and pressed his lips against mine. He pulled me closer, holding me tight, seeking a response. I relaxed my lips and he seemed satisfied.

When he released me he said hoarsely, "I'd do anything for you, Grace."

I thanked him and detached myself from his embrace.

The house was quiet when I entered the drawing room. I stood at the window and watched as David's carriage vanished down the avenue before retiring upstairs.

"Did you have a nice time?" Deirdre asked as she sat before the vanity brushing her hair.

"Yes," I said, forcing enthusiasm into my voice.

"Good." She slipped between the bedcovers, and before I had finished undressing, she was already asleep.

I lay awake, my mind buzzing with the notion of justice, both Irish and English, which sanctioned murders and rationalised hangings all in the name of freedom. I looked at my sleeping sister and wondered if she had escaped a fate worse than Conor's disappearance. If he were embroiled in some revolutionary society, she could end up like the demented Bridget Joyce, worried that her husband would be sent to the scaffold in the name of British justice, or worse, killed by Irish loyalists. Better to let Deirdre create a shrine to her lost love if it helped quell her loss. In time she would accept his disappearance and continue on with her life.

Tom and Olam took advantage of lingering warm weather to go swimming in the lake as summer began to wane. I stood on the bank, water beckoning me into it depths.

"Put on your swimming costume and come in, Miss Grace," Olam invited. He broke off two hollow reeds near the bank. "Let's see who can stay underwater longest."

"You always win," I said.

"I'll let you win."

"Another day."

Olam hung his head.

"We'll play chess tonight."

"I'll beat you," Olam said.

"We'll see about that."

"I will, just like in swimming—"

Tom glanced at me, mildly curious. I seldom objected to swimming, especially when the weather was perfect. I couldn't admit that images of Conor's decomposed body concealed somewhere below the surface deterred me.

From the time we were small I had spent countless hours in the lake helping Olam learn to swim, encouraging him while he struggled with coordination. I cheered him on when he stayed afloat. As we grew older he became an ardent swimmer and gradually out-swam me, his strokes more powerful and stronger.

I left Tom and Olam submerged in deep water and racing towards a target Tom had set up years earlier. I continued to the cottage where I promised to meet Deirdre. Most of the work was finished, and she wanted me to see its effect. It stood out now, no longer neglected and forgotten, its doll-like exterior whitewashed and cheerful.

Inside, flowered drapes were equally bright. A pale blue tablecloth covered the small square table with matched seat cushions on wooden-back chairs in the new dining room and kitchen combination. In the small front room the hearth had been cleaned and firewood lay in the grate, set to be lit. Two rocking chairs sat side by side next to the hearth and a long wooden bench was placed beneath the front window. A heavy desk occupied the space between the two back windows that overlooked the lake. In the bedroom a thick high-poster bed took up most of the space. A wardrobe stood against one wall and patchwork rugs covered the floor.

Deirdre looked at me anxiously awaiting my reaction. "What do you think?"

"It's remarkable," I said.

"It'll comfort me when life's pressures get too much. You may come here, too, whenever you wish."

I hugged her. "I'd like that."

"I was afraid you wouldn't approve."

"Of course I do."

"I'm not so sure Cecil does. He says it's time to forget about the cottage and start thinking about the future."

"Do you agree?"

"I'm at peace here. It's the only place that's truly mine." She paused. "Cecil has asked me to marry him."

Her words froze me where I stood.

Deirdre moved to a back window and looked out at the lake, her arms folded. When she spoke her voice was low.

"Conor's not coming back. He would've heard about the cottage by now and returned if he truly loved me."

She raised a hand as I opened my mouth to object. "Fixing up the cottage helped me grieve my loss. I'm grateful to Cecil. He's been considerate and patient. He accepts me the way I am. Other men might not be so generous."

"You're beautiful, and kind, and caring," I said staunchly. "Any man would be honoured to have you for his wife."

Deirdre smiled a tired smile. "I'll never love any man the way I loved Conor. I'll marry Cecil so I won't ever be hurt again."

I put my arms around her. It was clear she was struggling to fix her broken life; to find a reason to continue living. But a marriage of convenience to Cecil wasn't the answer.

"Don't listen to Cecil. He's deceptive, manipulative. Think carefully before you do anything rash."

Deirdre didn't answer.

Tom and Olam were busily attaching training ropes to young colts in the paddock. I slipped past them unnoticed and sneaked into the stables to saddle Spitfire. Easily, I trotted him out, easing past Tom and Olam, their backs pointed away from me, as they concentrated on the colts. I struck out across the fields heading northwards. I halted at the cove where David and I had picnicked and looked out at the island of Inchnaghoill, its ruined chapel visible from here. Walking along the water's edge I searched its banks.

Hardly a breeze blew and the lake embraced the earth longingly. "Where are you, Conor," I asked beneath my breath. Then louder, "Are you out there somewhere?" Unexpectedly a voice replied.

"Right here, I'm right here." A small boat, blocked by trees, came into view and pulled into the cove. To my surprise Ruairi Kineely stepped onto the bank.

"What are you doing here?" I asked, taken aback.

He grinned. "Weren't you calling for me?"

"No—I—er—"

"If not me, then who?"

"Er—nobody."

"Do you usually call out to the lake for nobody?"

I didn't like how he mocked me and words I wanted to hold back spilled out. "If you must know, I was calling for Conor Hagerty."

"Conor?"

"Yes. You remember Conor. He and Deirdre were planning to marry."

"Everyone in Brandubh knew they were betrothed. You think Conor's hiding on one of the Corrib islands to avoid marrying your sister?"

"That's not amusing," I countered. "He could've been killed and thrown into the lake."

"A bit melodramatic."

"It's melodramatic if an illegal society committed a murder."

Ruairi's eyes narrowed. "Grace, you shouldn't make statements concerning things you know nothing about. Revolutionaries didn't kill Conor."

"How can you be so sure?"

He put his arms around me and tilted my chin so that our eyes met.

"Conor is in no danger from anyone, except—"

"Who?"

Ruairi's eyes held mine. "I don't believe he's dead. That's all."

"Then where is he? Where did he go?"

"Maybe he took a break to think things over."

"If he had thinking to do, he should've done it before he pledged himself to marriage. He's done irreparable harm to Deirdre. She's devastated enough to consider marrying Cecil Sloane."

Ruairi squeezed my shoulders. "She can't be so stupid she'd marry Sloane. No matter what Conor did."

"Conor walked out on her on her birthday."

"What he did was wrong, but it doesn't change the fact that Sloane is unscrupulous. If your sister marries him, he'll abuse her. Keep her away from him."

"He's helping her get over Conor."

"Why are you defending Sloane? You know how dangerous he is. Have you forgotten he deliberately spooked Spitfire at Larcourt and could've gotten you killed? He's ruthless when it comes to getting what he wants. He'll destroy your sister."

"Conor already did that."

Instead of releasing his grip on me Ruairi pulled me closer, stroked my face with his fingers. We were so close I could feel his heart pulsing. His lips were inches from mine, his breath warm on my face. His eyes reached inside me, demanding my soul. At that moment I would have willingly given it to him. Instead of retreating from his touch, I yearned for it like a desert seeking rain.

Ruairi stepped away from me. "Conor didn't destroy your sister. The imperialistic government that rules our country did. Remember what I said about America, Grace. I hope you'll consider it."

He got back in his boat and for the first time I noticed the bottom was filled with fish.

I rode back to Kilpara more concerned than before, not only by Ruairi's touch, but by his defence of Conor and his hatred for Cecil. I knew he was right about Cecil. I had to find a way to prevent Deirdre from marrying him.

The next morning I stood at the paddock watching young colts frolic about with older, stronger stallions. Deirdre and Olam emerged from a building in the courtyard carrying garden tools. They were on their way to the cottage to do weeding. Mother joined them, her gardening hat tied under her chin, a picnic basket in her hand.

"It's a glorious day to watch the lake from the cottage," Mother said. She linked her free arm in Deirdre's. "Your great-grandparents would be proud of your interest in the old place."

"Thank you, Mother," Deirdre said, and the three of them set off towards the cottage.

I watched them leave; they had invited me along, but I wasn't much of a gardener. I didn't share Mother and Deirdre's interest in making plants grow.

When I went inside the house Maureen was busy dusting in the drawing room. "Where is everyone?" she asked. "Your mother?"

"They just left for the cottage," I said.

"Can we talk? Privately."

I gestured towards the settee.

"I must warn you," she began. I waited as she smoothed her apron and took a deep breath. "There's uneasiness in Brandubh. Rumours about Ellis—your father."

"What rumours?" I asked, surprised.

"That he disapproved of Deirdre's marriage to Conor."

"That's no secret."

"There's talk that he threatened Conor."

"Why would he do that?"

Maureen hesitated, then said in a rush, "Before Deirdre went away to Switzerland, your father told him to leave Brandubh, or else—"

"That was sorted out. Conor and Deirdre were getting married."

"Malcontents say Ellis viewed Conor as a schemer and used his power to get rid of him."

"There's no basis for such accusations," I said, rushing to Father's defence. "Conor left of his own accord. Father can't be blamed for Conor's shortcomings." I was surprised at the strength of my conviction.

Maureen clasped her hands. "I tried to defend Ellis by reminding people he's a decent and honourable man, but that doesn't satisfy the gossips. They insist he wanted Conor gone because his daughter's nuptials to a common upstart were a family embarrassment. I know that's not true. But they point to Cecil and Deirdre's courtship starting immediately after Conor went missing as proof. In their minds this puts your father decidedly on the side of aristocrats."

"That's insane. Conor will turn up and things will go back to normal. You'll see."

Maureen's face turned hopeful. "You really think so?"

"Yes, he'll come back when he hears how much trouble he's caused."

She looked crestfallen by my meagre rationale for Conor's return. Ever since Ruairi had suggested Conor needed time to think about the difficulties he and Deirdre faced, I clung to that possibility. But now it seemed weak and desperate.

"Have you told Father?"

"Yes. He dismissed the whole thing as nonsense. I'm worried." She rose slowly and walked out of the room. I watched her unhappy figure and wished I could say something to give her more hope. With this new turn of events I cursed the day Deirdre ever met Conor Hagerty.

One Sunday in early September, two months after the fateful day Conor disappeared, we sat relaxing in the drawing room after afternoon tea. Grandfather was immersed in the newspaper and Father played solitaire at the small table by the window. Normally he spent afternoons like this in the library, but today he was content to idle away the hours. Mother and Deirdre had retired to their studio. I sat on the settee reading *The Woman in White*.

We were startled when Anthony entered the drawing room and announced, "Master Sloane is here to see Miss Deirdre." Father told him Deirdre was in the studio, and he left to fetch her.

Moments later I went to the window and saw Deirdre with Cecil walking down the avenue. I sighed heavily, knowing he was due to leave for Dublin to continue his studies at Trinity College, now that he was formally enrolled there. He would no longer be a constant presence at Kilpara.

His departure would force Deirdre to depend on herself. She would become strong again. I recalled Grand-Aunt Sadie's words the day I went to visit Bridget Joyce and her children at Mercy Hospital. "Too much trial too soon can destroy a spirit," she had said. I wondered if losing Conor had destroyed Deirdre's spirit. In other circumstances Cecil's annoying attention would be a small price to pay if it gave her strength to move forward, but his manipulation to satisfy his own ends made her vulnerability more tenuous and worrisome.

Mother had joined us in the drawing room by the time they returned from their walk. They came in, Cecil holding Deirdre's hand and looking dreamily at her with puppy dog eyes. They stood awkwardly by the settee not speaking, which drew our attention to them. Something was amiss. Cecil's face was flushed from excitement, but Deirdre looked resigned.

Detaching himself from Deirdre, Cecil stood before Father. "I wish to speak with you privately, sir. I have a request to make."

Father answered without taking his eyes off the cards he turned over and placed on various rows before him. "Whatever it is, Cecil, you may speak here and now."

Cecil looked at Deirdre, who fidgeted with her hands. He heaved noticeably, and cleared his throat. "Very well then," he said. "As you know, Mr O'Donovan, my feelings for Deirdre are no secret, so I shall be direct. I'd like to ask for her hand in marriage."

Mother, Grandfather, and I stared at Cecil. Father continued to place cards one on top of the other. His voice broke the silence when he looked up at Deirdre and spoke. "You've agreed to Cecil's proposal?"

"Yes," she said, quietly.

"You're sure this is what you want?" Father's words snapped sharply.

"Yes," Deirdre said again, her voice devoid of emotion.

"Absolutely sure?"

"Yes."

"You're proposal is accepted," Father said to Cecil, whose lips broadened into a satisfied smile. "However," he continued, "after everything that's happened, I'm sure you'll respect my decision to wait a couple of days before I give you an official answer. At that time we'll discuss arrangements."

"Of course," Cecil said. He took Deirdre's hand, victory beaming across his face as he led her out of the room, oblivious of her detached resignation.

It took a moment for what had happened to take root. A gloomy mood had settled over the room. Mother was the only one who looked contented; happy her daughter would soon be married and settled with a man who adored her.

"Don't look so glum," she said, regarding each of us in turn. "It's obvious that Deirdre has recovered from her romance with Conor and is now ready to make a new life for herself. It's the sign of a healthy mind."

"Is she really over the boy?" Father asked. "I wonder. There are drawbacks to this idea of her marrying Cecil."

"It's too soon. She's on the rebound," Grandfather chipped in.

"You can't let Deirdre marry Cecil," I said. "He's not what he seems."

"Listen to all of you," Mother said, frowning. "Cecil adores Deirdre. He'll make a good husband. And, in all likelihood, Charles and Daphne will remain in England. Far enough away not to be bothersome. Larcourt will become Cecil and Deirdre's home. She'll be close by."

"If Deirdre marries that boy, Morrigan, you can be sure Daphne will be right in the middle of it," Grandfather said.

"Not if he makes Larcourt his home, which he will because he'll do anything to make Deirdre happy," Mother said. "He helped her get over that horrid affair with Conor. And we must think of *her.*"

"I don't trust the boy," Grandfather said "He always acts like he's up to something."

I looked at Grandfather in surprise. His vehement rejection of Conor was to be expected. He was convinced that any association with Conor would ruin our family name. After he disappeared, Grandfather accepted Cecil's presence at Kilpara without complaint. I was sure he'd receive Cecil's proposal with jubilation. After all, Deirdre would be marrying her own kind, which was tantamount to Grandfather. His objection left me uneasy.

"You're forgetting one thing," Father said. "Deirdre accepted his proposal."

"You have the final say in this, Ellis," Grandfather said.

"That's right," Mother said. "Let's forget the past and make a fresh start. Do what's best for Deirdre."

"That's the difficult part," Father said. "What *is* best?"

Nobody answered. Father needed to decide. And if his worried look was anything to judge by, it was a decision that troubled him.

CHAPTER 16

Deirdre studied herself in the mirror, pulling at her bodice as she dressed for breakfast. I attempted to reason with her. "You can't be serious about marrying Cecil."

"I'm dead serious," she replied.

"But he's calculating and devious. He can't be trusted."

She turned away from the mirror to face me. "He's changed. He stuck by me after Conor abandoned me."

"He knows how vulnerable you are. He's pretending, so you'll comply with his agenda."

"You're wrong. He says Conor made me a laughingstock when he jilted me. And knowing that, Cecil still asked me to marry him."

I threw out my hands in frustration. "If Cecil loved you, he wouldn't try to diminish your confidence. Can't you see that's what he's doing? There's a logical explanation for Conor's disappearance; why he hasn't contacted you. We just have to find out what it is."

"Cecil overturned every stone to find Conor. He says Conor became frightened by our class differences, and the division it would cause. He was too proud to admit his fears, so he took the coward's way out, and left. I don't love Cecil. But maybe I will. In time."

"Cecil is wrong."

"Everyone knew that marriage between Conor and me was impossible. But I was head over heels in love with him. I trusted him and thought I could count on him. I was especially proud when we stood up to Father together. Then he abandoned me."

I gathered her into my arms. "It's possible Conor was forced to leave. You should wait. Give it more time."

Deirdre drew away. "I gave Conor every chance to change his mind and come back. But he didn't. I'm marrying Cecil." She turned back to the mirror. "I don't want to talk about it anymore. And now I've lost my appetite. I won't be down to breakfast. Please tell Mother and Father. I'm going to the cottage."

She pulled a shawl from the closet and left.

I sat on the bed and stared out the window. Deirdre appeared outside moments later, walking quickly in the direction of the cottage. I felt saddened that we argued; it made us both unhappy. Thinking back to the simplicity of our childhood, those unhindered times made me ache at the sight of my sister's dejected figure hurrying away.

After breakfast I saddled Spitfire and rode to Mercy Hospital. I found Grand-Aunt Sadie busy with her mid-morning rounds in patient wards. I joined her as she checked on chronic cases in the long dormitory with small worn iron beds just feet apart. Grey walls did nothing to cheer the atmosphere, and slate floors were cold and bare. The air was heavily scented with disinfectant. As we moved from bed to bed, the intense suffering of these patients did not disquiet me. If anything, I was anxious to help ease their pain. Stopping at each bed I noticed how slowly Grand-Aunt Sadie moved these days. But her voice had lost none of its strength; she intoned orders as easily and quickly as ever. Together we checked each patient and I helped where commanded.

"Your smile does them good," Grand-Aunt Sadie said.

"A small comfort," I said.

"You're kindness means a lot to them. You learn easily, too. You'd have no difficulty becoming a nurse."

"A nurse, Grand-Aunt Sadie?"

"You could train here at the hospital, instead of going abroad."

"Abroad?"

"Yes, your father has mentioned sending you to finishing school."

"He didn't say anything to me."

"He will, I'm sure."

"I don't want to go away."

I followed Grand-Aunt Sadie into her small office with a desk where she kept official patient annuals that recorded their illnesses. She pulled two books with stiff covers from a bookshelf. "Perhaps you should read these. See what you think."

The books were thick and heavy; I tucked them under my arm.

She uncovered a tea pot beneath a multicoloured tea cosy the housekeeper had left on the desk for her after she conducted rounds. She took two teacups from a shelf and wiped them with a tea cloth.

"Now tell me what's really on your mind?" she said, after she poured the tea.

"I haven't been feeling well lately," I began.

"I'll check you over, if you like."

"It's not that kind of feeling. It's—well—it has to do with other things."

She nodded sympathetically. "I see. Is it of the emotional kind?"

"Yes, sort of."

"Is it a boy? Someone you're fond of who doesn't return your affection?"

"No, Grand-Aunt Sadie."

"Your father said young David Ligham has been paying visits to Kilpara. He's a nice lad."

"David and I are friends. Nothing more. But that's not what's bothering me."

"What is it then, child?"

"It's Deirdre."

"I see."

"She's agreed to marry Cecil Sloane."

"You disagree with her choice?"

"He's evil and distrustful. But he's convinced Deirdre he's changed."

"You don't think so?"

"No. Besides, what if Conor should return?"

"That's unlikely, since no one knows where he is."

"But nobody knows why he left. We have to find out."

I picked up the teapot and poured more tea.

Grand-Aunt Sadie raised her cup and sipped the steamy liquid. "His disappearance shocked Deirdre. Poor child. It's strange how the boy just dropped out of sight without a trace. If he intended to come back, he would've done so by now. It's possible we'll never see or hear from him again. Perhaps Cecil's proposal is a good thing. Deirdre needs permanency in her life."

"He's *pretending*," I said

"Maybe not. He deserves a chance."

"There's a rumour circulating that—well—that Father has something to do with Conor's disappearance."

"Hmm." Grand-Aunt Sadie was silent for a moment, then she said, "Gossip is for empty minds. Where there's doubt, malcontents will look for someone to blame."

"And they've chosen Father."

"That's disturbing."

"Maureen warned Father, but he ignored her."

"It'd be wiser to address the issue before it gets out of hand."

I nodded.

"I'll bring it up next time he comes to visit. In these troubled times, wrongful accusations could have serious consequences."

On my return home I was more worried than ever. A cancer seemed to be spreading through Kilpara, and I saw no clear way to stop it. Situations were evolving beyond my control that left me feeling defeated. I dismounted Spitfire and took him to the stable where I rubbed him down. Afterwards I went to the library and was glancing through the books Grand-Aunt Sadie gave me, when I heard Father come in the front door. Mother greeted him just outside the library.

"Cecil is coming at seven; he sent a note," she said.

"I see," Father said tiredly.

"Daphne and Charles will be returning to Larcourt to officially approve the engagement."

"I see," Father said again, only now there was agitation in his tone.

"Ellis, please pay attention. This is serious. Deirdre will be more settled when she marries Cecil. She'll start fresh."

"I'm not convinced she should marry him," Father said. "Daphne will gloat over this whole affair with Conor. I can't stand that woman. And I despise the son just as much. They stuck their damned noses into Deirdre's courtship with Thomas Roberts, the only match that showed real promise. Then when this fiasco with Hagerty happened, Cecil moved in like a vulture. He and his mother spread mayhem quicker than any wildfire."

"Ellis, you're overreacting. We should think about Deirdre. How much more disappointment can she stand? Cecil adores her and will do anything to make her happy, unlike Thomas—or Conor. She'll get over her disappointment if she marries him. It's the best thing for her."

"If Hagerty hadn't run off like the coward he is, we wouldn't be facing this dilemma."

"Ellis, that's another reason we should get this resolved. People are pointing fingers, saying that you're responsible for Conor's disappearance. It's not healthy."

Father strode into the library, his eyes cold, his jaw set. He ignored me and walked over to where two guns and a rifle hung above the mantel. I stiffened when he picked up the revolver on the left, the one that belonged to Uncle Francis who was killed in America's Civil War. "I won't give credence to the drivel of gossips," he announced.

Mother gasped, and fainted.

Father dropped the revolver onto a chair and grabbed Mother, as she crumpled towards the floor. I jumped up to help him.

"Get the smelling salts," he ordered, after we settled Mother onto a chair. But Mother waved a hand to signal she was all right.

Father asked for the sherry and I filled a glass half full. Father took the glass and held it to her lips.

"Drink this," he said.

Mother took a few sips then pulled herself up straight. "The sight of you holding that gun—terrified me," she said, her voice sounding low and terse.

Her fearful gaze held his cold one for what seemed like an eternity. Slowly, Father's features relaxed. "It's probably not a good idea to start packing a revolver," he said, gathering her into his arms.

She sighed. "It's a very bad idea."

Father drew back. "About Deirdre marrying Cecil, I still have reservations, but maybe their marriage will put an end to this Hagerty nonsense for good."

That evening at dinner Mother made an attempt at normalcy. She commented how quickly autumn had approached. She complained about upcoming winter days when she would miss fresh flowers from the garden. Grandfather took up the conversation, saying how cold weather bothered his rheumatism.

Shortly before seven we withdrew to the drawing room. Father handed Deirdre a glass of wine. She shook her head and he passed the glass to Mother. He poured himself a brandy, picked up the glass and swished the liquid around before speaking.

"You're sure marrying Cecil is what you want?" he asked.

"Yes," Deirdre said softly.

"Foolish child, you are," Grandfather admonished.

"It'll be my folly," Deirdre said flatly.

"It's a mistake."

"It's too late to worry about mistakes, Grandfather."

"Let's not debate this," Mother said. "Cecil has made every effort to be sincere. He loves you, Deirdre."

At that moment Anthony announced Cecil. He came into the room, his eyes resting on Deirdre and remaining there until Father spoke.

"We accept your proposal," Father said. "The announcement will be made, followed by an engagement party."

"No announcement and no engagement party," Deirdre intervened quickly.

Cecil stood beside Deirdre and took her hand. Addressing Father he said, "We'd like to get married right away. I wanted your approval before offering Deirdre this." He pulled a small box from his pocket and dropped down on one knee. "I'd be honoured if you'd become my wife, Deirdre." He opened the box and a large diamond sparkled. I thought Deirdre recoiled at the sight. If she did, she recovered quickly.

"I accept," she said. Mother looked like she might cry. Father and Grandfather shifted uncomfortably.

Cecil put the ring on Deirdre's third finger then stood up and looked at Father. "With your permission, sir, we don't want any announcements. We'd like a quiet wedding; in London."

"And deny me the pleasure of seeing my daughter married at Kilpara?" Mother said.

"It's best this way, Mother," Deirdre said.

"I'll take leave from my studies at the end of October," Cecil said. We'll get married in London then. Afterwards we'll spend a short honeymoon in Switzerland."

"I thought you hated Switzerland," I said, looking at Deirdre.

Her gaze went straight to Mother and Father. "I left something behind. I should return to retrieve it."

"Your doll?" I asked

"What?"

"Your favourite doll. You left it behind."

"Yes, I want to get it back."

Her words seemed to carry a meaning I didn't understand any more than I could make sense of the strange determination on her face. Her experience in Switzerland had been a huge failure that left her apathetic towards everyone and everything. Yet of all the places she could choose for a honeymoon she wanted to return there. It didn't make sense, but then nothing made sense these days.

An awkward silence lingered. Father looked at Mother before he spoke. "In light of everything that's happened, Morrigan, we should agree to the wedding in London."

Mother looked away.

"It's what I want. Please say you understand, Mother," Deirdre pleaded.

"I envisioned you getting married at Kilpara."

"I did too, but that was before— I don't want any fuss."

Mother walked over to the window. I could see tears brushing her eyes.

"As for the dowry," Father said, speaking directly to Cecil. "Your parents and I will agree on a sum of money, and you may choose two of Kilpara's prized horses, excluding Spitfire and Ceonig."

"That's agreeable, sir," Cecil said.

Father looked at Deirdre. "My wedding present to you will be the cottage and the three hundred acres that I had already promised. It'll belong to you and you alone. You may manage its tenancy as you see fit."

Deirdre went to Father and hugged him. "Thank you, Father," she said.

"My parents arrive at Larcourt next week," Cecil said.

"We'll finalise the agreement then," Father said.

Cecil took Deirdre's hand. "We'd like to get married on October 31st. Halloween."

I had been sitting in the library most of the day, attempting to concentrate on the journals Grand-Aunt Sadie gave me, but my mind kept wandering from the text to watch the mixture of sun and clouds colouring the landscape different hues of green. Father came in and poured himself a brandy. "What're you reading?" he asked.

"Books that Grand-Aunt Sadie gave me."

He looked over my shoulder. "Medical journals?" He raised an eyebrow when he read the titles. "Those were like bibles to your grandmother. A good thing, too, since her services were often needed."

"Will you be returning to America soon, to visit Stonebridge?"

Father looked down at his drink, swished it around then took a gulp.

"Possibly. Maybe next spring. You could come with me if you're not in Europe by then."

"What?"

"Your mother and I discussed your attending finishing school. Possibly somewhere in France. Your mother disapproves of you roaming the countryside unattended and wants you to prepare for your coming-out season."

"Olam accompanies me, most of the time," I offered lamely.

"We don't have to decide right away. We'll talk about it after Deirdre's wedding." He finished his brandy and left.

After he departed I sat staring at the open pages that described diseases in intricate detail, complete with images of medical procedures. With difficulty I turned my concentration fully to the complex text, conscious this was my lifeline to escape being shuttled off to some foreign school.

Ruairi, along with other local lads from Brandubh, was in the bog digging turf for Kilpara fires. Once, when I was riding, I saw him from a distance. It was one of those rare warm days as I rode Spitfire along the lakeshore. After my last meeting with Ruairi, I put aside the possibility Conor had come to physical harm at the hands of some rebel society, and his body was thrown into the lake. But I kept a vigil nonetheless.

Olam rode with me, and on our return to Kilpara, we paused on the ridge that looked down on the bog. We rested the horses among sparse trees, and from this vantage point I could see the men at work. They had removed their shirts in the sun's warmth. I could pick Ruairi out easily, dark hair curling down his forehead and along the nape of his neck. His agile body bent from the waist, strong arms digging blocks of turf out of the earth with the ease of uprooting a potato. I wasn't aware how long we lingered there until Olam complained. "I'm rested, Miss Grace. Let's go."

I nudged Spitfire. "Yes, let's go."

Ruairi chose that moment to look up. He must have sensed our presence. He waved, and I responded likewise, before galloping off down the hill.

I was unprepared for the next time I saw him. Several days later Father was late for dinner. We waited impatiently in the drawing room while Maureen hovered close by, complaining about his tardiness. We looked expectantly towards the front door when a knock sounded. But it wasn't Father. We could hear a man identify himself loudly as a worker from the bog. He asked for the mistress and was ushered into the drawing room by Anthony.

Without preamble he said, "It's the mister. He's been hurt. I was sent ahead to warn you."

"He's been what ...?" Colour drained from Mother's face. Grandfather put an arm around her and led her to a chair.

I rushed outside in time to see Father's chaise coming up the avenue. When it halted Ruairi dropped the reins and helped Father down. With Father's arm around his neck, Ruairi brought him inside the house.

Ruairi looked up at me from under Father's weight. "In here," I said, leading them into the drawing room. Ruairi eased Father onto the settee. There were bruises on his face and he was clutching his side.

"What happened?" I asked.

Mother, forcing aside her shock, knelt beside Father and took his hand in hers.

"Bring a basin of water," I told Maureen. "Brandy, Grandfather. And send someone to fetch Grand-Aunt Sadie."

Maureen ushered away servants that had gathered in the doorway, and returned with the water. "I was afraid this might happen," she said, setting the basin beside me. I washed away dirt from Father's face while Mother held brandy to his lips. Several times he winced. I felt around his stomach, there was no sign of swelling, but he let out a groan when I touched his ribs. I ordered a sheet and had it ripped into long strips. These I wrapped tightly round Father's mid-section. It seemed to give him some relief.

Ruairi stood by anxiously. Colour returned to Father's face, and when he spoke it was in a strained voice. "Thank you, young Kineely, for your help."

"What happened?" Mother asked.

"Vigilantes assaulted Mr O'Donovan," Ruairi said. "They weren't expecting company. We were moving a wagon-load of turf to Kilpara and came upon them by chance. They ran off when we started pelting them with rocks. We ran after them, but they had too much of a lead."

"Who would want to hurt you like this?" Mother's voice wavered as she stroked Father's cheek.

Maureen looked at her worriedly.

"It's about those rumours, isn't it?" Mother said.

"They weren't locals," Ruairi declared.

Deirdre came into the room and saw Father lying on the settee. She ran to him. "Are you all right, Father?"

"I should be going," Ruairi said, moving aside to let her get closer to Father.

"Thank you, again," Father said.

"Yes, we're indebted to you," Mother said.

"It's late. Do you have a horse?" Father asked.

"Not today, I'll walk home," Ruairi said.

"Grace, ask one of the grooms to find him a mount."

"I'm much obliged, Mr O'Donovan. I'll return the horse first thing in the morning."

Father nodded.

I went with Ruairi to the stables. Darkness had fallen and stars were present in the sky. None of the grooms were in sight, and I assumed they had retired for the night. I went over to where a brown mare was stalled. I began to remove the tackle from a hook, and Ruairi reached above me to lift it down. Our hands touched. He smelled of turf and earth. Our bodies brushed against each other, and when I turned to face him, only inches separated us. Neither of us moved; his eyes held mine. Slowly he bent and kissed me gently. A sigh escaped me, his nearness striking every nerve in my body.

The tackle dropped. My arms went round his neck, clung to his thick curly hair. He held me, his lips brushing my forehead. He pressed closer and his green eyes searched my face before his lips teased mine again. I yielded to his kiss.

Shakily we broke apart, surprised by the intensity that had overtaken us.

"I want to be with you, Grace," he said. "I don't have the right to say this to you. Soon you'll have fellows better educated than me with worthier prospects and manners clamouring for your favour. All I have to offer you is myself. I'll have the money saved soon for passage to America. I'm asking you to come with me."

"You don't know what you're saying. I can't leave Kilpara. We're letting the emotion of Father's attack affect us—"

His fingers brushed my cheek, stained from digging turf. I laid my hand over his. He savoured it for a moment, then took it and pressed it against his chest.

"You can't deny what's happening between us," he said. "It has nothing to do with your father's beating. But you know I can't stay here. There's only poverty. I want to make my fortune in America. Say you'll come with me."

I looked up at him. "I can't. You're asking me to give up my family. My home. I love them both. I'll never leave."

He drew me into his arms and pressed his lips to mine. My heart pounded in my ears. He pulled me closer, wrapping me in the heat of his passion. His eyes, filled with intensity, searched mine for an answer. "Think about it, Grace, that's all I ask. Think about it."

I nodded, unable to speak. He kissed me gently one more time before saddling the mare and departing into the night. Outside I sucked air deep into my lungs and watched him leave. In a single moment he had upset my world and filled it with confusion.

Father spent a restless night on the settee. Finding it impossible to sleep, I checked on him several times. Thoughts of Ruairi occupied my mind. Towards morning I finally dozed off from exhaustion and woke up late.

I came downstairs to find Grand-Aunt Sadie standing beside Father, who was now sitting up on the settee. "You did fine work," she said, pointing to rolls of makeshift bandages on the floor, replaced now with clean, strong binding.

"Thank you, Grand-Aunt Sadie. How are you, Father?"

"Sore."

"His ribs are bruised, but not broken," Grand-Aunt Sadie said. "His face escaped permanent damage, too."

Anthony announced the constable, who entered the drawing room with an official air. Father pointed to a chair. The constable's gaze roamed around the room before he removed his hat and sat down. Focussing his attention on Father, he pulled out his notebook and spoke in an authoritative voice. "Nasty business this, Mr O'Donovan. Tell me everything you remember."

"There's not much to tell," Father said.

"How did it happen?"

"I was driving the chaise home from Galway when four men in hiding jumped out from a ditch and startled the horse. One of them grabbed the reins and the others dragged me to the ground and started beating me."

"Did they rob you?"

"No, they just beat me."

"Did you recognise any of the attackers?"

"No, they wore black hoods. There was one thing—"

The constable leaned forward.

"One of them spoke with an English accent."

"How could you tell?"

"When Kineely and the other boys working at Kilpara showed up and began throwing stones, they struck one of the attackers in the head and he yelped 'crikey' with an English accent."

"He must've said that on purpose to throw you off. There's no English in this area except for the ascendancy. And they're only here on occasion."

"None of the attackers had spoken until that moment. They were taken by surprise when Kineely and the others came along. You know what this means?"

"What?"

Father smiled faintly. "It wasn't the locals."

"Sure it was. Who else could it be?"

"I don't know."

"Well, we'll catch whoever did it," the constable assured Father.

"Make it soon. The next time I go into Galway, I'll be toting this." Father pointed to Uncle Francis' revolver lying beside him in its leather holster.

"This isn't the Wild West, Mr O'Donovan," the constable remarked. "It's a civilised country. We'll get the job done."

"Civilised be damned," Father said heatedly. "If you don't catch who did this, I will."

The constable stuck out his chin. "Now, now, Mr O'Donovan, there's no need to be insulting, and don't go taking the law into your own hands."

"Then find the bastards, or I'll deal with this myself."

The discussion waned as I left the room. I dressed and went to the stables, grateful that Olam was nowhere around when I saddled Spitfire. I wanted to be alone with my thoughts. Taking the trail along the banks of the Corrib, I galloped hard near the lakeshore. Once I paused to look out at the lake, islands scattered in the middle like green gems. I found my thoughts shifting from Father, to Ruairi, to Deirdre, hoping to make sense of how mixed up everything had become. Unable to glean any insights, I turned away from the tranquil setting and galloped back to Kilpara. I was almost there when I saw David Ligham's carriage approach the house and rode over to meet it. The driver halted and David appeared at the window. "I heard about your father in Galway. I'm on my way to see him. May we talk later?"

I nodded and followed him to the house. News had travelled fast.

After David spoke with Father, Mother invited him to stay for lunch. All through the meal I compared him to Ruairi Kineely. His pale face, straight hair; how he constantly reached for his handkerchief. His eyes were languid, lacking the intensity so compelling in Ruairi's.

Following lunch we walked outside and David said, "Terrible thing to happen to your father. I wouldn't have suspected the locals were capable of this." He took my hand and held it. "It could've been more serious."

"How could it be worse than this? My father didn't deserve to be assaulted."

"Of course not. The constabulary will apprehend the culprits." He caressed my hand with his soft fingers. "May I share your company again soon? It's been too long already."

"With pleasure," I fibbed. I accepted his invitation for the sole purpose of staying informed because he was so closely connected to the law. I wanted him to share any news with me.

I stood on the doorstep and watched his carriage disappear down the avenue.

The incident with Father's attackers faded into the background during the next few weeks as preparations for Deirdre's wedding consumed our thoughts. During the whirlwind of activity, Lady Daphne and Sir Charles arrived at Larcourt. When they visited Kilpara the tenseness between Lady Daphne and Father was tangible. With an effort she managed to behave politely, her demeanour superficially chummy as she assumed the upper hand now that her son had won his prize. She pretended sincerity when she inquired after Father's health and expressed relief he would fully recover in time for the wedding.

Father improved with amazing speed. While he mended, Mother, Deirdre, and I made frequent trips to Mrs Collins's shop. Very quickly a wedding gown was produced for Deirdre and new ceremonial gowns were made for Mother and me.

I felt sad knowing I would not be wearing my purple silk gown at Deirdre and Conor's wedding. I tried to imagine the ceremony between Deirdre and Cecil, but it didn't feel right. It lacked the sense of pleasurable expectation that goes along with anticipation of matrimonial bliss. Deeply missing was the love that two people share. It was a marriage of convenience.

As arrangements were finalised for our passage to London, the situation became surreal. I avoided Cecil whenever possible, and he ignored me now that he no longer considered me a threat. I kept telling myself this was my sister's choice while using every opportunity to remind her it wasn't too late to change her mind. But she continued to stick by her decision. She even blamed Father's attack on Conor's disappearance, saying if he hadn't left so mysteriously, Father would never have suffered that brutal beating. I could almost hear Cecil influencing her thoughts.

Two weeks before the wedding word came from Mercy Hospital through Trista that Grand-Aunt Sadie was ill. Father and I went to see her immediately.

"It's nothing," Grand-Aunt Sadie said, looking pale and frail. "Trista's worrying and fussing too much."

"It *is* serious," Father said, taking her hand in his. "You're working too hard. It's not good at your age. You should be taking better care of yourself. Come to Kilpara where you'll be more comfortable."

"Stop fussing, Ellis. Trista and the Sisters are looking after me. I'll be all right in a few days."

As we were leaving, Trista walked with us to the carriage.

"How is she, really?" Father asked.

"She's been getting fevers on and off for no reason. This one is worse. It's hanging on longer. There are too many drafts in this old convent. And the building is damp. She should be somewhere drier. I'm concerned. My father isn't well, either, and I may be called to his side at any moment."

"Deirdre is getting married shortly," Father said. He looked at Trista. "If you think Aunt Sadie's condition is serious, I could insist she come and stay at Kilpara."

Trista nodded. "If she stays here she'll keep working and not rest like she should."

Nothing was decided for several days. Then Trista sent word from the hospital that Grand-Aunt Sadie's condition hadn't improved. She was concerned because, as she predicted, her family had summoned her home. Her father's health had worsened and she had to attend him. This news seemed to settle Father's mind. He called a family meeting and proposed that Grand-Aunt Sadie be brought to Kilpara. He said that it was unfortunate that her illness should happen so close to the wedding, but she needed looking after. Mother agreed. The question remained who should keep vigil.

"We could employ a nurse," Mother said. "And Dr Murphy can visit."

"We'll employ a nurse to oversee her care," Father said, "but a family member should be here. She's very stubborn and will demand to be taken back to St Bridget's the moment we're out of sight."

"I'll stay," I said. "I can handle Grand-Aunt Sadie, and I'll recognise the symptoms if her condition worsens."

Deirdre looked at me sadly. "But I counted on you to be my maid of honour."

I went to her and hugged her. "I know, Dee. I want to be there." I was being truthful. I disapproved of her decision to marry Cecil, but I would always stand by her. Still, it'd be a relief not to witness his satisfied gleam when she spoke those final words and became his trophy. It would be impossible to disguise my true feelings. By staying behind, my sister would be spared my despair.

"It's an omen, so it is," Grandfather said. "The wedding should be cancelled."

"Everything is organised, Grandfather," Deirdre said. "We need to get it over with."

"We should postpone the wedding," Father agreed.

"Cecil and I will go alone then," Deirdre said.

Mother looked helplessly at Father. "She can't do that."

An awkward silence ensued before Father said, "Aunt Sadie is too much responsibility for you to handle by yourself, Grace."

"You have to be at Deirdre's wedding, Father," I said. "It'll only be for a few days, and I have Maureen and Tom and Rengen to rely on."

After much discussion this was the only solution that everyone could agree to, so it was settled that I would stay at Kilpara with Grand-Aunt Sadie. The very next day Rengen went to the convent and brought a protesting Mother Superior to Kilpara. A novice and a nurse came along to help get her settled. One of the guest rooms was made ready and fires remained continually lit. She had only just adjusted to her surroundings when it was time to bid farewell to Deirdre.

I watched my sister as she readied to ascend into the carriage. I wanted to grab her and beg her not to leave. Instead I made one final attempt to change her mind. "It's not too late to say no."

"I know," Deirdre said, and hugged me. "I'll be happy, you'll see. Stop worrying."

She stepped back and brushed my cheek with her hand. "I'll miss you, little sis."

"I'll be thinking about you every minute," I said, my voice thick with emotion. "You'll make a beautiful bride."

She held my hand until she was seated inside the carriage. I kissed and hugged Mother, Father and Grandfather. Then the carriage moved forward down the avenue. I ran beside it, waving. When it finally pulled ahead I stopped and stared at its back, loaded down with luggage. Next time I saw my sister, she'd be Mrs Cecil Sloane. I felt a chill travel down my spine like someone raking my skin with an ice pick.

CHAPTER 17

On Halloween I thought about Cecil and Deirdre's wedding ceremony taking place in London. The preacher dressed in parochial robes greeting them at the altar in Temple Abbey, the organist playing Bach, notes resounding around tower walls unacknowledged by empty pews. Words recited by Deirdre and Cecil permanently uniting their lives as man and wife. I wanted to imagine Deirdre happy, her face animated and contented, the way she looked when she gazed at Conor. Instead, I envisioned her face masked with tolerance and subjection. On this most important day in her life, it pained me to think of her joined in a loveless union.

Grand-Aunt Sadie wasn't the best patient I could hope for. She refused to take her medicine and argued with Dr Murphy that it was the wrong kind. Gently, he stood his ground, and reluctantly she gave in. She spent her days in front of the fireplace or resting in bed. Under my watchful eye she showed general signs of improvement. I suspected her real dilemma was that she demanded too much of herself and ignored her own health.

We supped together in her room. I read to her afterwards, and once she was settled, I put the novice in charge. Many of the servants had already left to participate in the annual nighttime celebration when Celtic and Christian customs converged. I wrapped my cloak around me and sat outside on the steps in the evening chill. In the distance a parade of young and old climbed the torch-lit hillside to the bonfire that had been piled high for days with anything flammable. As was the long-time custom, cows, sheep, and horses were moved to eastern meadows in preparation for the festivity.

The black night came alive when the bonfire was lit, sparking flames that rose high above the hillside. Drawn by curiosity I wandered towards the path that led up to the blaze. As I drew close, costumed figures looked eerily medieval as they gyrated around the flames to the lively beat of bodhrans, uilleann pipes and fiddles. I stood well back from the dancers, mesmerised by masked faces unleashed in unseemly guises of goblins, witches and ghosts.

Suddenly a hand reached out and pulled me away from the crowd, leading me down over the hillside out of sight. I knew his touch even before the mask came off. Ruairi's arms went around me, his eyes compelling mine in the flickering shadows.

"Grace," he whispered, touching my cheek. "I wondered if you'd come."

I closed my eyes. He gently lifted my face to his, to a long kiss mixed with moist breezes and peaty flames. After we drew apart he picked me up and carried me to privacy below a nearby knoll. Here, sheltered in a clump of hedges shaped like a horseshoe, he unbuttoned his overcoat and spread it on soft, damp moss. Above us flames flew higher and wilder and heat spread over us like a warm blanket. Recklessness overcame me. I didn't protest when his lips pressed against mine, softly at first, then growing insistent. He teased my mouth open, his tongue flirting with mine until his dominated. He removed my cloak, then unbuttoned the neck of my dress and warmed my throat with kisses. Undoing my hair, he spread it above my head, his fingers dropping down to caress my cheek. "I could spend the rest of my days looking at you. You're so beautiful."

I giggled. "You'd get bored right away."

"I'd never get tired of seeing your face." He brushed my earlobe with his lips. "I love you."

His words were just the softest murmur that grew in force as their meaning spread through me. He pushed my shift up around my waist, his hands stroking me as he pulled himself flush against me. He removed his shirt, revealing taut muscles earned through hard work. I could almost feel blood pulsing through him as his warm skin filled me with longing. I repeated his name over and over, his kisses hot against my breasts, his fingers trailing down my spine, sending desire rushing to my head. He pulled off my undergarments. His hands caressed my hips and thighs, drawing our bodies together until I was nestled beneath him. I pressed against him unashamed, apprehensive, yet eager to experience our coupling.

Flames lit the night sky cutting through falling dew, bodhrans beat faster and louder, chanting echoed over the hillside. Our breath mingled, our hearts raced, our bodies joined.

Only once did he pause and ask, "Are you sure, Grace?"

I answered with my lips.

It was almost dawn when I crept back inside a silent house. I slipped into bed, sheets cold and starched after the soft moss and Ruairi's warm body. When a maid summoned me to breakfast I woke up disoriented, yet sensing a change had taken place, something wonderful. Within seconds I remembered the knoll, Ruairi's face, the passion we shared, and afterwards when he buried his head against my neck, his tears damp against my skin, emptying his heart and soul into mine.

I expected to feel remorse in the aftermath of our lovemaking, but it occurred so naturally that I was devoid of shame. I dressed for breakfast and went to check on Grand-Aunt Sadie before going downstairs. She sat staring at the fire, an empty tray sitting next to her on the small table. She greeted me and asked me to join her for tea. We had settled into a comfortable silence when she said, "It's difficult to think of Deirdre as a married woman. She's so young to be facing such responsibility." She looked towards the window. "I'm feeling much better now. I should get back to the hospital. Who knows how things are being managed."

"It's too soon," I said. "You know Rengen rides over every day. He hasn't reported anything amiss. Has he?"

"No, and he won't, either. He'll keep bad news to himself."

"If there were serious concerns, he'd tell you."

"Still, I should get back."

"We'll talk about it after Mother and Father return home."

"You sound like your great-grandfather Burke when you talk like that."

I smiled at her, knowing this was meant to be a compliment.

Later that morning the Ligham carriage pulled up outside. I was surprised, then it struck me, today was the day I had agreed to have lunch with David in Galway. He looked surprised to find me in my morning clothes when I met him in the drawing room.

"I've been distracted," I apologised. "What with Grand-Aunt Sadie convalescing with us, and Deirdre's wedding—"

"It's quite all right, Grace," he said gently.

"May I offer you tea?"

"Thank you." He removed his coat and gloves, and sat on the settee. I summoned a maid, and then sat in a chair opposite him. He talked about minor issues related to his work. I tried to remain attentive, but found it extremely difficult. In the end I gave up and just smiled and nodded politely.

Afterward we went for a walk, and I asked him to stay for lunch. He agreed and we walked on until we drew close to the cottage. During that period he sniffled often and employed his handkerchief to blow his nose. I thought about asking after his health but refrained. He appeared healthy except for this continual annoyance.

Presently he said, "You know I'm very fond of you, Grace."

I smiled my surprise.

"And your seventeenth birthday is coming up soon?"

"In January."

"Will this be your formal coming-out season?"

I didn't answer right away, my bubble of happiness bursting as I was reminded that Mother and Father would soon pressure me to attend finishing school. Now that Deirdre was settled, the question of my future would occupy their minds. More than ever I wanted to stay at Kilpara, to be near Ruairi.

"I suppose I'll go to finishing school first," I said morosely.
"Not for long, I hope."

We walked back to the house in silence. I was glad that Grand-Aunt Sadie felt well enough to join us for lunch. Every time I looked at David across the table there was a question in his eyes. I wondered what he would say if he knew I had lain in another man's arms the previous night. A man I yearned to be with and who occupied my thoughts.

"I expect Deirdre and Cecil will make their home at Larcourt," David said matter-of-factly.

"It'll be wonderful to have her close by, especially when the babies start coming," Grand-Aunt Sadie said. "What a delight it'll be to have children underfoot."

David looked at me, reached across the table and put his hand over mine. His intention was very clear. It took all my willpower not to withdraw from his touch.

Grand-Aunt Sadie smiled benevolently.

When Mother and Father returned from London, I greeted them with questions about Deirdre's wedding. Mother's eyes grew misty as she talked about the ceremony, the abbey and how beautiful Deirdre looked in her ivory dress trimmed with delicate lace. It was a shame, she lamented, that my sister couldn't be seen by all. A party should be planned to introduce the newlyweds as soon as they were settled.

The Sloanes returned to Larcourt to stay until the married couple came home. During that time they paid only one short visit to Kilpara and were received with forced cordiality. They journeyed back to England three days after Cecil and Deirdre arrived home.

I was anxious to see Deirdre and paid her a visit the moment I heard the Sloanes had departed. I found her the way I expected, reserved, lacking the usual exuberance shown by new brides, and disinterested in her new home.

Cecil escorted us to lunch in the large dining room and behaved unusually tender towards her. He encouraged her to explore her new surroundings and to make any changes she deemed necessary.

She agreed in a bored voice, seemingly uncaring about her new role as mistress of Larcourt.

Each time I tried to be alone with Deirdre, Cecil made it a point to join us, under the guise of the perfect host. We toured parts of the house I had never seen before. We visited the gardens, stables, and boat docks for which Cecil provided a running commentary. Deirdre hardly spoke a word, appearing distant, like she was miles away. Upon my departure I kissed her cheek and hugged her. She remained at the door while Cecil accompanied me to the bottom of the steps where the groom stood holding Spitfire. Cecil slapped the horse's flank softly, a deliberate motion meant to remind me of the hunt nearly a year ago. When he looked at me, all the tenderness he showed Deirdre disappeared. His gaze became dark and threatening.

"Don't expect to drop by Larcourt whenever you feel the mood, Grace. You'll wait until I invite you."

I didn't balk at his words. "What if Deirdre invites me?"

A sly smile crossed his mouth. "I'll have lots of excuses why you shouldn't come."

"She may insist."

"Then you'll refuse or suffer the consequences." He slapped Spitfire's flank again, a little harder this time. Spitfire snorted and moved away impatiently.

"You can't keep us apart. If I don't come to Larcourt, she'll come to Kilpara." I mounted Spitfire and rode away before he could utter another word.

The moment Cecil left for Trinity College, Deirdre began making frequent visits to the cottage. Sometimes I joined her there. I began to see a different Deirdre. Her face lit up when she stood by the window talking about how well the orchard, now bare, had come along under careful attention. Cool winds off the lake whipped around the cottage, and she would say how cosy and safe she felt inside. She reminisced about how beautiful the hillsides and lake looked in springtime; she was already making early plans for her garden during these cold-weather months.

She returned to Larcourt only when Cecil came home on weekends. He knew almost immediately how much time Deirdre spent at the cottage, reportedly from spies he had set up to watch her. He began to sound like the old Cecil as his frustration grew with Deirdre's infatuation with the cottage. She confided that he demanded she behave more like the mistress of Larcourt and not some peasant whose only ownership was a rundown cottage on a useless piece of land. His persistence increased her resistance to perform as the mistress of Larcourt, and instead provoked her to seek asylum whenever she could.

"If only she were obsessed with Larcourt the way she is with the cottage," Cecil complained to Mother one Sunday after dinner as Deirdre retired ahead of us to the drawing room with Grand-Aunt Sadie and Grandfather. "She spends far too much time there."

"Be patient," Mother advised. "It's only been a few weeks, and running a household as large as Larcourt is a daunting task. She'll come around, you'll see. Especially when you're home."

"You're right. If I were there to help her direct the household it would be different, but I must finish my studies. Mrs Spencer is an excellent housekeeper. She wants to please her new mistress. But Deirdre shows no interest."

"Things will change when the term is over. The Christmas holidays are coming up."

"But I must return to college in January."

"You'll be together for a few weeks, enough time to make a difference." Mother pressed a reassuring hand on Cecil's arm. "Deirdre could be lonely. Perhaps Grace should stay with her when you're away."

Cecil glanced at me, a frown darkening his face. But when he turned to Mother his voice was smooth.

"An excellent idea. But I worry if having Grace at Larcourt would create a distraction, giving Deirdre more reason to shirk her duties. She'll attain confidence sooner if she gets used to her new home by herself. Less disruptive."

"I see your point," Mother said.

He sneered at me and I stared back boldly.

Mother's plans were underway for the pre-Christmas gala to formally celebrate Deirdre and Cecil's marriage, and to introduce Deirdre as the new mistress of Larcourt. Feverish preparations overtook the household in readiness for the event. Servants dusted furniture, mopped floors and polished silver until it shone. Decorations were ordered and delivered, and the house took on a festive look. One afternoon Mother and I were in the vestibule watching a workman clean the chandelier when Father strode in. He gave Mother a peck on the cheek and continued towards the library, then stopped abruptly, and came back.

"Gilhooly says he's retiring," Father announced to Mother.

Mother nodded sadly. "I'm not surprised. He keeps saying he wants to spend more time fishing."

"I tried to dissuade him, but his mind is made up. He and his wife will move out of the gatekeeper's cottage and in with his widowed sister in Galway after the New Year. I've recruited young Kineely to learn the gatekeeper responsibilities until I decide on a replacement."

"I hate to see the Gilhoolys leave," Mother lamented. "They've been here for so many years."

"They'll stay through Christmas, so we'll have them awhile longer. I'll miss Gilhooly. He's very loyal."

"Especially to you."

They shared a secret smile and Father kissed Mother again, more tenderly this time.

I had feigned disinterest when Father mentioned Ruairi's name. We hadn't spoken since Halloween, but I found myself constantly riding towards the bog to watch him work. Often, he would pause on his shovel to look up at the hillside. We didn't speak, but the bond between us was unmistakable. I only had to think of him and I could feel his arms around me and see the tenderness and passion in his face.

His working at the gatehouse meant our paths would cross often, making it difficult to deny our attraction. Despite the problem that created, I saw a bright side to the situation. Ruairi's settling into the gatekeeper's position raised my hopes he would become more attached to Kilpara and forego his intention to go to America.

In this preoccupied mood I joined Grand-Aunt Sadie for tea in her room. After Deirdre's wedding Father had insisted she stay on at Kilpara through the winter. She argued that her health had returned, but Father disagreed and said it was better to err on the side of caution and avoid a relapse. She was explaining medical terms to me when Rengen interrupted us to give his report on the patients at Mercy Hospital. He happily announced that Trista had returned from caring for her father.

Grand-Aunt Sadie's face brightened at this news. "Rengen, I'd like Grace to go with you tomorrow when you visit the hospital. She's been studying my medical journals, and I'd like to hear her impressions."

"All right, Mother—" Rengen grinned. "We's happy you're here at Kilpara, Jasmine and me. She liking your company."

"Jasmine is a jewel." Grand-Aunt Sadie patted Rengen's big hand. "You are too, Rengen. I thank God every day for bringing you into our lives."

Rengen's pleasant face turned worried. "You know, Mother— we going back home soon to be with our kids and grandkids."

"I know, Rengen. It's all Jasmine talks about. I understand, but you'll be sorely missed."

"I's going to the hospital early in the morning, Miss Grace," Rengen said, turning to me.

"I'll be ready."

At dinner that evening Grand-Aunt Sadie asked Father, "Have the constables discovered anything new about the men who attacked you?"

"They've made no progress," Father said. "Whoever the villains were, they've covered their tracks well. The scant descriptions don't match any of the local troublemakers, which has the police puzzled."

"It could've been someone passing through," Grand-Aunt Sadie said.

"Maybe." Father stroked his chin thoughtfully. "I'm not giving up. I'll find the bastards myself whoever they are and make them pay."

Grand-Aunt Sadie frowned at Father's use of language, but he was too preoccupied to notice.

Two days later I deliberately rode Spitfire down the avenue. Ruairi appeared from behind the gatehouse when I stopped near the gate. He took hold of Spitfire's reins, his eyes smiling into mine. "Shall I get the gate?"

In answer I dismounted. Ruairi's hands went around my waist as he eased me to the ground. He didn't release me immediately and we stood inches apart. He glanced towards the cottage for signs of Mr Gilhooly. He whispered against my ear, "I've missed you, Grace. Can we meet tonight?"

"No. After what happened on Halloween, we can't be trusted alone together."

He caressed my cheek. "I'll never forget that night."

I knotted my hands tightly together lest they crept around his neck. His eyes came alive with longing as they searched mine. "We belong together, Grace. You can't deny that."

"I don't. But you're going to America, so there's no future for us."

"Not here, Grace. But in America the opportunities are endless. It would be different there."

"I can't."

"Are you afraid I won't provide for you?"

"It's not that—"

"What then?"

"I can't leave my family."

"I'll be your family. We'll have grand adventures. Think of all the things we'll share."

"I know what we can share," I said, sadly. "You make me feel so alive, that is an adventure in itself."

"Then come with me."

"It would devastate my family if I snuck off to America."

"They'll adjust to the idea. I'll look after you, I promise." His eyes pleaded with me.

"Stay here, don't go," I said. "You could take over as gatekeeper and stay at the gatehouse."

"That won't change anything. Mostly not the fact that I'll be forever poor, or the social barriers that will always stand between us. Emigration is our only choice."

There was no mistaking his determination, dashing my hopes that he would stay. I feared we were doomed to be apart.

"April," he said. "I'm booking my passage for April. You have until then to decide."

I shook my head. "I won't change my mind."

He put his fingers over my lips. "Just promise me you'll consider it."

I nodded.

Not wanting him to pressure me anymore, I blurted, "Deirdre married Cecil."

"Aw, Grace. No!" He grabbed his head between his hands as if struck by a blow and backed away. "Jesus! God! Don't tell me that." He doubled over, bringing his hands down to rest on his knees. "When did this happen? There were no announcements."

His reaction surprised me, and I stood staring at him. "They eloped to London and were married on Halloween. Only my parents, Cecil's parents, and both grandparents attended."

Ruairi straightened. "You didn't go?"

"No. Grand-Aunt Sadie was unwell and I stayed behind to look after her."

"Why didn't you tell me?"

"I couldn't bear to talk about it. Besides, we were otherwise occupied." A smile started across my lips, but faded when he slammed his fist into his palm.

"How could she marry that bastard? He's not fit to wipe her spit. Didn't you warn her?"

"I tried, but she was determined. She was devastated over Conor."

"This wasn't supposed to happen. It's typical Sloane not to advertise his intentions—snake that he is."

I looked at him in confusion. His hatred for Cecil ran deeper than I imagined.

"Is your sister at Larcourt?"

"Yes, but she's not happy. She prefers the cottage and goes there when Cecil is in college."

"This should never have happened. Clare didn't say a word. She would've told me."

"It was kept secret. The servants were told the family was going to London for the baptism of my second cousin Harold's son. They didn't take any of the help with them. Father apologised to the household for the secrecy after Cecil and Deirdre returned from their honeymoon. Everyone thought it was romantic and were understanding. Clare was absent then."

"My mam was having female troubles and Clare stayed home to help with the chores until she got better."

"Nothing serious, I hope."

"She's back on her feet now."

Ruairi looked at me with desperation in his eyes.

"I'm sorry your sister married Sloane. Keep a close eye on her. He can't be trusted, but you already know this."

"Is there something you're not telling me?"

He hesitated. "It makes no difference now. They're married." He squeezed my arms. "Grace, if we're to have any chance together, we'll have to leave Ireland."

I shook my head sadly, took hold of Spitfire's reins and walked back to the house.

That night I looked out onto the dark avenue and wondered if Ruairi was preparing for bed. Mrs Gilhooly had fixed him a place to sleep on the days when he worked late into the evening. Only a few hundred yards separated us, yet it felt like he was hundreds of miles away. We were distanced by the ever-present social barrier bearing down on our lives.

I avoided the gatehouse, knowing the very sight of Ruairi would draw me back into his arms. But by the evening of Deirdre and Cecil's celebration I knew I was losing the battle to stay away from him. He was all I thought about. I stood in the receiving line with my family and wondered how they would react if I were to leave Kilpara. They had survived Deirdre's wilfulness to marry Conor, his disappearance, her marriage to Cecil, and Father being accosted. Yet here they stood, cheerfully shaking hands with friends and neighbours, proudly introducing Deirdre as Mrs Cecil Sloane. Would they forgive me if I eloped with Ruairi to America?

Guests knew from the invitations that the party was held to honour the newlyweds. They offered congratulations, and exclaimed how fortunate Deirdre was to have married a man who was destined to add to his family fortunes. By now, they had recovered from their surprise and speculations that abounded around the impromptu marriage, although most would conclude the union had been arranged to bring together two powerful families and combine their wealth.

Cecil's face was a handsome mask, and after the introductions were over he escorted Deirdre around like a prized possession. The evening wore on, and towards the end she began to look strained. Later, as the men gathered into small groups to discuss politics and business, I was the only one aware she had put on her cloak and slipped away. I wondered what Cecil's reaction would be when he discovered she was missing.

David Ligham left a group of men and came over to where I stood. He took my gloved hand in his and kissed it. I smiled indulgently.

"You look as beautiful as ever, darling Grace."

"Thank you."

He gazed around the room. "I'm not the only one who's noticed." He leaned forwards. I took a step backwards. He moved closer and whispered in my ear. "Please remember I was first to show my admiration."

"Of course."

He left me then to go back to the company of men. Mother moved away from a lady's circle and came to join me.

"I've noticed the way David looks at you," she said.

"You're overestimating his attention, Mother."

"He's a serious young man. Not the type to be frivolous. He's clearly enchanted with you."

"Time will tell if you're right, Mother."

She went back to her group, and I went outside for fresh air. The night was cold, but I didn't care. Like Deirdre I, too, had begun to feel stifled. It wasn't until my fingers turned numb that I went back indoors. I found Maureen and asked for tea. I took this into the drawing room and stood by the window. I was there when Deirdre came running towards the front door. At the same time Cecil came into the drawing room looking for her. "Where's Deirdre?" he asked. "Were you two in here gossiping?"

I didn't answer.

"The party is almost over and I'm ready to leave."

"Deirdre is not here. You should look for her elsewhere."

He turned on his heel and left.

I followed him into the hallway where guests were gradually moving towards the front door, still continuing to express their gratitude to Mother and Father for a wonderful evening. I sighed with relief when I saw Deirdre already inside the house.

"There you are," Cecil said. "Ready to go home?"

Deirdre looked away. "Yes."

When she turned back I saw her face alight with contentment, a sense of pleasure that fleetingly restored her whenever she visited the cottage.

As Christmas approached I began to detect a definite change in Deirdre. We seldom talked intimately anymore, and even when the opportunity arose, we were too caught up in our own affairs to share confidences. Sadly, I wished for the days before she went to Switzerland when we shared every little detail about our lives. During our casual conversations and those that occurred when she and Cecil came to tea or dinner, it was obvious she continued to resist taking responsibility for the running of Larcourt. She must have found harmony in her new home somehow because, at times, she seemed almost happy.

Deirdre's disdain towards running Larcourt became even more evident during one of her visits when Mother reproved her dismissive attitude. "You're the mistress of one of the largest estates in Ireland, Deirdre," Mother emphasised. "Certain things are expected of you. You must begin planning parties to entertain Cecil's friends and acquaintances."

"I truly don't care about entertaining Cecil's friends or being mistress of Larcourt, Mother," Deirdre said stubbornly. "Mrs Spencer is an excellent housekeeper and quite capable of planning anything Cecil wants."

"I know this is a difficult transition, darling," Mother said gently. "But you know there are certain duties that go along with being the lady of the house."

Deirdre's face became pinched. "I despise Larcourt, all those relics taken as trophies from foreign places. It's depressing."

Mother continued to be patient, even though her face grew worried. "You can always redecorate. I'm sure Cecil won't mind."

Deirdre scoffed. "He may pretend to be agreeable in public, but his family is proud of their possessions. He'd never permit me to remove any of them."

Grandfather, who had been quietly reading said, "I agree with Deirdre. The house is like a mausoleum. It smothers the very energy that gives life."

Mother gave Grandfather a stern look.

"It does, Morrigan, that's all ..."

"I'm going to the cottage," Deirdre said. Mother opened her mouth to protest, but decided against it. After Deirdre left the room she said, "Cecil is losing patience with her, and I don't know what to tell him."

"Tell him the truth," Grandfather said. "Deirdre doesn't like Larcourt. She'd be happier back at Kilpara, so she would."

"It's the cottage," Mother said. "We were wrong to encourage her interest in it."

"If it wasn't the cottage, she'd find some other project."

Mother didn't say anything, just pulled out her hanky and dabbed at tears that appeared around the edges of her eyes.

On Christmas Eve, Deirdre arrived at Kilpara to help Father and me give out presents to the local children in the annual custom. Cecil stayed behind at Larcourt with his parents. He had voiced his disapproval weeks earlier when Deirdre and I giggled about how much we looked forward to the event.

The investigation into Father's attack had been dragging on for months, with the authorities convinced the culprits would be found in Brandubh. Father disagreed with them, strongly believing his attackers were English. To show strength in his conviction, he decided to go ahead with the Christmas Eve festivities for the servants. The only change to this year's ritual was that Olam would dress as Santa's helper.

Olam loved being surrounded by the children. Maureen and Tom looked on proudly at their affectionate son who gave a loud "Ho, Ho, Ho" every time he handed out a present.

When the dancing began Ruairi picked up his fiddle and joined with other musicians. Deirdre and I were pulled into a circle of foot-tappers. My partner twirled me, and whenever I looked up at the musicians, my eyes met Ruairi's. He smiled back. Eventually the band took a break and Ruairi motioned to me as he left the room. Minutes later I followed him into the hallway and he steered me out the back door. Under the eaves, away from prying eyes, he pulled me into his arms and kissed me. He kissed me again and this time with a deeper hunger.

When we drew apart he said, "You've been avoiding me."

"You know we shouldn't be together. It will only make things harder when I'm sent to finishing school and you go to America."

"It doesn't have to be like that, Grace. You can come away with me." He looked around to make sure we were alone. "Mr and Mrs Gilhooly are spending Christmas with Mr Gilhooly's sister. Say you'll meet me at the gatehouse later. We should talk more. I won't take no for an answer."

I hesitated, but only for a moment, before whispering my agreement. We returned inside separately.

After everyone left and the house grew quiet, I slipped out into the darkness and walked down the avenue to the gatehouse. With each step I told myself I was being unwise, yet I kept going, propelled by a desire so strong it was difficult to control. When I reached the gatehouse, lamplight and soft music welcomed me. I unlatched the door and slipped quietly inside. From the entrance I watched Ruairi standing by the fireplace in the cosy room; he played a haunting melody on the fiddle. When he finished he looked up and saw me.

He came over and unhooked my cloak.

"That was a beautiful tune," I said.

"It's about an impossible love." He kissed me then, his lips lingering on my neck. He had placed a thick rug in front of the fireplace and gently pulled me down beside him. Slowly, he removed my clothes, his lips moving over my body, igniting exquisite sensations in their wake. His mouth closed over mine again, and I became lost in the sweep of his tongue thrust deep into my mouth in a long, lustful kiss. I unbuttoned his shirt and he shrugged it off. My fingers entwined thick dark hair at the nape of his neck, tasted the roughness of his skin when my lips dropped down and kissed his chest. He slid off the rest of his clothes and pulled me closer to his warm body until I felt his nakedness pressing against me.

His lovemaking was unrushed. His fingers trailed over my body, exploring its intricate territory, my skin seeking more from his touch. I quivered when he traced the curves of my breasts with his lips, and lingered there. Each touch, each sensation, became an act of love, until our arousal demanded satisfaction. We joined together, our passion exploding into shattering euphoria.

Afterward, when I lay in his arms, Ruairi handed me a small box. "Merry Christmas," he whispered. "I wasn't sure you'd come, but I got this for you."

"I didn't get you anything," I said.

He kissed me passionately. "Your presence is my gift."

I opened the box and inside was a delicately designed gold Claddagh ring. I took it out and admired it. "You shouldn't have. It must've cost you a fortune."

He put his fingers on my lips, then took the ring from me and placed it on my finger.

"I love you, Grace. This ring symbolises my pledge to you. Say you'll marry me."

Longing and despair filled me. He had mistaken my decision to be with him as confirmation of my willingness to elope. I struggled to find the right words to respond, but he pressed his fingers against my lips and stifled my answer with a kiss.

Flickers of dawn lightened the night sky when I was ready to leave. Ruairi took the ring from my finger and attached it on a chain around my neck. "Keep it close to your heart, my darling, until the day I can openly declare my love for you."

I longed to tell him my mind was still unchanged, but tonight was so precious I wanted to treasure it in my memory; so I remained silent. Even as he held my cold hand in his warm one when we walked back up the avenue, I wondered if I possessed the courage to watch him leave and not be at his side.

Christmas Day passed in a pleasant dream. I was wrapped up in my thoughts of Ruairi. We gathered in the great room for Christmas dinner. Mother talked about the New Year celebrations, and Father expressed his desire to go to America in the spring.

"Rengen and Jasmine are returning to Stonebridge in March," Father said. "I'll accompany them on the journey. Tom can oversee the spring foaling."

"You should visit your brothers and their families," Mother agreed.

She exchanged a glance with Father then looked at me. Father took a deep breath. "Grace, your mother and I have made inquiries into finishing schools. There's a good one in Paris that comes highly recommended. We've written to them. They'll have an opening in March and can take you then. It's a good program that will prepare you for the following spring's coming-out season in Europe and then here. What do you think?"

I had expected to hear this news for so long I shouldn't have been surprised, yet the shock of his words crushed me. "Do I have to go, Father?"

He looked at me uneasily. "I know you love Kilpara, but finishing school will broaden your mind and widen your horizon."

After art school in Switzerland had proven such a disaster for Deirdre, I wondered how he and Mother could feel so sure finishing school would help me.

"I think Grace belongs in the medical profession," Grand-Aunt Sadie pleaded. "She already knows more than most trainees."

"You know women aren't accepted as doctors," Mother said.

"Grace might be the very woman to change all that."

I listened quietly, distracted while they discussed my future. My only thoughts at that moment were with Ruairi Kineely. I felt below the neckline of my dress for the ring. I looked around in turn at the faces of my family and felt myself being slowly pulled away from them by a man I hardly knew. Yet in my heart I trusted him completely.

CHAPTER 18

On New Year's Day Mother and I argued over who should attend my birthday party. I wanted a family gathering like last year, but Mother wanted a grander affair. Not only was I against a big party, I also hated the prospect of being sent to Europe and expressed my objection. Mother complained she didn't understand her daughters' reluctance to agree on even the simplest of family matters. At almost seventeen, she said, instead of riding all over the countryside and behaving unladylike, I should be thinking about a coming-out season.

Huffed after the argument, I went riding out of sheer frustration. I blamed my involvement with Ruairi for my quarrelsome mood as I rode Spitfire across frosted ground, over bleak hillsides dotted with lifeless trees. On my return the sky had darkened and low clouds threatened snow. Approaching the cottage I noticed an oil lamp lighted inside. This was unusual, since Deirdre was otherwise engaged at Larcourt with Cecil still home from college and the Sloanes visiting from England. I stopped to investigate.

I tied Spitfire to a tree in the orchard and looked around for a sturdy stick. Finding one near an oak tree that was straight and strong, I picked it up and walked cautiously through the open gate and up the repaired pathway. I peeked inside a front window and saw the remains of a meal on the small kitchen table. Whoever broke in had made themselves at home. I tightened my grip on the stick, ready to strike the intruder as I tested the front door latch. The door was locked. The window didn't budge, either. I went around back and tried the back door. The top half of the door was latched but the bottom half creaked open. I peered around it before crawling inside. There was no sign of anyone, yet a fire burned brightly in the hearth. The cottage looked lived in.

Softly, I pulled the half-door closed behind me and tiptoed back towards the bedroom. I paused at the bedroom door that was slightly ajar. Moving cautiously, I pushed it further. That's when I received the shock of my life.

Deirdre and Conor lay in bed together, asleep in each other's arms. They awoke, startled by my sudden scream and the stick clattering to the floor.

Deirdre looked at me dazed. "Grace—wha—what are you doing here?"

"I—uh—was out riding. I saw a light through the window. I thought you were at Larcourt, so I stopped to investigate." I stared at their naked bodies and couldn't take my eyes off Conor. He was alive and he was here. "You—how—?"

"Turn around," Deirdre ordered. I did as I was told, confused by the vision of Deirdre and Conor together. They dressed and followed me into the front room where I stood awkwardly beside the small table. Deirdre went to the fireplace and hung a teakettle on the pothook. She stirred up the coals around it.

I continued to stare at Conor.

"I know this is a shock, Grace," he said gently. "I can explain—"

"Explain! Everyone thought you'd left. Or were dead. Father was beaten because of you."

He pointed to a chair. "Sit down, Grace. There's a lot you don't know."

Deirdre placed a tray with teacups on the table then scooped tea into the teapot. I was reminded of that day in Dublin when I had followed her and Conor to his uncle's house. I had the same feeling then that I had now of the domestic intimacy they shared together.

Deirdre waited for the water to boil, then filled the teapot. She looked lovingly at Conor when she handed him his cup and saucer, as if she was his wife instead of Cecil's. I almost choked on my first sip of tea as the gravity of the situation struck me.

"I think it's time Grace knew the truth," Conor said. Deirdre nodded and put down her cup.

I sat very still, looking from one to the other.

Conor leaned forward and touched my hands. I stared at my small hands next to his very large ones. I thought I should remove them, but was too stunned to act.

"You remember when I left Kilpara?" Conor looked at me closely. "The first time?"

"To go to America," I replied.

"Yes."

"You never went?"

"No, I cashed in the ticket and went to Europe instead; to be near Deirdre while she gave birth to our baby."

"Ba-baby?" Shock ran through me and I looked to Deirdre to contradict Connor.

She nodded. "Please forgive me for not telling you. I wanted to, but I couldn't. I thought you'd turn against me."

I rose and waved my hands in protest. "No. No. No. You didn't have a baby. You went to Switzerland to study art and learn proper etiquette. You stayed there a whole year. You couldn't have had a baby. And if you did, where is it? *Where is the baby now?*"

"Yes, I went to Switzerland, but not to study art or prepare for a coming-out season." Deirdre's voice shook. "I was pregnant with Conor's baby. Father sent Conor away; gave him passage to America and told him never to show his face around Kilpara again. We pleaded with both Mother and Father to let us marry and have our child, but they refused. They said Conor could never support me, and a baby would ruin my future chances of marrying well." Her mouth compressed into a thin line. "My baby was a stigma—a blight on our family name. They sent Conor away and me to a private home for unwed mothers on the Continent."

I choked back tears. "How could they be so cruel? You should've told me."

Deirdre shook her head. "Mother and Father thought I was too young to have a mind of my own. I was fixated on my happiness and that of my child. And I was afraid you'd be revolted if I told you. As it was, you were the only stabilizing factor that made my life normal. I'm so sorry."

"And the baby?"

"Father arranged for her to be fostered by a very good Swiss family."

"Her—a girl?"

"Yes. We called her Giselle. She has the most precious face and beautiful fair hair."

I remembered that Deirdre had taken her doll with her to Switzerland and didn't bring it back. "Your doll—?"

"It was the only thing of mine I was allowed to give her. That, and a locket with my portrait, which she'll get on her eighteenth birthday. Conor never emigrated to America. He came to Switzerland instead. We planned my escape from the home, but they were watchful. I was caught trying to leave. After that they kept me under close scrutiny. I discovered the name of the foster family from a kind nurse who also took messages to Conor. After Giselle was born he went to the family and gave them what money he had left to allow him to see her. She's beautiful, Grace. We want her so badly."

I went to Deirdre and held her trembling hands. "That's why you tried to run away together after you came home."

"Yes, we began meeting in secret when I returned from Switzerland."

Conor squeezed Deirdre's shoulder. Tears gleamed in his eyes. "I had to find a way for us to be together. I would never leave Deirdre. You must know that, Grace. After she returned to Kilpara without the baby, I came back as often as I dared. The rest of the time I stayed with relatives in Dublin. I couldn't stay in Brandubh—people would discover I hadn't left. When I got Deirdre's letter saying she was visiting Dublin, we agreed to meet and make plans about our future. We were both heartbroken that we didn't have our little Giselle."

"That's when I saw you together."

"Yes, in Stephen's Green," Deirdre said. "My mind was made up then that I would marry only Conor and no one else. Mother and Father had insisted I forget him and our baby's existence. But I just couldn't. I continued to argue that I wanted to be with them, but Mother and Father wouldn't listen. Around that time Cecil and Lady Daphne became suspicious and investigated my sojourn in Europe. They discovered I didn't study at La Croix art school like I pretended, but that I'd been sent to a home for unwed mothers. Cecil didn't care that I'd had a baby. He was determined to marry me and thought I should appreciate his gesture. After all, I was tainted.

"He convinced Lady Daphne he had his heart set on this. She came to Mother and Father demanding that I end my courtship with Thomas Roberts, even though I never intended to marry him. She insisted that I marry Cecil instead or she would disgrace me before our family, friends, and the whole community. Even with this hanging over my head, I still couldn't stand the thought of marrying Cecil, so I ran away with Conor—"

"And Father brought you back."

"Yes."

"But you both got your wish. Father gave his permission to let you marry. What happened, Conor? You were invited to Kilpara for Deirdre's birthday party. Why did you leave?"

"I didn't," Conor said tightly.

"I don't understand."

"Sloane paid the Lighams a casual visit and came to the forge to congratulate me on my upcoming marriage to Deirdre. To show there were no hard feelings, he offered to arrange a carriage to take me to her birthday party. 'You should arrive in style,' he insisted. He was being conciliatory and I didn't want to act like a cad, so I accepted. I was on my way there when I was abducted."

"Abducted?"

"Attacked by four or five men. The carriage stopped at what I later realised was an appointed spot. I was ambushed. They were too many to fight off; they beat me up badly."

Conor went to a back window and looked out onto the lake. "They dragged me to the lake right down there." He pointed to the bottom of the hillside. "They were going to throw me into deep water, but fishermen were fishing on the lake and they became anxious about getting caught. They figured I was done for, anyway. They'd beaten me nearly unconscious. They threw me into what they thought was the deepest spot. They didn't know the Corrib well. The water was fairly shallow. If it had been any deeper I would've drowned. The shock of cold water was enough to revive me briefly. I grabbed hold of a tree limb jutting out into the water and pulled myself onto the bank. I tried to get the attention of the fishermen, but they were too far away, and I was too weak to yell for help." Conor paused and Deirdre looked at him pitifully.

"I passed out then, and when I awoke again it was nighttime and I was shivering. Somehow I managed to crawl up here on my belly to the cottage and get inside. I passed out again—I may have lost a full day. I knew I had broken bones because of the pain and swelling. I was also losing blood. I thought I was going to die, and all I could think about was that Deirdre would never know what happened." He grinned then. "But I found the strength to hang on."

"I struggled out to the garden and pulled up wild onions and shook down crab apples, then crawled up the attic steps and yanked blankets from the trunks Deirdre had discovered. I managed to keep warm with them."

I looked at Deirdre with sadness. "That day we were here and thought there was an injured animal in the cottage, it was Conor. If only we'd known—"

Deirdre nodded, her eyes misty.

Conor smiled. "You saved my life, anyway. Tierney Lynch came to investigate. He's a Fenian. He recognised me. He knew my uncle and assumed I was given a beating by government investigators trying to force information from me about my uncle's whereabouts. He got me to a safe house first in Galway, then in Dublin. A doctor came and treated me. I remember little. For days I hovered in and out of consciousness, and when I did come round, it was still touch and go. It was a long road back to recovery."

"You almost died," I said. "The constables found no evidence of foul play."

"Sloane covered his tracks well," Conor said. "I recognised his foreman. The others had English accents, so I presume they were brought over from England. I told this to my protectors as soon as I was able."

I gasped.

Deirdre's expression was one of frustration and sadness.

"Sloane's foreman was long gone by then. Word has it that Sloane paid him for getting rid of me, and then sent him to work at one of his parents' estates in England. Once I was well enough to identify him and discovered he'd skipped the country, Kineely volunteered to go after him."

"Kineely? Ruairi Kineely knew about this?" I tried to keep my voice impassive.

"Yes, you know him then?"

"He works for our father."

Conor nodded. "Kineely wanted to tell your father, but the Fenians discouraged him. They convinced him if news leaked out I survived, it could jeopardise my recovery. Sloane could hunt for my whereabouts to finish the job. My death was imperative to his marriage with Deirdre."

"Cecil's cunning and dangerous," Deirdre added. "We suspect he arranged Father's beating and paid people to start rumours. To get me to agree to marry him, he promised we'd get Giselle back. I complied. I had convinced myself I would never see Conor again, and Cecil offered me a chance to bring home my baby. That's why we went to Switzerland on our honeymoon.

"After Cecil saw Giselle, he paid the foster family money to hire a nursemaid, and insisted we should wait until we were established at Larcourt before bringing her home. At first I believed him, but every time I mentioned her homecoming he went into a tirade about how I cared more about her than I did him. I knew then he never meant to bring her home, and I began to fear he might hurt her."

I stood transfixed, unable to absorb everything at once.

Deirdre hiccupped as she tried to hold back tears. "I know you tried to warn me about Cecil, but all I could think about was getting Giselle back, and nothing else mattered."

A shiver went down my spine. "I thought Cecil was vengeful and possessive, but I never imagined he would stoop so low. You must go to the authorities. You're taking a huge risk meeting here."

Deirdre looked at Conor, "I only learned everything myself a few weeks ago. Conor came to me as soon as he was well enough. We can't go to the authorities. They won't take action against the Sloanes. Not even for us. It would be our word against Cecil's. And I'm his wife who bore an illegitimate child for her lover. Who do you think they'll believe? They would crucify me, and put Conor in shackles."

"But Cecil could find you here as easily as I did. He has spies." I was really worried now. I thought back to the rider watching us from shadowed trees when Father first gave his permission for Deirdre to marry Conor.

"I was cautious," Deirdre said. "Cecil doesn't suspect me. He believes he got away with murder. And more. He and his parents are in Galway today visiting the Lighams. They're having an afternoon New Year's Day celebration. This morning I deliberately ate bread with honey and later complained of a stomach illness. You know how honey always gives me cramps."

I nodded, sympathetically. "What're you going to do?"

"I'm almost completely recovered," Conor said. "Plans are underway for us to leave for France soon. From there we'll go to America. The Fenians have already arranged to move Giselle from Switzerland to France the moment we depart. After we meet up in France we'll sail for America."

Deirdre put her arms around me. "You must keep our secret, because if Cecil—or his mother—finds out, we don't know what they'll do. Promise you won't say anything to Mother and Father, or that you know about Giselle, until after we're safely away."

I hugged her and made the promise. But I was worried. Deeply worried.

I winced when I remembered the scene in the cottage. I avoided it when I went riding for fear I would draw attention to it. I had begun to get used to the idea that Conor was alive and well when Deirdre and Cecil came to tea two days later.

Deirdre looked pale, but she was as attentive to Cecil as she had been in recent weeks. She did such a good job pretending, that she would have fooled me, if I didn't know the charade was for her and Conor's sake. Someone would have had to pay close attention to see that Deirdre's motions were automatic, the actions of a good actress. But her face told the true story. There was no laughter in her eyes, no lightness in her voice; she remained stiff when Cecil touched her instead of lingering in the moment. They seemed like a normal couple to the unpractised eye. With one exception. Today Cecil was beaming, and he didn't begin with his usual laments about Deirdre's lack of interest in her role as mistress of Larcourt. He held her arm and led her to the settee.

"Are you comfortable, darling?" he asked.

"Yes, thank you," Deirdre said.

Mother and Father looked pleased for once.

"I have a confession to make," Cecil said, looking around at everyone. "I suspect Deirdre is pregnant. But she's not convinced."

I choked back a gasp.

Deirdre squirmed on the settee. "I've just been under the weather lately. Cecil is jumping to conclusions."

"My mother says you have all the signs," Cecil said. "Women know these things."

"Can it be true?" Mother asked hopefully.

"If Dee says she's under the weather, then she is," I defended.

Cecil snickered. "Don't you want a niece or nephew, Grace?"

"Yes, if that happens."

"It's happening *now*," Cecil snapped, then turned to Deirdre. "I'll ask Dr Murphy to come to Larcourt and examine you."

Deirdre patted his hand. "Let's not overreact, darling. I'm sure it's just a passing malady."

"On the contrary," Grand-Aunt Sadie chimed. "If you're pregnant, you should begin taking proper care of yourself right away."

"I'm *not* pregnant, but if I don't feel better soon, I'll consult the doctor," Deirdre said.

"Wise decision," Grand-Aunt Sadie agreed.

I studied the pride on Cecil's face and decided it was fake. What I didn't understand was why he took pleasure in creating this pretence. Father remained silent throughout the discourse.

In some warped way I wondered if Cecil wanted to remind Father that his plan to dispel of Deirdre's baby and save her reputation had failed. A subject off-limits by Father, but not Cecil, who found satisfaction in testing everyone's emotional limits.

"You're coming to my birthday party, aren't you?" I asked.

"Yes, of course," Deirdre said, anxious to divert attention from herself.

"It'll be an intimate gathering."

Mother sighed. "Only because Grace refuses to have a proper birthday party."

Cecil leaned over and kissed Deirdre's cheek. "How fortunate. I shan't have to compete with admirers tripping over themselves for your attention, darling."

Deirdre's fingers tightened into a fist, but she smiled back charmingly.

On the evening of my birthday Deirdre and I escaped to my bedroom for a few moments. She confided that arrangements had been finalised for her and Conor's departure in a few days. She explained Cecil was packed and prepared to return to college the following day. I hugged her tightly. The strain between us that existed since she returned from Switzerland had evaporated now that the truth was out in the open. We were closer than ever before. With everything set in motion, I was relieved that she and Conor would soon be safely away.

"What'll you do for money?" I asked.

"I sold some of my jewellery," Deirdre said.

I noticed she was only wearing a simple gold necklace instead of the diamond one Cecil always insisted on.

"It'll give us a good start," Deirdre continued. "Please explain everything to Mother and Father after we're gone. I'll contact you when we're far enough away and out of danger."

"Be careful," I warned, overcome with sadness of not knowing when I would see her again.

Now that I was fully aware of Cecil's evil misdeeds, I found it almost impossible to be civil to him. But I had to pretend for Deirdre's sake. That evening I made every last effort to be pleasant.

Two nights later I awakened to the sound of someone running through the halls shouting, "Fire! Fire!" I jumped out of bed, but couldn't smell any smoke. Cautiously, I placed my hand on the bedroom door. It didn't feel hot so I looked out into the corridor. All was clear. No smoke, no heat. I ran downstairs and joined Mother and Father in the vestibule with the rest of the household.

"What's happening?" I asked.

"I'm not sure," Father said.

Rengen came through the front door, shaking all over, his dark eyes wide with shock. "Look," he pointed. "Outside … Larcourt … Miss Deirdre …"

We followed him outdoors, and in the distance we could see the sky lit up orange.

"Oh God, no," Mother squeaked in a hoarse whisper. "Larcourt's on fire."

"Get the carriage," Father ordered Rengen. "Take Morrigan. I'll ride my horse. It'll be faster."

Rengen obliged.

Grand-Aunt Sadie limped outside. "What's all the commotion?" She looked into the distance at Larcourt and made the sign of the cross. "May God have mercy on our souls."

I stood rooted to the spot, staring at the orange sky. A hand grabbed my arm urgently. I heard my name being called somewhere in a fog.

"Grace! Grace!" It wasn't until Ruairi shook me that I registered his face and realised that he was trying to get my attention. "Get on your clothes. Your shoes. Your cloak. Hurry! We have to get to Larcourt."

I nodded numbly. He followed me through the pandemonium to my bedroom. Everyone was running in different directions, trying to leave as fast as they could and get to Larcourt. Ruairi helped me pull my clothes on and we ran to the stables. Mother, Grand-Aunt Sadie and Grandfather were ascending the carriage. Tom ordered one of the stable hands to go into Galway to make sure the fire brigade had been alerted.

Ruairi saddled Spitfire and Ceonig. We rode as fast as we could towards Larcourt.

As we got closer, numbness began to wear off and my heart sank. The house was totally engulfed in flames; heat carried towards us on the winds. The roof had collapsed inwards, and flames soared out of the crater like a boiling cauldron.

The fire brigade had already arrived and was trying to squelch the flames, but their efforts were hardly making a dent. People were running around the courtyard trying to find survivors, and onlookers stared at the flames in awe as the majestic structure crumbled before their eyes.

I found some of the servants in the courtyard, still clad in their nightclothes. "Where's Deirdre?" I asked. They shook dazed heads. I worked my way through the crowd, searching for my sister's face. Then I caught sight of Father on his knees, his head resting in his hands. I ran to him. "Father—" He looked at me through dazed eyes. Deirdre's limp body lay on a pile of hay in front of him. Two other bodies lay next to her. A man I recognised as Nolan O'Leary stood with his hand on Father's shoulder. I fell down on my knees.

Gently I touched Deirdre. She didn't move. Why didn't she get up? We had to help her. I took one of her hands and tried to rub warmth into it. Then I took my cloak off and covered her thin nightclothes with it. She looked beautiful even with her face smoke-stained, and burns covering most of her feet and hands. I tried to remove some of the soot from her face with a corner of my hanky, but only succeeded in smudging it.

Prayer found its way to my lips and I asked God in his mercy to let her live. Something inside of me snapped then, and Father put his arms around me. I felt Ruairi's hand squeezing my shoulder. His voice sounded distant when he asked someone, "What happened?"

A man spoke hesitantly, while sobs retched from deep inside my chest. Still, my beautiful sister didn't move.

"I don't know how the fire started," the man said in a thick country accent. "The house was already in flames before anyone noticed. Several of us tried to get to the missus and her two housemaids, but flames cut us off from the stairs. They tried to escape through the skylight onto the roof. We got the ladder, but it didn't even go up halfway. We loaded hay bales from the barn onto a wagon and scattered them on the ground, hoping to break their fall. Flames were already through the roof. We could hear them screaming and we still couldn't get to them—" The man stopped, wiped his eyes and blew his nose. "They jumped. The fire was already burning at their heels." His voice turned tearful. "The hay wasn't thick enough to break their fall. They crashed to the ground."

His words echoed through the night as Father moved closer to me and we held each other. I don't know how long we stayed that way before we heard a piercing scream. Mother had discovered Deirdre. She rushed towards us and threw herself on my sister.

"My baby, my darling baby," she cried, cradling Deirdre's broken body. Father, his face flooded with pain, tried to pull Mother away. I stood up, feeling numbness spread through me again. Ruairi held me, momentarily blocking out the horror. His cheeks were wet against my own.

An hour later, flames still burning high, a priest arrived and performed the last rites for my sister and her two housemaids. Mother wouldn't let go of Deirdre until Grandfather gently pried her away. Dr Murphy gave her a sleeping powder and she was then taken back to Kilpara in the carriage. I don't remember much about the journey home. All I know is Ruairi rode on one side of me and Father on the other.

Early next morning I watched in a daze when my sister's body was brought to Kilpara to be dressed and taken to the chapel for people to pay their last respects. I hadn't slept all night; it was as if my eyes were permanently propped open. I sat in the drawing room with Father, Grand-Aunt Sadie and Grandfather not saying a word, just drinking cup after cup of tea. When it came time to dress Deirdre for viewing, I insisted on tending to her myself. Grand-Aunt Sadie joined me as I washed her body and brushed her long hair, and at last, cleaned the soot off her beautiful face.

I went to the cottage still filled with her presence, my thoughts full of how perfectly she and Conor fitted together here. I took one of her few dresses she kept there because Cecil had mocked her, telling her she looked like a peasant in them instead of the mistress of Larcourt. I chose a pink muslin dress and put it on her limp body. As she lay in her padded coffin among lighted candles, she looked like a sleeping princess.

I had forgotten about Cecil until he came running into the chapel. Someone must have gone to Dublin to give him the news. He fell down on his knees and sobs racked his body. I watched him without sympathy. It never occurred to us that Cecil might have other plans for Deirdre's burial, but for once he accepted she belonged at Kilpara.

Mother floated in and out of consciousness during most of the first day. Throughout the house servants tiptoed about and spoke in whispers. Kilpara was in mourning. That night sleep still eluded me. I stood at the window just staring out into the darkness. When two riders approached and pulled up under my window, I had no difficulty recognizing them. One was Ruairi's dark shape, the other was Conor, his fair hair illuminating the night. Ruairi picked up a pebble to throw at my window. I opened it as he readied his aim. He beckoned me to come down.

I opened the door and they came in out of the cold. Conor put his arms around me, and I sobbed against his chest. We shared the same deep love for my sister. When I finally looked at him through my tears, I saw shock and despair in his eyes. Wordlessly, we went to the chapel. Ruairi and I stood silent as Conor took Deirdre's cold hand in his.

"My darling wife," he said, and bent over and kissed her cold lips. "All I want right now is to die with you, to ease the pain that I know will stay with me the rest of my life. But, my darling, that would not be your wish. You would want me to get our daughter back like we planned, but instead of running away I will bring her home. I will bring her back to Ireland where she belongs and where she will get to know you—her mother. Every day I will tell her how wonderful you were and how much we loved each other. And I promise you, my darling, I will be the best father any man could possibly be. Together, we'll make you proud."

He reached beneath his shirt and pulled out a strand of rope with two wedding bands. He took the ring off Deirdre's wedding finger that had bound her to Cecil, opened the church window and threw it into the darkness. Then he took the rings from the rope and placed one on her finger and one on his own.

He kissed her hand and then her lips. "Good bye, darling wife. Someday we'll be together forever. I know this in my heart."

He walked out of the chapel and we followed. On the steps he said, "Sloane will pay for this. After I get Giselle, after I bring her home, I'll take care of him myself. *He did this and he'll pay!*"

There was no reasoning with him and I didn't know if I wanted to. We had no proof this was Cecil's doing. He was away at college. I wanted to implore Ruairi to stop Conor from doing anything irrational, but hatred smouldered as deeply in his eyes as it did in Conor's.

And I couldn't deny the hatred burning in my own pain-filled heart.

CHAPTER 19

Our shoes crunched on frozen ground when we walked in a procession to the O'Donovan graveyard, a cold wind beating against our pale, inconsolable faces. We watched silently as Deirdre's coffin was lowered slowly into the ground. The priest's voice hummed monotonously, commending Deirdre's soul to a happier realm, free from afflictions and problems of this imperfect world. Mother keened sorrowfully throughout the service. His words, meant to provide comfort, only made me angrier; my sister had died too soon. Happiness had been within her grasp, only to be snatched away. Memories of her trudging over the path to the cottage wrenched at my soul. I envisioned soft breezes lifting her long fair hair and caressing her smiling face. Delight sparkling in her eyes as improvements brought the cottage back to life. She and Conor would have been content there.

In the weeks that followed our tearful farewell to Deirdre, we each sought solace in our own way. Mother withdrew further into herself, and Grand-Aunt Sadie sent Rengen to Mercy Hospital to recruit a nurse to be in attendance. Father neglected his business in Galway for days at a time. When he wasn't working, he retreated to the library and spent hours there with the door closed.

Rengen buried his feelings in talk about his family and longing to see his grandchildren. He reminded us he would sail for America in just over a month. Tom and Maureen crept about the house quietly, afraid that any noise would bring the walls caving in. Olam couldn't quite understand what had happened; only that Deirdre was now with the angels. Cecil returned to Trinity College and resided there. Larcourt was nothing more than a pile of rubble. I moped from room to room, at times picking up medical journals, but unable to study them. It was impossible to focus on complex information as thoughts of Deirdre constantly broke through my concentration.

When the constable came to the house, we all gathered in the drawing room to hear the authorised report of what had started the fire at Larcourt. In his most sombre voice he told us the incident had been ruled an accident. It began when a relative, who had lingered at Larcourt after the New Year, fell asleep and left an oil lamp on near the bed. He must have knocked it over accidentally during the night, and it caught the bedding on fire. With everything so old and dry, the blaze spread quickly through the house.

The constable shook his head, saying how tragic it was to lose someone as young as Deirdre in such circumstances. The people of Brandubh were praying for our family and had asked him to relay their sympathy.

Father thanked the man and said we were grateful to the community for their compassion. The constable acknowledged this with a sad smile, put away his notepad and took his leave.

Near the end of February I began to feel a hint of spring in the air, the earth's first sign of awakening after the harsh winter's slumber. I had been numb and morose since Deirdre's death, but on this morning I felt restless. I wanted to ride, something I had lost any desire to do until now. I dressed and went to the stables, intending to saddle Spitfire for an early morning canter along the Corrib before breakfast.

I stepped inside Spitfire's stall, patted his neck and spoke softly to him. He nickered as I tightened the saddle. I thought I was alone until Ruairi whispered in my ear from behind. "Good morning, Grace." I jumped at the sound of his voice and turned around. His arms went around me and pulled me to him. He brushed my lips softly with his. "I was unclogging a ditch near the gatehouse when I saw you walk to the stables," he said.

I sighed and leaned against him. We hadn't spoken since Deirdre's funeral. I had detached myself from everyone except my family, wanting to be alone with my thoughts and memories of my sister. I hadn't needed, or wanted, to be with anyone else. But as the sun had awakened the sleeping earth, Ruairi's touch stirred desire dormant inside the tomb of my heart.

He took my hand and led Spitfire into the quiet courtyard. Helping me onto the saddle, he pulled himself up behind me. We rode out over the hills and along the banks of the Corrib. In the little cove where we had met months earlier, we sat on the moist bank, holding each other and staring at the morning mist hovering on the water. Here in the comfort of his arms, I released tears that had been bottled up inside me.

We spoke little, yet upon our return to Kilpara, I felt emotionally drained. That was the first step. Later, I felt a change gradually take place as energy began to seep through me. I arose each morning at dawn and headed to the stables while the household was still sleeping. I met Ruairi and we rode to the little cove and watched the sun rise over the lake. Each day brought renewal, and with it came the bittersweet longing to live, and an increasing need to be with Ruairi.

"Time's getting short, Grace," Ruairi reminded me one morning.

"I know."

"I leave for America in April."

There was an unspoken question in his voice and with Deirdre's death still fresh in my mind, I wondered if I could bear to lose Ruairi, too.

"Say you'll give me your answer soon." He lifted my chin to look into my eyes. "Can you do it? Can you leave Kilpara?"

His gaze gripped me, holding me steadfast by its sheer force. Tears gathered around my eyes as I saw purpose and strength in his. "I don't know," I said honestly. "It's too soon. We're still grieving Deirdre. There's Cecil to deal with. And now that I know about my niece, I want to see her."

"Leave Cecil to Conor. He'll see that Irish justice is done. Losing your sister has been a terrible shock, but you can't change what happened. She fought for the life she wanted to live. She'd understand if you did the same."

"It's not that easy."

"I love you, Grace." His lips passionately claimed mine. It was a kiss that told me he had committed himself to me and wanted nothing less in return. "I'm asking a lot of you. But you know I have to leave."

I nodded sadly.

We mounted Spitfire, and as we rode back I was conscious of how confident his strong hands felt on the reins and how his body protected mine. I lingered in his arms after we dismounted near the gatehouse, digging my face into his jacket, letting the warmth and smell of him shut out the world.

He kissed me lightly on the forehead and looked at me tenderly. I found love brimming in his eyes. We parted reluctantly, renewing our promise to meet at the stables every morning. It was all we had for now.

Thoughts of our morning meetings were the only thing that made life bearable. I watched Mother sink deeper into her silent world; she barely spoke these days. Dr Murphy said she could talk if she wanted to, but that she lacked the inclination.

After dinner one evening I approached Father in the library. Our conversations about Deirdre since her death had been only about fond memories. But now I was ready to broach the subject of Conor and their baby. He looked up when I stood before the desk where he sat answering correspondence. I plunged right in. "Conor is here—in Brandubh," I said. "Deirdre planned to elope with him the day after the fire at Larcourt."

Father looked at me astonished. "What are you saying?"

"He never ran away, he's not dead."

"Son of a ..." Father beat his fist on the desk, causing me to jump. "How do you know this?"

"I saw them together."

"When?"

"Before the fire."

"Hagerty just couldn't leave her alone. That scoundrel. He practically leaves her standing at the altar. Then, coward that he is, waits until she's married to worm his way back into her life. He deserves the hangman's noose."

"It's not what you think," I objected.

Father's eyes narrowed. "The man was nothing but trouble in her life. If I could get my hands on him I'd—"

"There's more," I said.

With a thrust of his arm Father swept everything off the desk, sending ink and papers crashing to the floor. "There *is* no more."

He stood up and faced the window, shoulders slumped. "Deirdre's gone. And we can't bring her back."

"I know." I was fearful of his next reaction, but I continued. "That's why I must tell you what I know."

He turned to face me. "Conor never came to Deirdre's party because he was ambushed by men hired by Cecil, not because he ran away. One of the abductors was the Sloane's foreman."

I waited for Father to say something, but he just stared numbly at me. I continued quickly.

"They beat him up and left him for dead. They threw him into the Corrib, but he managed to survive and crawl up to the cottage. Deirdre and I almost discovered him when we saw blood around the cottage a few days later. We thought it was from a rabid wild animal, so we didn't go inside.

"We reported it to you, and Tom sent Tierney Lynch over to take care of the problem. He told Tom he found an injured feral pig and had to kill it. But it wasn't a wild pig he found; it was Conor. Mr Lynch is a Fenian who assumed Conor had fallen prey to authorities seeking information about his uncle, who is rumoured to be connected to the Phoenix Park murders in '82.

"He took Conor to a safe house in Dublin and got him medical care. Conor stayed there until he recovered, which took some time because his injuries were extensive. During that period Cecil connived Deirdre into marrying him. I'm sure he felt certain Conor was dead. After Conor recovered sufficiently he contacted Deirdre. He was shocked to find out she had married Cecil. He told her the truth about what happened, and afterwards they started meeting secretly at the cottage."

Father sat down heavily in his chair and put his head in his hands.

"They made plans to elope. They couldn't tell anyone because they feared what the Sloanes might do—or that someone else might stop them."

"Why didn't you tell me this before Deirdre's accident?"

"Deirdre and Conor swore me to secrecy. Deirdre was Cecil's wife. Her situation was precarious. I was going to tell you everything after they were safely away."

Father looked at me through shocked eyes. "The fire?"

"You heard the constable say it was an accident. Cecil was at Trinity College when it happened."

"Very convenient. He could've had a hand in it. I'll make him pay if he did."

I gave a hard laugh. "Conor is already planning revenge."

Father nodded as if this was an appropriate course of action. I didn't agree and was glad that Cecil was in Dublin. This was a matter for the constables. I couldn't bear it if Father or Conor went to jail. I wanted to tell Father that Cecil was also responsible for the attack on him but decided that news could wait. First things first.

"I know about Giselle," I said evenly.

Father's face crumbled. "We never should've kept the knowledge of her existence from you. But your mother and I thought if we handled the situation discreetly, you and Deirdre would not be scarred by this one unfortunate incident."

I wanted to lash out at Father that I didn't consider my niece's birth "one unfortunate incident." She was my sister's daughter, to be welcomed and loved as our own flesh and blood. But the torture in his face made me hold my tongue.

"We were wrong," he said shakily. "Ever since Deirdre's death all I've thought about is the child. We should never have sent Deirdre away to face—the birth—alone. It almost killed your mother, yet we were convinced we had to spare your sister from a scandal that was sure to ostracise her from society for the rest of her life."

"She didn't face Giselle's birth alone," I said. "Conor went to Switzerland and stayed close by."

"Instead of using his passage to America?"

"Yes. He wouldn't let Deirdre have their baby alone. He wasn't allowed to be with her, but he was there. He never left for America."

Father shook his head. "We were wrong to send her away."

"Conor wants to bring Giselle home. I do, too. She belongs here with us."

Father didn't speak immediately. After a short silence he said, "Considering everything that's happened, perhaps we should. It is the one thing we can do to honour Deirdre's memory. I also have a selfish reason for bringing her here. She could be the medicine that will cure your mother."

"She's not some convenience, Father. She's Deirdre's daughter, your granddaughter, my niece." I felt the anger creep into my voice that I had been holding back. Yet I had to admit my own motives were selfish. Giselle would help fill the void Deirdre's death had left in my heart.

Father sighed. "I meant that by bringing Deirdre's daughter into the house we would find the healing and forgiveness we so badly need for the mistakes we made."

"Thank you for that, Father."

"I blame myself for Deirdre's death. I should've protected her, and I failed. I let her marry Cecil Sloane against my better judgement." He began picking up papers off the floor. "I'll draft a letter to Hagerty. I've misjudged him and I want to correct that."

I managed to hold back the sobs in my throat until I was outside the library.

The appearance of a live, breathing Conor at Kilpara left the servants gaping in surprise. I laughed for the first time in weeks. I hadn't seen Conor since before Deirdre's funeral and wasn't prepared for his gaunt face and vacant eyes. Her passing had taken its toll. He was not a well man. Father greeted Conor and they retired to the library. They were there a long time before Father summoned me to join them.

"Hagerty is going to France to bring the child back as quickly as he can arrange it," Father said without pre-emption.

I looked at Conor, and Father smiled faintly. "He has taken precautions to remove her and her nursemaid from Switzerland. He will spend a month or so with the foster family in France and the child herself, getting to know her. We don't want to frighten her. It'll be hard enough to take her away from people she knows and bring her here among strangers. I'd like you to go with him."

I wasn't prepared for this suggestion and stammered, "Is—is that wise, Father? It could be too much for Giselle to absorb both of us at once. Perhaps it's better if Conor establishes a relationship with her first. I could join him later."

Father considered this for a moment before nodding his agreement. Until that moment I had not consciously registered my decision to leave Ireland with Ruairi, even though he was constantly in my thoughts.

The next few days were filled with meetings with Conor to discuss plans for his departure and Giselle's eventual arrival. Father had grown considerably hopeful that once she was settled, her presence would have a positive effect on Mother. Neither Father nor Conor discussed Giselle's permanent residence once she arrived in Ireland. It was enough for now just to know Deirdre's baby was coming home.

On a fine spring morning Father and I accompanied Conor to the railway station in Galway and bid him farewell. Conor smiled for the first time since Deirdre's death, and I saw a spark of hope in his eyes. He waved goodbye when the platform attendant blew the whistle and the train began its retreat from the station. Shouting from a window above the engine's noise he promised to send news of his progress with Giselle, and to cable and write from each stop along his travel.

After his departure Father and I rode the carriage to the Travellers' Inn for lunch. By sheer coincidence we bumped into David Ligham, who invited us to join him at his table. I had not seen him since the funeral. He expressed his condolences again, and his delight to see us in Galway. He and Father lapsed into discussions about current events while I picked at my food. My thoughts were still with Conor on his way to see my unknown niece. I wanted to meet her. To touch her face, see her smile, hold her, knowing that Deirdre had held her, if only for a brief time, before she was taken away. I wondered if I could leave with Ruairi for America knowing I would miss her homecoming.

Sitting next to me, David repeatedly reached over and touched my hand. I felt too disconsolate to withdraw it. Later, as we left the restaurant, an acquaintance stopped Father to offer his condolences. David and I continued outside without him. On the sidewalk David took my hands in his. "I know your sister's death has been a terrible shock, Grace. Know that I'm always available if you need anything."

"Thank you, David." I was moved by his consideration.

"When the time comes that you're ready to think about the future, please remember me."

"You're a kind and gentle man." I leaned forward and kissed his cheek.

Father joined us and we bid each other farewell.

In no time at all we were back at the railway station in Galway, only this time it was to say goodbye to Rengen and Jasmine. Father sent letters with Rengen to my uncles along with a promise to visit as soon as Mother was well again. Grand-Aunt Sadie hugged Rengen and Jasmine, sadness lining her face. Taking a rosary from her pocket, she put it around Rengen's neck.

"May God guide and bless you," she said.

"Mother—" Rengen replied huskily.

"Shhh. We'll carry each other here." She put a hand over his heart. "And in our prayers."

"Yes, Mother—"

Grand-Aunt Sadie hugged Jasmine tightly. "I'll miss you, dearest."

Jasmine nodded, her lips quivering.

We each hugged Jasmine and Rengen in turn one last time. We watched as they became lost among the passengers boarding the train.

After Rengen and Jasmine departed, Grand-Aunt Sadie decided it was time for her to return to Mercy Hospital. She missed her patients and the other nuns. Father tried to convince her we needed her at Kilpara to help with Mother's recovery. She patiently pointed out that she had done all she could for Mother and the rest was in God's hands. Her patients needed her. She knew, as we did, that once she returned to the hospital, her health would deteriorate again. But taking care of the sick had been her lifelong work, and the hospital was where she was happiest.

Tom and I accompanied her to Mercy Hospital. She was met by joyful nuns who ran out to meet the carriage and helped her to her quarters that had been cleaned spotless for her homecoming. When Tom and I returned to Kilpara, the house seemed even more morbid and sombre than before. So many people who contributed to its vitality were gone, leaving an empty imprint within its walls. It was as if the house was in mourning from a different kind of death, not sudden like Deirdre's untimely demise, but something broken that couldn't be mended.

I felt the pain of abandonment and loss everywhere I went, except on those early mornings when I met Ruairi before anyone was up. It was no use pretending anymore that I could live without him. I needed him; his arms were the only place I found peace. We spent time galloping through the countryside, then lying by the lake digging deep into our souls for understanding about our ideas and destinies.

"This is it, Grace," he said at the end of March. "I sail for America in two weeks. Have you decided?"

Panic rose in my throat. "Can't you postpone your departure? I need more time."

He pulled me into his arms and held me. "I know everything you've been through." He pressed his lips against my forehead. "But I can't wait any longer. This existence is killing me."

"How can I leave? Mother is still in the same catatonic state since Deirdre's death. Rengen and Jasmine have gone back to America, and Grand-Aunt Sadie is back at Mercy Hospital. I'm all my parents have. It would devastate them if I left."

"Grace, your staying won't change anything. I love you. I'm tired of us having to sneak around. As long as we're here, I'll never fit into your world and you won't fit into mine. Our only chance to live a normal life is in America."

"Please—just a few more months. Enough time to get over the shock of losing Deirdre."

He stroked my cheek with the back of his hand. "I'm sorry, Grace. It has to be now."

"But so much has happened. I have responsibilities."

"I have responsibilities, too. My family lives on subsistence. If I do well in America, I can help them. I'm useless here."

"We could talk to Father."

"I don't want a handout, Grace. People will assume I used you. The looks, the sneers, the rumours, would tear us apart."

His green eyes held mine. I felt powerless against the wall of pride I saw in his gaze.

Despite Ruairi's ultimatum, I wondered if he was wrong; if by talking to Father we could be together at Kilpara. It was difficult to know how such a request might affect Father these days. He was so detached he failed to notice any change in me, never once questioned me when I arrived late to breakfast every morning. Yet deep down I knew I wouldn't talk to him. Ruairi had made it clear he would never accept anything less than being master of his own destiny.

I handled the looming future by ignoring it. I pushed it so far from my mind that I was taken aback the morning Ruairi produced a passage ticket to America. He pressed it into my hand along with two other tickets.

"This is it," he said. "The ship to America sets sail day after tomorrow."

"Day after tomorrow? That can't be."

He looked at me closely. "Grace, I've been telling you every day for weeks now when the ship leaves. First, we'll take the train to Dublin, then the boat to Liverpool and afterwards the ship to America." He pointed to my hand. "All three tickets are here."

"I want to go with you," I said, "but—"

"There can be no buts, Grace. Meet me at the top of the avenue tomorrow morning at dawn. I'll have the carriage waiting for us next to the gatehouse. If you don't show, I'll know you changed your mind."

Ruairi held me for a long time, then sighed and walked away without looking back.

I returned to the house and wandered listlessly from room to room. I went to see Mother, and as I brushed her hair, I remembered Dr Murphy said to talk to her as if we were having a normal conversation. "You just never know when something will catch her attention and unlock her mind, setting her on the road to recovery," he said.

But if I hoped for any reaction when I spoke to her, I was left disappointed. "Forgive me, Mother," I said. "I'm leaving you to go away with Ruairi. You've met him, but you don't know him well. I love him and want to be with him. His future in Ireland is bleak, so he's going to America to seek better opportunities. You see, we could never marry here because our worlds are too different; our only chance of acceptance is to emigrate. I know it will be hard for you and Father when I go, but I can't live without Ruairi. I love him that much. Please Mother, tell me I can go." She didn't utter a word, answering me instead with her permanent vacant stare.

Desperate to make her understand, I took her out into the garden, hoping to find something that would provoke a response. Narcissus and crocus had come into bloom, and pots of hellebores, Mother's favourites, were set about in the spring sunshine. They brought a faint smile of recognition to her face. I fussed with the flowers, explaining and reminding her about them, hoping to draw out interest. Grandfather joined us and interjected stories about Mother's childhood. How she loved to run among the flowers, stopping to smell the blooms and picking a flower she liked best to put in her hair. But our attempts only provoked a slightly more alert, yet still empty look.

That evening Grandfather, Father and I ate a silent meal together. I looked closely at Father and saw how lines had deepened his smooth face, and how quickly hope rose in his eyes when I told him Mother had recognised the hellebores.

"That's good news," he said. "Maybe she's starting to come back to us. She'll do better tomorrow." The intensity of his words conveyed how deeply he needed Mother, his anchor in life. I wondered how he'd react if he knew I was about to desert him, too.

That night when the house turned silent I made up my mind. I couldn't stay at Kilpara without Ruairi. I opened the closet and reached inside for my valise. I stopped when I saw Deirdre's lone blue dress hanging there tucked away in the back of the closet. It was the only one she left behind when she packed to go to Switzerland, and again when she left to live at Larcourt. It had been one of her favourites, and I never understood why she left it behind. I touched the cotton fabric, letting its smoothness flow through my fingertips. I wondered if this dress held the memory of the day she conceived Giselle, a reminder of her love for Conor and her daughter's abandonment. I pressed it against me, seeing my sister's image in the mirror instead of my own.

An overwhelming longing overcame me to see my niece, to touch her soft baby skin, to feel her fingers curl around mine, to see my sister in her eyes. I had already missed more than the first year of her life. By leaving I would miss getting to know her permanently; miss discovering if she was artistic like Deirdre and Mother or if she possessed the same fondness for horses that Father and I did; if she held the human antidote that would bring Mother out of her mindless haze and back into the living world. I wouldn't be here to witness this. I would be in America with Ruairi discovering new things and making a new life, just like my grandparents had done. Could Father ever forgive me for leaving? Maybe not right away, but in time he would understand my decision.

I couldn't sleep, so I opened the window to let in the cool air. Somewhere in the distance lambs bleated. Horses neighed in the stables. Not long now till I met Ruairi. I sat down at the desk and began to write.

> *Dearest Father,*
> *I'm sorry you must find out like this that I have emigrated to America. By the time you receive this letter I will already have started my journey. I'm not going alone. I will be accompanied by Ruairi Kineely, whom I love and plan to marry, either with the help of the ship's captain, or when we reach the shores of America. I know you'll find this a shock. Believe me when I say I never meant to fall in love with him, it just happened. There is no way we can live together happily in Ireland because of our different upbringings, and we can no longer stand to be apart. So we're going to America to build our future together. I will send you a letter when I arrive there and let you know my address. I hope you will find it in your heart to forgive me for leaving this way.*
> *Your loving daughter,*
> *Grace.*

The hours ticked by and the letter grew hot in my hand. I remembered when Father first taught me to ride, how my enthusiasm delighted him. He was so proud that my love of horses had grown to match his own. Those were happy times, his face content and proud, so different from his grieving indifference of late. I knew how it pained him to watch Mother, who he loved so dearly, trapped in her mindless world, unable to speak. It seemed like eons ago that we all sat together as a family in the drawing room whiling away lazy Sunday afternoons. A lifetime had passed since those simple days. My thoughts drifted to Deirdre and how the life she wanted to live had been snatched from her. I wouldn't let that happen to me.

It was still dark when I picked up my valise and looked around the bedroom one last time. As on those many other mornings when I stole out of the house to meet Ruairi, nothing or nobody stirred. I reminded myself that I was leaving to be with the man I loved. I walked outside and down the steps and stood staring at the long avenue that stretched before me. Endlessly. Never before had it seemed so long. I put one foot in front of the other, forcing myself forward.

As I did, Mother, Father, and Deirdre's faces pushed their way foremost into my consciousness. Mother's empty eyes stared at me. Father's grief-stricken face haunted me. And Deirdre, poor sweet Deirdre, who would never see her daughter, Giselle, looked at me sadly. Shadows of a small child peeked at me from behind her skirts. Did she resemble Deirdre? I couldn't tell.

"No! No! No!" I screamed into the darkness. "Leave me alone. I want my happiness. I *deserve* my happiness."

I dropped to my knees and beat the pavement with my fists. Dew soaked the hem of my travelling clothes. I continued to beat the ground until exhausted. I leaned back on my heels and tears spilled unchecked down my face. I wanted to be picked up, lifted into the carriage and galloped away to the railway station. I stared ahead into the receding darkness, watched the sun begin its slow assent over the horizon until it was broken by Ruairi's outline walking towards me, dressed in a dark suit and overcoat.

He came and knelt down beside me. Gently he wiped the tears from my face with the sleeve of his coat. I didn't have to ask him if he saw the invisible hands tearing at my heart, ripping it wide apart till the pain was so great that I could scarcely breathe, and with each breath the pain deepened. He knew. Tears continued unchecked down my face, and now they were running down his cheeks, too.

"You can't leave, Grace," he announced simply. He drew me to my feet and cupped my face in his hands. He kissed me long and slow and passionately. Then his hands dropped to his sides and he turned and walked back down the avenue.

I watched him go until I could no longer distinguish his shape, dark and straight, against the brightening rays. I clutched the Claddagh ring warm against my neck. Through thickened tears I murmured, "Goodbye, my love."

CHAPTER 20

Later that morning I stood staring out the drawing room window at the spot where Ruairi and I had said goodbye. Father sat quietly reading the newspaper. The door opened after a soft knock. I turned slightly to see Clare come forward and thrust an envelope towards Father.

"My brother, Ruairi, asked me to give you this," she said, then exited quickly.

"Looks like Kineely is bound for America," Father said, after reading for a few moments. He laid the open letter down. "We lose all the good ones."

Feigning mild curiosity, I picked up the letter and scanned Ruairi's brief apology for his hasty departure. My name wasn't mentioned. The sight of Ruairi's determination set down in words only intensified my feelings of pain and regret that I couldn't be with the man I loved.

At this moment, more than ever, I missed my sister's companionship. Gathering a wool shawl, I tossed it across my shoulders and went to the place where I could still be close to her. The previous night's coarse temperatures had been replaced by mild spring air. It brushed my cheek like a soft voice whispering my name. I knelt down beside Deirdre's grave and plucked at new blades of grass sprouting up, a sad reminder this was now her permanent home.

My hand touched the cold smooth stone that bore her name. "Dee, I wish you were here so I could tell you about Ruairi Kineely. I fell in love with him and hoped we would marry someday. But, like Conor, he is not a man of means, and Ruairi is too proud to be beholden to Father—should Father have agreed to our union. Ruairi is determined to shape his own destiny in America. So he left this morning.

I wanted to leave with him. Desperately. But I couldn't bring myself to go, not with Mother like she is. She has turned inward and won't speak to anyone. She needs me. Father does, too, in his own way. He's blaming himself for the tragedy, attempting to cope with it, but doesn't know how. Kilpara is a sad place now.

"An unusual thing has happened, though. Father agreed that Conor should bring Giselle home. Father's grief is stronger than his need to protect our reputation. I promise you, we'll look after your baby girl in a way that will make you proud. She'll be a bittersweet reminder of how much we love and miss you."

I paused and looked out towards the lake. A voice sounded behind me. I turned to see Olam.

"Are you all right, Miss Grace?"

"I miss her, Olam."

"Me too, Miss Grace." He looked at me sadly. I rose and laid my head against his shoulder.

He patted my back. "Don't be sad, Miss Grace. The angels are taking good care of Miss Deirdre."

"It hurts, Olam."

"She had to go because God called her home."

"I know. It's natural to feel this way when we lose someone we love."

"You'll never go away, will you, Miss Grace? I wouldn't like that."

"No, I won't ever leave without saying goodbye."

I meant what I said. In my desperation to elope with Ruairi, I hadn't thought clearly about how my absence would affect others. I was heartsick over Ruairi and loved him completely, yet deep down I was bound to Kilpara and my family, and my conscience wouldn't let me to desert them at this difficult time. But once life returned to some kind of normalcy, I would be free to follow my heart and share a new life with Ruairi.

I touched my fingers to my lips and placed a kiss on Deirdre's headstone. I turned away and together Olam and I walked back to the house.

With Rengen no longer around to help at Mercy Hospital, I rode over to visit Grand-Aunt Sadie more often. I found solace in helping patients. It kept my mind off Ruairi and my grief over Deirdre. During these lengthening days, hope occasionally uplifted my spirit as grass turned vibrant springtime green and trees blossomed into full leaf.

Today, as usual, when I visited Grand-Aunt Sadie, she asked the same question. "Is there any change in your mother?"

"None. We're trying everything to stimulate a reaction."

"Strange thing, mental illness. People snap out of it after a devastating shock sometimes, or they never come out of it at all. You must keep trying. Have you learned anything new from the medical journals?"

"I've been studying them. But it's difficult to focus."

She laid a hand on my arm. "You've a gift for understanding medicine. Keep trying."

I pulled the sketch of Giselle from my pocket that Conor had sent in the post, and set it down in front of her.

"Did you know the real reason Deirdre was sent away?"

Her hand trembled as she picked up the sketch, and her voice quivered when she said, "Yes, I knew."

"Did you try to persuade Mother and Father not to send her away?"

"Your parents did what they thought was best for Deirdre. Lesser parents would have disowned her. Un-wedded pregnancy brings disgrace on a well-bred family. Your mother and father tried to protect Deirdre's reputation. They supported her in every way possible."

"Not enough to agree to her marrying Conor."

"They did relent to her persistence in the end—a difficult decision for them. Deirdre chose unwisely. She should have stayed within her own class."

"Sometimes the heart is stronger than the will."

"It is, dear. But the heart must resist the passion of desire or the consequences can be dire. Women are the virtuous race. They're the strong ones when it comes to matters of moral dignity."

"Not always," I said quietly.

"They bear the disgrace. The sin of impurity can wreck their lives."

"Deirdre didn't commit a sin. She bore a child with the man she loved and wanted to marry. How can that be a sin?"

"Her union was not blessed by God."

"She was in love."

Grand-Aunt Sadie ran her hand over the portrait of Giselle. "She was young and impressionable. But the sins of the parents should not be borne by the children."

"You agree that Giselle should be brought to Kilpara?"

"Yes, of course. Right or wrong, Deirdre was devoted to this beautiful baby girl. She was willing to make every sacrifice for her. The child will feel her mother's love at Kilpara."

I hadn't been to Larcourt since the fateful night of the fire. Giselle's portrait, her fair hair and wide blue eyes reminded me of Deirdre and compelled me to go back to where she had spent her final days. I saddled Spitfire and rode to Larcourt.

Beneath the blue sky, the wind gusted, tinged with the promise of summer. As I rode closer, memories of that fateful night crowded my thoughts, and I felt again the heat of overpowering flames, the acrid smell of smoke. The avenue was overgrown and deserted, what was left of the massive structure stood roofless and open to the sky. Ivy clung stingily to broken walls, the charred interior visible through broken windows. The scene was one of desolation.

Securing Spitfire to a tree, I walked to where the blackened ruin faced a restless lake, to the spot where we found Deirdre's lifeless body. She never wanted to be mistress of Larcourt. It was almost as if the house knew it and rejected her, sealing her fate from the first day she set foot inside its walls.

I looked up at where she climbed onto the roof ledge when escape was cut off from below. She stood there teetering between life and death, fire searing at her flesh as she pleaded for help. The ledge was no longer visible, having broken away after she leapt into the hay that wasn't stacked deep enough to break her fall. I knelt on the cold stone surface and touched the place where her body had lain, the cracks now covered with weeds. It had been a vain attempt at survival. Deirdre's hopes had perished with her in one fateful moment.

I ran my hand along the outline where she had fallen. "Dee, oh Dee, I wish you were here," I said to the grey pavement. My fingers brushed against something, and I looked down. Stuck inside a crack was the bracelet I bought Deirdre for her birthday. She must have been wearing it when she tried to escape, and it came loose in the fall. I held it to my breast and rocked back and forth crying, "Dee, oh Dee."

A voice startled me out of my mourning. "Very touching, Grace."

I got up and turned around. Cecil stood staring at me through narrowed eyes. He looked villainous in his dark suit with corners of his open jacket catching on the wind, his moustache twitching unevenly.

"I thought you were in Dublin," I said.

"I come back sometimes and stay at the gatehouse. The fire didn't touch it."

"I should go."

"No, stay, Grace. I was hoping you'd come. You were instrumental in Deirdre's and my marriage—always the busy little meddler. Couldn't resist interfering, could you?"

"I know all about you, Cecil. So did Deirdre. You plotted to have Conor murdered."

He walked around me. I stood without flinching.

"You don't know everything, my prying nuisance." He stopped directly in front of me. "I hired vagabonds for a few pounds to get rid of him, helped by generous promises to our foreman. They were English and not entirely comfortable here in Ireland. Too bad they didn't stick around to make sure they finished him off."

I resisted the urge to spit in his face.

He stepped closer; inches away. I commanded myself not to cringe.

"You didn't think I'd let Deirdre choose a peasant over me."

"And Father's beating?"

"The same vagabonds. They were paid only to rough him up. It would've delighted Mother if police had charged him with Hagerty's demise after the way he insulted her. However, I wanted him all nice and healed up for my wedding. Wedding indeed!"

"You're insane."

In a flash he grabbed my hair and wrapped it around his fist so tight my temples throbbed.

"You're hurting me, Cecil," I said.

"You helped Hagerty survive."

"Deirdre and I thought an injured animal had taken shelter in the cottage. But it was Conor."

Cecil gritted his teeth. "Hagerty would've died if you'd minded your own business, and my darling wife would still be alive. This was all your fault."

I tried to twist around but he drew my hair tighter. His knuckles dug into the back of my head.

"You knew, didn't you?"

"Knew what?"

"Hagerty returned and they were meeting at the cottage."

"Yes, I knew."

He tugged on my hair and I yelped.

"Deirdre didn't think I noticed when she began singing happy little songs to herself, a departure from her sullen detachment. I suspected she was up to something so I had my manservant keep an eye on her. I was sure she was scheming to reclaim her bastard child behind my back. Imagine my shock when he reported her meeting a man at the cottage. I saw her with Hagerty myself, laughing, touching. She wasn't that way with me. She pushed me away, complained of headaches, backaches, anything to sleep alone. Pretended she didn't want to disturb me with her restlessness. I didn't let her get away from me that easy. Even the locked door couldn't keep me out. There were other ways into that room, and I snuck into her bed."

I squirmed. "Let me go."

"Shut up. She married me, thinking I would rescue her bastard child and we would live together like some happy little family. All I ever wanted was her. I intended to make her mine and had no intention of sharing her with some peasant's bastard. She never wanted me, only *him*."

"You shouldn't have married her."

He yanked my hair again, bringing tears to my eyes. "Don't you understand I wanted *her*. I gave her everything money could buy, but she wasn't satisfied. She betrayed me with *him*. She deserved to die."

"You set the fire?"

He jerked my face around so I was looking into his icy stare. Shudders shot through me, and if he hadn't been holding my head tight I would have retched. As it was I swallowed bile rising in my throat.

"It was easy. Everyone thought I was in Dublin. No one would ever suspect I deliberately destroyed Larcourt, not even my parents. It's one of our family's beloved homes. I came back that night when everyone was asleep. I made sure cousin Dennis extended his stay after the New Year through an invitation to go duck hunting with Lord Blakely. I snuck into his bedroom disguised in peasant clothing and upset a lamp. He was a sound sleeper."

Sickened, I didn't want to hear any more and attempted to squirm away, but he held my face close to his.

"The fire took hold and I watched it rise through the house. Chaos erupted. Servants didn't notice me in their panic to get outside. The fire roared through the house, and I heard Deirdre and her maids scream when they discovered they were cut off from below. I went outside and saw her and her maids climb through the skylight onto the roof and stand there screaming for help. I felt every sear of burning flesh as pain ripped through her the same way pain ripped through me when I discovered her treachery.

"Fools stacked hay on the ground, as if that could save her. It didn't. Pity she jumped. I wanted to watch her burn alive. I wanted her to be consumed by the same agony I felt."

My eyes filled with tears. "You're demonic!" I spat in his face. "You tried to kill Conor. You hurt Father. You killed Deirdre!"

He slapped my face hard with the back of his hand. Pain shot through my head.

I tried to break free, but it was no use. He slapped me again. My cheek began to swell from the sting of his blow.

"Don't try to escape, Grace. I have plans for you. I know about you chasing after peasants like Deirdre did. Spreading your legs for Kineely. You're a whore just like she was."

He repositioned his grip. Seizing this momentary distraction, I broke free and bolted across the overgrown gardens. He recovered quickly and in no time caught up and overpowered me. His hands went around my throat and I thought he was going to choke me. He let go suddenly and I fell to the ground, gasping for air. He straddled me, pulled my hands together with his left hand. With his right hand he undid his cravat and bound my wrists tightly together. I screamed when he dragged me to my feet.

He laughed. "Scream all you want, there's no one to hear." When I screamed again he pulled out his handkerchief and stuffed it in my mouth. Yanking me towards the tool shed that was scorched by the fire but otherwise undamaged, he kicked open the door with the heel of his boot. As my eyes adjusted to the dimness he gave a satisfactory grunt and grabbed a length of twine off a workbench. Jerking me back outside, he pulled me towards stone steps and down to the private dock where a small rowboat was moored. "Get in," he ordered.

The boat was weather-beaten from exposure. Frothy spray pushed it against the walled inlet, rocking it from side to side. Steadying himself inside the boat, Cecil shoved me down on a seat. He drew my feet together and tied them.

"I don't know why I didn't think of this before," he said matter-of-factly, like we were going for a leisurely boat ride. He looked at me with cold malice.

I couldn't move, but when I glanced down I saw several life vests beneath the seat. This gave me comfort that was short-lived. Cecil saw them too and threw them onto the boat landing, except for one, which he put on.

He untied the boat and pushed off from the dock against a stiff wind. We proceeded about ten yards before the right oar became tangled in reeds. Cecil let out a string of curses. Placing the left oar in the oarlock, he set about untangling the right one. I stared at the parked oar, contemplating if I could grab it and knock him overboard. The water here was no deeper than three feet. He would recover before I could manoeuvre the boat back to the dock with my hands and feet tied. Who was I kidding? I was a prisoner with no hope of escape.

Every breath I took punctuated a lifetime. My surroundings grew in enormity. Whiskers of spray whipped off the lake. Reeds bent and thrashed against wind that carried with it the sweet scent of grass and snatches of fuchsia. Grey clouds slid over the blue sky like a door closing, and islands hued in multiple shades of green gave wisps of life to an otherwise desolate lake. Warm air seemed to have been sucked out of the atmosphere, because my body felt like it was wrapped in ice. Despite everything, I was determined to fight with every last breath, and if I died, Cecil Sloane would die with me.

The oar broke loose from the reeds, jolting the boat forwards. Cecil began rowing again with gusto. We rounded the jetty and stretched out onto the stormy Corrib. I watched land and security slowly slip away. I banged my feet against the bottom of the boat, and then stood up, rocking it precariously on the harsh lake.

Cecil raised an oar and pointed it at me. "Sit down. Don't make me knock you unconscious. That would be a pity. I want you to see your watery grave."

I sat back down, but continued to bang my feet.

"Why bother, Grace? Look around you, there's no one here to save you. Not even your precious Kineely."

The Corrib was a virtual layer of tossing water, no fishermen in sight, no ferry traversing the lake between Cong and Galway, no turf boats headed to the islands. I looked towards Inchnaghoill, the closest island, its inhabitants nonexistent on the shoreline. Angry tears brushed against my eyelids. I banged my feet furiously.

Cecil guffawed.

He rowed against the wind, which sometimes stirred the boat in a different direction. We were a good distance from shore before he said, "I'll make sure *you* don't survive the Corrib."

I tried to make sounds around the gagged handkerchief.

He pulled in the oars and stood up in the boat. He dragged me to my feet. I struggled to free myself from his grip, but he held me firm.

"Prepare to meet your end," he sneered.

I twisted against him frantically; he gripped me harder.

"Pay for your nuisance." He took the handkerchief from my mouth. "Scream, you meddlesome bitch. Scream! You're going to die."

He pushed me against the side of the boat, forcing me backwards. It tilted sideways. I grabbed for the shoulder strap of his life vest and fisted my fingers around it. The boat tilted more. I prayed it would overturn. Holding one hand against my chest, he undid my grasp with the other hand.

With a satisfied smirk he pushed me overboard.

I closed my mouth automatically as I hit the cold water. The shock hurt my head. As I floated downward on my back, I looked up and saw Cecil's face through a watery glaze, peering down at me. Then the oars splashed into the water and the boat moved away. I would drown and he would live.

I struggled to hold my breath and free my hands, twisted them inside the cravat, which rubbed my skin raw. I kicked the water with tied feet, punched at it with tied hands. My efforts raised me towards the surface, but not above it.

It wasn't so long ago I believed Conor was buried at the bottom of the Corrib, fish eating away at his flesh. No one would think to look for me here. They would assume that I ran away, unable to face the pressure of recent months. It was better for Father to think that, instead of wondering when my body would wash up on shore. Mother would never know I was gone.

I couldn't hold my breath any longer. Lough Corrib was going to claim me. I was about to join Deirdre in death.

A shape appeared beside me. A hand grabbed the collar of my riding jacket and yanked me above the surface.

Air! I could feel it filling my lungs as the hand kept my face above water that frothed all around us. I was being propelled backwards with the aid of a strong grip on my collar. I couldn't do anything to help, so I relaxed my body and floated on the current.

Cecil's boat ploughed towards the mainland. The wind was at his back. Arduous strokes of my rescuer made slow progress in the opposite direction. I knew if we didn't get help or reach land soon we would both drown or die from hypothermia.

We had been in the water for what seemed like an eternity, but it was less than fifteen minutes, when my head bumped against something solid. I rolled my eyes backwards and saw Olam's face beaming down at me, his free arm resting on what looked like a floating log. He grinned. My hopes soared at the sight of him. I tried to grin back, but sputtered water. I twisted around, raised my tied hands and rested my wrists on the rough wooden edge. I nodded my head towards the flat surface.

Olam understood my meaning. He loosened his grip on my jacket and hoisted me onto the log. It was a section of wooden landing that had remained bound together after it split apart from land. It was about two feet wide and six feet long. I positioned myself horizontally on my stomach, praying this beat-up wooden float would hold together.

Olam caught his breath. He was wearing a life vest. I began untying the knotted cravat around my wrists with my teeth. If I was going back into the water, my hands would be free.

Olam helped finish untying my wrists, bobbing against the float. With my hands untied I paddled the conveyance, and Olam kicked from behind with his feet. We worked our way towards the nearest island, and as we drew close, my muscles began to feel like rubber. We hit shore and everything went black.

I became conscious lying face-down on a muddy bank. I gasped for air. Above me a moisture-laden cloud splashed rain onto my face. I was on firm ground. I checked my limbs and they moved. Next to me lay the twine Cecil had used to tie my feet. Olam sat huddled beside me, rocking back and forth in wet clothes, his fearful eyes glued to my face.

He looked at me hopefully.

"Olam?"

"Yes, Miss Grace. I'm glad you're not dead," he said, through chattering teeth and blue lips. "We're on Inchnaghoill."

I looked around at stone walls roofless from age. "The old church?"

Olam nodded.

The broken landing sat a few feet away, blackened from lying in the water so long. It seemed impossible that something so flimsy could bring me to safety. Uncontrollable shivers started through my body and wouldn't stop. Olam bent over and rubbed my shoulders and arms with cold hands. Slowly they subsided. "I was in a boat—"

"Yes, Master Sloane's. I saw him try to hurt you. You screamed."

"How did you know where I was?"

"I followed you. I saw you ride towards Larcourt and came after you on Ladybug. She's slow. I saw Master Sloane drag you to the boat. He tied your feet together and said nasty things to you. I got scared when he wouldn't let you go. I didn't know what to do. Then he started rowing and got stuck in the reeds. I grabbed one of the life vests and crawled to the edge of the jetty, then waded through the reeds and hid. When Master Sloane rowed past, I grabbed the mooring line." Olam grinned. "You kept banging your feet and making noise, so he didn't see me."

"You could've drowned."

"So could you," he said simply. "After he shoved you into the water, I knew you couldn't swim all tied up. He started rowing towards shore and I swam to where you were. I saw your red jacket and grabbed hold of it. We floated, just like when we go swimming, except the water was rough. I was glad the broken wood drifted by. We paddled it here, only you stopped when we hit the island and I thought you were dead."

I threw my arms around him. "You saved my life."

Olam nodded, his teeth chattering even more. "Why did Master Sloane want to drown you?"

"His mind is sick."

Olam looked confused, but didn't say anything. I tried to get up. My legs wobbled and I plopped back down.

"We have to get help," I said. I looked around at the old stone building. If we were on Inchnaghoill, there were inhabitants here. We had to find someone to help us. "Was I asleep long?"

"Not long." Olam looked at me worriedly. "I didn't know what to do. I was afraid you wouldn't wake up."

"You did just fine, Olam." I tried to stand again. My legs seemed slightly stronger. Olam put his arm around my waist and helped me up. His feet were bare where he had kicked off his shoes. He was shivering badly. Spotting a sturdy stick on the ground, I pointed to it. Olam picked it up. I leaned on it and began to walk. Slowly we limped our way along the uneven path that ran around the boundary of the island. At last we saw grey smoke curling from a chimney and walked towards it. The wind had turned stronger, and I became weak with relief when a whitewashed cottage came into view.

We went through the white gate and up to the front door. A grey-haired woman opened it after we banged on it with our fists. Her faded eyes grew round in her small face when she saw us.

"Jesus, Mary and Holy Saint Joseph, where might ye be coming from in such a state?"

"Our boat sprung a leak and sank," I lied.

Olam looked like he was about to contradict me, but I gave him a stern look and he remained silent.

"Glory be, dearies, come on in. You're lucky to be alive. 'Tis a fierce day to be out on the Corrib. Whatever possessed ye to try such a thing? We'll get something warm into ye. What a terrible fright ye must've had."

We went inside and the woman called out, "Marlow, we have two childer here who are almost dead from drowning in the lake."

A man came from a small adjoining room. "Indeed, Eileen, there *are* two childer here. Almost drowned, ye say?"

The woman disappeared into the small room and came back with sheets. "Out of those wet clothes wi' the both of ye." She went over to the fireplace to a pot that sat there. "I've got a wee bit of stew left over from the dinner, will ye have it?"

We nodded. She anchored the pot on the pothook and stoked the flames so that they flew up around it.

"Where might ye be from then?" she asked.

"Kilpara," I said.

"Kilpara, ye say." She looked at me harder. "Over yonder side of the lake? Aye, I recognise the red hair. Do a lot of riding along the shore, don't ye. I've seen ye in the distance."

We handed her our wet clothes from beneath the sheets. She took them and hung them on a wire stretched across the hearth.

She took two bowls off the dresser and spoons from a drawer. "Come over to the table with ye and get this wee bit of stew."

Olam and I sat quietly at the small table. Marlow filled mugs with hot tea and handed them to us. The woman got out a breadboard and cut thick slices of soda bread and spread them with yellow butter. "Eat up," she ordered.

Her husband sat down opposite us, a tall bony man with a straight nose and hawk-like eyes. He looked to the woman for more explanation. "Ye say their boat sank, yonder in the Corrib?"

"Aye, that's what happened." She filled two bowls with thick brown soup full of lentils, potatoes, carrots and chunks of meat. She placed them in front of us, and her husband watched us curiously. I had no appetite, but didn't object to the meal out of politeness. After tasting the first spoonful of soup I couldn't stop eating until I finished every last morsel.

Olam did, too. Colour came back into his face and lips, and his shivering stopped.

"I can't get ye back to the mainland this evening," Marlow stated. "The wind's blowing too hard and a mist will roll in soon for the night. I'll take ye there in the morning."

"There isn't much here in the way of a bed," the woman said. "But I'll set up what I can for ye in front of the fire."

We thanked her. With her husband's help she brought out thick blankets and set them in front of the fireplace. Gratefully Olam and I lay down by the warmth. Soon all the candles were extinguished and the cottage sank into darkness, the smell of stew and soda bread lingering about the room. I dreamt of Deirdre standing on a roof with flames licking her feet, of Conor sinking to the bottom of the lake, of Mother staring vacantly into space, of Cecil's menacing eyes. I knew he was going to kill me.

I must have been moaning in my sleep, because I woke to a soothing touch on my hair. I could barely make out the old woman in her nightdress as she crooned. "There now, dearie, 'tis all right, 'tis safe ye are." I relaxed beneath her comforting touch and drifted back into a dreamless state.

Dawn was sending faint rays of light through the cottage window when I heard the door latch lift and cool air seeped inside. I looked up and saw a tall shadowy figure go out into the semi-darkness. I rolled towards the lingering heat of the fire, and when I awoke again it was to the sound of ashes being stoked in the fireplace. I stretched, and Olam opened his eyes.

"Will ye have a sup of tea?" Marlow asked. "The mist is still curling about the lake this morning. It'll clear off shortly."

The woman added turf to the ashes, and when it took flame she hooked a pot above the fire. Once again we sat at the hard kitchen table wrapped in sheets with mugs of tea. This time we ate boiled eggs with our soda bread. Afterwards the woman checked our clothes.

"Ye may put these back on," she said. "Looks like they've dried out by the fire."

As soon as we were dressed the man wordlessly handed Olam a pair of old slippers, then led us down to the lake. Fog still hovered over grey milky water. I hesitated when Marlow took my hand to help me into his small boat. I began to shudder. He squeezed my hand so tight that his grip hurt. The shudders stopped.

"No need to fear the Corrib, missy," Marlow said gently. "She took care of ye. She brought ye to us."

Once seated, he rowed the boat deftly across the lake with the experience of many years of practise. We docked at Kilpara just below the cottage. It sat in darkness. We thanked Marlow, and I asked him to come to Kilpara so he could be repaid for his kindness.

"No. Indeed not, missy," he said. "No reward necessary."

With those parting words he pushed off to return to Inchnaghoill and the little grey-haired woman who, I was sure, waited anxiously for his return.

Upon seeing us, the usually quiet-mannered Anthony shouted, "It's them! They're *here*!"

We walked into the house and were immediately surrounded. Maureen, Tom, Father and Grandfather came rushing out of the drawing room. There were hugs and sighs of relief. Father's face was haggard, his eyes pools of distress. My knees weakened at the sight of worry on everyone's face.

"We've been up all night," Maureen said. "People are out combing the hillsides for you."

She turned to the butler. "We should send out word they're back, unharmed."

He nodded, but didn't move. He kept staring at our unwashed faces and sagging clothes.

"We feared the worst," Father said. "We found Spitfire and Ladybug wandering the fields, but there was no sign of you. Are you hurt?"

I began to cry in his arms.

"Don't, Miss Grace," Olam said. "We're home now. Please don't cry."

"You're both suffering from shock," Father said. "I'll send for Aunt Sadie."

"I'll fetch a groom," Grandfather offered.

Tom looked at him gratefully as he and Maureen led Olam away to get cleaned up. Maureen turned to me on her way out and said, "I'll send someone to your room with hot water."

I thanked her.

Before Father could order me upstairs I said, "I must tell you what happened."

"You should rest first," he said.

"I can't until you know."

He nodded.

The words spilled out, and Father's face turned incredulous when I told him how Cecil, in his demented state, accosted me at Larcourt. How he knew Conor had survived the attack. How he plotted Father's assault. That a spy discovered Conor and Deirdre at the cottage and Cecil deliberately set the fire at Larcourt because he felt betrayed by Deirdre's infidelity. I explained that he blamed me for interfering in his and Deirdre's marriage, his forcing me into a rowboat and his attempt to drown me in the lake. My voice grew tearful when I said he would have succeeded if Olam hadn't bravely rescued me.

I told him about the old couple in the cottage on Inchnaghoill who allowed us to spend the night and gave us shelter and food.

By the time I'd finished, Father looked like a man bored into by an auger. His face had turned white and his lips were compressed into a thin, angry line.

CHAPTER 21

A constable stood with his hat tucked under his arm talking to Father when I entered the drawing room.

"Well now, Miss Grace O'Donovan," he said, after I sat down, "your father tells me you were abducted the day before yesterday, May 15th, by your brother-in-law, Mr Cecil Sloane. Your hands and feet were bound and you were taken out on the Corrib in a rowboat and pushed overboard. Is that correct?"

"Yes."

"And you survived?"

"Yes."

He licked the tip of his pencil and wrote something on a pad.

"What was your purpose for going to Larcourt?"

I hesitated. "I was grieving my sister, Deirdre, and I wanted to trace her last steps."

"Like when she died?"

"No. What she had endured at Larcourt."

"She had an idyllic life, married to the prominent young Mr Cecil Sloane. She was the mistress of Larcourt and the envy of every entitled young woman."

I looked at the constable, but didn't answer.

"Did you expect to find Mr Sloane there?"

"No. He was in Dublin at Trinity College."

"But you knew he returned occasionally to attend to business. The tenancy, for one thing. His parents are in England, and he oversees leftover business at the estate. Isn't that correct?"

"I thought Larcourt was deserted. The house is in ruins."

"You didn't see a caretaker? There had to be a caretaker to keep vandals away."

"I didn't see anyone."

"You didn't go there to take the boat out on the Corrib yourself, then discovered it was more than you bargained for and abandoned it?"

"No, I didn't."

"How did you escape from drowning?"

"Olam, our maid's son, followed me to Larcourt. He saw Cecil Sloane abduct me and he rescued me."

The constable raised an eyebrow. "In another rowboat?"

"No, he clung to the mooring line of Cecil's boat. After Cecil pushed me overboard Olam saved me and kept me afloat."

"It must've been difficult for Mr Sloane to row the boat with someone dragging his line. Don't you think he'd have noticed?"

"It was a stormy day and the lake was tumultuous. And he was distracted because I kept stomping my feet in protest."

"He continued rowing while you stomped your feet?"

"Yes."

"He wasn't afraid someone would notice your shenanigans?"

"No, the Corrib was deserted because the water was rough."

"How did you and er—Olam—get to Inchnaghoill?"

"Olam kept me afloat until a lump of wood drifted by. It was a broken piece of wooden landing, probably washed away from one of the islands. He helped untie my hands after I positioned myself on top of it. Then he propelled it from behind and I used my hands to paddle it ashore."

"An average swimmer would have difficulty keeping himself above water on the lake in bad weather, never mind keeping himself and another person afloat for any length of time."

"Olam is a powerful swimmer. He wore one of Larcourt's life vests, which helped."

The constable frowned at me. "And where did he get this life vest?"

"Cecil threw several out of the boat onto the landing before he rowed away."

"He didn't give you one?"

"Of course not. He intended to drown me."

"Continue."

"Cecil rowed out quite far. Inchnaghoill and some of the other islands were visible when he pushed me overboard."

The constable tapped his pencil on his notepad. "Saved by a bit of floating wood, were you?"

"Yes."

"And it got you ashore?"

"Yes."

"A miracle, I'd say."

"We were fortunate."

"Indeed. Why do you suppose your brother-in-law wanted to harm you?"

I squirmed uncomfortably. "He thought I interfered in his and my sister's marriage."

"Did you?"

"He thought so."

"Was there a particular incident that bothered him?"

"My sister and I were close; *that* bothered him."

The constable squinted. "Give me an example."

"Constable, you can stop berating my daughter," Father interrupted. "Cecil Sloane tried to drown her, that's the only thing relevant here. He admitted to her that he plotted to kill Conor Hagerty, to have me beaten, and he set the fire at Larcourt. You should find him and arrest him before he does more harm."

The constable sniffed. "Begging your pardon, Mr O'Donovan, those are serious complaints to make against Mr Sloane, a citizen of extreme prominence—as you are yourself. I intend to proceed with the utmost caution, as I would in any inquiry. However, I will be even more judicious in this case because Mr Sloane's father, Sir Charles Sloane, also happens to be a close friend of Chief Secretary Mr Henry Campbell-Bannersman.

"Besides, we know there was no mystery surrounding Conor Hagerty leaving Brandubh. He left to seek his fortune elsewhere, as people are apt to do from time to time. We have proof the fire at Larcourt was accidental. It's unthinkable that Mr Cecil Sloane would deliberately set fire to his own home, a landmark property, with a fortune in valuables inside. He suffered a tremendous shock when his wife, your older daughter, died in the fire.

"And it doesn't seem plausible Mr Sloane would want to drown Miss Grace O'Donovan, or that he is responsible for any of the other charges you allege. From my perspective it appears Miss O'Donovan has a jealous streak. She was envious of her sister and brother-in-law's marriage. She craved Mr Sloane's attention and was upset that he preferred her sister over her. She's making these outlandish claims so he'll notice her. It's a case of sibling jealously. I experienced a similar situation myself." He straightened his necktie and stuck out his chin. "Two young ladies from the same family got into a fight over me because I couldn't decide which one I wanted to court. In the end I courted neither young lady."

Father pounded his fist on the fireplace mantel, shocking the constable into silence. "Have you been listening to anything my daughter said? Are you calling her a liar?"

The constable's expression remained impassive. "Calm yourself, Mr O'Donovan. I'm only stating the facts."

"No, you're ignoring the facts and stating what you think. I'll calm myself when you arrest Cecil Sloane."

"We can only do that if there is cause to believe a crime was committed."

"He tried to drown Grace, his latest of *many* crimes."

The constable pursed his lips. "I have only Miss O'Donovan's word to back up her allegations against Mr Sloane."

"It's your job to establish a case. Start with Olam, our maid's son, who will corroborate Grace's story."

The constable shifted his stance. "The same boy who stole a life vest from Larcourt and is complicit in this melodrama conjured up by Miss O'Donovan. Mr O'Donovan, if you'll let me have a word with your daughter in private, I'm sure I'll get to the bottom of this quickly."

"You're through speaking to my daughter." Father went to the door and opened it. "You'll hear from my lawyer. We're done here."

The constable shook his head and left.

Father slammed the door. "Fastidious idiot. I'll talk to David Ligham and ask him to hire a private detective to gather evidence against Sloane."

My mind was no longer on Cecil. I was thinking about how indebted I was to Olam for saving my life.

After the Corrib incident I kept to the grounds around Kilpara. I craved leaving, but dreaded it at the same time. I retreated inside a shell and was anchored there by fear. To occupy myself I set up a daily routine to find ways to stimulate Mother's reaction to things she loved. Every morning I took her to the paint studio, hoping the sight of her easel and canvasses would stimulate a reaction. Instead, she looked at them as if she didn't know what they were. I was sitting with her in the paint studio one morning when Anthony announced David Ligham had been shown into the drawing room. "Is he here to see Father?" I asked.

"No, he requested to see you, miss," Anthony said.

I walked into the drawing room. David rose immediately to embrace me. "Dearest Grace, I had to come and see for myself that you were all right. Your father told me what happened. It's hard to believe Cecil could do such a heinous thing."

"Believe it," I said, extracting myself from his embrace. "Have you spoken to him?"

"No, but I've hired a professional detective on your father's behalf to trace him. We'll know his whereabouts soon."

"He's not in Dublin?"

"He doesn't appear to be."

This was disturbing news. It left me feeling uneasy. If Cecil was confident I had drowned, there would be no reason for him to change his routine. "Perhaps he's in England with his parents."

"That's the first place we're looking."

"The constable who interviewed me thinks I'm making things up because I craved Cecil's attention," I said.

"He doesn't know you."

"Cecil wanted to take revenge on me for interfering in his marriage."

"When he discovers you've made charges against him, he'll give himself up."

"I think your expectations are naive. Cecil won't ever admit to wrongdoing."

David embraced me again. "The truth will win out. You'll see."

"He's already gotten away with murdering Deirdre, an attempt to murder Conor, and beating Father. He's too cunning to be caught."

David held me at arm's length. "Take heart, we'll get Cecil. What you need is something to take your mind off this terrible experience. What about a picnic sometime soon by the sea?"

A simple invitation to a picnic sent me crawling back inside my shell. "I'd like to, but not just yet. We could have lunch in the gazebo, if you like."

David's lips broadened into a smile. "I'd like that, dearest Grace."

On a warm day almost two weeks after my near-drowning, Mother sat comfortably on the garden bench as I moved among delphiniums, clipping a bouquet for the dining table. Father came out and sat down beside her. He took her hand in his and she smiled at him without speaking. He kissed her forehead. "Giselle, Deirdre's baby daughter, is coming home," he said.

Mother continued to smile blankly at him. I stopped clipping and stared at Father. He silently handed me a telegram. "Conor's been anxious to get back home ever since he heard about the incident with Cecil."

Giselle's arrival two days later, her fair hair framing a heart-shaped face and bright blue eyes, brought servants out onto the front steps to inspect and admire her.

"Looks the image of Miss Deirdre," they murmured.

"Poor little mite must be terrified to come among strangers."

"Don't stare, lest you frighten her."

Conor lifted Giselle into his arms and together they ascended the steps. She looked fearfully at the overpowering stone structure and people lining the way to the front door. She buried her face against Conor's shoulder and began to whimper.

"Don't be afraid, Giselle," Conor soothed, stroking her hair. I could see she clutched Deirdre's old doll tightly against her.

The servants called out words of welcome as Conor carried her inside the house. When Giselle looked up again at her surroundings, her eyes rested on her nurse. She stretched out her hand and said, "Berthie."

"I'm right here, dahling," the woman said in a strong German accent. She was tall and slim. She wore a white cardigan over a plain black dress that seemed stark against her chiselled features. She took her eyes off Giselle long enough to rove them over the building. It must have met with her approval for she said, "Eet is very beautiful here, Giselle."

Grandfather and Father stood waiting to greet them in the library.

"I do declare, so I do ..." Grandfather exclaimed when we all trudged in. "Image of Deirdre, so she is."

He held out his hand. "I'm your great-grandfather."

Giselle drew her hands tighter around Conor's neck. The nurse brushed Giselle's hair with her hand and said, "Opa." Giselle turned her face sideways to look at Grandfather.

Father pointed to Deirdre's doll. "I know where there's lots more dollies like that one." Giselle pulled the doll closer, fearful Father meant to take it from her. "They were your mommy's. Would you like to see them?"

Giselle indicated to Conor that she wanted to be put down. She took the nurse's hand and stood before Father.

"Opa?" she said pointing.

The nurse nodded.

Father looked at us in amusement. "Opa," he repeated, smiling. Giselle offered him her free hand, and together they went upstairs. Grandfather followed close behind.

Conor and I watched as they made slow progress up the stairs, the nurse and Father matching Giselle's small steps.

When they reached the top, Conor and I went into the drawing room. "You don't look well, Grace," Conor said. "I came home as soon as I could."

I looked away. "I didn't tell you everything in my letter."

"There's more?" Conor's voice sounded bitter.

"You know Ruairi left for America, like I wrote."

"He wanted to marry you. Why didn't you go with him?"

Tears stung my eyes. "How could I? Deirdre's gone, and Mother—well, you'll see for yourself how she is."

"I understand, Grace." He put a hand on my shoulder. "I'm sorry."

I looked down at my hands. "That's not all. You know Cecil tried to drown me, but I didn't tell you he admitted to setting the fire that killed Deirdre."

The air tensed. I looked up at Conor and his forehead seemed to bulge before my eyes. Blood rushed to a vein at his temple. His gaze became fixed like a wild animal's about to attack its prey. I feared I had sent him over the edge. I threw my arms around his waist and pent-up tears overflowed against his chest. I could feel the rapid beating of his heart begin to slow against my ear as I sobbed uncontrollably. When I stepped back, relief washed over me. Sadness mixed with regret had replaced the strange animal look that possessed him minutes before.

Conor wiped the tears from my face with his hand. "Sloane will pay for what he did, Grace, I promise you that." He drew me back into his arms. "I feel responsible. If you'd been in France with Giselle and me, this wouldn't have happened."

"You couldn't have known—nobody could." I wanted to confess that Ruairi was my reason for staying behind, but as Conor's arms tightened protectively around me, I held back my secret. We stood motionless, partners in heartache.

Mother brightened at the sight of Giselle and began murmuring, "My baby." We hoped she would say more, but were encouraged even by this small reaction. Giselle immediately took to Mother and brought everything she could find to lay on Mother's lap. Mother hugged each item as if it were a present, which encouraged Giselle to find something new.

The nurse, whose full name was Beatrice Braum, had been raised by a German father and a French mother. She learned English when her parents worked for an English family in Zurich. From her stern exterior I would not have guessed her to be a warm and engaging woman. But her affection was obvious as she gazed upon Giselle and Mother with patient interest.

When it came time for dinner Conor stiffened, and with good reason. Mealtime at Kilpara was an extravagant affair and he was used to a simple family repast. I had asked Maureen to simplify the menu to put him at ease. But even a simple meal at Kilpara was elaborate.

Giselle toddled into the great room, her small hands tucked inside Mother's and Beatrice's. When Deirdre and I were little we took our meals separately in the nursery, but this was an unusual situation and no rules had been established. With everyone's attention on Giselle, Conor's discomfort went mostly unnoticed.

Dinner began with oxtail soup, followed by mutton cutlets, mashed potatoes, and cauliflower, then apple tart for dessert. At each serving Clare appeared discreetly at Conor's side to prompt him which spoon or fork to use. He ate little for someone I was sure had a large appetite. Throughout the meal Giselle giggled, pointed, and banged her spoon on the table, delighted by the sound it made. Whatever strangeness she felt just hours before had disappeared.

After the meal Father drew Conor and me into the library. "There is much to discuss," he began. He poured two drinks and handed a glass to Conor. "I can't tell you how grateful we are that you brought the child home. Her presence has already begun to heal the grief felt from Deirdre's sudden death." He paused as sadness passed over his face. "What are your living arrangements?"

Conor cleared his throat. "I've rented a cottage in Brandubh, and I will return to work for the Lighams. The cottage is small, but adequate."

"I see." Father laid his glass on the mantelpiece and faced Conor. After a long moment he said, "I have a proposition I hope you'll consider. I promised to deed the cottage and three hundred acres to Deirdre upon your marriage." He hesitated. "I deeded the cottage and the acreage to Deirdre *alone* upon her marriage to Cecil. The land now belongs to the child and will be held in trust until she reaches the age of consent. You are my granddaughter's father, and I'd like you to be the executor until then. You can work the land as you see fit." He picked up his glass and studied the liquid. "Deirdre loved that cottage. She would want you and the child to live there. It would require more renovation to accommodate a family, but it's yours, if you'll have it. The child can spend her days here at the house with her nurse."

Father's words hung in the room as we waited expectantly; I held my breath.

Conor cleared his throat. "Sir, I appreciate everything you've done to bring Giselle back to Ireland. Your offer is very generous, but I must decline it. I will make sure that Berthie brings Giselle to Kilpara often to visit you and her grandmother." He looked over at me. "And Grace too, of course. That's the best I can offer right now."

Father and I both nodded. We didn't have to ask why Conor declined the offer. It was obvious his pride would not allow him to agree to such an arrangement, no matter how practical it seemed.

When we returned to the drawing room a surprise awaited us. Berthie sat playing the piano and Giselle wiggled her little body in front of Mother. Mother had risen from her chair and she was imitating Giselle's moves. Father and I laughed out loud, and Conor looked on with silent pride.

Giselle spotted Conor, and opened and closed her fist in a come-hither motion. "Papa—up," she said.

Conor grinned and swooped her into his arms. They danced around the room. Grandfather eased Mother back into her chair, and she clapped her hands. After the music stopped, Giselle padded over to Mother.

"We must be going," Conor said soon afterwards. "It's long past Giselle's bedtime."

Berthie obeyed grudgingly, but nobody was prepared for Giselle's sudden clinging to Mother when Conor bent to pick her up. "Stay—Oma," she said and repeated it through fitful sobs.

Mother held Giselle in her arms. "My baby."

We watched, amazed, as Giselle clung to Mother and laid her head against Mother's chest. Nobody knew what to do.

After a delayed silence Conor beckoned Father outside. When they returned to the drawing room it was obvious from their faces they had reached an agreement. Conor motioned for everyone to sit. Already Giselle's eyes were drooping in the warmth of Mother's embrace.

A faint smile crossed Conor's face. "It looks like we'll be living at Kilpara. For now. Berthie and Giselle will remain here while I make the necessary accommodations for them at the cottage. I'll survey the best way to tenant the land bequeathed to Deirdre on her behalf. Mr O'Donovan and I agree this arrangement will best suit everyone."

Berthie and I jumped up and hugged Conor. Grandfather murmured, "hurrmph," that sounded more like a concession than an objection. Giselle had fallen sound asleep in Mother's arms.

Giselle's presence breathed new life into Kilpara. Conor divided his time between the cottage and the house. Mornings began with cheerful sounds coming from the nursery where he ate breakfast with Berthie and Giselle. Everyone gravitated there instead of the great room, filling up the small dining table. Conor looked more at ease in this familial setting. Berthie, Giselle, Mother and I would go into the garden afterwards. Giselle played while Mother watched and Berthie read. I wandered through the flower beds, cutting Mother's favourite flowers to be placed around the house, always picking out a special flower to be worn by Giselle in her hair.

Conor appeared beside me one warm afternoon when I was returning to the stables with Spitfire after I had put him through his paces in the paddock. It occurred to me how healthy he looked, so different from the bereaved man who left Ireland to retrieve his daughter. France and Giselle had brought him back to life. He seemed pleasantly serene now that he was working on the cottage. At times he and Father walked the fields together, inspecting crops and talking about the harvest.

"So why don't you ride him?" Conor asked, patting Spitfire's flank.

I didn't want to admit I was afraid to venture beyond Kilpara demesne, but Conor guessed it anyway. "We'll find Cecil," he said. "It won't be long before you'll feel safe again."

I didn't ask for details. I just wanted justice. I wanted Cecil locked away where he would pay for his crimes, yet I didn't wish him dead. "Don't do anything rash," I said. "I couldn't bear it if anything happened to you or Father."

Clare had begun sleeping outside my bedroom door at night. She would have her bedding cleared away when I awoke the next morning. I tried to calculate how long letters took to get to America and back again to decide if this was Ruairi's idea. I couldn't be sure and Clare refused to say. The first night I heard noises in the corridor I grabbed the poker from the fireplace and sneaked to the door. I opened it just a crack and peeked outside.

"It's only me, Miss Grace," Clare said.

"You gave me a fright," I said. "What're you doing lurking in the corridor?"

"I'm sleeping here."

"Why?"

She looked at me as if I was dense. "I'm keeping watch."

"There's no one to fear at Kilpara."

"If you say so."

"The house is locked up tight."

"It still pays to be careful."

"You should go home."

"If it's all the same to you, Miss Grace, I'll sleep here."

"Did someone ask you to do this?"

She grinned. "It was me own idea."

"Does Maureen approve?"

"It's me own time. I don't need Maureen's permission."

I pointed to the floor. "That's where you're going to sleep?"

"Yes, Miss Grace."

With that she settled herself between blankets she brought along and laid her head on a pillow.

She was being deliberately cheeky. Ruairi's face flashed into my mind, sending a physical ache through me so forceful it buckled my knees. If Clare had written to him and told him about Cecil, he would ask her to watch over me. She would think her sleeping in the corridor protected me. Albeit impractical.

I expected her to give up her vigil after a few nights, but she stubbornly continued to bed down outside my door and didn't seem to tire of her commitment. I contemplated asking Father to offer her a live-in position, but that wouldn't solve keeping her out of the corridor at night. The bedrooms were only for family and visitors; none of the servants occupied this part of the house. Matters worsened when she developed a hacking cough.

I gave her medicine, but she continued to cough. One night I couldn't sleep because her cough had grown so loud it kept me awake. I lit the lamp and knelt down beside her in the corridor. "Come on," I said, "you're sleeping in my bed tonight."

"I can't do that," she argued. "I've never slept in a lady's bed before."

"You're sick. You must do as I say."

"Where will you sleep?"

I had requested that Deirdre's bed be removed from the bedroom after she married Cecil. It was replaced by a settee.

"I'll sleep on the settee."

"I can't bother you like this, miss." Anxiety made her cough even harder.

"And I can't have my protector getting sick," I insisted.

"I'll go down to the servants' quarters and ask one of the maids to let me share a room."

"It's too late to disturb the household. Come on. I'll fix you a mixture that will ease your cough."

After I coaxed her into bed and gave her a cough mixture, I fixed up a makeshift bed on the settee. I left the lamp on low so I could monitor her without waking her and cracked open the window. Soon her heavy breathing eased into a noisy rhythm.

Still, sleep didn't come easy. I had just started to doze when a squeak on the floorboards brought me fully awake. In the shadowy light a figure tiptoed steadily towards the bed where I should be sleeping. Instead of bedtime clothes, the trespasser wore a morning suit and appeared to be male. My heartbeat throbbed rapidly as I watched the intruder slip a pillow out from under Clare's head, then hold up a knife. I clamped a hand over my mouth to hold back a scream.

He stood still for a moment with the pillow in his left hand and a knife in his right hand. I gasped when I heard him whisper, "You're not so clever now, are you, Grace? You won't escape me this time."

He brought the pillow down over Clare's face and held the knife against her throat.

I leapt up and yelled, "Stop!"

Cecil froze in mid-motion, loosened his grip on the pillow and turned to face me, pointing the knife out in front. Clare startled awake and coughed fitfully. She crawled to the other side of the bed and slid to the floor.

Cecil advanced towards me. "How did you do that, Grace?"

"Do what?"

"Be in bed, yet over here at the same time?"

"I wasn't in bed, Cecil."

He looked around and saw Clare. She gave a hoarse scream.

I made a dash for the door and had my hand on the doorknob when Cecil grabbed my hair and dragged me back into the centre of the room.

Clare stood against the wall screaming, "Help! Help!"

Cecil yelled, "Shut up." Clare's mouth clamped shut.

He pushed me down on the bed and brought the knife down against my throat. I could feel its cold edge against my neck. "You should've drowned in the Corrib, Grace. Imagine my disappointment when I found out you eluded your death."

Something smacked against Cecil's back and he jerked upward. He stood dazed for a second, then turned and advanced towards Clare, who held the poker between herself and Cecil. She screamed and shakily pointed it at his chest.

He laughed a demonic laugh and kept advancing.

"By God, I'll ram this through you if you come any closer," she said.

She slipped one hand on the doorknob, opened the door, and just when it seemed she would draw him out into the corridor, he rushed at her, yanked the poker away and threw it on the floor. He dragged her back into the room and slammed the door shut. He pushed her up against the wall.

I had slid to the end of the bed, moved to the fireplace and grabbed the coal shovel. I raised it, ready to hit him from behind.

"Drop it, Grace," he said without turning to look at me, "or I'll slit this common bitch's throat."

I knew without a doubt he intended to carry out his threat. "Let her go." I weighed putting down the shovel or hitting him with it. "It's me you want, not her."

"Do you think I'm stupid?" he said, over his shoulder. "The minute I let her go she'll run for the door. Put down the shovel and get around here beside her."

I had made up my mind to take my chances to hit him with the shovel when the door burst open and Father stood in the doorway, holding Uncle Francis' revolver. He pointed it at Cecil. "Let her go or you're a dead man."

Cecil backed up towards the window then threw down the knife. He picked up the lamp and pushed open the window.

He pulled off the globe, set the flame on high. Fire licked the air—strengthening. Cecil held the lamp up, aiming it at us. Father cocked the revolver. Their eyes locked. Nobody moved a muscle. My heart thudded in my chest and shivers started through me. With slow precision Cecil lowered the lamp, held the flame against his coat sleeve. It teased the wool fabric before taking fire. He threw the lamp to the floor then turned and leapt towards the windowsill. His laughter echoed through the eerie light as flames ignited around him and the smell of paraffin filled the room.

Father bounded across the room, avoiding the fire. He coldcocked Cecil with the butt of the revolver as he climbed onto the windowsill. Cecil fell to the floor in a plume of flames. Father yanked the rug next to the vanity and rolled Cecil in it. I fought back mounting panic as I picked up the water jug and doused water on flames catching fire to the floor, wallpaper, and drapes. Clare joined me, beating flames with blankets.

"What the …" Grandfather exclaimed, appearing in the doorway. He disappeared for a moment then returned with more water. Servants arrived, and soon the flames were contained before they had a chance to get out of control. Smoke smouldered as Grandfather gathered Clare and me into his arms. Cecil lay still on the floor, wrapped in the charred rug. Father glanced around the room and blew out a long breath of relief.

Cecil had passed out, but his pulse was strong. Father, who suffered superficial burns, assisted Anthony in getting Cecil into the carriage. Tom roused a couple of grooms, one to be his eyes on the ride to Mercy Hospital, the other to fetch Dr Murphy and alert the authorities.

Grandfather accompanied Clare and me into the library and was urging us to drink sherry when Conor burst into the room. A stunned look passed between him and Father before he put his arms around me.

"This should never have happened, Grace," he said. "I promised you I'd take care of Cecil."

"I thought I was safe here," I whispered in a broken voice. "How did he get in?"

"I don't know, Grace. I don't know."

With dawn came the smell of eggs, bacon, and sausages from the great room. People sat around the Georgian table who normally would be too timid to touch anything so grand. All of Ruairi's family were there, as were Conor's parents, who came to Kilpara out of concern for their granddaughter.

Even in my distressed state I noted when Father greeted Ruairi's father, Kegan Kineely, how much his face reminded me of Ruairi. His likeness made me want to reach out across the ocean and touch Ruairi.

"I'm sorry Clare was put in harm's way," Father said. "Without her, Grace might not be alive."

"It was Clare's choice to protect Miss Grace," Mr Kineely said, simply. "Besides, it's our family that's indebted to you."

Father looked puzzled.

A faint smile crossed Mr Kineely's face. "Think back nearly twenty years ago. You were bringing your mother home from America on *The White Lady*. I was on that ship with my family. Our food rations were depleted when an unexpected storm hit. My son, Ruairi, just an infant then, was in danger of becoming deathly ill. You arranged food for us and medical attention for my son. It is I who owe you thanks."

"You weren't supposed to know. I swore the captain to secrecy."

Mr Kineely's smile grew wider, a stark reminder of Ruairi that tore at my heart. "It was obvious someone had done us a kindness, and it wasn't the captain. I wanted to thank our benefactor. Just before we docked I asked the captain who had helped us. He said he was sworn to secrecy, but would share the information for a price. I told him I wasn't giving into blackmail, that I had fought in the Union army and knew ways to make even the toughest men squeal. He told me then. I never did thank you. There was never an appropriate time. Until now."

Wordlessly, Mr Kineely held out his hand. Father shook it.

CHAPTER 22

Fate had denied me the satisfaction of watching Cecil pay with his life for his crimes, denied me justice for Deirdre's loss, and left me fearing for my life. I shrank from the horror of knowing Cecil had watched my movements while he plotted to kill me; that he survived an attempt to commit suicide in a horrible twist of providence after his scheme failed.

I moved about the house restlessly, unable to settle in one place. When I entered the drawing room, Berthie looked at me with disquiet on her face and in her eyes. She opened her mouth as if to speak, then changed her mind. Instead, she wordlessly handed me a cup of tea—as if that could soothe the terror that made me tremble at my very core. Even Giselle's happy little voice and innocent face could not lift me from deep gloom.

Nothing interested me anymore. I knew from reading Grand-Aunt Sadie's medical books I was suffering from shock. I was unable to talk about the attack, afraid its reality would shatter my fragile shell. Father avoided the subject, too, but I overheard him tell Conor that the lousy bastard hadn't been burned badly enough. His skin would heal. Despite everything Cecil had taken from us, he was at Mercy Hospital under the care of Grand-Aunt Sadie.

Lost in contemplation, I stood at the drawing room window, not paying attention to anything in particular, when the Sloanes' carriage came to a halt out front. I watched Lady Daphne dismount and walk up the steps. In my mind I was already outside pulling the silly-looking hat off her head, shoving her back inside her carriage, screaming at her never to set foot at Kilpara again.

If she was here to beg leniency for her son from Father, she would be disappointed. Father was away in Galway, just as he had been the previous day. I presumed he was there to provide the constabulary with details of Cecil's attack.

Lady Daphne's exchange with Anthony echoed from the vestibule, not loud and boisterous, but sober and firm. The butler explained the family wasn't receiving visitors, but Lady Daphne insisted she was at Kilpara to offer sympathy. Silence lingered before the butler showed her into the drawing room.

Numbly I turned around.

"My dearest child," she said, crossing the room to take my hands. I shrank from her touch; she sat down on the settee. I remained standing.

"I've come to offer my condolences for Deirdre's accident. Poor Morrigan. And to say I'm dreadfully sorry that Cecil, in his grief, tried to kill himself in the same way Deirdre died. And in her very bedroom. He would have succeeded if you and your father hadn't intervened and stopped him. I'm here to thank you for your prompt response. In his present mood Cecil is a danger to himself. He is so distraught is he over losing Deirdre. We'll get him the best treatment for his uncharacteristic behaviour. I'm hopeful that, in time, he'll learn to live with Deirdre's tragic demise."

The only thing I noticed about Lady Daphne's appearance was her silly-looking hat that didn't match her outfit. But there was something else that was odd about her; she looked pathetic. She wasn't the same woman of my childhood who took pleasure in conniving and scheming. She had always been well-dressed, well-coifed in her appearance, and had the confidence of someone with a shrewd mind. Never once did she assume a beseeching manner, or allow her appearance to become unkempt. Strands of hair escaped from under the wide-brimmed hat, and her clothes were wrinkled in places. Her eyes darted from side to side as she waited for me to speak.

"Your son tried to kill me. Twice," I stated coldly. "And he set the fire at Larcourt that killed Deirdre. He doesn't belong in some convalescence facility that cures *uncharacteristic* behaviour disorders. He should be tried in court for his crimes, and hanged."

Lady Daphne's mouth opened and closed without speaking. She jumped up and faced me, her eyes turning hard as coals. "You cruel girl. How dare you make such malicious accusations to accuse Cecil of criminal behaviour? We've shown nothing but tolerance and respect for your family. Cecil's no monster. He loved Larcourt, and your sister. He would *never* destroy his home that contained so many ancestral heirlooms. He's a kind, sensitive boy, who in his grief over your sister's accident, attempted to join her in death. He's not guilty of harming anyone. Only himself."

She produced a hanky and dabbed at her eyes.

"He *is* guilty," I said. "He came here, snuck into *our* home, intending to smother me with a pillow and to slit my throat with a knife. He didn't reckon on a sick housemaid asleep in my bed, or Father foiling his plan and coming to our rescue. It was only after he was cornered that he set himself on fire. He did it to avoid the hangman's noose."

Lady Daphne held her head up and puffed out her chest. "You twisted, demented girl. To stand there and accuse Cecil of harming you. What rubbish!"

I was feeling drained and didn't have any strength left to wrangle with this woman. "The authorities will decide Cecil's fate."

"Now listen to me, you little strumpet." Her voice turned pure ice. "If you or your father involve the authorities in this affair, I'll make your lives a living hell. Don't think I don't know about *you*. You've bedded commoners. You're sinful and immoral just like your sister who couldn't keep her hands off that boy, Hagerty. You tried to force Cecil to engage in a vile sexual act involving you and that servant girl. You invited him up to your bedroom on the pretence that you wanted to console him, then sprang your fiendish trap on him. When he refused to engage in your illicit rendezvous, you became outraged and threw the lamp at him, setting him on fire."

Lady Daphne pointed a finger in my face. "If you or your father pursue charges against Cecil, that's the story I'll tell at the inquiry—and I'll produce witnesses. It would be in your best interest to go along with the truth that Cecil is suffering a mental breakdown due to his grief over your sister. I rue the day he ever got involved with—that—that—"

I began shaking from head to toe. Before I could stop myself my hand shot up and would have struck her face if David Ligham hadn't appeared. He came out of nowhere, smoothly catching my hand in mid-air as if he was responding to my greeting. He brought my arm down level and kissed my hand.

Then he turned to Lady Daphne and kissed her hand. "You must be here to give Grace the good news about Cecil's condition," he said casually. "I hear he's recovering quite well."

Lady Daphne's face changed into a disarming smile and her voice turned pure silk. "Yes, poor boy. I have Grace and Ellis to thank for saving him from the same fate that took poor Deirdre's life. We'll arrange for Cecil to convalesce in a good facility where he'll receive treatment not only from his physical wounds but from his broken heart, too." She nodded conspiratorially at David. "We must get him released from that dreadful Mercy Hospital as soon as possible. Such a depressing place."

David looked from Lady Daphne to me, then back at her. His sudden appearance had shocked me into silence. "I have contacts who will gladly recommend an excellent facility for Cecil's recovery, in England, of course. Would you like me to intercede with them on your behalf?"

Lady Daphne laid a gloved hand on David's arm. "Thank you, David. You're so thoughtful. That would be wonderful. Shall I see you tonight at dinner?"

"Of course."

She turned to me, her eyes boring into mine. "Thank you again for your quick action on Cecil's behalf, my dear. Give my greetings to your mother and father." Her words were soft-spoken, but there was menace in her undertone.

She kissed my cheek then turned and swept out of the room.

I stood in the same spot without moving. David led me to the settee. "Where does your father keep the sherry?"

I pointed to the library.

He came back with a glass and handed it to me. I took a sip and coughed on the strong taste.

"Good," David said. He took the glass from my hand and put his arms around me. I could smell the starch in his shirt mixed with scented soap. He held me in his embrace, not moving or saying a word until I withdrew.

"I didn't hear you arrive," I said.

"I told the butler you were expecting me." He brushed my hair aside and looked into my eyes. "I think you should eat something."

He left to find Maureen and arrange lunch.

I stood up and walked over to the window. My mind was thawing from its shocked state. I had misjudged Lady Daphne. Her mind was still sharp, her connivance as thwarted as ever. I had been deceived by her appearance. She had effortlessly convinced David Ligham that Cecil suffered an emotional breakdown over Deirdre's death and was a danger to himself. If David, who knew about Cecil's attempt to drown me and had heard about his latest attack as well, could be swayed by Lady Daphne, what chance was there the constabulary would believe in my innocence, or Cecil's guilt?

I began to suspect Cecil never intended to commit suicide. He made it look that way and had fooled even me. Having failed at his second attempt to murder me and knowing he was about to face the authorities for his crimes, he concocted a brilliant plan. He appeared to set himself on fire then attempted to jump out the window to his death. He assessed the situation correctly when he gambled that Father would pull him to safety.

His damaged skin would serve as an honour badge, sure to earn people's sympathy for the devoted and broken-hearted husband who tried to join his wife in death. It all sounded devastatingly romantic—if it were true. Instead, it was the self-serving act of a twisted mind. But a jury wouldn't believe me if Cecil stood before them suffering from self-inflicted wounds. My heart sank, knowing I would have to leave Kilpara if I were to feel safe again

Grand-Aunt Sadie wrote to say she missed my visits to Mercy Hospital, and she hoped I would return after I recovered from the horrific events that led to Cecil's near-fatal accident. I didn't know what Father had told her, but Lady Daphne seemed to have delivered her message with lightning speed—which was sympathy for Cecil. Common consensus was already forming that he was mentally unbalanced from his grief over his dead wife and had tried to join her in death. In one sense I was relieved. I didn't know if I could survive the strain of a lengthy prosecution process that ended in a verdict rendering Cecil delusional at the time of his attack, and ordering him into a treatment facility. A jury of men would never believe Clare's or my testimony over Cecil's. Without a legal conviction, I had only a finite time to make a decision about my future.

The morning of Cecil's release from Mercy Hospital I went to the stables. Spitfire whinnied and stomped in his stall, restless to ride. Calming jagged nerves, I removed the tackle from its hook and went through the motions of attaching Spitfire's saddle and bridle. Before I stopped to consider my actions, I climbed into the saddle and we struck out for Mercy Hospital.

I rode in behind the orchard where I had a view of the hospital entrance without being detected. I didn't have long to wait until I saw Lady Daphne, Sir Charles, and a tall distinguished-looking man, who I assumed was Cecil's physician, come out through the hospital doors. Among them was Cecil in a wheelchair pushed by a nurse. White bandages covered the left side of his face and were wrapped around his left arm. Lady Daphne held his right hand. Before they got into the carriage, Cecil paused to look around as if he sensed a presence. A slow smile creased his face, and then the physician gently assisted him into the carriage. The contents of my stomach disgorged and rose in my throat. I felt the urge to retch when a horse snorted behind me.

I turned to find Father, who looked just as surprised to see me as I was to see him. He nodded towards the carriage.

"How did you know he was being released today?"

Tamping back nausea I said, "Grand-Aunt Sadie mentioned it in a letter."

Father dismounted and so did I. We stood in the grove of apple and pear trees, watching the carriage move towards the gates.

"Where are they taking him?" I asked.

"To an institution in England. The physician diagnosed him as being emotionally and mentally overwrought from grief and a danger to himself."

"That's not true."

"Of course it's not." Father looked thoughtful for a long moment. "I went to the police. I wanted the bastard thrown in jail. But legal justice is slow, if they'll even believe the evidence against him."

"You showed them the knife?" I had recognised the surgical knife immediately after the attack. It was stored in a medical bag in the library along with other instruments Grand-Aunt Sadie had given me to study.

"Yes. The one Aunt Sadie gave you. The police were sceptical when I produced it as the intended murder weapon. They questioned how Cecil knew where to find it, and what it was doing in the library."

"You told them that's where I study Grand-Aunt Sadie's medical journals and kept the knife in a medical bag?"

Father nodded. "But the police were unconvinced that Cecil would know its whereabouts."

"They probably think I staged my own murder," I said sarcastically.

"They also questioned how he got into the house without force. I explained there must be a hundred windows at Kilpara, and Cecil could've found one that was unlocked."

"He was planning to kill me for some time."

"Possibly. Your appearance at Larcourt gave him an unexpected opportunity. Imagine his shock when he found out that you didn't drown. What were the odds? It likely made him reckless. He thought he'd escape suspicion if you were killed with your own surgical knife at Kilpara. Fortunately, his plot failed. Setting himself on fire was a desperate act to convince everyone he intended to commit suicide by jumping out of Deirdre's own window on fire—like she died."

"It was a calculated risk?"

"He was out of options, and his scheme paid off."

"You should've shot him, or let him burn alive."

Father grimaced. "Justice will be served. He'll rot away in an insane asylum."

I held Father's gaze. "Only until he's pronounced cured. Then he'll come after me again."

"He'll never leave *this* institution."

"Yes, he will."

"It'll be seen to that he won't." Father firmly set his face.

I waited for him to explain further, but all he said was, "Let's go see Aunt Sadie."

One evening at dinner Father said, "I've arranged for us to go to France."

I stopped eating. "France?"

Father leaned forward. "We've been through so much I thought we should get away from Kilpara for a while. I've a lot to apologise for, Grace. I should've sent you to finishing school when your mother first suggested it. But you looked so dead set against the idea that I procrastinated. Aunt Sadie, well, she had her own ideas about where your talents lay. If I'd listened to your mother, none of this might have happened."

"It's not your fault," I interrupted. Finishing school and coming-out parties seemed superfluous after all we had been through. My waking thoughts were filled with Deirdre, Cecil, or Ruairi. Lately I thought more about Ruairi, especially now that I had received a letter from him. Father knew of the letter, but didn't question it. I wondered if it prompted his sudden decision to take the family to France. Perhaps he feared I would soon request to go to America and spend time with relatives I hardly knew; where I could feel safe from Cecil.

280

"David Ligham has arranged for us to stay with his uncle at his home, La Fontaine, in Paris," Father continued. "From there we'll travel down to the Riviera and stay in Nice in a house an agent located for us. It's very pleasant at the Riviera in summertime."

"Will Giselle come?" I asked.

Father smiled a rare smile. "I don't think we can separate your mother from her. Aunt Sadie, Giselle, her nurse, and your grandfather are coming. We'll take Clare to help."

"Seems quite a troop to impose on David's relatives."

"Not at all," Father said. "They're anxious to have us as their guests. And Giselle's nurse speaks French. It will also give you a chance to practise the language yourself."

After the announcement the house became abuzz with preparations. Clare, who had turned quiet and serious after Cecil's attack, was back to her smiling and giggling self. She was the envy of the other servants.

On my walk to the cottage I made a point to tell Olam we were leaving on a holiday, but would not be gone long.

"Can I come too?" he asked.

"Your father needs you here. He'd miss you too much."

"I know. And I'd miss him and Mam."

"So it's better that you stay. I'll write you every day."

Olam grinned. "I've never received letters in the post before."

"You'll write to me, too?"

"Every day."

I stood back and looked at the cottage. It had almost doubled in size. Conor had made renovations with Deirdre's approval in mind. I could almost feel her presence beside me, agreeing it was turning into a fine home. Conor laid down his tools and came over.

"It's coming along well," I said.

Conor smiled. "I feel like Deirdre is here guiding everything I do."

I nodded.

After a brief silence I said, "Thank you for allowing Giselle to spend time in France with us."

His smile widened. "Don't stay away so long that she forgets me."

"That won't happen."

I didn't expect to enjoy our visit to Paris. I thought it would be fraught with obstacles and problems. But it went smoothly and turned out to be pleasurable. Maryann and Gilbert Ligham lived at the edge of Paris in a sprawling brick house with a fountain in front and willow trees leading up a gravel avenue. Gilbert resembled Lord Henry Ligham. He, like Lord Ligham, was a pleasant man whose hearty appetite resulted in a thick waist. His wife, although English, could pass for French. Her hair was the colour of corn silk, her skin smooth and lightly tanned. Her eyes were warm hazel, and her voice, soft and melodious, hinted of a French accent.

The servants rushed to our assistance upon our arrival and escorted us inside where everything was light and airy. It was obvious our hosts loved flowers, because they were displayed in large and small vases throughout the house. The colourful bouquets accented dark furniture, their scent intoxicating.

Gilbert and Maryann were wonderful hosts, seeing to our every comfort and constantly fussing over Mother and Giselle. At first Mother seemed confused by the attention of these new people surrounding her, but gradually she became accustomed to it. She loved the vividness of the flower gardens with so many species of plants not seen in Ireland. I encouraged her to walk through the gardens with me. At first she took only a few steps, but as we ventured farther each day, her legs grew stronger.

The Lighams owned a small French poodle who became fast friends with Giselle.

"We must get Giselle such a pet," Father said.

"Pifou is expecting puppies soon," Maryann said. "We'll be happy to bring one with us for Giselle next time we visit Ireland."

Father smiled his agreement.

Paris was unlike any other city I had ever seen. We stood in awe of the Arc de Triomphe that was commissioned after the victory at Austerlitz by Emperor Napoleon. We climbed the steep streets to Montmarte, and visited the cathedral, a strange Romanesque building. We explored the markets and walked along the Seine River in the evening, gas lamps reflecting on the water.

When Mother was resting and Father talked business with Gilbert Ligham, one of the grooms escorted me into the city where I explored museums and cathedrals. I particularly liked the Louvre and stood in the Grande Galerie before Leonardo da Vinci's painting of the *Mona Lisa*. A physical ache squeezed my heart as I imagined Deirdre here beside me, her face alive and animated revelling in the *Virgin of the Rocks*, another Da Vinci painting. It showed the child Jesus meeting the infant John the Baptist, who is in the care of the angel Uriel. Both were on the run to evade Herod's massacre of innocents.

Before our visit ended, the Lighams organised a party for us. We were to be introduced as their guests of honour. A surprise awaited me when I descended the stairs the night of the party. David stood at the bottom, looking up. I hadn't seen him since the day Lady Daphne came to Kilpara. I despised him then for succumbing to her influence, for cordially assisting to get Cecil out of Ireland, never once showing concern that he should be charged for his crimes.

I had since concluded that David, like Father, believed it was better to remove Cecil from Ireland and our lives than to go through a prolonged court process. They were both wrong if they assumed Cecil no longer posed a threat. Thoughts of Cecil brought back images of fear and horror, destroying the pleasure of simple freedom I'd tasted in France.

"When did you arrive?" I asked, frostily.

"Early this afternoon," David said, his warm smile wavering. "You look stunning."

"Thank you."

"I mean it. I've never seen you look more beautiful. You seem relaxed and healthy."

"Thank you."

"I intend to dance every dance with you this evening," he said, determined to remain cheerful and ignore my detachment.

That evening was the most carefree one I had spent since before the day Conor disappeared and life at Kilpara spiralled downward. By the end of the night my face hurt from laughing and talking. I caught Father looking at me several times with pride and contentment. Even Giselle had been allowed to stay past her bedtime. She stole everyone's heart.

When our visit ended and we bid farewell to the Lighams, I expected to say goodbye to David, too.

"I'm not leaving quite yet," he said.

"You're not?"

"No, I'm accompanying you to the Riviera and spending a couple of days there before I return to Ireland."

I looked at him quizzically.

He grinned. "We never had that picnic by the sea. There's no better place than the Riviera to fulfil that promise."

Two weeks at the Riviera flashed by as we spent days by the sea and pleasant evenings sitting on the veranda of our rented lodging. David and I had our picnic on white sand in a small cove. This time I was careful not to drink wine, which David seemed to anticipate. I noticed whatever nose irritation he suffered in Ireland didn't bother him here, and I wondered why. I stored the question in the back of my mind to ask Grand-Aunt Sadie later. After we cleared away our picnic lunch, David drove the chaise back to the harbour. He invited me to walk with him. We strolled leisurely along the pier, admiring sailboats of different sizes and types anchored in clear blue water. David stopped at a large white sailboat with its sail hoisted, and looked at me. In large black letters *Espoir* was painted across the side.

"This belongs to my family," he said.

My stomach tightened and nausea rose in my throat. I started to walk away. David stopped me and turned me round to face him. He stroked my cheek tenderly.

"You're safe with me, Grace," he said. "If you can't face going out on the boat, I'll understand. But if you want to put that terrible memory of what happened behind you, what better place to do it than here and now?"

"Why should I listen to you?" I flared. "You knew Cecil tried to drown me and intended to kill me in my bed, yet you behaved like nothing happened that day Lady Daphne came to see me. You acted cordially, so it's clear you never believed me; that you thought I made up the whole thing. Your promise to find Cecil and make him confess was all a *lie*."

David's soothing strokes stopped. He ran all ten fingers through his hair, walked away a few steps then turned and came back.

I hadn't moved.

He took my hands in his and held them. "My actions seem unforgivable, I know, but let me explain. I hired a professional detective. He found Cecil several times, but before I could get to him, he took off again. I feel responsible he eluded me and made a second attempt on your life."

David's words were measured, but his eyes flashed austerely. "After Cecil was taken to Mercy Hospital, Lady Daphne and Sir Sloane stayed with my parents at Ligham Downs. The day Lady Daphne came to see you, I overheard her tell the groom to take her to Kilpara. I knew your father was in Galway and I suspected she knew, too.

"I sensed she was up to no good, so I followed her. I informed your butler you were expecting me, and he pointed me towards the drawing room. I overheard everything. She is without conscience and will go to any lengths to cover up Cecil's crimes. I'm sorry if I belittled you. Can you forgive me?"

"You stood by and let Lady Daphne berate and insult me, instead of standing up for the truth. Instead of seeing that justice was done."

David winced. "I acted as I did only because I wanted her to agree when I suggested a reputable institution for Cecil's recovery."

"And why was that important?"

"To control where he went."

"He should've gone to jail and hung from the gallows."

"He'll be institutionalised forever."

"And Lady Daphne knows this?"

"No, she thinks Cecil is at a recovery institution where he'll receive the best treatment and be declared cured in a few months."

"You're not making sense."

"It was important that I get Lady Daphne to agree with my recommendation. Cecil won't ever be released."

"From this particular place in England?"

"Yes, but I don't know where it is."

"If you don't know where this place is, how can you be sure Cecil isn't released?"

"I can tell you with absolute certainty he won't ever leave there."

I was silent for a moment. "That's what Father said."

"Then trust your father. Trust me. Now please, say you'll come out on the boat."

"Is my father behind some scheme to get Cecil out of Ireland?"

David looked out to the harbour.

"I see. I'm afraid your word isn't good enough. I need a guarantee."

"Grace, understand I would do everything in my power to protect you."

His eyes pleaded with me. I didn't believe his promise, or his conviction that Cecil would be incarcerated at some institution forever. I would never feel safe again. Fear consumed me. "I can't get on the boat."

David ran his hands down my arms and held my gaze. "I know you, Grace. You're brave. Take this step to undo the nightmare Cecil put you through." He tipped my chin and brought my face closer to his. "Please."

I slipped from his embrace and paced back and forth. I stared at the name *Espoir*. It meant hope. If I took this first step forward, possibly, I would find the strength to turn the tide against the terror that consumed me and take back control of my life. To lack courage now, I may be forever locked in the past and unable to face the future without fear. I walked unsteadily to the boat. A crew member stood by the gangplank and reached out for my hand. I stood immobile for several moments before extending it.

A shadow of a smile passed over David's face when he joined me on board.

The experience on the *Espoir* masked the day Cecil dragged me onto the small rowboat, rowed out onto Lough Corrib and pushed me overboard. It was like a caring hand was erasing an ugly picture and painting a pleasant one in its place. Here, I gazed into clear blue water and the sandy bottom below, smelled sea salt in warm Mediterranean air; watched the sail flap in the breeze as the boat cut smoothly through the surface. David stood with his arms around me, saying little the whole hour we circled the bay.

I admired the painted villas sitting against the hillside, at times veiled by palm trees lining the promenade. People swam in the ocean or sunned themselves on the strand. Children built sandcastles. The picture before me was so serene with the boat easing through water like a glove covering a hand that I was surprised when we returned to the pier to dock. Yet the moment I stepped off the boat, I felt drained and tired. For the first time since Cecil's attacks I slept that night without waking, my dreams filled with happy faces and warm sea breezes.

I thanked David the next day as he prepared to leave. He paused to stroke my face lightly with his hand. "You're my Mona Lisa," he said. He bent and kissed my lips lightly.

CHAPTER 23

When the carriage turned into Kilpara, I expected my newfound peace of mind to shatter. Instead, intense longing to be home engulfed me. The servants were not only on the steps to welcome us back, they came down the avenue to wave the carriage into the courtyard. Inside the house, the familiar smell of lamb cooking made me salivate at the meal that was to come.

"You've grown a foot," Maureen said to Giselle, nuzzling her nose in Giselle's tummy and making her squeal.

"That's an exaggeration for sure," Father said.

Maureen drew her brow together, but her eyes were playful.

Anthony opened my bedroom door slowly when he brought my luggage upstairs. I stood on the threshold in stunned surprise at the sight inside. Scars from the fire had been removed. New wallpaper covered the walls in yellow and white daisies, and matching drapes hung on the windows. The floor had been sanded and varnished and was covered with white and yellow rugs. A large bed dominated the middle of the room draped in a white bedspread. Pillows in white and yellow frilly pillowcases sat plumped against the headboard. A white and yellow flowered water jug stood in the washstand. The wardrobe, small table, writing desk and vanity covered the rest of the room.

"Conor and Maureen's doing," Anthony said proudly.

It felt different to be home, yet the same. I was different, yet the same. I wasn't sure I knew myself anymore.

I returned to riding Spitfire after Father assured me I wasn't in imminent danger. I stretched out farther each day, sometimes going as far as the sea, and then stopping to visit

Grand-Aunt Margaret. I walked along the strand in front of her house where I knew Father and Mother first met. As I looked out across the sea, I wondered what it would be like to cross it; to reach Ruairi's waiting arms on the other side. As the weeks passed I thought about this more and more. At other times I was content to sit with Mother, play with Giselle, or go over to Mercy Hospital and help Grand-Aunt Sadie with her patients.

But I was growing restless. I blamed this on my desire to be with Ruairi and increasing anxiety that time was growing short before Cecil was released from his convalescence. I disagreed with Father and David's certainty that the recovery institution was strong enough to hold him. He would find a way to convince doctors he was cured and be released.

With panic and longing battling inside me, I found myself drawn to Deirdre's grave. I lay on the ground next to it and looked up at the sky. "What should I do," I asked, willing her face to burst through the blue screen. "How can I abandon everyone and everything? I can't stay, knowing Cecil won't stop until he kills me. I have no choice but to leave."

"You do have a choice."

I shielded my eyes against the sun with my hand. A silhouette moved into view and I recognised Conor's tall, confident figure standing upright. The sun shone around him, cloaking him in shining gold. I shivered, not from fear, but from something I didn't understand.

"Conor?"

He hunkered down beside me. "You do have a choice," he repeated.

I raised up into a sitting position. "Only until Cecil is cured and can come after me again. Odds are I won't survive his next attempt."

Conor looked at Deirdre's headstone as if asking her permission to speak his mind. Then he looked down at the ground before looking back at me. "We'll only have this conversation once, Grace. You must promise me you'll never repeat what is said here today. To anyone."

He waited and I nodded.

"Cecil won't ever leave Sturgess Conventry."

"What's Sturgess Conventry?"

"The place where Cecil was taken."

"How do you know where he is when no one else does, and how can you be so sure?"

Conor ran his hand over Deirdre's headstone. "Cecil signed his death warrant when he agreed to go to Sturgess."

"But he'll only be there until he's declared medically fit."

"That's what Cecil was counting on when he feigned his suicide in your bedroom. And what he was led to believe when he entered Sturgess Conventry."

"I don't follow."

"When I came back from France with Giselle, your father and I had a long talk. He was more informed about my family than I thought. He knew about the Phoenix Park murders in '82, and that my uncle was a suspected member of the Invincibles. He was implicated in that crime, but never caught for questioning. Your father also knew that the Invincibles, a revolutionary group pledged to remove British tyrants from Ireland, were responsible. I confided in him it was the Invincibles who nursed me back to health after I was beaten. I spent some time in Dublin recovering from the assault, but was later secretly transported to Dover and admitted to Sturgess Conventry until I was fully recovered. My uncle is superintendent of that treatment centre."

He waited a moment to let this information sink in.

I let out a long sigh. "And that day in Dublin?"

"My uncle was never sick. He was there on a mission and stayed temporarily at the house in Stephen's Green. He was out that day. But he was due back, and I had to get you away from there."

"So you offered to take Deirdre and me on a sightseeing excursion around Dublin?"

"Sorry, but yes. "My uncle was meeting with Invincibles suspected in the Phoenix Park murders who were still at large. The British authorities were closing in on them, and he had to convince them to flee to Sturgess Conventry or most definitely face the gallows.

"The Invincibles are often forced into exile when their identities are discovered. Sturgess Conventry has been under the control of the Invincibles and Fenians for a long time. It's a treatment centre in Dover that caters to wealthy people who spend time convalescing after surgery or an illness, or who need therapy for mental sickness. Beneath the façade, it's a hiding place for revolutionaries facing execution for their crimes against the British government. My uncle was groomed to take the position of superintendent there. He altered his appearance and learned to speak like an Englishman.

"Immediately after Cecil was taken to Mercy Hospital, your father went to the constabulary and made charges against him. When Lady Daphne arrived at the Lighams' from England, she insisted on going to see Cecil immediately. Sir Charles, who hadn't fared well on the voyage, wanted to rest first. Lady Daphne called him uncaring because he refused to ignore a little travel sickness and go visit their son who had almost burned to death. She stormed out of the house, stopping just long enough to ask David to take her to Mercy Hospital. He agreed out of courtesy. She insisted Cecil be released from Mercy Hospital as soon as possible, and made lurid comments, even after she knew your grand-aunt Sadie had accommodated Cecil in her private quarters."

I let out a breath of pure disgust. Grand-Aunt Sadie had sacrificed her own comfort for a murderer.

Conor pinched his brow with his forefinger and thumb. "I know what you're thinking. But her hospitality had its advantages. Cecil informed his mother the constabulary intended to launch an investigation into what happened at Kilpara. The moment she heard this, Lady Daphne ordered privacy. Your grand-aunt Sadie pretended to close the door, but she left it slightly ajar.

"She and David stood outside and listened as Cecil told Lady Daphne the truth about how he meant to kill you, calling you an interfering little witch."

My lips trembled and Conor hesitated. I gained my composure and nodded for him to continue.

"He said your attempts to turn Deirdre against him, and the bungled job those witless bums did to dispose of me, were what doomed his and Deirdre's marriage. When the constables came to the hospital to question him, he pretended to be too shaken to see them. That was part of his scheme to foster sympathy for his supposed emotional collapse after Deirdre's death.

"Lady Daphne offered up the notion to convince authorities that you had lured him to your bedroom for a lurid sexual encounter involving not just you, but Clare Kineely, too."

My hands flew involuntarily to my mouth.

An angry flush crept up Conor's neck. "Cecil agreed this was a good scheme, one she should use to force your compliance, but emphasised that if he was charged with any wrongdoing, an emotional collapse defence would set him free."

Conor studied my face to make sure I comprehended everything he had said.

Silence lingered before I responded, "This doesn't change anything."

"It does," Conor said. "David knew your father wanted Cecil in jail or out of the country permanently. He told your father Cecil intended to plead emotional and mental instability to account for his bizarre actions, and deny any accusations to murder you. Your father came to me and asked if we could turn this information into a plan to get Cecil out of our lives. Everything came together the day Lady Daphne visited you at Kilpara."

In a quiet voice I said, "That day, David let Lady Daphne believe he sympathised with Cecil having a mental breakdown by proposing to recommend a private care institution."

Connor nodded. "Exactly. Lady Daphne didn't know David's offer was a ploy to get Cecil into a place where he'd be incarcerated for the rest of his life—Sturgess Conventry. Your father and I couldn't believe our good fortune when David dropped this in our laps. I contacted my uncle and he sent over Dr Anderson, who had no problem convincing

Lady Daphne that Sturgess Conventry was the best place for Cecil.

"Your father dropped all charges. He pretended he was cowed into believing it was useless to pursue the case in court. Lady Daphne was bursting with victory because she believed she and Cecil had outsmarted both your father and the authorities."

"What if Cecil tries to leave?"

"He'll end up committing suicide. It will be credibly done with statements and evidence that document his suicidal nature. In her efforts to corroborate Cecil's story, Lady Daphne voiced concern that he might injure himself. All an act on her part to keep him from answering to authorities."

After a long silence I said, "Cecil won't ever be released?"

"No. You'll never have to fear Cecil Sloane again."

We rose and stood looking at Deirdre's grave. A sense of tranquillity settled over me. "Thank you for giving me back my life," I said.

Giselle and Berthie joined Mother and me in the garden as the long summer days began to wane.

"Brush," Giselle said, handing a hairbrush to Mother. She sat on a small stool in front of Mother, who took the brush and began combing Giselle's long fair hair.

"My baby, my sweet baby," Mother said in a childish dreamlike way.

Grand-Aunt Sadie came into the garden. Trista had insisted she return to Kilpara before cold weather returned. This time she didn't resist; she even agreed to be assisted by a novice, a quiet girl.

Grand-Aunt Sadie sat down beside me. "It doesn't seem that long ago your grandmother, Ann, and I sat here together with your mother's father. She asked me to take care of her family after she left this world. I hope I didn't fail her."

"You didn't," I said softly.

"Thank you. I'd hate to see disappointment on Ann's face when we meet in heaven. So much has happened since she returned to Kilpara."

CORRIB RED

I smiled at Grand-Aunt Sadie and patted her hand. I looked out beyond the garden to fields of long grass, bent by the warm gentle breeze as if paying homage to the red sun sinking over Galway bay.

I had been sitting on the strand for hours waiting for the sun to set. The time had come to decide if I would stay at Kilpara, or if I would go to America. I took Ruairi's Claddagh ring I wore around my neck and put it on my finger, then pulled out Ruairi's letter tucked inside the breast pocket of my dress. It read:

My Dearest Grace,

I think of you constantly and wish I could show you all this rugged country has to offer. I'm keeping a journal so I remember to tell you everything when I see you again. I don't want to leave out a single detail. My only regret now is that I wasn't in Ireland to protect you from Sloane. The bastard. He's in a place where he'll never hurt you again. You can rest assured about that. I know that doesn't make everything you've been through any easier to bear, but it gives me more reason why I should make my fortune in this land. I want to offer you a secure future.

My brother Hughie and I are saving every penny we can and we dream of owning our own farm. They say Texas has good farmland. It is our goal to move there as soon as we have enough money. You would like it, Grace. I hear it has lots of wide-open country. Everyone rides horses. You could bring Spitfire and we could ride him together the way we did along the Corrib.

Life in Boston is crude and not befitting a lady. There's lots of Irish here, all homesick for the auld sod. This has given me an opportunity to put words to my music and I sometimes sing and play in small music halls and bars. The words must touch people's hearts for they return over and over to hear them.

These tunes come easy because they are about you, my love. You are always close to the

*surface of my thoughts, dearest Grace. I live for my
memories of you and Lough Corrib—it's what keeps
me going. I think about you lying next to me nestled
in my arms, your touch and the smell of your hair.
I ache to see your face again and this makes me
want to do my damnedest to deserve you. I truly
wish that we'll be together soon. Please say you'll
come ...*

> *I love you,*
> *Ruairi*

I read the letter over and over, touching the paper, the dried ink, knowing Ruairi held this same paper where my hand lay now. My fingers tingled as I moved them over the thick letters, each one penned carefully.

I traced where his hand had been. He still loved me and I loved him.

His face came before me, so clear that I reached out to embrace the love in his green eyes. His fingers touched my face with soft caresses that stirred longing, and when he kissed my lips, fevered sensations swept through me like a tidal wave. I stood, kicked off my shoes and walked out into shallow water shimmering warm against the sand in the looming sunset. Waves brushed my ankles like silky kisses as Ruairi pulled me closer, pressing me against him.

As quickly as it came, his image faded, leaving me alone and aching for his touch. I waded deeper into the water until I was waist deep. Around me the sinking sun reflected red hues. The tide would soon be going out. I took Ruairi's letter and laid each page carefully face-up on the ocean bed. Water smeared the ink, turning the pages black, drifting each one farther out to sea as each footstep backwards guided me home towards Kilpara.

❤

75598324R00168

Made in the USA
Columbia, SC
21 August 2017